BESIDE US

A Supernatural Mystery

STEPHEN W. BRIGGS

Black Rose Writing | Texas

ISBN: 978-1-68513-287-3
PUBLISHED BY BLACK ROSE WRITING
www.blackrosewriting.com

Printed in the United States of America
Suggested Retail Price (SRP) $23.95

Beside Us is printed in Garamond Premier Pro

*As a planet-friendly publisher, Black Rose Writing does its best to eliminate unnecessary waste to reduce paper usage and energy costs, while never compromising the reading experience. As a result, the final word count vs. page count may not meet common expectations.

To my fellow conspiracy theorists,
who have sacrificed so much searching for the truth.

PRAISE FOR
BESIDE US

"This mesmerizing novel spins down wheels within wheels, wheels that turn out to be crop circles with the bloodless bodies of children at their centers. Follow this maze of conspiracies into magical portals to adventure and wonder.

It begins when Canadian detective Simon Elliott, out for a bike ride, witnesses a mysterious kidnapping of three children, made all the more puzzling when their parents were not taken. When Simon reluctantly agrees to investigate for the parents, his quest takes him to England, and leads to a series of harrowing events. He hooks up with new companions, and they are pursued by two competing, but equally frightening, groups. Unsure of what is real, or who to trust, Simon refuses to give up the search. It takes him and his friends into a hidden world, with portals into other places and times, a blood-tinged elixir promising eternal life, and war with those less altruistically motivated. Buckle up and put on your tinfoil hat for this journey, it's a masterfully-written five-star adventure full of fun, fear, and unexpected twists."
–Bill Schweitzer, author of *Doves in a Tempest*

"Buckle up and put on your tinfoil hat for this journey, it's a masterfully-written five-star adventure full of fun, fear, and unexpected twists.

A supernatural mystery chock full of frenzied action across two continents, numerous dimensions, and tackling current conspiracy theories head on. Stephen W Briggs' well-crafted protagonists will have you questioning everything as you follow them throughout their ethereal journey."
–Ken Harris, author of the *From the Case Files of Steve Rockfish* crime fiction series

"In *Beside Us*, Stephen W. Briggs delivers a gripping thriller that takes readers on a riveting investigation from Canada to England and throughout Europe. When a missing person case leads a Canadian police officer on leave to investigate mysterious crop circles, he finds himself caught up in a battle between good and evil. With an intricate plot and masterful suspense-building, Briggs keeps readers guessing until the startling conclusion. Fans of Dan Brown's Angels and Demons won't want to miss this page-turner."
--Cam Torrens, award-winning author of *Stable* and *False Summit*

"*Beside Us* is a Dan Brown-esque mystery for readers who like a good, juicy conspiracy theory. There are plenty of twists and turns in the complex plot, and supernatural elements that feel logical and integral to the story. I also appreciate the very real stakes for the main characters, and the difficult choices they're forced to make."
–Amanda Waters, author of *With You*

"If you enjoy novels that keep you guessing, *Beside Us* is the book for you. Briggs does an admirable job arousing the reader's continual interest in a mystery involving two detectives, three continents, kidnapped children from three families, crop circles, vanishing men in black hoodies, others in blue tunics, and a time span that begins in 1490 before jumping to the 21st Century. It's all very complicated, but the two lead detectives, who are as perplexed as readers may be, make sense of the complications at a satisfying pace.

This is a page turner, with plentiful chases interspersed with minor characters revealing wild secrets, some true, others false. The most powerful sections are set in the fields with crop circles. Who made them and why? How were they constructed overnight? Can the fake ones be differentiated from the real ones? When the detectives discover the answers, there are several chapters to go as more is unravelled and the greater mystery beyond the kidnappings is explained."
–**Carolyn Geduld, author of** *Who Shall Live*

"Investigator Simon Elliott was out for a leisurely bike ride when he witnesses three children being kidnapped. One of the children is mysteriously found dead in the middle of a crop circle. After talking to the devastated parents, Elliott promises to find their still missing twins. The search opens a world he could never have imagined with strange people trying to kill him, even more missing children, a number of crop circles, conspiracy theories and the nagging feeling that someone is always watching them. Beside Us is a gripping tale that extends across the ocean in a search for answers to questions, some of which are centuries old."
–**LeeAnne James, author of** *Justice for Loretta* **and** *The Dusty Road to Homicide*

"Briggs takes you on an action-packed, supernatural journey to solve this mystery.

A simple kidnapping turns into an international quest for the children, but produces only more questions. Who else is looking for the children, and why? The journey leads them to a supernatural world where they are forced to make impossible, but necessary choices. You won't want to put this book down until the final secrets are revealed."
–**Gary Gerlacher, MD, MBA, author of** *Last Patient of the Night*

BESIDE US

PROLOGUE

Amesbury, England 1490

Satisfied with the work on the ground, Gus Chapwilk inspected the large hole for the foundation of his home, Chapwilk Manor, on the land King Henry VII gifted him. Having spent ten months in France and Spain successfully negotiating the Treaty of Medina del Campo, the land and the title of Baron was a symbol of his king's ongoing gratitude.

He climbed into the hole where his men had worked hard over the exceptionally warm winter. Gus, a tall, slender man, with dark wavy hair and dark eyes, stood with his hands on his hips, looking twelve feet up to the ground. His one hundred hired men had made substantial progress while he was abroad, removing the soil in the enormous manor's footprint.

"Sir." His master architect greeted him. "Are you pleased with the progress? They have worked hard on your behalf, but they will need to dig an additional six feet to find bedrock."

"Yes, I am pleased. Have they found any artifacts?"

"Only a few, but I assure you they are eagerly searching."

With the primordial pillars of Stonehenge thirty miles away and the market for old world artifacts growing in England and throughout Europe, the workers screened the soil for items of value. Much to their delight, Gus had promised to share any profits amongst them.

"Good, keep looking. Find me a shovel, I will help dig," said Gus, with a jovial manner of a man freed from all obligations.

After the long days of traveling back to England, Gus enjoyed moving soil and digging alongside his workers. The son of peasants, he wasn't afraid of manual labor and working hard, rare behavior for one so financially blessed.

His workers viewed his participation with suspicion, changing their habits along with their language until they saw the hard earned callouses on his hands and knees and him eating the same rough meals alongside them.

Gus' wife had died in France at twenty-nine. Pneumonia took her and the five-month fetus inside her. Friends from an early age, they grew up as neighbors in their village of Salisbury. Gus courted her from the age of ten, marrying at sixteen. The love of his life, she supported Gus and traveled with him as he gained favor with the king. The physical work helped take his mind off the loss.

Work progressed slowly but steadily. Twenty days after Gus' return brought them close to the sixteen-foot depth mark.

"Come! Come quickly!" A foreman's voice broke the typical din.

In the southern corner of the hole, a group hastily gathered. From the shadows of the hole, Gus detected a glow radiating from around the men. He pushed through his men, eight deep and all standing in stunned silence. When he broke through the line, he saw a pulsing light, piercing blue with white arcs as bright as the Lord's sun above. The light, only partially exposed, glowed through the soil. He pushed his men back and stared into the light.

Come to me.

He spun his head around. "Who said that?" he asked, knowing the answer but not willing to accept it. "Who?"

Eyes stared back at him, but no one acknowledged speaking.

More men assembled around him, but Gus pushed them back. "No, back away." He pointed as far away from the light as the hole would allow.

A sudden sound snapped him back to the light. An audible hum and crackle, accompanied by the smell of a busy blacksmith's shop, sent terrified workers clambering up the ladders and running to their tents. Only Gus and a handful of men remained.

Their voices from the tents echoed down into the hole as the sun set.

"We have dug too deep and exposed the gates of hell."

"Yes, the devil himself wants our souls."

"No, it must be something else, or we would all be dead."

"Is it an ancient relic? Related to Stonehenge?"

"No, no, it is evil. We must leave here."

Gus motioned the men around him to gather close, purposely shrugging off the overheard dialogue. "Gentlemen, unlike the workers above us, I believe we have uncovered a light from the heavens. Who shall stand with me and see the job done?" he asked.

Gus looked from man to man, seeking their commitment. One by one, they nodded their heads. "Good. I thank you. Understand, no one will touch the light. With care, dig around it. We must show it respect, as we respect our Father in Heaven."

Three men approached the light, shovels in hand. They vigilantly dug around it, each man waiting to be struck down as it pulsed and crackled. Lanterns were unnecessary. The light from the object filled the hole with an eerie blue hue.

As the moon hung high over their heads, Gus instructed, "Stand aside, men. If our Lord calls it back, best not be in its way." Approaching with a shovel while motioning the others away, he said, "I will complete the work myself." He removed the soil around the light, sweat ran down his face— none of it from exertion. Wiping his brow, he thrust the shovel at the dirt. It caught on a rock and slipped forward, touching the blue center, the blade of the shovel vanished into the light. As the blade passed into the light, it brightened, causing Gus and his men to protect their eyes.

A deathly silence filled the hole. Gus held his shovel tightly by the shaft. The sound of arcing filled the night air. With all his strength, Gus pulled back on the shovel, the blade appeared from the light. Gus stumbled backwards and fell onto the ground. A few loyal workers helped him to his feet while more men headed for the ladders.

He labored cautiously through the night. Finally, as the sun rose over the surrounding hills, Gus had exposed the entire ball. Astoundingly, it hovered inches above the ground, standing eight feet tall and wide.

Gus took his shovel and deliberately pushed the blade into the light. The ball glowed brightly as it swallowed the blade and part of the wooden shaft.

He expected the wood to catch fire, but it just slid into the light. He pulled back, and his shovel returned, whole.

"Do one of you wish to earn four ounces of gold and retire to your family to live a wealthy life?" Gus asked, as he turned to the few men who dared to stay with him throughout the night.

Most took a step back. "I will, Master. You want to ask me to step through the light?" A young man, short and stout, said from behind the others.

"I am. What is your name, lad?" asked Gus.

"My name is Paul Bridge. Master, if I do this and I pass, will my family receive the ounces of gold?"

"I promise you, if you do not return, I will treat your family as my own. My word I give you," said Gus.

"Then I will take your offer." Paul bowed his head and prayed. He stood before Gus and smiled. Looking at the workers surrounding Gus, he nodded and turned to face the light. After a deep breath, he placed his hand into the light and watched the brilliance absorb it. He pulled his arm back and stared at his hand as he moved his fingers.

"It has a feeling I do not remember ever feeling," said Paul, looking back at Gus.

"Do you wish to back away?"

"No, sir." He stepped into the light and disappeared. The light pulsed white, then returned to a blue glow and hum.

Gus listened as all the surrounding men inhaled together. Some dropped to their knees and prayed, others ran to the ladders, but a few men stood with Gus in silence.

After hours of watching and waiting for Paul to return, men walked away, assuming he would never return, absorbed into the light of God, or captured by the gates of hell.

As the sun shone directly above them, a hand appeared, then bit by bit, Paul revealed himself. A reassuring smile grew as he stumbled onto the dirt. Voices lifted, calling to the workers of his return. Gus took his hand and helped him find his balance. Paul stepped away from the light and sat on the ground.

Gus sat beside him as a crowd gathered around. "How are you, lad?"

"Master, I am very well. Tomorrow those in there want to meet you. They have many things to tell you."

CHAPTER ONE

Guelph, Ontario, 2016

Simon Elliott pedaled his bicycle along the wooded path beside the Speed River in the early morning. Sweat dripped from his chin as the rain overnight had made the trail muggy.

A day earlier, he wrapped up a drug investigation with a large search and seizure of three grow houses and the arrests of four major drug dealers. The money and weapons recovered in the basement shut down a large Asian drug ring that had been operating in his town of Guelph. Unfortunately, he knew there would be larger, more violent groups moving in to replace the void he and his team created, but for today, he still had an accomplished glow from his first large bust.

The trail opened to a park where, later in the day, families would gather to have picnics or walks with their dogs. Simon pulled off the trail and turned onto Neeve Street to head to police headquarters. With the physical work completed yesterday, he would spend his day tied to his desk completing reports, forms, and, if he was lucky, a vacation request.

• • •

All morning, co-workers stopped at Simon's desk. They gave him pats on the back and congratulated him for the large bust, as he shuffled papers and clicked on his keyboard. A sticky note hanging below his computer screen reminded him the upper brass had scheduled two meetings and a press conference in the afternoon, where his attendance was mandatory.

Twisting his chair from side to side, he thought how proud his parents would be if they were still around. His dad, a former police officer himself, died six months earlier of cancer and his mother passed when he was twenty-three in a tragic car accident.

He thought about calling his kids to tell them the big news, then looked at the clock.

In school.

He picked up his phone to call Helen, his ex-wife, and paused. His career was the reason she was his ex-wife. She wanted a husband to be home at night, sober, and be there for their boys, Kyle and Richard. But his aspiration to be a staff sergeant before retiring took precedence over everything else—family, friends, and finances. After years of disagreeing on their priorities and future, Helen took the kids and moved out, way out, to British Columbia and her sister's small farm north of Vancouver. Simon was upset but buried himself in his work, his first love anyway, for comfort. Except for a week at Christmas and two weeks each summer where the boys visited him, his only communication was through video calls. This summer he canceled their visit because of the drug investigation. Just another reminder to Helen how his work always came before his family.

· · ·

The day passed with the accomplishment being noted by all except anyone close to him or, more accurately, anyone who was once close to him. The end of his shift came faster than he expected.

Noticing most had already left for the day, Simon headed to the locker room, changed into his bike clothes, and collected his bike in the underground parking garage.

He took the long way home, adding kilometers to his monthly cycling distance by riding out of town along gravel farm roads. With an hour of riding behind him, he took an old rail trail back into town.

A kilometer ahead of him, he noticed a family on the trail biking away from him. "My rabbits," he said to himself. He drew in a deep breath, shifted his gears to increase his speed, and gave chase.

The family, traveling at a snail's pace, approached a road crossing. Simon's goal was to catch them before they reached the road. He sped up and, with his heart rate increasing, closed in on the family.

The man, tall and muscular, pulled a trailer behind his bike and the female had a child's bike attached to her seat post. The child pedaled hard, looking at the trailer as he and his mom attempted to pass it. They entered an area where the trees created a tunnel effect, closing off the sky and darkening the area just before the crossing.

Simon closed in on the family, about a quarter of a kilometer behind them. His lungs burned as his legs pumped the pedals.

The smile on his face suddenly changed. He stopped pedaling and squeezed on his rear brake. From the trees, three men in black hoodies stepped out behind *his rabbits.* Their hoods covered their heads and black gloves covered their hands.

Overdressed for the weather.

He looked ahead of the family he was chasing. At the mouth of the trail, a blue van stopped, blocking the exit of the path. The driver's door and side door slid open and three men, dressed like the others, jumped out and walked onto the trail. The father slowed, then moved protectively ahead of his wife and son.

Simon slowed and pulled to the edge of the trail. He looked behind, to see if others were around. The trail was empty.

The family slowed, approaching the three pedestrians spreading across the trail and blocking their ability to pass.

Simon cautiously rode towards the group, unsure of what he was witnessing. One hundred meters from the interaction, he stopped, pulling off to the side and into the shadows.

The three men who emerged from the trees closed in behind the family and circled them. There was a conversation, but their voices did not carry in the dense treed area. The father motioned with his arms for the men to move. He looked over his shoulder, troubled to see the others behind him.

Being careful to stay hidden from view, Simon walked his bike towards the gathering.

The man who spoke with the couple stepped closer to the father, raised his hand, and opened it. A cloud of powder discharged into the man's face. He dropped immediately to the ground, his bike toppling over him.

Another man stepped forward towards the lady. She screamed for help, struggling to get off her bike.

With the same motion, he released his handful of powder towards her. She fell over, her bike and her child on the come-along bike crashing onto the packed dirt and stones.

The hooded men looked around the trail. One spotted Simon and pointed. Two others bent and reached into the trailer, removing two children, their legs kicking in the air and crying. They ran to the van with their hands over the children's mouths. Two of the men warily watched Simon.

Simon reached for his cell phone.

No signal.

The oldest child, behind his mother, kicked and screamed as the driver of the van lifted him to his feet. He pulled at the grip of the stranger as they followed the others to the van.

"Eh, what's going on here?" Simon yelled. Placing his phone back in his jersey, he threw his leg over his bike and rode towards the group. The men with the children entered the van. Simon could hear all three kids screaming for their parents. Their shrieks reminded him of his own boys the day Helen left him.

The remaining three men took a stance between the parents and Simon.

"Stop! Hey, everyone, just stop!" he yelled, as he closed on them.

The middleman reached behind his back and revealed a pistol. He raised it towards Simon.

Simon locked his brakes and turned to the side of the trail, looking for protection from the trees. The three men spun on their heels and ran to the van. Jumping through the open side door, the wheels spun, the sliding door closed, and the van pulled away. Simon rode to the mouth of the trail, attempting to chase the van. After a quick sprint, he stopped. The dust stirred up from the shoulder of the road, blocked the license plate and choked him.

From his jersey, Simon pulled his phone.

Still no signal.

He looked at the sky. "What the hell, I'm in town and no signal? Excellent job, Star Cellular and your nationwide, reliable service." He placed his phone in his jersey pocket and rode back to the adults lying on the ground.

CHAPTER TWO

Simon placed his bike against an old maple tree. Working to catch his breath, he looked through the trees and up the trail for any signs of motion.

Still, no one around.

The two parents lay motionless on the ground, entangled in their bike frames. He kneeled beside the lady and checked for a pulse. Finding one, he crawled to the man and repeated his action. The man had a cut above his eye, scrapes on his knee and elbow, but he was alive.

"Hello, hey wake up. Hello?" He gently pressed on the man's shoulder.

His eyes fluttered, then opened. They were bloodshot and glassy.

"Hello, what's your name?" asked Simon.

The man stared through Simon, struggling to focus his eyes and mind.

"Lay there. Don't try to move, please. I'll move your bike." Simon removed the bike from his legs. "Is that your wife?"

His head slowly turned to where Simon pointed. He looked at her and nodded, trying to focus on her.

Simon crawled to the lady. "Hello?" He gave her a gentle nudge on her shoulder, then a stronger one. Her eyes slowly opened, bloodshot and glassy, like her husband's. Simon watched her pupils dilate, then she smiled at him. A baby blue powder stuck to her nose and cheeks.

"Are you okay? My name is Simon. I witnessed the whole thing. I tried to chase them, but they all got in the van. Then I tried to call 911, but I've no cell signal."

"Chased who? What are you talking about? Witnessed what?" The man sat up.

"Sir, please—please stay on the ground," said Simon.

"Sir? No, I'm Robin. That's my wife, Susan. What did you witness?" he asked, his voice drawn and slurred.

She sat up and took in her surroundings. She looked towards the road. "What happened? And who are you?" She looked at Simon, then at Robin, confused. She pulled her legs from the bike frame. On her calf was a grease mark from her chain.

"You both should stay seated. Don't try to stand. My name is Simon Elliott. I'm a police officer here in Guelph. I witnessed them take your children."

They both glanced at Simon, then at each other. The lingering effects of the powder hung over them.

"Well, I'm not sure what you..." said Susan.

"I'm sorry, honey. I took my eyes off the trail and must have hit a stone or branch and wiped out, bringing you down with me. Are you okay? Lucky, we weren't going too fast. I must've hit my head. I have a terrible headache and my mouth is very, very dry. Simon, is it? Tell me, is it a crime to have an accident on the trail?" asked Robin.

"Yes, I remember. I swerved to miss you and I guess I dumped my bike. Look, the streamers on Ricky's handlebars ripped off," Susan said. She clawed at the streamers lying behind her and held them up. "I never noticed the colors to be so vibrant."

"What? No, *no*, that's not what happened. Nothing like that happened." Simon checked his phone again, no signal. "Your kids were just kidnapped." He looked at Susan. Her bloodshot eyes and dry mouth looked like the drug users who entered the station, usually with their hands cuffed behind their backs.

"Sure, sure. Susan, your arm is bleeding," said Robin. He dusted the dirt from his arms and reached for his water bottle, still in the cage on his bike's frame.

"We both have scratches on our arms and legs. Robin, you have a cut above your eye." She leaned to get a closer look.

Robin's hand searched his forehead for the cut. He found it by his right temple. "My blood is so red," he said, staring at his hand.

Simon watched them. Their movements and speech were slow and labored.

"We need to go. My parents will be worried. We're late picking up the kids," said Susan.

"Huh. Your kids were with you. A van full of men took them. I witnessed the whole thing," said Simon. He stepped back to allow them to lift their bikes.

"Simon, are you sure you aren't the one who fell off your bike?" asked Robin.

"Listen to me. I know what I just witnessed. Six men just took your children. Men, all dressed in black, came out of the trees and a van stopped on the road—they were talking to you. They blew powder in your face and then took your kids. *One of them pointed a gun at me.*"

Susan threw her leg over her bike. "Please, we need to be going. Thank you for stopping, but as my husband said, he caused our crash. We've had a long day." She adjusted her helmet.

"I don't think either of you should bike," said Simon. He glanced at his phone and shook his head in disbelief.

Robin turned his bike around to head back on the trail.

"There, why are you turning the bikes around? You were coming from that direction. Why are you going back that way? Two kids were just taken from your trailer and the older one from the come-along bike you're pulling. *Susan*, they kidnapped your children. *I know what I saw.* You two were unconscious when I got to you. Please, *please listen to me.*" Simon moved to the middle of the trail with his bike, blocking the trail.

"Simon, I don't doubt you are a police officer and maybe under a lot of stress right now. I think we would know whether we picked up our kids or if someone knocked us out. Neither of those things happened." Robin glanced at his watch. "Let's go Susan, we're really late for the kids." He stumbled as he tried to get his feet on the pedals. "Whoops, I feel a little lightheaded. But honestly officer, I haven't been drinking." He smiled at Simon.

They both looked at Simon. Their faces asking him to move.

"Robin, look at Susan. She has powder on her face. Susan, you see powder on Robin's face too. That trace of baby blue. Actually, don't touch it. I would like to take a sample," said Simon. He reached into his backpack.

"A sample of what? Rock dust from the trail. Can we see a badge, please? You're scaring us," said Susan. She leaned on her handlebars and held her forehead. "Wicked headache."

"Sure, anything, just don't touch your faces." From his backpack, he pulled out his wallet and tossed it to Robin, then continued to search his bag for something to take a sample. At the bottom of his bag was a travel pack of tissues. He took a few out.

Robin completed his investigation of Simon's badge and handed it back.

"Okay, you're a cop. Nevertheless, we need to go. Or are you arresting me for crashing and knocking over my wife?" he chuckled.

"I suspect they drugged you two. Six men took your kids in a van, and I found you lying on the ground. You don't remember any of that?"

"This is very unusual. But..." she stopped when Simon placed a tissue under her chin. She pushed his hand away. "Please..." she suddenly gasped and stumbled back.

"What is it, Susan?" asked Robin.

"I—well, I just had a vision of men in black hoodies. One blew a powder at me." She looked at Simon. "Okay, quickly, take your sample. Robin, let him take his sample—there is something, no it's gone. I feel stoned." She looked at her husband and chuckled.

Simon heard the doubt in her voice. "See this light blue, almost white powder, Robin? You have it on your face too," said Simon.

Like a parent wiping food off a child's face, Simon gently stroked Susan's face, letting the powder drop to the tissue. "Stay still, Susan. You have more of it around your nose. Let me just get it."

He wiped at Robin's cheek and forehead. "I know this all seems weird to you both, but trust me, I know what I saw. There, hopefully, that will be enough. Try not to touch your faces until I can get the rest."

"Simon, we appreciate all this, but we need to get our kids. I'm surprised my mom hasn't called yet," said Susan.

A group of cyclists weaved their way around the trio, still blocking the trail.

"Hey idiots, move to the side next time you want to have a chat on the trail. How about a bit of curtesy for us who want to ride?" the last guy yelled. He sprayed water from his bottle at Simon's legs.

"Screw you," Simon said. He turned to Susan. "Huh, call your mom, please. Then we can all be on our way. I'm not crazy. I know what I saw."

"Yes, call her. Call your mom," echoed Robin.

"No signal. Robin, you got anything?"

"Nothing, weird."

"I have no signal either," said Simon. "I'll come with you. Neither one of you is steady enough to be biking alone. I can tell you exactly what I saw. Then when we get there, we can end this. How about this? If we get to your mom's and your kids are there, supper's on me. Wherever and whatever you want."

"Sure, Simon. Nothing better than a police escort and a free meal," Robin said, smiling. "Can we go slowly? I feel a bit off balanced, lightheaded, and my legs feel weak. Or maybe I'm stoned, as Susan put it, but we don't use drugs." He shook his head.

"I hope we aren't coming down with something right before vacation," said Susan.

"Even better reason for me to stay with you. I can't believe there is no phone service. We're in town," said Simon, looking at his phone and shaking his head.

They pushed off on their bikes. Robin and Susan struggled, needing to stop twice to catch their breath and balance. As they rode, Simon recounted the events that led to him kneeling over them. Even with the proof of a substance on their faces, they denied any memory of the events Simon spoke of. One kilometer away from the incident, a melody of rings played on their phones.

"Can we stop for a minute? Seems all our phones have come back to life," said Susan.

"Yes, I'm not sure what's wrong, but my heart's racing, and I could throw up," said Robin.

"Me too," said Susan.

"I think the powder has affected you two more than you understand. We can walk if you want," Simon said.

She smirked at Simon and shook her head. "Let me check my phone and get my breath. It's like the flu was just sprung on me."

They checked their phones. Simon missed a call from the station. Robin had a text from his work, and Susan had a call from her mom.

"See, my mom is wondering where I am. I missed her call."

"Call her," said Simon.

She did as Simon requested. "Voicemail. We're five minutes away. Let's get over there and put an end to all this confusion. I can get a couple of pills from my mom to help with how I feel."

• • •

After a precarious ride on the groomed trail, they arrived at Susan's parents' house. Simon could hear children playing, screaming, and laughing behind the house.

"I can already hear them playing. See, nothing to worry about," said Susan.

The front door to the house swung open. "Robin, Susan, what are you doing here? Where's Ricky? I didn't see him get off the bike?"

"Not you too, Mable. How are you in on this little joke?" asked Robin.

"What joke?" she replied. Her eyes shifted to Simon. "You're the police officer on the news. You just had a major drug bust in the west end of town. Why are you here?" asked Mable. "I didn't know you two knew him."

Susan looked at Robin. The wrinkles on his forehead told her he was thinking the same thing.

"Mom, we are here to pick the kids up. I can hear them out back. Can we put an end to this little joke?" Her voice cracked as she said the last few words.

"Susan, did you forget something?" Her father asked as he stepped onto the porch.

"What, Dad?"

"Why are you back here, and where are the kids?" he asked.

Susan looked at Robin, then at Simon. Her face shifted from confusion to panic. Blackness filled her vision. Her mind struggled to understand what was happening. She leaned on her dad's car as her legs struggled to support her.

Simon took his phone out of his jersey and called the police station. "It's Simon Elliott. I just witnessed a kidnapping." He nodded to the response.

Susan and Robin dismounted their bikes and dropped on her father's lawn, hearing Simon on his phone.

"Send a couple cars to—" He turned and looked at the house. "To 43 Armstrong Avenue. Prepare an AMBER alert for three missing kids. They were taken in an early 1990s Chevy van, pale blue and in mint condition for its age. Six men in black hoodies were in the vehicle. They're armed, one pointed a pistol at me." He nodded as dispatch read back his information.

He glanced at the couple staring at him in disbelief. They were pale and shaking.

"Huh, when the cruisers get here, we'll have a lot more information on the kids, but get the van intel out now, please. Also send over paramedics. We'll need them too." He nodded and disconnected.

"Mom, this is Simon. As you know, he's a police officer, and unless you two are in on one horrible hoax, he witnessed my children being..." she stopped and buried her face in her hands. Mable put her arms around her daughter.

Robin looked up at Simon from where he'd collapsed on the grass. "Help us, please. Get our kids back."

CHAPTER THREE

The police and ambulance arrived together. Simon directed the paramedics to Robin, Susan and her parents, all who were in various stages of shock.

"What's going on?" Gary Davis, an officer, asked as he approached Simon.

A second officer, Mark Walker, hollered from the open trunk of his cruiser. "Hey, Simon, what do you need?"

"Mark, grab me an evidence bag. I think there might be some dust left on Robin's face." He turned to the paramedics. "Don't touch their faces."

Susan was crying, her tears washing any evidence from her face. But he hoped Robin still had residual powder around his nose and mouth.

From his backpack, Simon retrieved the tissues and placed them in the evidence bag Mark handed him. "Mark, the kidnappers blew this powder on their faces. We need to know what's in it." Kneeling next to Robin on the lawn, he said, "Just a quick second. This is Mark. I want him to swab your cheek and around the base of your nose. I hope there is still some powder there."

"Sure, Simon. What powder?" asked Robin.

"There was some powder blown into your face. We're going to help you, okay?"

Robin nodded.

Simon motioned to a paramedic to follow him to the side. "I'm not sure what they had blown in their faces, but they dosed them with some kind of mind-altering chemical. Just be careful what you give them. They were both out cold for almost five minutes."

"Thanks. That's good to know. Do you know anything else about the powder?"

"Nothing. It was blown at them, and they collapsed immediately. Sorry, I wish I had more—it looks to be baby blue."

"Okay. Did you come in contact with it?"

"I don't think so. For the sample I collected, I used a tissue. I tried to be careful, not to come in contact with it."

"Good. Let us know immediately if you feel ill."

"Will do," he said, as they rejoined the others.

Mark had moved Robin into the passenger side of his cruiser. Carefully, with a cotton swab, he wiped around Robin's mouth, nose, and eyebrows.

Gary and the paramedics tended to Susan. Her face was wet from tears, and she continued to shake. Carefully wiping her face, Gary placed his cotton swab in an evidence bag.

"Simon, I was able to get a sample," said Gary.

"Good. I'll take it," said Mark.

As the paramedics began evaluating the distraught woman, the two men made their way to Mark's cruiser.

Neighbors had left their dinner tables and televisions to stand on their wooden porches trying to see and hear what all the commotion was about. "Hey, Mark, can you calm all these people down, maybe get them back into their homes?"

"Sure."

Leaning into the front seat, Simon said, "Robin, look at me. Tell me what you saw."

"Simon, we had just crossed the street. I remember Susan coming beside me on the trail. I swerved to miss a rock or something I saw at the last second. We touched handlebars. I fell one way and she over corrected and dropped her bike. We must have banged our heads because it knocked us out cold. So much for our helmets protecting our heads."

"No, that isn't what happened. Before this becomes a proper investigation, think. Do you remember seeing three men in dark clothes approach you on the trail?"

"No, what are you talking about? We were coming here to pick up the kids…" He paused. "But we…" He looked around the street. "But we picked up the kids and then…"

"Simon, let him tell me the story. I'll get your statement later. You know better than this," said Mark.

A high-pitched wail sounded throughout the street. Everyone stopped, reached for their phones, and read the AMBER alert.

"No, no, no!" Susan screamed. *This isn't true.*

She fought away from the paramedics, running to her husband. "Robin, how can you be so calm? *Where are our kids?*" she screamed.

Despite Mark's efforts, the nosy neighbors gathered around the cruisers and ambulance. Three more cruisers showed up, and the on-duty sergeant, seeing all the spectators, directed some uniformed officers to help Mark move the crowd back and establish a safe perimeter for the family.

Two more cars arrived.

"What the hell is going on here, Simon?" Terry, Simon's sergeant, asked. "And what are you wearing? Are you undercover in spandex?"

Simon smiled at him. "Terry, I've no idea what's going on. What I do know is, I was out enjoying a late afternoon bike ride until—you can get my statement at the station. Right now, we need the van with their children found. What they think happened is completely different from what I saw. I'm starting to doubt myself."

"I trust you over a couple civilians any day," said Terry.

"Well, I'll let you talk to them yourself. This way." The paramedics had moved Robin to the rear of the ambulance. "Terry, this is Robin. He is the father of the missing children. He needs to…"

"I'm *not* going anywhere," Susan yelled, over all the noise on the street. "I *will not* be getting into any ambulance. *I need to find my children. I need you to find my children, now!*"

"Robin, can you recall what happened this afternoon?" asked Simon.

Again, Robin told the story of how he and Susan had crashed on the trail. When he finished, Simon said nothing, but raised his eyebrows at Terry.

Terry asked a uniformed officer to stand with Robin. He wanted them both, Robin and Susan, brought to the hospital and looked at, under guard. He instructed another officer to take one of Susan's parents and check Robin's and Susan's house for a break in. With their permission, he wanted the inside checked for kids, drugs or anything that would explain their strange behavior.

"Simon, can we leave and talk?" asked Terry. He looked around the scene. "Ashley, come over here, please."

A uniformed officer with two stripes on her shoulder approached.

"You're the sergeant in charge here?"

"Yes, Terry."

"Okay, I'm taking Simon back to my office. I've asked for an officer to stay with them at the hospital and another one to check out their house."

"Okay, Simon, I'll need a statement. I've sent a couple of officers to the trail too," said Ashley.

"Good, good. Come see us when you get a minute," said Terry. "Simon, let's go."

"Sure thing, boss, let me just tell them I'm leaving."

"Sure, I'll put your bike in the trunk."

"Carefully Terry, one scratch and the station buys me a new bike."

"Uh-huh," Terry said.

Simon found Robin sitting on the rear bumper of the ambulance. Susan arrived at the ambulance with her father's arm around her shoulder. He had calmed her and reassured her the police would do everything they could to find the boys. She sat beside Robin. He opened the blanket draped over his shoulders. She moved closer to him and lay her head on his shoulder.

"Guys, are you okay?" asked Simon.

"Where are my kids, Simon? How did this happen?" asked Susan. "Why can't we remember any of what you said happened?"

"We're going to work on this. I need to go back to the station to answer some questions and fill out a report or ten. This is my personal number, call me anytime. I'll call you tomorrow, sooner if I hear anything."

CHAPTER FOUR

Terry's office, on the third floor of the station, looked over a city parking lot. The sun had set, and the sky had a ribbon of blood red left on the horizon. Simon sat across from Terry, reviewing his attempted bike ride home and the details of the kidnapping.

"Okay, why did you stop when the men came out of the trees?"

"Terry, it's not normal for three men in hoodies to appear like they did. It startled me."

Terry wrote on a yellow pad of paper. "Did you hear any of the conversation?"

"No, nothing. Just—just an opinion. But I wonder if the man who talked to them fed them the story they're telling. They're both telling the same story, like they heard it somewhere instead of experiencing it."

"Good point." Terry scribbled a note on the pad. "Anything else?"

Simon sat back and reviewed the episode in his mind. "Wait, when the last man jumped into the van he yelled, *'go,'* as the door closed."

"Okay. But..."

"No, no, wait. He had a German or Italian accent."

"Are you sure?"

"Yes. It was—it wasn't Canadian. Not even French Canadian. Definitely European. Italian, I think."

"Anything else?"

He looked at the ceiling. "Nothing, Terry. It happened so quick."

"The powder?"

STEPHEN W. BRIGGS   19

"The guys with the powder had gloves on, those blue medical gloves, and the rest had black leather gloves."

"Your cell? You said you couldn't call. You had no service?"

"Right, we all checked. Nothing, not even basic 3G. The phones had no signal. We were five minutes away from her parents' house when I felt my phone vibrate."

"Do you think the van had a scrambler?"

"I suppose. Was an outage reported?" asked Simon.

"Not that I heard. I'll have Ken in IT check."

"Call someone back to the scene and have them check. I've never noticed it before, but maybe there's a dead spot there on the trail."

"Ashley can confirm it for us," Terry said.

They sat quietly in the office as Terry flipped his pages over. Simon jumped when Ashley knocked on the door. Terry waved her in.

"We finally got them to the hospital and partially sedated. The doctor was careful of the dosage in case the powder was a potent drug. He'd like to know what was in it. They're doing some blood work, too."

"In case? They *were* drugged," said Simon.

"The blood work will hopefully confirm that. Their stories are identical, almost too identical, if you know what I mean. Mable, Susan's mother, said Susan and Robin picked their kids up at the regular time today. The three children," she looked at her notes, "Ricky, ten, and the twins, Doug and Don, aged eight, were picked up at the same time as every other day. Today they played in the backyard with a neighbor's grandkids until approximately 5:15 pm, when Robin and Susan collected their kids. The neighbor, John Harrow, helped buckle the twins into the trailer. They left for home, giggling and waving." She briefly consulted her notes. "John said he was eating supper out back with his grandkids when Robin and Susan returned. He heard some commotion and went to investigate. They'd returned without the kids, but he was confused when he saw you, Simon, with them. Simon, I am going to need your statement at some point."

"It's right here and nowhere near what you have documented from them," said Terry.

"Who's on the trail, Ashley?" Simon asked.

"Barry and Jen. Why?" asked Ashley.

"Call their cells to see if they get a signal," said Terry. "We're wondering if the van had a scrambler running."

"Straight to voicemail. It could very well be a dead zone. I'll have it investigated." She pulled out her notebook. "I'll ask Ken to help."

"Ashley, what do you have Gary and Mark doing?" asked Simon.

"Gary's at the hospital now, taking statements from the parents, and Mark's with Chris at Susan and Robin's residence. One other thing, there have been no reports on the mystery van Simon reported."

"Where's the powder I collected?"

"I just packaged it. Someone will take it to the lab in Toronto for testing once I find a free body. The lab knows I need answers tonight, for medical purposes." She looked at her watch. "But we know it will probably be tomorrow, hopefully before noon."

"Okay, Ashley, anything else? I'd like to send Simon home," said Terry.

"Nothing right now. But if I need anything, we all know where you live, Simon." She smiled. "Don't go anywhere."

"Am I a suspect, Ashley?"

"Number one, as always. How perfect. The criminal is within the police station."

He reached out his arms and pressed his wrists together. "You're good Ashley. Terry, I give up. Take me away. I will disclose everything."

Ashley shook her head and laughed. "Don't leave the city," she said, as she left the room.

"Simon, head home. Report back to work tomorrow as usual. We'll need to review your statement, but you can't be part of the investigation."

"No, I want to stay and keep working this. I can head out to the trail or up to the hospital."

"I can't have you do that. You're our only witness. You're not running this, nor can you be involved in any part of the investigation. Understand? So, please go home. Come back tomorrow. We can talk more then. Do you want a ride?"

CHAPTER FIVE

Sleep did not come easily for Simon. He replayed the events of the past evening through his mind over and over, searching for a small forgotten detail—each time sitting at his kitchen table writing what he witnessed, then comparing it to his last set of notes. He kept wondering why he stopped instead of charging in and attempting to stop the kidnaping. The children calling for their parents played in his mind. He tried to call his boys, but no one answered the phone. He headed to bed, lonely, confused, and frustrated with his actions.

. . .

Simon returned to the station early, looking for Ashley.

"Good morning, Simon. You're here early," Ashley said, seeing his reflection on her computer screen.

"I couldn't sleep," he said, leaning on her desk. "I wanted to see you before your shift ended. Are there any updates from overnight?"

"Nothing. The van has disappeared, and they released Robin and Susan from the hospital around one this morning. Her mom is with them at their house."

"How are they?"

"I'm not sure, they haven't updated me on that. With the meds the doctor gave them, I assume they slept. We left a car outside their house, so I'll get a report before my shift ends."

"Any findings on the powder?"

"Simon, this isn't your case, right?"

He stood and looked down at her. "Huh. No, I know, but I'm the only witness and, well..."

"Hey, don't. I know where you're going and don't. No one is blaming you for your actions. So don't Simon. You did what you needed to do."

"I know. Easier said than done. I don't know why I hesitated and didn't just ride to them."

"Don't worry. We'll get you what you need to accept this, even if the bosses want you out of the loop. I'll be handing the case to your department when Terry gets in. I'm assuming Gary and Mark will run with this one."

"Thanks Ashley."

• • •

He sat at his desk and reviewed documents from the drug bust while waiting for Terry.

With his gym bag swinging from his shoulder, Terry passed Simon's desk heading to his office. Simon followed him.

"Simon, let me get Ashley's updates from the night, then we can talk. She needs to head home," said Terry.

After a half-hour, Ashley tapped on Simon's desk. "You're up to bat."

After a brief review of his night, Simon asked the first official question. "Do you think we have a professional kidnapping ring happening? Or, and this one's out there, could this be payback for the drug bust? The first of a series of kidnappings in the area to let us know—what? They're still around, proving they weren't defeated? There could be a ransom or worse. I've run the whole thing over in my head many times. They weren't amateurs. It wasn't an estranged uncle or friend. Those guys were pros. They were so precise and to have a powder ready. They had it all planned out."

"Let's not get into conspiracies just yet. We have three missing kids and parents with no memory of what happened. There are news crews here looking for answers, and the chief's statement was vague last night. Today's going to be a PR nightmare if we don't get a handle on things early."

"I agree."

"At nine, I'll call the lab and start pushing for the results," said Terry.

"Okay, I'd like to see them myself. Would you have an issue if I visited the family later?"

"Don't leave the station until the results come in. I want Gary to sit with you one last time to review what you witnessed, then yes, you can go visit the family. It might help you both. Also, on your way, stop at the trail and see if your phone works. Call me."

"Thanks, Terry. If there is anything..."

"Simon, you need to be hands off on this one. You're a witness. Know your role, please."

"Okay. One last thing. I was wondering, can I have a few days off? I'll be available for questions and meetings, but I need a break. You know better than anyone here what I'm going through. Quitting smokes in June was hard. Not seeing my kids this summer has also taken its toll on me. The drug bust was worth it, I guess, but I need some time to binge watch a show and eat pizza for breakfast. Ya' know what I mean? Take the bike out on a tour for a couple of days. And if she lets me, head west to see my boys."

Terry looked up at him. "Yes, I have no problem approving your leave. Just make sure you're around if we need you. Keep your phone with you, especially if you're out biking alone. Whoever or whatever took those kids is aware there was a witness. Before you go to see the boys, let me know. Other than that, stay away from the case. Leave starts at the end of your shift. Until then, clean up anything on your desk, review the notes from the bust and then clock off for two weeks. You've earned it."

"Thanks Terry, I'll check in before I leave."

"Hold on, I just got an email from the lab." Terry sat quietly as he clicked his mouse. He moved it around on the mouse pad with a worn-out photo of him and his family standing on a dock in Cozumel with a large cruise ship behind them.

"What's it say?"

"Well, no wonder they can't remember anything. The powder has a few unique items in it. They found three main chemicals comprising eighty-nine percent of the sample—Domoic Acid, PCP and Salvia Divinorum. The remaining eleven percent are trace chemicals, but not enough to be identified. They assumed road dust and other nonmedical chemicals."

"That's quite the cocktail. No wonder they've no memory of the incident or picking up their kids."

"We should be happy they didn't overdose."

"Do we know if the hospital took blood?"

"Unless they give us permission, I doubt the hospital will pass on their findings. But when you visit them, be sure to ask them if we can have the results. It'd be nice to confirm this report with a blood sample."

• • •

Simon pulled the car up to the mouth of the trail. From his pocket, he pulled out his phone.

Four bars

Stepping out of the car, he dialed Terry's number.

"Terry, I'm at the mouth of the trail. How clear is the call?"

"Crystal clear," said Terry.

"Stick with me. I'll walk in to where I first checked my phone. This is strange, I'm roughly where the interaction happened. There's a hole, it's fresh, about two feet deep and a foot wide. That was not there yesterday. Follow-up and see if we dug it. I doubt we did, it's too fresh. You there?"

"Yes, you haven't dropped."

"I'll keep moving. I'll snap a couple of photos on the way back."

He arrived where he checked his phone the day before. He still had four bars. Terry never heard any distortion as he talked. He walked back to the hole and took photos of it and its location on the trail.

As he stepped back into the car, he looked around. He had a strange feeling someone was watching him.

• • •

Simon arrived at Robin and Susan's house as he ended a phone call with Gary on the latest updates of the case. He looked at the house and hesitated. He dialed his ex-wife's number.

"Hello, Simon."

"Hi, Helen, how are you?"

"I'm very busy right now. The kids are out with friends playing if you want to call back later."

"I was just approved for vacation, now that my drug investigation is complete." He paused. "I was thinking of flying out to see you guys, you know, spend some time with the kids and you, maybe?"

"Oh, umm? When?"

"Later this week? I just need to get a flight and clean a few things up around the house." He smiled, having expected a hard *no* right away.

"Well, I don't think that's going to work. Sorry, Simon. With school started and other things going on right now. How about this? I could take them out of school on the Thursday and Friday before Thanksgiving and let them fly to see you?"

His hopes dashed, he blurted out before thinking, "But, Helen, I have a right to see…"

"*What?* Where was your concern this summer when I had to tell them they weren't going for a visit? Where was that concern when the station would call, and you would run out the door years ago? Don't you tell me you have a right, Simon. *Don't you start.*"

He sat in silence and hit his steering wheel.

"Plus, I didn't want to say anything just yet, but why not? I met someone a year ago. We moved into his house last month. He's good with the kids and me."

"What?"

"I need to go, Simon. I have errands to run. This weekend I'll have the boys call you, Saturday, at 9 a.m. my time."

The phone disconnected. Simon threw his phone into the passenger side floorboards. He dropped his head onto the steering wheel, struggling to stop shaking.

CHAPTER SIX

Simon knocked on the front door of the Easton's. Robin answered the door. The black lines under his eyes and messy hair made him look older than he did the previous evening. With a handful of tissues, Susan arrived behind Robin. She was pale, her eyes bloodshot and puffy.

"Simon, we weren't expecting you. Do you have news about my children?" asked Susan.

"No, I wish I did. If I had any news, I likely would have knocked the door down to get to you two. I thought I would stop by and see how you are doing. But this is unofficial, just a check in."

"Please, come in Simon," Robin said. "Coffee?"

"Sure. How are you guys holding up? Sorry, stupid question," Simon said, entering the house and following them to the living room.

"How do we answer that? Really, what do we say? They poked and prodded us in the hospital. I swear they treated us like a couple of druggies."

"That reminds me. Would you mind releasing your blood samples to us? It would confirm our analysis of the powder."

"Sure, if it'll help," Robin said.

"Great. Gary will have a form for you to sign when he returns."

"You know, no matter how hard we try, we don't remember anything from about 3 p.m. yesterday afternoon until you picked us up off the ground on the trail. If someone planned to kidnap our kids, why not kill us? It would've been better than living like this," said Susan, from the kitchen.

Simon stood and looked at the family photos on the mantel of the fireplace. Each 5x7 frame had a photo of a vacation or a trip around southern Ontario. The five of them smiling, laughing and happy as a family. Two thoughts ran through Simon's mind. *They were a close family* and *I wish I had memories with Helen and the boys like these.*

Pointing to one photo, Robin said, "That was Disney about three months ago. Our first trip there with the kids." He turned away from the photo with pain in his eyes. "Will we see them alive? How do things like this go?"

"Have you followed all the steps we asked? Have you called every friend, family, and estranged person you can think of?"

"Yes, we finished this morning. My mom and dad made most of the calls," Susan said, handing Simon a mug of coffee.

"Just so you both are aware, I am not investigating the case. You don't have to tell me anything. Being a witness, I can't investigate. But I'm taking a leave. I've had a crazy year and need some time off."

They sat quietly, sipping their coffees. "Simon," Susan hesitated and looked at Robin. "Simon, why didn't you stop them? Why did you let them take my kids? You watched as they stole my children. You stood and watched as they threw them in a van. *Why?*"

"Susan, I told you not to do this." Robin attempted to embrace her, but she pushed him away.

"No, Robin, no. He's a police officer. What happened to *serve and protect*? It doesn't say stand and watch, it says, *serve and protect.*"

"Simon, I'm..." Robin said.

"I should go. It was a mistake to come here so soon. I tried to stop them. It was just such a—you know." He looked to the floor, then at Susan. "You know that feeling when you just can't believe what you are seeing? And I know when I describe it with the details it sounds like a lengthy time, but it wasn't the whole interaction was less than a minute." He shook his head. "Thank you for the coffee. I wish I'd done more, believe me. I should have done more with my own family, too." He quickly stood and walked to the door, but felt a tug on his arm and turned.

"Sorry, really, I am. I shouldn't be thinking like that. You did what you could. I don't think anyone else would've reacted any differently. Please come back and finish your coffee," said Susan.

He looked past her at Robin, who was nodding his head. He followed her back to the living room.

"Please tell us one more time how it happened," said Susan.

Simon reviewed his evening from leaving the station to picking them off the ground.

Susan cried, and Robin sat quietly, looking out the window to his backyard. The swings gently moving in the wind.

"We were talking before you came. We're thinking of hiring a private investigator," said Susan. "This might sound strange, but can we hire you while you're on vacation to investigate this?"

Simon looked at them both and smiled. "Well, yes and no, sorry. I would need to get a PI license to start. The two officers on your case are very good. If they find anything, they'll be all over the leads. I'll be involved a bit when I go back, I'm sure. So as much as I'd like to help, I can't."

"Okay, is there anyone you would recommend?" asked Robin.

"Let me think about that one. I know a few investigators, but they're more the cheating spouse, insurance fraud type."

"What about the vehicle you saw? Anything on it?" Robin asked.

"Nothing. It's an old vehicle, so there aren't too many around. I believe we've contacted the owners of all but three within a hundred-kilometer radius. Mostly older contractors who don't know how to put their tools down and retire."

"Did the AMBER alert receive any calls?" asked Robin.

"No, nothing. That's just it. An old van like that would stick out in people's minds. It would for me anyway."

"Maybe it means they were close to the area where our children were taken. Maybe they're still here in Guelph," said Robin.

Susan returned carrying a tray with cookies and a fresh pot of coffee.

"We can sit outside." She motioned to the patio door and slid it open.

"You should keep a bar on the rails when you're not home. Those doors are easy targets for criminals."

"Little late now, they stole everything from us yesterday," said Susan.

"Listen, you need to keep the faith. Both of you remain positive. For each other. The universe works off positive vibes. If there's one piece of advice I can give you it's, don't start blaming each other or doubting each other. I've seen it in other cases where an event like this destroys a marriage. Please, if you feel anything like that, talk to each other or get professional help."

They sat at a wooden table looking out at the trampoline, swing set and sandbox. Robin opened a large umbrella for shade while Susan placed the mugs around the table.

"What about the men you said came out of the trees? Aren't there a few houses on the other side of the tree line?"

"Officers are checking with the owners for cameras or if they heard or saw anything. We won't leave any stones unturned."

"We want to do something, but we've been told to stay here. I want to be out looking for the kids. Shouldn't we be organizing search parties, hanging posters, or searching the fields and parks inside and around the city?" asked Susan.

"I know what you're saying, and I understand your anxiousness, but we need you here in case your phone rings or they appear in the driveway. Every local channel on the TV and radio has reported it to their audience. If your children were targeted, there could be a ransom request."

Simon took a drink of coffee and examined the fluffy white clouds passing over them, like giant balloons.

"Can you delay your leave and help, assist, poke around on this case?" asked Robin.

"No, because I'm a witness, they won't let me work the case. And in all honesty, I need the leave. I was going to go out to Vancouver and see my kids."

"Oh, that will be..."

Simon shook his head. "My ex told me it's a bad time. She just informed me today she's now living with someone." Simon dropped his head. "Well, I guess we're all VIPs of the worst couple days club."

Robin patted him on his forearm.

"You know what?" Simon raised his head. "Yes, I need some good fortune, good vibes, whatever you want to call it in my life. I'm going to do it. Yes, I'll take your case. I'll search for the kids. I don't know how far I'll get, but yes, my leave starts tonight at five. We need to keep this quiet. Canadian law differs from what we see on TV from the States. I'll let Gary and Mark know what I'm doing. They won't have a problem with it. But anything you learn has to go to them first. We'll keep it between us and only a few others at the station, understand? I'll start working on my PI application tomorrow to keep everything legal."

"If it means bringing my kids home, not a word to anyone," said Robin.

"Thank you, Simon," said Susan. A weight visibly lifted from her shoulders.

Simon finished his coffee, looking at the clouds.

CHAPTER SEVEN

Hayfield, Northern England

Norm Shoemaker happily bounced on the seat of his tractor, just minutes behind the rising sun, inspecting his fields of wheat, beets, and barley. For a change, he could get an early start to his day and the work he had fallen behind on. Over the last week, he hadn't felt well, spending a few days in bed. The days he could get up and move around a horrible headache kept him in darkness and silence.

Stopping in his first few fields, he found his wheat crops were growing well in the late summer heat, but pests, the beet leaf miner, had infested his beet crop. He spot checked the field of beets to ensure he wouldn't lose them all to pests. Priding himself on using the old ways of farming he learned as a boy, he kept some chemicals and fertilizers only as a last option. Returning from Germany in 1944, he had married, raised three children, and now had grandchildren. In 2003, his wife passed. His children left for college, and not wanting the *farm life,* they all relocated to the more prosperous southern England, around London. In the summer, he worked on his crops, and in the winter, he spent time with his children and grandchildren.

Pulling onto his third field of golden wheat, from the corner of his eye, he noticed the motion of what he thought was a fox. Turning his head, he realized it was a grown man in a black hoodie sprinting through a field of barley towards the fence that separated Norm's farm from a windy, narrow road.

"Now, what's this?" Norm said. He shifted up the tractor's transmission and headed toward the intruder. Watching the man run, he headed towards the barley field, hoping to intercept the stranger. Two other men in black hoodies joined the man he was pursuing. They ran through the field sure footed on the old dry soil, looking over their shoulders at Norm and his tractor.

He chased them as quickly as the old tractor would go without damaging his crops.

Come on, old girl, give me more.

The trio arrived at a small wooden fence and hopped over it. Norm had to stop, back up and head to a gate, not as direct as jumping a fence.

He drove his tractor, now overheating, into the field. He stopped and surveyed his land.

Where did they go?

"Damn kids, what have they done?" He pulled out his flip phone and dialed the local precinct in Hayfield.

"Hello, it's Norm Shoemaker. It looks like a large crop circle has miraculously appeared in one of my fields. Damn kids, they don't understand how much this hurts me and the other farmers. Can you send someone over to investigate?" He paused and listened to the reply. "Yes, it's field seven and yes, have him come up that road. Thank you." He closed his phone and wiped his forearm across his wrinkled and tanned forehead.

The last few years had been tough on Norm and his farm, and to lose any of his crops this year would mean having to sell a field or two to one of the bigger corporations. To lose a field to what other farmers were calling the new Druid society doing ancient rituals boiled his blood. Climbing off his tractor, he traced the perimeter of the design, stepping over his crops. He kneeled down and inspected the bent barley, noticing how it followed the patterns of the circles. The standing barley looked completely untouched, while another stem beside it was carefully bent and woven into other plants.

He stood and looked to the road. A police car stopped on the road beside the field. Norm took out his phone and called the station. "Hello, it's Norm. Can you radio the officer you sent? He's on the road by the field." He paused. "Yes, thank you for the quick response, but I need him to go about a quarter of a kilometer up the road and open the gate, then follow the muddy path to the tractor. Tell him not to leave the path or you'll be pulling him out. The lower land is very mucky. When he gets to the tractor, it's dry. Tell him I'll meet him there."

• • •

Fifteen minutes later, a ginger haired, pimply faced bobby shook Norm's hand.

"I called the police, not the Boy Scouts, son," Norm said.

"Yes sir, I get that all the time. My name's Jeff Spence. Even though I look like I should be sitting in class doing my sums, I'm a police officer in my second year on the force. I just have a youthful face," he said, changing his shoes to Wellington boots.

"You're not from around here?"

"No, born and raised in London. I get that question a lot, too."

"Jeff, you have a young everything. Is this your first crop circle call? They don't seem to happen as much as they did years ago."

"Yes, sir. First one. I'm a big crop circle fan. I've been following them since I was a lad."

"Jeff, I hate to tell you, but you're still a lad."

"I'll take down the details for my report and then, with your permission, well—I have a small drone in the cruiser. It's my personal one. Can I fly it over to get a video of the circle?"

"A drone? Isn't that what Obama used to blow up people in the Middle East?"

"Well, yes and no, mine is just a camera, nothing special," he said.

Norm pulled a map from his tractor and located the field they were in, showing Jeff his property line.

Jeff turned and looked over the land, shading his eyes from the sun.

"Go ahead, son. Let's get a look at this crop circle," said Norm.

They struggled around a side of the circle.

"Okay, it's muddy. Instead of struggling through the field, why not just let my drone be our eyes?"

Winded from the walk, Norm nodded in agreement.

• • •

Jeff stood with his controller and phone in his hands. Norm stood behind him, looking over his shoulder as the drone lifted into the air.

"This will cost me a few quid in damages," said Norm.

"Actually, Norm, you might be surprised. You have a pretty secure fence line. You can sell tickets to people. Set up a website, sell photos of it. I know one farmer who sold the seeds to people. They were bean plants, and he called them *magical beans*. Sold enough to buy a new tractor and upgrade some other equipment. There is some science that proves seeds harvested within a crop circle will over produce the next year."

"Son, I just want what I have to produce for me this year, and a large crop circle isn't helping me."

"It looks like four large circles, connected to look like a four-leaf clover. It's an interesting pattern. Two large circles have smaller circles within them, with opposite shading. Look, I can zoom in on one for you. It's pretty cool with the barley pushed over the circles have an illusion of shading. The other two large circles have triangles. No, it's more like six-sided stars with a smaller triangle inside them, there that's a better angle of this one. Again, the shading is opposite from each other, amazing. Look how the stem of the clover curls out and away from the circles, with a circle within a circle. Then how it fades out to a point. You've a nice design here, Norm. Definitely worth selling tickets to."

Jeff flew over the center of the crop a few times.

"I wouldn't know where to start," said Norm.

"If you want, I have some friends—Wait, there's something in the middle. See here where the two large inner circles overlap. I'm not sure if it's an animal or..."

Jeff struggled to keep the drone airborne as his hands shook and his breath quickened.

"Jeff, is that a person?"

Through the small screen on his phone, they both peered at a body. A child's body lay in the fetal position, bare except for a white sheet wrapped around his waist.

He lowered the controls, hovering the drone a few meters above the body. "Yes, it's a body. A child's."

He raised the drone to a height where it could hover.

"We need to examine it. Here, hold this while I radio into the station." He handed Norm the controls to the drone. "Don't move anything. It will hover."

Norm clung to the controllers as he looked into the screen. He raised his head and looked into the field. The sun glistened through the swaying plants.

Jeff informed the station what he found. He tapped Norm on the arm, pointing at the drone dropping towards the earth. Norm leveled his hands, stopping the drone's nosedive and allowing it to hover again.

"They're sending an emergency team, and a team from Manchester will arrive later. Sorry, Norm, but this is now a crime scene."

Jeff landed his drone and placed it in his satchel. They carefully walked into the circles. From the distance, it looked like one of Norm's shaved sheep sleeping. But when they arrived, it was what the drone had shown them, a young boy, preteen.

Norm looked at Jeff. "How the hell did a child get here? Then again, how the hell did this whole thing get here? I was on this field four days ago."

"Norm, I've no clue how any of this happens. I've some theories but so do many others, but science calls us all conspiracy theorist. Just stay back if you can't handle it. Try not to move around. Hopefully, we can find a boot print or two."

In the distance, the wailing of sirens grew louder. Jeff kneeled beside the body. Putting on a purple pair of surgical gloves, he touched the skin.

Cold and stiff.

He took his hand away and shook his head.

Norm stood behind him. "Dead. Dead on my property in the middle of a crop circle. What witchcraft is going on here, Jeff?"

"Norm, look. It looks like his blood has been drained. See the incision just above the collarbone?"

Jeff radioed the station. "Tell the responding team there is no need to rush. The body can't be revived. No one should drive past my car. Otherwise, they'll likely get bogged down."

While waiting, Jeff took a couple of photos with his cell phone.

●   ●   ●

When the emergency vehicles entered the field, Norm and Jeff could hear voices calling to them. Jeff's sergeant, Garret Holmes, was the first to arrive to them.

He looked at the body, then at Jeff. "Did you move it?"

"No, sir."

"Right, make sure you note it in the report. Is this the owner of the land?" asked Garret.

"Well, we all know the queen owns all the land on the island, but yes, this is my little piece to tend to. I was the one who reported the crop circle," said Norm.

"Jeff, make sure you get his statement, too."

"Already done."

"Did you fly your drone over the circles?"

"Yes, sir. I did."

The inspector looked at Norm. "Kids these days, I can't keep up." He turned to Jeff. "I will need the file."

"Of course, sir. I didn't complete a full grid flyover. I stopped when we found the body."

"Before you leave, please do it."

"Yes, sir."

"I want this place secure. No one in or out. The lads from Manchester will want to do a thorough investigation when they arrive. They're sending down a forensics team. Until then, get your drone up and complete the flyover. I'll get my camera and snap some photos."

●   ●   ●

The team from Manchester arrived and took over the scene later that morning. Norm stood back and watched as they trampled through his good crops. Once the forensics officers completed their investigation, the body was removed and driven to Manchester for an autopsy.

"Excuse me, could it be possible for you men to stick to one route in and out of the circle and my fields? Every plant you step on is money out of my pocket. There's no insurance for crop circles or city officers trampling healthy crops."

Timothy, the lead forensics officer, stood by Norm. "Sir, we found a body in one of your fields. Do you know what that means?"

"I'm the number one suspect?"

"So, I understand you have a business here, but we also have business. We need to find how a body got here."

"Right."

He stepped back and looked at Norm. "Garret, have you questioned him?"

"Timmy..."

"It's Timothy. We are not back in the schoolyard here."

"Timothy," Garret said with a touch of sarcasm. "We have completed our investigation. It's in your hands now. This is a big city investigation."

"Garret, with all due respect, you sent a child to investigate a murder scene? How old is constable Jeff?"

Jeff looked at Timothy and then at his partner. "Umm, my age is not germane to the case. This started simply as a crop circle, and since discovering the body, we have determined it's not a murder scene. If you noted, they drained the body of blood. The incision above his right collar bone would be your first clue. Second, there isn't a drop of blood anywhere inside or outside the crop circle. So, at best, the body was placed in the crop circle. Third, they placed the body in its last location early this morning. There are too many wild animals looking for free meals around here. There's no way someone or something left the body alone overnight or for an extended amount of time. Oh, and it's obvious *they* made the circle before bringing the body here. Then the fact his head was shaved. Typical of ritual killings and a quick way to change the appearance of a child to move him around the country. Finally, the footprints we found match Norm's from the other day. They are not fresh and match the boots he's currently wearing. They go nowhere near where the body was located. So why don't you men go back to your offices in the big city and find out who is missing a child?" He took in a deep breath and looked at his sergeant.

Everyone looked at Jeff. He met the eyes of the officers, Garret, and then Norm.

Norm nodded and smiled at him.

"Now, Norm is likely hungry as I know I am. It's almost dinner time, and we have been standing around this circle since seven this morning."

Timothy looked at Garret. "Okay, well, I guess you can handle securing the field tonight. If we need to, we'll be back tomorrow, but like the kid said, we need to find where the body came from. It's *obvious* someone didn't kill him here. We just want to fly our drone over the field, and then we will be on our way."

The large drone flew over the entire field in a grid pattern. Everyone stood around the monitor watching for anything that seemed out of place. Norm sat directly in front of it, knowing his fields like the back of his hand.

With the drone secured back in the vehicle, the forensics team headed back to Manchester.

"What a bunch of assholes," Norm said. "I didn't realize there was a rivalry between the police around here and the city boys."

"Yes, it's not just the general population. It trickles down to police, contractors, every profession. I've broken up my share of pub fights around here when the city folks come out for a weekend trip, then all they do is put down the locals and tell everyone how great living on miles of asphalt and concrete is," said Jeff.

"And we all know I'll have those people crawling over my fields once the news releases the information on this crop circle."

"Well, Norm, I'm sorry about this. If there's anything you need, just call. If you see anything suspicious or have too many visitors, let me know. We don't have enough constables to put a watch on the field," said Garret.

"Jeff, if you come back to the main house, I'd like a copy of the drone's file. Plus, if you don't mind, I could use your help to fly over my barn so I can see the condition of the roof. If you don't need him elsewhere, Garret."

"Not at all. Glad to help. Plus, both our shifts ended about two hours ago."

"You're welcome to come too. There's a free meal in it. Lamb?"

"Thanks, but I need to get home to see my kids before they head to bed. I miss enough nights as it is." They walked to the cars. "One last thing, Norm." He bent into his car and pulled out some papers. "Here, take these. A farmer gave me copies of this a few years ago. I dug it up before coming out to the call. Fill the forms out and send them to the address on the top of the third or fourth page. You'll get money back for the damages to your crops."

Norm took the papers and quickly scanned them. "Thank you, Garret. I appreciate this."

CHAPTER EIGHT

Jeff took his drone from the trunk of his car. "What barn needs reviewed?" he asked Norm after he finished parking his tractor in the maintenance barn.

"If you have time, all three," said Norm. "But the one I just parked the tractor in is the worst, I would think."

"Right." He raised the drone with the controllers.

"I should text my kids and tell them about my day," said Norm.

"I'll be about half an hour to forty-five minutes, then I have a couple more questions for you, unofficial."

Norm went into the house and sent texts to his kids, telling them about the crop circle and the forms for a rebate. He received "*that's cool dad*" from his oldest as he cooked lamb chops in the frying pan.

Jeff knocked on the door, then stepped into the house. "All done, Norm. Can we talk a bit more?"

"Yes, come in. Bathroom is just down the hall, you can wash up in there. I have dinner waiting for you."

Jeff breathed in the smell of lamb. "One of my favorite meats."

Norm welcomed him to his old wooden table, where he set a place for Jeff. "First, it must be a London thing, but who puts that much tomato sauce on their chips?"

Jeff laughed at Norm's comment. "Habit, I guess. Norm, this is just me speaking, not Officer Jeff. I'm off the clock. I need to be sure we are on the same page."

"Right, the kid, not the copper."

Jeff smiled at the comment. "Aye. This is why I came up here. For the crop circles. They have fascinated me since I was a kid. Not just crop circles, but anything outside the norm."

"UFO's and assassinations?"

"Yes, I know what you're going to say but, yes, all that stuff. I find it fascinating."

"Do you think the royals are reptilians?"

"What?" Jeff asked, tomato sauce teetering on his chin.

"The elite control the world?"

"Norm, you're one of us?"

"Maybe a little." He laughed at Jeff's surprised reaction. "My middle son has been into it since he was a young boy. Couldn't—wouldn't stop talking about UFOs and other conspiracies. I believe it was the Rendlesham Forest UFO sighting that hooked him."

"Okay, I wasn't expecting that from you, but *okay.*"

"Everyone has their secrets. Remember that."

"So, what are you going to do? I could help you with a website and promotion of the circle. You could sell tickets to people that want to…"

Norm raised his hand. "No, none of that. Maybe, and it would be a hard sell, but maybe if a child wasn't found in the middle of the circle, I would consider it but no, I will harvest my crops, or what's left of them and then turn the soil for the winter crops."

"I understand, and I respect that."

They sat reflecting on the boy and where he came from and what horrors he might have seen before dying. Jeff broke the silence. "Norm, would you mind if I did some extra investigating before you clear the field? I have some friends I'd like to bring, too." He took a bite of the lamb, loosening the tomato sauce from his chin. It landed on his pants. "They don't make food this good down south."

"Thank you. As for my fields, just no messing with my good plants. I need to keep what I have in the fields. Respect the fields and my crops and then, yes, you can bring over some friends."

"Thank you."

They sat at the table discussing conspiracies until dispatch called the house asking if Jeff would return the much needed cruiser before midnight.

•   •   •

The next evening, Jeff stood on Norm's porch with two friends.

"Hi, Norm, I was wondering, before the sun goes down, could we go back out to the crop circle? We promise not to damage anything. This is Al, he's a chemical engineer, and this is Tom, he's a specialist in crop circles, and hosts a conspiracy podcast."

"Come in here, you three. What is this, the *Scooby Doo hour?*"

They followed Norm into his parlor and sat on the sofa, expecting a scolding for disrespecting the life of a child. From behind the door, Norm pulled a rifle.

Tom pressed himself into the couch.

"Now, Norm..." said Jeff, raising his hands to shoulder level.

"You lads need to be careful if you are going out there." He placed the rifle on the table. "I'm coming with you. Jeff, there was something I didn't put in the report. I saw three men in black hoodies running through my field as I approached the crop circle. I wasn't doing a routine ride on my property, well I was when I started out, but it turned into chasing three men. It was strange, they seemed to disappear. I lost sight of them when they moved from one field to the next because I had to go around to the gate. But where could they have gone? When I saw them, they were in no rush. They ran, more of a jog or trot, I guess. They were all about the same height and build, with broad shoulders. It was weird how they, well, they almost looked transparent."

"What? Why didn't you include it in your statement?" asked Jeff.

"It was likely the way the sun was hitting my tractor's window and reflecting, but they seemed to just disappear. I didn't see them run up the road. No car drove away, just *poof,* into thin air. I knew if I put it in the report, it would create a larger investigation, and, well, at my age, they would check me to see if I was senile. Here's the strange thing. There were no footprints again, like at the circle."

"Sir, that's why we're here. We investigate circles in our free time. Jeff sent us the file of his flyover. We haven't seen one as magnificent as yours in years. And four large circles, very rare. But I have in the past heard the same stories. Men in black hoodies seen around the circles. You're not the first to report that, or not report it." Tom winked at him. "Please, we have no money to pay, but we'd love to spend a couple of hours out there before the sun sets. If possible, be the only ones you allow to investigate your circle."

"I never said no, did I? You need to be careful, that's why I'm coming too. I'm also curious as to what you find."

•   •   •

They all climbed into Norm's Range Rover and took a route through the fields to the location of the crop circle. They watched as news helicopters flew over his fields.

"Can I shoot at them?" he asked Jeff, a smile grew on his face.

"I'd prefer if you didn't. I'm not sure I want my boss to know I'm back here, allowing you to shoot at the local news. And if you pop off a shot, they'll be asking us all questions."

"Can I put a complaint in about it?"

"Again, it will be my co-workers attending the complaint."

"I suspect once we get out and start our investigation, they'll leave," said Tom. "I have a mirror in my bag. The sun reflecting into their cockpit will move them away, I would think."

Watching the helicopters, they climbed from the vehicle and opened the hatchback. Each person took their shoulder bags and set up beside the crop circle. They passed through the first circle and in silence, moved into the second circle where the boy's body was found.

Tom and Al examined the barley. "No damage, just like the other ones. There's no stress on the plants. Norm, you can harvest these plants if you wish. They'll not erect themselves fully, but—would you mind if I take a few seeds?" asked Al.

"Sure, why?"

"I would recommend you collect all these seeds by hand if you can. Some studies I've seen show the seeds usually produce anywhere from three to five times the crop production when planted the following year. It seems to only last one generation, but you'll be thrilled next year with what you collect. It's as if they're supercharged as a thank you for the use of the field."

"What are you talking about? How's that possible?" asked Norm.

"Norm, we're standing in a complex design humans can't understand, where the plants are flattened but not ruined and it all took place in one night, possibly within minutes. And you are asking how it's possible?" asked Al.

"Right," said Norm.

"Hey, come over here," Tom said.

They walked to where the boy was found.

Tom was on his knees. "Look, is it me or…"

"No, I see it too. The soil's disrupted. We know there were a lot of footprints from the investigators, but you're right, the soil has been turned and the plants look like someone or something, placed them back into the soil," said Jeff. He crouched down and picked up the soil. "It's loose. It hasn't been packed down."

"I've seen that in other circles," said Tom. "But only a couple."

"I don't think we've been to a circle this close to its creation or before multiple gawkers have trampled through the fields," said Al. "Norm, are you okay with me taking samples of the soil and maybe a plant?"

"Lads, we are here to do what you need. I just want answers."

"Right," said Jeff.

"Pull out the compass," said Tom.

Al pulled out his compass and lay it in the palm of his hand. Norm peeked over his shoulder.

"Your compass is broken, son." Norm turned to his right and pointed. "There's north."

"Norm, watch this." Al stepped outside the crop circle. The needle moved and pointed to the magnetic north.

"Keep watching," said Al.

He stepped inside the crop circle, the needle moved. It pointed towards the center of the circles, where they found the boy. "Follow me, Norm."

They moved to the center of the crop circle. The pointer shook and turned as they passed where the boy was discovered.

"Watch the compass. No matter where I am, in here, the needle points to where you found the boy."

"How's that possible?" asked Norm.

"This will wear off over the next few days. It's as if the plants have been magnetized. That's why your seeds are precious now," Tom said. "It's the best I can do to explain it."

"We're running out of light. Tomorrow is a scheduled day off for me. Can we come back, Norm?" asked Jeff.

"I suppose it's not going to hurt if you do. Collect me though, I want to be here too. You have me hooked. My son called today asking for an update. He tried to get off work to come for a visit," said Norm. "I'll need to call him tonight with all these additional notes."

With the sky darkening, they gathered their equipment and loaded the vehicle.

"I suppose there will be more people crawling over my fields again tonight, lighting their candles and playing their games of one with the Earth. Now that it's a news story." said Norm.

"Suppose they will," Jeff said, sitting in the passenger seat.

"Wait, one last thing to check. I forgot. Someone run out and see if you lose signal on your phone when you enter the circle," said Tom.

Al jumped out with his phone in hand. "Nothing," he yelled to the group. He stepped out of the circle. "Four bars."

• • •

Norm woke to his cell phone ringing. The green background of the phone and the white letters showed Jeff's number.

"Jeff?"

"Norm, I have to go into work for six. We won't be out this morning. I need to cover a shift. I've been told the autopsy report arrived last night. It'll be one of the first things I look at. Are you not up? It's four-thirty. I thought you farmers were up at the crack of dawn working."

"Son, look outside. Do you see dawn's crack?"

"No."

"Exactly. Call me later or stop by." He closed his phone and lay looking at the empty side of his bed. With his wife gone, he still hadn't migrated to the middle of the bed or removed her pillow. He placed his hand where she used to lie and fell back to sleep.

•   •   •

Norm headed out to the barn to let the sheep out to graze for the day after his usual breakfast of bacon and eggs. He pushed and prodded the last few out the barn door and through an open gate to the field. With the fields' gate closed, he leaned on his shepherd's staff and watched a police cruiser approach.

With a friendly smile on his face, Jeff stepped out of his car. "Morning, Norm. Sorry for the early morning call."

"What brings you here on duty? I thought you would call if you had any information."

"I'm on break and was in the area. You're still a free man. I thought I would pass on the autopsy report and a few other notes on the boy. It's gruesome, Norm. Some weird stuff."

"Satanists?"

"Possibly. Or something stranger, if that's possible."

"Let's go into the house and talk. There are still choppers flying over the fields, and I saw lights out there last night. I was going to get my tractor and head over there to assess the damage. Do you have time?"

"No, I wish I did. Just be careful. You'll see why when we get inside."

They sat at the table, and Norm placed a full kettle on the stove. "You have time for tea, I assume?"

"Yes, please."

"Do you want to wait for the kettle to boil?"

"I can start. These are the reports from forensics and the labs." He opened a blue folder. "What we found was a ten-year-old boy. He has been dead for approximately forty-eight hours."

"He died the night before we found him?"

"Yes. When his body arrived in the circle, it was already deceased."

Norm stood and took out cups and some pastries. "Keep going. I'm listening."

"The autopsy showed no sexual abuse."

"That's good."

"Right. It also reported there was no blood left in the child. Drained dry. It looks like he died from an empty heart. Like his blood was pulled out of him, mechanically, when he was still alive."

"I didn't see any cuts besides the one you pointed out on the collarbone."

"Exactly. That was the only incision found. They found marks on his legs and wrists, like they strapped him to something before his death."

"What are you saying, Jeff? They drained the blood from this child, then left him in my field. For what reason?"

"I don't think there's a simple answer, but yes."

"Where's his blood? Or what would they need it for?" Norm placed the plate of pastries and mugs of tea on the table.

"Norm, both excellent questions. But I don't have any answers. I wish I did, and hopefully I will. It gets stranger. We have no report of a missing child fitting his description."

"How? It's been at least four days. Someone must have reported their child missing," said Norm.

"You would think, unless it's a cult and, well, this was a ritual killing of one of their own."

"What?"

"I spoke to Timothy this morning. The team from Manchester searched the open cases of missing children. No missing kids in the area or in the Isles fit this one's age and description. They sent the information to Europe this morning, and later today it will go out to North America and Australia."

"You don't think he's local?"

"I'm sorry Norm, but I—we—just don't have many answers right now. None of this makes any sense." Jeff swallowed his last bit of tea. "I have to go. I'm covering the area alone today. A few guys called in sick. The bug that's going around hit the station. Can I come back later with the others? We would like to dig around where you found the body."

"I'll have the kettle on. Just call me."

CHAPTER NINE

Guelph, Ontario

Simon was ending his second week of vacation. He had found a daily routine he enjoyed. Early morning bike rides, then some chores around the house, a quick visit or phone call with Susan and Robin before heading out for a walk to let his mind wander. He repeatedly rode past the scene of the kidnapping, checking his phone for a signal and recalling the event.

Robin and Susan's case had, like most kidnapping cases after a couple of weeks, stalled. The community searches and group support were in the past and the reality of never seeing their children again had settled deep into their hearts. Simon spoke with them daily to discuss the lack of updates on the case. They had grown close, having meals together and walking the streets handing out posters.

On his bike, his mind turned over, reviewing the case. He was on an old rail trail between Guelph and Elmira with *54-40* and *Matthew Good* blasting tunes in his ears. The ring of his phone interrupted the song, "Blue Sky." He reached for his phone in his jersey's back pocket. The headphone cable wrapped around his fingers and phone, trapping his hand in the jersey's pocket. Reaching for the brake, he hit a tree root. The front wheel kicked to the right on him. He pulled his left hand free and planted it on the handlebars, steadying the bike while his phone bounced off his back wheel, then rolled on the ground.

He stopped, muttering, "This better be a damn important call."

The call went to voicemail before he could pick his phone off the ground. He looked at the screen. It informed him he had missed a call from Robin. He tapped the screen to return the call.

"Hello?"

"Robin, it's Simon, you called?" In the background, he could hear Susan crying.

Robin's voice was disjointed and quiet. "Simon, they—Simon, they found Ricky."

"What? They did? Where? Is he—alive?"

"Simon, where are you? How soon can you get here? Gary and Mark are at my door. Can you come, please?"

Simon looked at the trail and the wind blowing up it. "It will be a half hour before I can get there. I'm just past Ariss out on the trail. Robin, is he alive?"

"Please get here as soon as you can." Robin's voice broke as he finished the sentence. The phone went dead.

Please let him be alive.

Simon put his phone in his jersey and headed back to town. He thought of calling the station to get more information, but had already been cautioned about being too involved in the case and asking for favors. Pedaling as hard as he could, he weaved between kids on their bikes and people walking their dogs.

• • •

Two police cruisers, an ambulance and an unmarked car were in front of the Easton's house. It told Simon all he needed before he talked to anyone.

They found a body, not a child.

Simon opened the front door to the house.

"Hello."

"Simon, back here," Gary answered.

He followed the voices to the living room. Two paramedics stood with their oversized bags at their feet. Robin sat with his arm around Susan. Both with red, puffy eyes and their noses running. Susan had a blood pressure band around her upper left arm, and Robin squeezed a cup of water.

"Simon, they found Ricky," said Susan, as she attempted a smile.

Gary grabbed Simon's arm and pulled him into the front hallway.

"Why didn't you guys call me?" asked Simon.

"Terry told us to let them break the news to you," said Gary.

"How bad is the body? And what about the twins?"

"Simon, this is beyond weird. They found Ricky in a field. We got the call this morning from Manchester."

"Manchester? Where's that?"

"England."

"*England?* How did he get to England? I was thinking somewhere in Ontario, not halfway around the world."

"I know. Manchester sent the information they have from their investigation."

"The twins?"

"Nothing, nothing at all."

"I'm not done. They found him in the center of a crop circle." He looked back to be sure no one was listening. "His body was void of blood."

"Like he bled out? They would see the wound. Did they torture him?"

"No, it was drained slowly. So yes, he bled out, but more like his blood was collected. There wasn't a drop of it where they found the body. Just a small incision above his collarbone."

Simon looked over Gary's shoulder towards the living room. "Do they know all this?"

"No, we were waiting for you. You know them. How much detail should we give them?"

"Wait, a crop circle? Like the ones we see on TV made by aliens?"

"Yes, the very thing. Alien made or whatever. But yes, a traditional crop circle."

"This sounds made up. Drained of blood in a crop circle." Simon shook his head. He looked into the room at Robin and Susan. "Looking at the shape of the two of them, I would say you have said enough. Right now, I don't think they need to hear all these details."

Simon pushed past Gary. Mark nodded at him.

Simon kneeled in front of Susan and took her hand. "Susan, Robin, I am so sorry about this. It wasn't the results we wanted. The good news is, it's a small piece, but it's a form of closure for you. But now there are so many other questions to ask. What can we do to help you? Are you okay with all these people around?"

"Simon, you tried to—prepare us for this." Susan cried uncontrollably.

"Simon, I think what she was saying was, even with your talks and preparing us for the worst, we still had hope that our children would come home safe and alive."

Susan nodded as tears dripped off her chin. A paramedic went to the kitchen and brought her a glass of water.

"I think we're okay now. Obviously not, but if we could have everyone leave except you two and you, Simon." Robin pointed to Gary and Mark.

Mark stood and whispered to the paramedics and the uniformed officers. The paramedic with the glass of water whispered into Susan's ear, then shook Robin's hand. Each person, as they left, shook Robin's hand and hugged Susan.

Simon went to the kitchen and took a bottle of water from the fridge. "Sorry, I feel a little underdressed in my bike shorts and jersey. Does anyone want a coffee?"

"Yes, please, Simon," Robin said.

The group sat in silence, waiting for the coffee to percolate. "Would it be better to sit at the table and talk?" asked Gary.

"Yes," said Susan.

Simon brought out cups and a pot of coffee to the dining room. Susan slowly moved around her kitchen and found some cookies and a tray of brownies to serve.

"Susan, sit. We..." said Simon.

"No, it's fine. I could use some comfort food right about now," she said.

"I have filled Simon in on the details of Ricky," said Gary. "We will have his body brought back here."

"Can we go to England and see the officers and where they found him?" asked Robin.

"You can, but you would have to arrange it all yourself. I suggest you let us organize this," said Mark. "It's too much to travel and then return with, well, with your son in the plane's cargo hold."

"But…" said Susan.

"I agree with Gary. Neither of you are in any form to be traveling," said Simon. He poured coffee into the cups.

"Simon, can you go then? We will pay for it," said Robin.

Simon looked at Gary and Mark. They had both been supportive of him investigating the kidnapping. He had helped by running around for them when they were working on the other three cases sitting on their desks.

"Susan, we would like to speak to Simon alone. We're just going to step out on the deck to talk. Do you mind?" asked Mark.

"Fine. Robin, could you get me another glass of water?"

A cool breeze welcomed them as they stepped outside. "What's up, Gary? Is there more?" asked Simon.

"Yes, one last thing." He paused and looked at Mark. "Terry wants you to travel to England to do some unofficial poking around and see what you can find. Preferably without getting too close to their cops. I have some files for you in the car, if you agree. He says between overtime, vacation and what he can manipulate, he can get you six weeks of leave, maybe eight. But this goes no further than this house."

"Terry knows how close you are to the family and wants to give you and them time to investigate this and the unusual circumstances," said Gary.

"We have to let them know," said Simon.

"Agreed, we, or better yet, you can tell them," said Mark.

"This is the strangest, old world hocus pocus stuff I've ever investigated, so I fully agree. You need to see this crop circle and see if there is anything to look into over there," said Gary. "We can only hope the twins are still alive."

"Okay, I assume we'll be communicating with updates?"

"I don't think we'll have much for you, but yes, if we get anything to help you, we'll let you know. I think you'll be the one gathering information," said Mark.

"And Terry is okay with this?" questioned Simon. "He will approve all this time off?"

"Yes, I know it's hard to believe, but he will. It's his idea to have you go there," said Gary. "Once he read the report and how the body was found, he changed. You just need to call him to finalize the dates."

"Well, let's get back in there and break the news to them," said Simon.

"I think they might already know." Mark pointed to a window on the second floor. "Susan has been standing upstairs looking out the bedroom window this whole time."

•   •   •

Simon was the first back to the table. Susan sat back in her seat and Robin poured everyone a fresh cup of coffee.

"Susan, I'm not sure if you heard what we were saying," said Simon.

"I tried, but no, nothing. Maybe next time you could speak a little louder." She attempted to smile.

"Okay, here's the deal. But this stays in this room. No one can know what we are about to talk about, understand?"

"Yes. I guess," said Susan.

"Robin?"

"Anything to get more answers," said Robin. "Can you tell us what you know about Ricky?"

Mark looked at Simon. "They found Ricky in a crop circle just outside of Manchester."

Susan erupted into a crying fit. Robin put his arm around her.

"No, I'm—I'm not ready. Please, no more," Susan pleaded.

Simon looked at Gary and nodded. Gary told them the plans of having Simon head to England.

"Simon, you were hoping to have your kids for Thanksgiving. You can't give that up for us," said Susan, wiping the tears from her cheeks.

"Susan, Helen and I talked, well fought, again this morning. She decided not to take them out of school to come for Thanksgiving." He paused and took a drink of coffee. "I want to do this. If I can help you two find closure, then it can only help with my place in the universe. We all have a fire to walk through, and my relationship with Helen is mine right now."

Susan hugged him. "You are a good man, and friend, Simon."

Gary's phone rang. He moved away from the table and took the call. After a few minutes, he returned to the dining room.

"Mark, we need to get back to the office. Simon, we have some things for you in the car. Do you want to throw your bike in the trunk? We can drop you off at home."

"No, I'll bike home. It'll give me some time to process this." Simon looked at Robin and Susan. "I'll leave. You two need some time alone, but I'll come by tomorrow morning and talk. In the meantime, I'll book a flight to England and review the files."

At the car, Mark handed a thick stack of files to Simon. "This looks like some kind of ancient cult ritual killing. Be careful, we don't know what is happening over there. And remember, you are on your own. Terry said he can't help you, so don't be breaking any laws."

"Right, can you drop the files off at my place? I'll be home in twenty minutes. Here's the key to the front door."

"Will do, Simon."

CHAPTER TEN

The connector plane landed at Manchester Airport two days later. Robin had a rental car and a bed-and-breakfast reserved for Simon.

Simon struggled on the way to his bed-and-breakfast. Jet lagged, he kept drifting to the right side of the road and turning through intersections to the right. A few honks, a couple fingers pointed at him, and one irate man helped Simon quickly learn the new rules of the British roads.

His bed-and-breakfast was twenty miles from the farm where Ricky's body was found. The family who owned the B&B welcomed Simon, gave him a quick tour of the grounds, and showed him to his room. It was a large bedroom with a small kitchen overlooking a field of grass and flowers in raised beds. In the distance, the rolling hills of Northern England went to the horizon, only broken by small stone walls and wooden fences. He had his own bathroom and a separate entrance to his small apartment. Robin booked the room weekly, renewing every Saturday for as long as Simon needed. He unpacked his clothes and placed his notes and files on the old English writing desk to review. Sitting at the desk, he glanced at the notes, but with jet lag clouding his mind, he closed the files and climbed into bed.

•   •   •

The next morning, he woke at ten, refreshed and hungry. The owners left a note under his door to call when he was ready to eat. He called the number on the paper and half an hour later, he was sitting with the owners of the bed-and-breakfast, a large plate of bacon, eggs, breads, and fried tomatoes before him.

"So, what brings you to our little part of the world, Simon?" asked Fredrick.

"I'm an author and just want to be away from my friends and family to get my book done. And since I have some research to do in the area to complete a few chapters, this seemed like the perfect place to hold up. My publisher has tight deadlines, and I have a ridiculously small attention span, at times," said Simon, hoping they believed his lie.

"What's it on?" asked Greta.

"The book? Well—"

"He can't give that away, Greta. Most authors don't want to talk about their work. Not until it's ready," said Fredrick.

"It's okay. I'm writing a sci-fi novel on aliens," Simon said, mopping up egg yolk with a slice of homemade bread.

"Crop circles. You're here about the crop circles and the connection to aliens. Are all you Americans like that?" asked Fredrick.

"Sorry, Simon, Fredrick has his ideas on crop circles, aliens and how the queen is in on it all, as are most leaders in the world, like the pope. Right hon? And if we don't feed the Loch Ness Monster three virgins a year, it will destroy the world with Satan riding on its back," she said, with a sarcastic tone.

"Okay, that last one is new for me," Simon said, chuckling.

"Don't listen to her. Greta's eyes are sealed to what really happens in the world. But if you want some help or need to see a place or two, I can help you," Fredrick said with a wink.

"Oh yes, sit in the car for an hour with him, Simon, and you'll have enough material for your next four books. Is there anything else I can get you? More coffee?"

"Huh, no, this has been wonderful. I might not eat again until tomorrow. Same breakfast tomorrow?" asked Simon.

"Yes, unless you want something different? Right now, you are our only guest, so we can customize it to whatever you would have in America," said Greta.

"No, this is fine. I can't understand how people live to be in their eighties around here eating this, but…"

"Simon, just another myth they like to lie about. This is good healthy food. We've been living off it for generations," said Fredrick.

"Just one minor point. I'm Canadian, not American. It's not a big deal but…"

"It's all the same to us, America land of the free," said Greta

"Not really," said Simon and Fredrick in unison. They looked at each and chuckled.

"Oh, be quiet, Fredrick. You and your theories."

"Simon, come see me later. We can talk without the interruption of…" Using his head, he nodded to his wife. Simon winked at him and laughed.

•　•　•

Simon repeatedly drifted to the right side of the tight windy roads as he drove to the farm where they found Ricky. He thought about how he would introduce himself—investigator, curious family member, or crop circle enthusiast.

Turning into the laneway, he passed by barns and a field of sheep to his right, searching for the owner of the farm. Further along the laneway was an old stone house, and a large area to park. He pulled the car to the barns and surveyed the area. No one was around. He honked the horn three times and got out.

Should have called ahead.

He walked towards the barns. The first one had the large doors wide open. Looking into it, he could see a tractor was missing. He glanced at his watch and wandered to the next barn. He opened the man door and yelled in. With no response, he moved between the buildings to the fence holding the sheep. In the distance, the constant drone of a tractor's engine was the only man-made sound around.

A car turned into the laneway and the billowing cloud of dust approached Simon. The driver honked and waved, then parked beside

Simon. He stopped waving and his expression of happiness changed to confusion.

Jeff rolled his window down. "Can I help you?"

"Umm—yes, do you own this farm?"

"No, I am a friend of the owner. Are you a reporter? Wait, that's an American accent."

"Well—Canadian, but you guys don't differentiate the two, I've noticed."

"Canadian? Well, what brings you here? Long way to come for a visit to a British farm. And why this one?"

"I was hoping to meet the owner."

"If you are a crop circle investigator, I've claimed this one. I know you don't get many in Canada, but this one's not open to the public. There's an older one about fifty miles away. I can give you directions. Norm, the owner, is not allowing anyone on his fields. Plus, it's secured by the police."

Simon shook his head. "No, I—would you mind if I wait to see the owner? Please?"

"Canadian? I guess you guys really are polite. We've had others from America just march onto farmers' fields. The last one was a year ago when we had a small circle appear south of here. Park your car over there by the house. I'll meet you there."

•   •   •

"I'm Jeff Spence." He extended his hand for a shake as Simon approached after moving his car.

Simon shook his hand. "Simon Elliot, I am—do you know when the owner will return?"

"Norm is his name. Real nice guy. I won't let you take advantage of him or push your way into his fields. I'm a local constable."

"Really? I'm an officer in Canada, from Guelph, Ontario. I assume you know about the boy? He was from Guelph."

The sound of a tractor grew louder, then over the hill a blue Ford TW20 tractor appeared.

"Are you here to investigate the crop circle or the body that was found in it?"

"I'm here..."

"I saw nothing in the report about an investigator from Canada. Did you check in at the station?"

"No, I didn't. I'm not here on any official investigation. The family of the child asked me to come and see if I can make any sense of what happened."

The tractor stopped beside the two men. Norm swung open the door and jumped down.

"Jeff, how are you? Another friend?"

"Simon Elliot. We just met." He stepped to Norm with his hand leading. "I assume you are Norm, the owner of the farm?"

"Yes, that's right. Simon, that certainly isn't an English accent."

"No, sir, I'm Canadian. Do you have somewhere we can talk?"

"Canadian? Did you know the family of the child?"

"Yes, that's why I'm here."

Norm glanced at Jeff. "I was back here to grab lunch, then head to the crop circle with Jeff. So why not sit with us and have something to eat? I can only imagine what questions you have for us."

Norm made a pot of tea and a few tomato sandwiches before he sat at the table with Simon and Jeff.

"Jeff, I feel like you're turning me and my farm into a restaurant."

"Norm, you always offer me food. I just don't want to be rude and say no to you," Jeff said. He helped carry the plates to the table.

"Eat up, you two. Simon, tell me why you're here," said Norm.

Simon explained how he witnessed the kidnapping and how he was unofficially there to dig a little deeper and hopefully find the twins. By the time he finished his story, Norm had made a second pot of tea and Jeff had taken notes.

"I have a few questions. We can start with these and expand from there," Jeff said. "First, you witnessed the kidnapping of three siblings?"

"Correct."

"If I call your station, they will confirm you are on leave?"

"Yes. Only a few people know I'm here. If you wouldn't mind, I'd like to keep it that way."

Jeff nodded as he wrote. "The family has you here to look for their twins. Is there anything special about this family that their oldest child was found here, in a crop circle?"

"That's the question, isn't it? And, yes, you're correct. I'm helping them get answers, closure and if I'm lucky, their missing twins. Again, I'm here as a favor to the family, not as an official police officer. My boss knows I'm here, as do the two investigating officers. But I'm just a civilian here looking to stay under the radar. As of right now, there's nothing any of us can think of that makes their family or children special. But unofficially, of course, it looked like they were targeted."

Jeff looked at Norm.

"Just a gut feeling," said Simon.

"Can't argue with that. And the details you shared would make it sound planned to me," said Norm.

"I was hoping to see the crop circle. Where you found the body and maybe gather any information you or your station has on the crime."

"Mate, I've only met you. Now you want me to reveal what we've found? Baby steps."

"I'll clean up from lunch. Simon, where are you staying?" asked Norm.

"At a B&B about twenty miles away. Why?"

"Just a question, son, that's all. Isn't that Greta and Fredrick's place?"

"Yes, the very one, good people from the little time I've spent with them. I assume you will call them to confirm I'm a guest?"

Norm stared at him.

"I told them I was an author finishing a book."

Jeff looked at him, confused.

"Just being open and honest with you two. I have nothing to hide."

"Simon, if you wouldn't mind just waiting outside while we talk?" said Jeff.

"Sure, take your time. I know this has to be strange for you. Not just me showing up, but the whole crop circle and body situation, too."

Jeff smiled at him. Norm shook his head.

• • •

The front door opened, and Jeff followed Norm onto the porch.

"Simon, we've talked. We'll show you the crop circle and where Norm found the body. But not today. I'll be back at the same time tomorrow, and you're welcome to join us then. I feel we can share more with you if you come back."

"Huh, thank you. The twenty-four-hour delay is for you to check out my story, I assume. I appreciate that, Jeff. I'd do the same if I were in your shoes. Honestly, I've nothing to hide from you or Norm."

"I hope not. This was a tragedy for the child's family and if we think you're taking advantage of the situation, you'll not be permitted on the property. Let that be your first warning for trespassing."

"I understand. No chance of a peek today?" asked Simon.

"Why don't we wait 'til tomorrow? I need the family's phone number, your contacts at your station and a way to get hold of you," said Jeff.

• • •

The phone rang the next morning at seven, waking Simon.

"Hello."

"Simon, come out to the farm at nine. Looking forward to working with you."

"Jeff?"

"Yes, did I wake you? Sorry, I guess jet lag takes a few days."

"It seems to. Nine? See you then. Thank you."

Simon prepared his backpack. He skipped breakfast and headed to the farm.

CHAPTER ELEVEN

Four people stood by the barns waiting for Simon as he drove up the dusty laneway. He climbed out of his car and approached the group.

"Simon, we weren't sure if you were coming or not," said Jeff.

"Well, I wasn't expecting rush hour around here. I was stuck behind a tractor and then stopped as what seemed like a thousand sheep crossed the road. Now, you don't see that in Canada."

Everyone smiled at his comment.

"Let's start with some introductions, shall we? I have a pot of coffee on. I can whip up some food too, if any of you are hungry. We can sit inside and talk," said Norm.

"Sounds good to me," Jeff replied. "Norm's restaurant is open."

The group sat around the kitchen table as Norm placed a plate of scones and butter on the table.

"Okay, I've filled these guys in on you, Simon. And yes, I did a bit of work on you last night. I spoke to Gary and Mark. You must pay them very well or have some dirt on them. According to Gary, you're a top notch officer and investigator."

"Thank you. I'm sure you'll be disappointed," Simon said with a smile. "They have very low standards."

"This is Al. He's a chemical engineer working mostly in the grain world, developing better, stronger seeds for farmers."

"Nice to meet you, Simon." He shook Simon's hand. "Just so you know, I don't do any of the genetic manipulation like some companies. The company I work for tries to keep to the old ways of selection. We work with farmers on soil strength and seed choices, not poisoning the soil or manipulating the seeds' DNA to cheat nature."

"Gotcha."

"This is Tom. He's been studying crop circles with his dad and uncle since he was a child. He's a bit of a conspiracy nut."

"And a popular podcaster." Tom shook Simon's hand. "You witnessed the child being taken?"

"Yes, there were three children. I'm here to look for the twins who are still missing. And figure out why the oldest was found in a field without any blood."

"Must have some special blood, I guess," said Norm. "Now that we are all working together, Simon, you mentioned the men that kidnapped the children were all in black hoodies. I guess it's time for us to reveal what we witnessed here." Norm told him of the three men in hoodies running across his field.

Simon sat in silence, writing in his notebook what Norm revealed. "I'm not trying to jump to conclusions, but you possibly saw the same people I saw in Canada in your fields? If not the same people, the same outfits?"

"It's strange, I know," said Jeff. "Is this an international kidnapping ring? But then why kill one of the three children and leave him in a crop circle?"

"Sounds like a form of ritual killing. But why travel to Canada, randomly take three kids and bring them across the pond? Then leave one in a brand new crop circle?" said Al.

"I don't think it was random," said Simon.

"A sacrifice to the alien overlords that run this planet?" said Tom.

"What?" asked Simon.

"Simon, sorry, but if you are going to stay here, you might as well know he really is deep into conspiracies. He hosts a large conspiracy podcast around the world. He's written a couple of books, too. One on 9-11 and the other on how NASA faked the moon landings and are the biggest money laundering company in the States. If you want to waste the day sitting here listening to him, just ask one question about 9-11. I dare you," said Jeff.

"We should head out before Tom gets going. I'm not saying he's wrong, but we can have that conversation at the pub tonight," said Al.

They left the house and headed to the vehicles.

"Hey Tom. About 9-11. I have a friend who's a pilot for a large airline. Been a pilot since he was..." said Simon.

"No, no, no, save it for later. They're calling for rain this afternoon. You can get into it then," said Jeff. "Let's focus on the job at hand."

Simon winked at Tom as they all entered the Range Rover.

•   •   •

Norm drove to the edge of field seven. The first thing he noticed was his gate was open and someone knocked part of his fence over. "See, this is what happens around here. No respect for property," he said, pointing to the damaged fence.

"Probably a bunch of kids playing Druids last night," said Jeff.

"Druids?" asked Simon.

"Yes, there has been a small resurgence of the Druid society since 2000 or earlier. They never went away, but with all the climate change talk, they're having a resurgence," said Al.

"Propaganda," said Tom.

"People are engaging with the Druid society again. We've a small one in town now. They believe getting back to nature will fix everything happening in the world today. I don't disagree," said Jeff. "They believe the crop circles are the planet asking for help. They seem to be in competition with the Freemasons around here for members."

"I don't think wrecking a man's fence and gate is getting back to the way things were," said Norm.

"All this is the great climate conspiracy. It's all about making us poor and the elite richer," said Tom.

"Later Tom," said Al, shaking his head.

The others chuckled at Al's dismissal of Tom's comment.

"We're here, Simon," said Norm.

Simon followed Norm and Jeff through the rows of barley to the edge of the circle. The others took bags and cases of equipment from the Range Rover.

"This is it, Simon. Doesn't look like much from here, but you saw the photos earlier and I assume the aerial videos on the news. It should help to show how big this crop circle is."

"Can we enter it?" asked Simon.

"Yes, remember, it's been a few days. The barley is already bouncing back. It won't become fully erect and will need to be hand-picked, but just be careful where you step," said Norm.

Jeff led Simon to the middle of the circles. He stopped where Ricky's body was found.

"It's incredibly quiet here. I feel like I have earmuffs on," said Simon. "The soil is so dry compared to some of the other fields we drove through."

"Yes, the soil has good drainage in this field and the next one. I usually plant the wheat and barley in these fields. The roots are stronger, and the plants don't require as much moisture," said Norm. "But right there," he pointed behind the vehicle, "turns into a bog with the littlest of rain. It always has."

Simon nodded his head.

Tom walked through the circle with his compass held out in his palm. He spun and turned. He looked at the sky, then the ground. "Weird. The other day, the needle was pointing to the center of the circle. Now it's back to normal." He turned to face north. "Nothing. How's that possible?"

"Simon, this is where we... Hey, come look at this, guys," said Jeff.

"What?" asked Norm.

"Someone dug a hole here. Look, the plants are all disturbed and there's a hole about a foot deep."

Everyone gathered around Jeff. They stared at the hole, shocked by the audacity of whoever did it.

"Well, Simon, here's exactly where we found the child. Right on top of that hole."

"Did it look like there was a hole dug under the child?"

"No," said Jeff. "That is new."

"Yes," said Norm. "We did note earlier the soil looked like it was turned. You know the loose soil?" He looked at Jeff. "Remember?"

Jeff looked at him with a raised eyebrow.

Norm mouthed back to him. *"No secrets, we agreed."*

"But it didn't look like this. This has been dug," said Jeff.

The wind picked up and the bit of blue sky overhead disappeared behind dark, thick clouds.

"Let me get my drone up before the rain comes. I'll look for other holes."

Jeff moved away from the group to prepare his drone. Simon walked to the next circle, being careful not to trample the barley. "This all happened overnight?" he asked. He turned to see who was behind him to answer, but no one followed him.

I was sure someone was with me.

He inspected a bent plant, running his hand over the stem. The outer skin of the stem was stretched but not cracked. He thought of a bow and how the wood arched by the pull of the string. "What do you think makes them stay bent? Shouldn't the stem have cracked here at the bend?" He turned and surveyed the vastness of the fields. His head snapped to the right. He saw Norm and Tom standing in the other circle, talking. Al was at the vehicle placing a plant in a bag, and Jeff stood on the outside of the circle, raising his drone. He spun around, looking for the person he thought he was talking to.

Someone was behind me. I'm sure.

A cool wind blew in his face as the smell of rain filled his nose. He waved to Norm and Tom to come to him.

"Everything all right? You look pale," said Norm.

"Yes, just a strange feeling. I was sure you two were behind me, so I was asking questions. Then it felt like, I don't know, someone was standing behind me."

"No one answered, did they?" asked Tom.

Simon smiled at him. "I don't think so."

"Simon, I'll admit I've had the same feeling when I've been out here since the circle appeared," said Norm.

"Me too," said Tom. "Almost like a feeling of déjà vu."

Simon looked around the fields. "So, this is all your land, Norm? This is your first crop circle."

"Aye, I've the honor of working all this land, year after year. All to make enough money to do it again the following year. As for the circle, there have been a few over the years in the area, but this is my first. And from what I've been told, the first where a body was found since the sixties."

"Really? I'd never heard of bodies being found in crop circles," said Simon.

"It happens more than you think," said Tom. "They just don't report it. And from what I've researched, the bodies usually aren't identified. This one and the one in the sixties were the only bodies they could tag a name to, but it goes back to the 1500s."

"Strange they keep it hush-hush," said Simon. "But I guess if they can't explain how the circles appear, it would scare the public even more if they knew authorities found bodies in them."

"It's the government. We know it's what they do. Probably some military tests that went wrong."

"Tom, is everything a conspiracy with you?" asked Norm.

Tom looked at him and opened his mouth to answer.

"And you saw three figures run through the field the day you found the circle?" asked Simon, cutting Tom off before he could respond.

"Yes."

"Can you show me where they were and the path they took to the road?"

"Follow me, Simon," said Norm. "And just to be clear, they never made it to the road from what I saw."

He walked through his field with Simon beside him. "Simon, what are you thinking? You have years of experience over those boys. And of course, the police here aren't equipped to investigate the death of the child from Canada or any connection to the circles. Identifying the child was more work than they've done in years, I think. Do you think the men I saw are the same ones you saw in Canada?"

"I don't know, but it can't be a coincidence that they had the same body type and were wearing the same clothes. I know it would make sense to take kids from Canada and move them to another country, but why here? In the

STEPHEN W. BRIGGS   69

nineties, there were rumors of a large kidnapping ring. They took the children to the Middle East to be sold as slaves. But why would you leave a kid in a field to be found? I would think the time and energy to make the crop circle would be better spent digging a deep hole to hide the body."

Norm opened the gate to his beet field.

"We assumed the kids were somewhere close to where they were taken. It's so strange. Even if it was a ritual killing, why travel to Canada to take three kids, kill the oldest and then leave him in a field? What makes them so special? Sorry, I'm just repeating myself now," said Simon.

"I know this land is ancient, and we don't know what happened here a thousand years ago or more. But this has to be the strangest thing these fields have seen." He stopped at his beets. "The first man I saw was about here. He ran that direction, and about a hundred meters away, he met his two mates."

"Where did they come from?"

"I don't know. They just appeared."

"From where?"

"Come along," he said, motioning. "Roughly here. But from where I was," he pointed to the field slightly uphill from their location, "I should have seen them before here."

"Have you ever been out here working and felt like someone was with you?"

"No, not until the other day. The day after I found the crop circle, I had a feeling someone was beside me as I inspected the beet fields. I see wildlife, but never people or feel that I'm with someone."

Simon scanned the fields as they headed back to rejoin the group. At the circle, he paused. Something looked out of place.

"Hey! Over here." He turned and whistled with his two fingers in his mouth.

Soon, Tom and Al had joined him, staring at the ground. "Is this hole the same as the one in the middle of the circle, or is it an animal's den?" Simon asked.

No one had an immediate answer. Simon quickly motioned to Jeff, who sent the drone towards them.

Jeff hovered it over Simon's head. Simon looked at the camera and pointed to the hole by his feet, and then made a large circle with his arms indicating the surrounding perimeter. Jeff responded by lowering the drone then sending it in a wide arc.

"Well, Norm, I'm not sure, but this might have something to do with our little mystery."

From the middle of the circle, Jeff yelled and pointed to his drone. Another hole, partially hidden, precisely dug, a foot in diameter and two feet deep, was under the stems of the barley.

"We need to mark these," said Simon.

"I can go back to the barn and get some stakes," said Norm.

• • •

When Norm returned with an assortment of wooden and metal stakes, Jeff had located eleven new holes—all the same diameter and depth. They tasked Simon and Tom with driving stakes into each hole.

A typical British day, the skies opened, and the rain came down. Everyone finished what they were doing and climbed into the waiting vehicle.

The ground was slick, and the Rover struggled to make it through the fields to the road. Simon, already wet, volunteered to open the gates. Once through, they drove back to Norm's house in silence.

After everyone dried off, and with hot cups of tea in front of them, the crew sat in Norm's kitchen. The rain bounced off his large window. Looking out to his barns, Norm asked. "Okay, so what were those holes?"

"We need to go back and survey the sticks. They seemed to follow the outline of the circle," said Jeff.

"Yeah, we need to draw a proper site map of that. Could *they* have placed something as markers to make the circle?" asked Tom.

"It might explain why my compass was all over the place the other day. They didn't have time to remove the markers, or whatever was in those holes," said Al.

"Whatever was in them just might explain how the circles are made without damaging the plants," said Simon. "Some theories suggest a strong magnetic field, man-made or natural, causes the circles."

"Or, as is very popular on many tv shows, alien aircraft," said Tom.

"You know, those holes look exactly like the one I found on the trail, too. I know what you're thinking a hole is a hole, but the depth and how neat the hole was dug are the same. I don't know, it's just a thought," said Simon. He showed them a photo of the hole on the trail. "It might explain why the phones didn't work, just like the compass in the circle."

"You have a point, Simon. I don't think we should throw that thought away," said Jeff.

"The holes are almost identical," said Tom.

"Well, fellas, we won't be going back out there today. And as much as I enjoy the company, I have chores to do. You are more than welcome to stay and help," said Norm.

"You know what? I'll stay, Norm. I've used up your time. So, I'd like to give something back," said Simon.

"Simon, you..."

"I insist," said Simon. "A little manual labor is good for the soul, good for the mind."

The others looked at each other. Al wanted to get his samples back to his office to have them reviewed. Tom had a scheduled guest for his podcast he needed to prepare for, and Jeff, who had done very little physical labor growing up, decided he needed to check in with the station on any updates. They invited Simon and Norm to their local pub for dinner and drinks later that evening. Simon accepted. Norm declined the invitation.

CHAPTER TWELVE

Simon sat in his car across from the pub and phoned his kids. They talked about school and how they missed not seeing him. Twice he had to cough to prevent himself from breaking down. Richard, his oldest, told him about his mom's boyfriend's house and how he picked them up from school every day and took them out on boat cruises on the weekend. Helen took the phone from the boys. After a few minutes of small talk, the conversation broke into an argument about the same things they had fought over for years—his time at home and his time with the kids. Simon brought up the new *boy toy,* who was trying to replace him. When he mentioned meeting his new friends at a pub, the conversation escalated to levels he had only heard when she finally left. She threatened him, "You have been sober for the last five years. It will all go to waste if you enter the pub. If you drink, you will never see the kids. *Do you understand, Simon?*"

When Simon tried to change the conversation to what was happening in England and calm her down, she would have none of it. "You put everyone and everything before your kids and me. Nothing has changed, you selfish bastard. If you ever want to see your kids again, *you will not enter that pub.*"

Simon sat in his car and looked at his phone, stung by how quickly she hung up. He knew prioritizing his job as a police officer would cause marital issues, many co-workers had warned him in his rookie year, but to be hearing about the new adventures of his boys, her new friend and his drinking problems of the past, tore at his soul. He started the car to leave, wanting to be alone.

I'm here searching for two children while my own are becoming lost to me.

He turned the car off and picked up the phone and called Mark. They discussed the day's activities and his call with Helen. Mark had been one of Simon's main supporters during his separation. They also walked the road to sobriety together. After a twenty-minute talk with him, Simon felt better. Mark encouraged him to go into the pub and order a pop, only a pop.

He made one last call to Robin and Susan to update them on his day.

With the three calls completed, he headed into the pub.

• • •

Jeff, Al, and Tom sat at a table in the back corner of the pub. An old building erected around 1830 held the dampness of the rain from the afternoon, even with a large fire crackling in the corner, giving heat to the room. The bar had a large mirror behind a series of bottles lined up on glass shelves. Etched into the mirror was a large family crest of two lions, and two long swords crossed behind a shield.

Simon sat at the table with his back to the bar. "Al, can we change seats?"

"Sure, why?"

"I don't feel comfortable with my back to the room. I'd rather be seeing the people."

"It's my round to buy, anyway. Take my seat when I'm gone. I'd rather not see what's coming my way. What can I get you?"

"Coke, please."

Simon moved to Al's seat and studied the walls covered in history. Helmets hung on a memorial wall from the world wars. A sword that looked like it came right out of an ancient knight's hand hung on another wall. Above the door, a shield made of steel, its painted coat of arms had faded, but the dents on it proved it had seen battle long ago.

Al returned with three stouts and a Coke in large, frosted glass cups. This will keep us going for a bit. "What did I miss?"

"Nothing. Simon sat down and hasn't said a thing. He's just staring at the walls," said Tom.

"Sorry, I'm just amazed by the items on those walls. It's like history coming alive right before me."

"All authentic, too. The sword and shield are at least five hundred years old. But I want to know about history that is a little closer to us. Simon, tell me about your pilot friend," said Tom.

Jeff rolled his eyes. "Well, that didn't take long, did it? What about the crop circle and the child found in it? Or better yet, what about you, Simon? Can we get a quick rundown?"

"Huh, well, I'm a cop in Guelph, Ontario, a city about an hour from Toronto. I have two kids who live with their mother, now on the west coast of the country. I put my job over my family and paid dearly for it. Be careful Jeff, all of you, if you have kids and a wife, don't take them for granted, put them before all else. I love cycling and have been sober for five years."

"Oh sorry, we shouldn't..."

"I'm a big boy. You can enjoy your drinks. Let's see what else. I lived in Guelph my whole life. I never traveled until I was married and went on our honeymoon," he paused and looked around the room, "and sitting here, I think I've missed a lot by just staying in southern Ontario." He smiled, then chuckled. "But I have to say the damp cool air is wrecking my back and knee. I feel crippled since the weather changed this afternoon. When I was younger, I hurt my back. Hit by a car on my bike, doctors didn't think I would walk again. But here I am, still in one piece, feeling every ache and pain. How about you guys?"

"I'll go," said Jeff. "I was brought up in London. My aunt and uncle raised me. We traveled up this way for holidays every summer. So, I decided when I could, I would live here. I saw my first crop circle when I was eight and I've been fascinated with them ever since. When I turned twenty, I got on the police here. That was two and a half years ago. Not much else to tell. And yes, the damp weather will not be friendly to your back."

"I'm from Manchester. I went to university there for chemical engineering. Now I work in a lab trying to make people, like Norm, better plants and soil. We're all natural, trying not to change what Mother Earth perfected. My role is to make those things a little more perfect. I met Jeff and Tom through a mutual friend who was also into conspiracies and a fan of Tom's podcast. My girlfriend and I live together. I work long hours, and, except for the last few days, my life is pretty boring," said Al.

"Okay, my turn. But only if you promise to tell me about your pilot friend after."

"Deal," said Simon, a smile growing on his face.

"Okay, as you can tell, I am much older than these two. I'm also a divorcee. It was a nasty, nasty separation. Luckily, we had no kids to fight over. I grew up in Oldham, just north of here. I have a podcast on conspiracies that I do weekly. It gets about thirty thousand hits."

"Is that good? A good number of downloads?" asked Simon

"Good enough to concentrate on it and writing books," he said. "I got to know these two through the show and our mutual friend. It worked out well. I needed some information, and Al had all the technical details to help me produce that show. Jeff helps with legal stuff. In our free time, Jeff and I investigate crop circles, haunted buildings and any other odd occurrences which happen around here. Al comes when his girlfriend will let him out." Al shot him a look of displeasure. "So, when they say their lives are pretty plain, we have our moments of excitement. Now, about your pilot friend."

"Okay, are you guys okay with this? I can talk about it later," said Simon, looking at Al and Jeff.

"Get it over with," said Jeff. "He won't let it go until you tell him. He's like a child for stories like this."

"I have a friend who works for a large airline. They do a lot of simulator work every month. Especially when moving to a different plane. After 9-11, some pilots didn't believe a bunch of amateurs who apparently failed flight school could fly those planes into the three buildings. One day, when the simulator schedule wasn't too busy, my buddy, who was an instructor for those 737 planes, and a few of his co-workers, tried to fly the same flight patterns into the towers and the Pentagon. It was impossible to do the Pentagon. Even with their years of experience, no one hit the Pentagon, no one. The spiral down at speed and then to slide it into the side of the building, well—the physics alone. Then when they attempted the two towers at that speed and angle, they were only successful forty percent of the time, and he's been flying planes for over thirty years. It isn't as simple as what the news made it out to be."

Tom bounced in his seat like a child ready to blow out some birthday candles. The smile on his face stretched his skin around his mouth, showing his crooked teeth.

"Remote control. Would you like to do a podcast with me and explain that again in more detail? Would your pilot friend come on the podcast too?"

"I don't..."

"Tom, can we stick to why he's here?" asked Al. "You got your story as promised."

"Sure, sure, but we need to talk more, Simon, please. A lot more. I think we have many podcasts in our future."

"You got it, Tom," said Simon, chuckling.

"Okay, so there was some weird stuff happening around the crop circle today."

"Can I ask?" interrupted Simon. "What about Norm?"

"If you are asking if he's a suspect?" asked Jeff.

Simon nodded.

"Not in my mind. I've asked him all kinds of questions. He is a very simple man. Not in a bad way. In fact, his life sounds very appealing. He gets up, works most days in his fields and with his animals, then goes to bed exhausted."

"Was he ever a suspect?" asked Simon.

"I think if I were to find a body in your backyard, you would be a suspect. No?"

"Yeah, I guess," said Simon. "Norm seems to check out with me, too, the little time I've spent with him. I'm looking at this as a friend of the family who lost a child to a murder and who still don't know where their twins are. This is just too strange. I can't apply my usual logic. I need help here, especially if I'm to talk to the locals, but we all need to remember there are two kids still missing somewhere on this planet. If we can work together, I think we can all help each other out. I need to find those twins and get them home to their parents. I'm more than willing to help with the crop circle conspiracy or the bigger one of Ricky and who left him there. I have some thoughts, but nothing worth discussing."

"Another podcast," said Tom.

Simon glared at him and his childish interruption. "The focus has to be those two kids. Maybe even more are out there."

"Do you think they're here in the area?" asked Al.

"Why would someone take three kids from Canada, bring them to a small village in England, drain the blood from the oldest one and leave his body in a crop circle? Why?" asked Jeff. "We know how these small towns work. Everyone knows everyone's business. I have a hard time believing a group of strangers are in the area without someone talking about it. Half the town knows Simon is here."

The group sat in silence, staring at their glasses.

"They shaved his head, too. Why?" asked Tom.

"Likely to place a wig on him? Change his identity to transport him," said Simon.

"Possibly, but the head was shaved bald. That would take time and isn't necessary for a wig. If you use a razor, the child would have to be still, not fighting you. Even with an electric razor, he couldn't be shaking his head. There were no nicks on the head. I think the body was already dead or unconscious," said Jeff.

"I can't believe they flew the three kids here on a commercial jet. Within twelve hours, all the airports and border crossings in southern Ontario knew of the kidnapping," said Simon.

"How else would they get here? Boat?" asked Al.

"Okay, I'll add that to our questions to be answered," said Simon, writing in his notebook.

"Have they had the funeral yet?" asked Tom.

"No, not until the weekend. The funeral home received the body yesterday morning," said Simon.

"I doubt anyone thought of checking for glue on the head or body," said Al.

"Glue?" asked Jeff.

"You know, when they stick electrodes on the body, they use a glue to make them stick."

"What are you thinking?" asked Tom.

"I don't know. I just don't know why anyone would take such care to shave him. It doesn't make any sense to me."

"Huh," said Simon. He called Gary and asked him if it wasn't too late to check the body for any glue or strange markings.

"And how did they carry a body through there without leaving footprints?" asked Jeff. "Better yet, how were the circles made without any footprints?"

"These are all good questions. Keep thinking that way. Another round?" asked Simon.

"No, I need to be leaving," said Al.

"How familiar are you guys with this pub?" asked Simon.

"I wouldn't say we're regulars, but we come here weekly. The food is good," Al said.

"Look but don't look. Those three guys, four tables over. Have you ever seen them before?" Simon asked.

Tom had the best view of them without turning around. He looked at the three men. They were muscular, with military haircuts and square jaws.

"No, not that I can remember. They look military. There's a base not too far away," said Jeff. He bent down, tying his shoe and checking out the men in question.

"Well, there has always been talk that crop circles could be military," said Simon.

"Or alien or man-made or created by the Earth," Tom commented, glancing over Jeff's shoulder. "What're you thinking?"

"Nothing really, but here are three men with the same build as the men Norm and I saw. Dressed in blue. Do we approach them?" asked Simon.

"And say what? Were you in Canada a month ago kidnapping some kids? Do we actually believe three men who possibly kidnapped three kids in Canada would be dumb enough to come into a pub and sit twenty feet away from us?" asked Al.

One man walked to the bar and took a plate of chips. He looked Simon in the eyes as he returned to his table. Simon nodded to him. There was no response.

"Maybe we're getting a little too far into our own heads," said Tom.

"The guy just stared me down," said Simon. "That I didn't mistake."

"I best be going. I'm on the early shift tomorrow. At some point, I'll see if we have anything new in the system. I think I know the answer, but are we all going to work together on this?" asked Jeff.

"Yes, for sure. I think we can all work together," said Tom. "Even expand the podcasts."

"Yes, welcome Simon. I have to work tomorrow, but we can all meet here for dinner tomorrow night. See if those three show up again," said Al. He checked his phone.

"How many?" asked Tom.

"Four," replied Al. "She just wants to spend some time together before bed."

"Uh-huh, keep telling yourself that," said Tom. "I told you it's how my life was with the missus. Take advantage of my experience and break it off."

"Tom, she's not like that. We enjoy spending time together," said Al.

Tom winked at him and nodded his head.

"Text me if you think of anything, or need anything," said Simon. He finished his pop.

Leaving the bar, Simon looked the three men in their eyes as he passed.

CHAPTER THIRTEEN

Simon woke to the chirp of his phone. A text message from Jeff had an address where he was to meet him at 10 a.m.

He stumbled around the room, gathering his notes before eating breakfast with the owners of the B&B. They asked what he was up to and if he was enjoying the sights of the area when he wasn't writing. With a belly full of food, he loaded his car and, using the GPS on his phone, headed to the address Jeff had left him.

. . .

Pulling into the laneway of the farm, Simon noticed two police cars and an ambulance parked by the house. Jeff directed him to park over to the side of a barn away from the emergency vehicles.

"Morning, Simon. Thanks for coming out. We're just wrapping up here. Another crop circle. Looks to be a day old. The owner has given you permission to look at it," said Jeff.

"Okay. What's with the ambulance?"

"The owner took a fall off his tractor when he rushed back to call us. Bump on the head and scratches on the arm and leg. Precautionary really. He's eighty-five."

"Are you staying?"

"No, we're backed up with calls today. I'll come when my shift ends if you're still here. If not, we can meet at the pub. Tom might make it out later."

"Okay. So where am I going?"

"Joseph will take you."

Jeff introduced Simon to Joseph, the owner of the farm. He had his right arm wrapped in gauze and a bandage on his head. He directed Simon to climb onto the old tractor and hold the door.

Simon wasn't sure with the rust and age of the tractor if the door would hold him if he leaned the wrong way, but he climbed aboard anyway. They bounced and slid out to a field of wheat.

The cut of Joseph's sleeve revealed a tattoo. Simon noticed a large Ankh cross, it had a black outline filled in with a gold color. The loop at the top of the cross was colored in, blood red. Under that, and running across the horizontal arms of the cross, was a series of markings, נפילים. Then, below the markings, was an acorn inside a circle.

"Where'd you get the tattoos from?" asked Simon.

"Back in the war, they stationed me in Northern Africa," he said, tugging at his sleeve. "Just some youthful memories." He stopped the tractor. "Here ya' are, mate. Can you walk back? I want a bit of tea and some pain pills the medics left me. Take your time, the field is yours to discover, just don't trample my stock."

"Thank you, Joseph. I won't do any more damage than what's been done."

"Aye, you better not," he said. He lit a cigarette and climbed up to the cab of his tractor. "Just be done by dark. You don't want to be out here at night." He drove away, leaving Simon in the field.

Simon paced around the perimeter of the circle. A feeling of déjà vu blanketed him. He looked around the field, searching for movement.

Should have taken the drone.

He took out a notebook and drew two large circles. Inside each circle was a right-angle triangle that was filled with a series of bubbles, some from the wheat being bent and others from the wheat standing. The circles were not as complex as Norm's, or as big. He studied the way the wheat bent, cracked, almost forced or trampled, unlike Norm's. He searched around the circles for holes but found none. Slowly, he moved through each circle, sticking to the emptiness between the rows of wheat. He noticed the transition between bent stalks and straight ones was also not as clean as Norm's circle or as precise where they wove together.

A shiver raced down his spine, and he felt eyes glaring at him. He looked around the field. He was sure he wasn't alone.

"Hello," he called out. Spinning to see who was behind him.

From his bag, he took out a compass. With it leading him, he moved around the circle. The needle stayed true to the north, not bouncing or turning to the center of any circle. Once again, making his way around the largest circle, he noticed something. The soil was tossed in the center of the circle and the plants were dug up.

He snapped a photo with his camera and sent it to the other three. Lowering himself down on his hands and knees, he lightly brushed away the soil. His fingers hit a hard object. Gently, he dusted around the object, carefully tracing it in the dirt. Suddenly, he pulled his hands back.

What is this?

He fumbled in his pant pocket for his phone and called Jeff.

"Hey, Simon. is everything okay?"

"Jeff, you need to get back here. I found a bone, looks like a human femur. But I'm just going by the size. I have nothing to back that. I didn't dig it up. That's your job. Also, I need you to confirm, but the plants look different this time. Some are broken. I didn't see a single damaged one at Norm's. Just an observation. And there are no holes around the perimeter. Could it be a fake? It just wasn't as neat as Norm's was. If I were to guess, this looks sloppy, not as precise. It looks like a bunch of drunk farmers attempted to make a circle. But you or Tom would know better. This is only the second one I have ever seen in person."

"What? Where was the bone?"

"Center of the larger middle circle. I noticed the soil was turned, I took a photo before I dug at the soil. There is a bone under the surface, but I don't see any blood. Like a dog hid it in the yard. I sent you a photo."

"Okay, step out carefully, and I'll be there soon. I'll call it in to the station. I guess the lads from Manchester will come for a visit."

"Can I text Tom and Al to let them know what I found?"

"Sure. We'll have a lot to discuss if I'm not working. I'll be a bit. I just pulled up to a domestic, and I'm sure you know how they can go."

"Enjoy," said Simon.

He took a series of photos of what he uncovered, treating the area as a crime scene. With the basics of a phone and notebook, he began an investigation. He looked closer at the bone, noticing scratch marks.

He rushed back to the farmhouse, and his car as his mind raced with theories.

Waiting for the police, he called Robin. After a few minutes of updating Robin, he sensed Robin was upset. "Robin, is everything okay?"

"Yes, fine. I'm just, well, we were hoping you would have more information on the twins. We didn't send you over there to become a crop circle expert."

"Robin, it all takes time. The bone I found this morning could be the next step in this investigation. It's not like I can wrap this up in an hour-long episode of *Murder She Wrote*. It all takes time."

"I know, I know."

"Is there anything else I can answer for you?"

"No—well," he paused. "There is one other thing. Susan isn't doing well, and honestly neither am I. It's—it's just—this stays between us, understand?"

"Sure, what is it, Robin? Are you guys hiding anything from me?"

"Simon, I'm serious. This goes no further than this call."

"So, the police haven't been told this information?"

Robin paused. "No, they would lock us up, claiming insanity."

"What is it?" Simon leaned on the roof of his car.

"Well, okay. We keep seeing Doug and Don."

"What? I need more than that, Robin."

"When we see them it's like they're here but—I don't know, it's like they're beside us, but only behind a veil, or a dirty window might be a better description. They're fuzzy. Think of a TV in the eighties when they had antennas. Remember, you could get a good clear image, then it would slowly fade, or a better word is washed out, before the static would come. Yes, that's it, Simon. That describes how they look to us."

"Like ghosts?"

"No, not that faded. Somewhere in between. I think my dirty window analogy is as close as I can get. Not all the time. But daily, for maybe a half-hour or a little longer. Susan saw them first. She was in the kitchen making breakfast the other day. She turned, and they were standing watching her. They waved at her. When she told me what she saw, I thought she had a breakdown. The next morning, she wouldn't let me leave her. We sat drinking coffee and then I felt the air change. Susan dropped her mug and pointed to the living room. I turned to look, and there they were, washed out, faded but there."

"Robin, this is understandable with what..."

"Stop, let me finish. Susan's parents have seen them too. It's brief, and they say the kids look happy. In fact, this morning when Doug appeared, he gave me a thumbs up. He was in a white golf shirt and smiling."

"Robin..."

"It all started the day after you left for England. First it was these powerful feelings of, I don't know, of being watched, I guess is how to explain it."

"What? Robin, slow down," said Simon. "Being watched?"

"Yeah, like there are people in the house sometimes. I swear I saw a man in blue at the bottom of the basement stairs one night. I checked the house. Susan was ready to call the police when Doug and Don appeared. I think they both had haircuts, too. I know I'm going crazy. Susan believes they're alive. Is this normal?"

"I have never investigated a kidnapping, but I haven't heard or read of this in any reports or classes I took. No, this isn't normal. Are you saying you see their ghosts?"

"No, no. I don't know. If they're ghosts, they don't look like the ones described on TV or in books." He paused. Simon could hear Susan talking to Robin. "Yes, yes. It's like they're observing us from that eighties television analogy. That's the best way to explain it."

"Who have you told?"

"You. Susan is freaking out, thinking she's crazy, but she's also happy to see them. When it happens, we get warm and relaxed. It's not scary. It's comforting. Her parents said the same thing."

"Robin, I don't think you're going crazy. If you are, I might be too. That feeling of being watched, you have, I've had it too. Out at the crop circle where Ricky was found, I was sure there were people around me. I even spoke as if there were. Then when I looked around, everyone I was with was too far away to hear me. The circle I am at now, same thing."

"Simon, really?"

"Document these occurrences, please, you, Susan, and her parents. Keep an accurate record."

Simon watched a car approach. Jeff's cruiser turned into the laneway.

"Robin, I hate to have to go, but Jeff just arrived."

"Simon, they *are* alive somewhere. Please, believe me. I know this sounds crazy but, please find them. Please bring them home. *Find them.*" He hung up.

"My sergeant is on his way."

"Garret?"

"No, he's off today. Today is Wayne."

"Should I leave?" asked Simon.

"No, he knew you had permission to be here. It's fine, Simon. We all know why you're here. And if it weren't for you, we wouldn't be coming to investigate a bone, anyway."

"Right."

"Are you okay? You look very pale."

"Yes, I'm fine. Just a strange call from home," said Simon.

"The ex?"

"Sure. Yep, at it again," Simon said, his cheeks turning rosy red.

Jeff opened his trunk and took out a pair of Wellington boots. He sat in the passenger seat and took his shoes off and pulled on his wellies.

"I tried not to make too much of a mess of the scene. But with you guys walking on it earlier, I couldn't find any old footprints," Simon said.

A cloud of dust appeared at the entrance to the farm and approached them. "Wayne is here."

"Any chance your drone is with you today?"

"Already did the fly over this morning. But now that it's a potential crime scene, I'll have to do a more detailed one."

. . .

Simon entered the circle, with Jeff and Wayne following.

"Right here. The ground was disturbed, so I dusted at it and thought I hit a stone. Then, well, as you can see, that's no stone. The bone looks new. I don't think it's been here long. Plus, when the farmer turned the soil in the spring, it would've popped up, you would think."

"So, just by chance, you found this by dusting the soil with your hand?" asked Wayne.

"Don't start with the questions. Why would I fly across the world to hide a bone?"

"I don't know, you tell me."

"You or someone at your station already vetted me. Am I some sort of suspect?"

"No, Simon, just pulling your leg." Wayne let out a large guffaw, which Simon did not appreciate. "Let me have a closer look." He kneeled beside the bone.

"Wayne, I'm going to get the drone in the air," said Jeff.

"Okay, get some wide shots, will you? But try to get low and follow the lines of wheat. See if there's anything else you can identify."

"Yes, sir."

"Look at this, Simon. See those marks?" said Wayne. "My dog makes the same marks when I give him a bone. Like he's trying to break it."

He stood and took a step back. From his shoulder bag, he pulled out a camera. "Let me snap some photos of it, then we can pull it out. Manchester is burning today, so they have no one to send."

"Burning?"

"Busy, not actually burning."

"Right."

Wayne took a series of photos and then instructed Simon to continue to dig around the bone. With his hands, he worked at the loose soil, following the shaft of the bone. Then, about ten inches in, he stopped. He pulled the bone out. Holding it up, Wayne videoed him.

"Do you want me to keep digging?" asked Simon.

"Do you feel anything in the hole?"

"Nothing. It isn't loose like what I just dug."

"I think we can leave it for now. If it was another broken end, I would say to dig deeper, but you pulled out the complete tip of the bone."

"Strange how it was placed in the ground, almost perfectly vertical. It looks human, maybe a femur." Simon placed the bone into a plastic bag Wayne handed him.

"Hey," Jeff called from the outside of the circle. "Carefully walk out to where the drone is hovering. I think I see something."

Simon, Jeff, and Wayne walked to the circle and then another seven rows of wheat.

"There," said Jeff.

"I see them. Paw prints. You guys have coyotes?" asked Simon.

"No, isn't that an American animal?" asked Wayne.

"We have foxes, but those prints are too big for a fox," said Jeff.

"Wild dogs?" asked Simon.

"No, no, not that I can think of. We have this newly introduced animal called a raccoon dog. Let me look it up on my phone."

"Does the farmer have any dogs?" asked Wayne.

"I didn't hear any barking around the house," said Simon. "But that means nothing. Where did this bone come from? And whose bone is it?" Simon scratched his head.

Wayne studied the bone through the clear bag. He turned it over in his hand and with his flashlight looked at the marks. "It's not human. I'm certain of it. It's a leg bone, but I'm sure it's the bone of a deer." He pointed at the broken end, exposing the marrow. "Look how dense it is, and the shape. As a hunter, I've seen that bone plenty when we're cleaning a deer. I'll need to get back to the station and report this. Can one of you check with the farmer to see if he has a dog?"

"Are you sure the bone isn't human?" asked Jeff.

"Not fully, but pretty sure. The lab can confirm this pretty quick."

"I'm still confused about how it's buried," said Jeff.

"There's no report of a missing person or a person missing a leg. That being said, the child was from Canada," said Wayne. He looked up at the drone. "You've got a knack for it, Jeff."

"Exactly," said Simon.

Jeff smiled at them as he dropped the drone. It buzzed past Simon's head.

"Jeff, can you run the drone over the entire field? I need to leave, but you two see what you can find."

"Are you considering this a crime scene?"

"No, I'm not sure there's a need to. If this comes back human, then we will. Just keep this quiet until I can confirm the bone."

"If we find anything else, I'll call right away, Wayne," said Jeff.

"Simon, help the kid out. You have a lot more experience with these types of investigations."

"I'll do what I can," he said, saluting Wayne.

Wayne took his camera and the bone and waved goodbye.

Simon watched Jeff as he continued to fly over the circle and surrounding field.

"I think this could be a fake or man-made circle, for lack of a better term. The plants are damaged, and they look to be trampled instead of neatly placed. I also ran the compass over the area. It stayed true to the north the whole time," said Simon.

"I agree, this is sloppy work compared to Norm's and no body just a bone. So why would someone make a *fake* crop circle and place a bone in it?"

"I guess that's up to us to figure out," said Simon. "How high can the drone go?"

"How high do you want it?"

"I wouldn't mind a quick scan of the other fields in case we're missing something," said Simon.

"Consider it done."

CHAPTER FOURTEEN

Simon was the last to arrive at the pub. The others were gathered around the same table as before. When Simon approached, Tom gave up his seat to allow Simon to have his back against the wall again, and Al went to the bar and picked up chips and a plate of curry.

Simon surveyed the other patrons. "No military boys yet?"

"No, not yet. We'll see if they arrive now that you're here," said Al.

"What? Do you think they're watching me?"

Tom shrugged his shoulders and reached for some chips.

"It sounds like you two had a busy day. Can we get more details than a couple of photos from Simon?" asked Tom.

Jeff recalled his morning with the call from Joseph to the station and then contacting Simon.

Simon then took over, describing the differences between the two circles. The broken stems and how the whole crop circle looked trampled or pressed, unlike Norm's. But he really piqued their interest when he brought up the bone they found, and how it was found in a hole vertically.

"First, I have seen circles like you described before. They're not as detailed as the *real* ones we see. By real I mean like Norm's neat and proper circle. Although not proven, I would agree with your theory of drunken farmers trying to make a quick quid to unsuspecting fans of crop circles. Second, an animal lays a bone in a hole. It doesn't dig a narrow hole and place the bone in it vertically," said Tom. "I can head out there in the morning, to further investigate the circle. Simon, can you join me?"

"Again, I just want to remind you all I'm here for a different reason. I checked in with Robin today. They..." he trailed off.

"What? They what?" asked Jeff.

Shh, don't say it.

"They just reminded me of why I'm here. It's not to become a crop circle expert." He took a hand full of fries. "Ketchup?"

"No, Simon. Dip the fries in the curry," said Tom.

"What? I was waiting for some naan bread."

"No, try it. You'll love it. You guys don't do this in Canada?" asked Al.

"Not that I know of." He dipped a single fry in the curry and slowly bit off the end. His eyebrows raised, and with each bite, the smile grew on his face. His head nodded as he threw the last bit of chip into his mouth. "Okay, that's amazing. Who would of *thunk* it?"

The group laughed at his comment.

"So, do we have any theories on today's findings?" asked Al.

"I don't know if you noticed Jeff, but Joseph had a strange tattoo on his arm. It was a combination of items that I have no idea why they would be together."

"No, I didn't see it. What did it look like?"

"It was a cross, an Ankh cross filled with gold. The inside of the loop was colored red. Below that was some hieroglyphics or I don't know what they would be. I wish I'd took a photo. Below that was an acorn. I'm not sure why it stuck with me."

Jeff's phone rang. He sat back and answered. The group looked at him as he listened to the person on the other end of the call. "Right, okay, thanks for the update, Wayne. Oh wait, I forgot, the farmer today has a dog."

He placed his phone back in his coat pocket and reached for some chips.

"Well?" asked Al.

"Wayne was right—it was a deer bone. An animal had chewed on it."

"Well, that's a relief. But it still doesn't explain the location Simon found it in," said Al.

"Could it have been lying in the field, and to throw us off, whoever or whatever made the crop circle put it there?" said Tom. "If you believe the circle is fake, or man-made, maybe they used it as a marker."

"If that's the case, it's working. Look how much we've talked about it already tonight," said Simon.

"There's more," said Jeff. He looked around the table.

"Are you all right?" asked Al.

Jeff placed his hands on the table. With a breath in, he cleared his throat. He looked Simon in the eyes. "We're not sure what it means. But when they cleaned the bone and examined it closer, there were two marks inscribed on it," he paused, taking a drink. Everyone leaned in to hear him clearly. "Well, it said, or showed, the number four and what looks like a maple leaf."

"Huh," said Simon. "*For the Canadian.* I assume we're all thinking the same thing? The broken bone is for me, as a warning. Go away or we'll break your leg?"

"We can open this up and have it investigated, Simon," said Jeff.

Simon leaned back in the seat. He sat quietly in his thoughts.

"I think we should look at it as a threat, Simon. But we don't need the police involved. I have an idea. Why don't we start to document this on my podcast? I think we're into something bigger than we can imagine. If that's the case, and please don't take this the wrong way, but if we are into something sinister, it's better to have it out there," said Tom.

"So, it's harder to make us disappear," said Jeff.

"Yes," said Tom

"Huh, makes sense. I don't want the police to investigate, Jeff. But I think we all need to be aware of what we're doing here. Someone doesn't want us poking around. Well, me at least," said Simon. "I'll go get another round of drinks."

Once Simon was out of earshot, Al said, "I guess it could be that simple."

"There's nothing simple about carving a threat into a bone and leaving it in what I believe was a fake crop circle. We need to be careful and watch out for him," said Tom.

"For now, let's see how Simon is when he returns and change the subject. Last thing we need is for any of us to be the next one in a circle."

"What were you guys discussing?" asked Simon, placing the frosted glasses on the table.

"I have a theory," said Jeff. "It's a bit far reaching, and it's not about the bone. Do you think the holes around the perimeter of Norm's circle had a device in them that's programed to make the circle? And what if all the *real* crop circles have a body left in the middle?"

Tom shook his head. "Where are the bodies, then? There's been too many circles over the years that look like Norm's. That's a lot of bodies to hide or even retrieve before anyone sees them."

"Let me finish. We know Norm's was fresh. Maybe if we don't find the circles right away, animals eat at the body."

"I don't know, most animals would leave something. A part of a bone, some flesh or muscle. Maybe, if we were in Canada out west where there are wolves and bears. But here, it doesn't sound like you have many large predators that could eat a human in a short period of time," said Simon.

Al handed his phone around the table.

"What's this?" asked Tom.

"A raccoon dog," said Al. "They're not much bigger than a fox. Just my opinion, but they would have to be starving to eat a human. Plus, there is no way they are breaking and eating large bones."

"I was just throwing it out there for discussion. But you're right, we have nothing big enough to eat a human. So, if bodies are left, first—why? Second—where do they go?"

"Or are only select circles used for bodies? I don't know the one Ricky was in had four large circles. I'd have to do some digging, but four seems rare. They are usually one, three, five," said Tom.

"Add it to our notes of questions to be answered. Next question, why are there crop circles appearing?" asked Tom.

"I did some research while I was waiting for you earlier, Jeff. There have been thirty-three circles this year around the world. That's slightly higher than last year, but far from 2012, when eighty-eight were reported," said Simon.

"Ricky was the only one found in a circle that I can see documented, other than that time in the sixties we talked about."

As they finished the fries and curry, Al nodded toward the door. "Look who just arrived. Two of our military friends," said Al.

Simon watched as they sat at the bar, conveniently in seats, allowing them to see Simon's table in the mirror.

"Okay, I'm going to go engage them," said Tom. He strolled to the bar and ordered drinks and another plate of fries and curry.

"Evening gents, another beautiful day around here."

"Aye, 'tis," the man closest to him responded. His friend nodded his head but said nothing.

Returning to his table with fresh food and drinks. "Scots, from his thick accent. I would say from the east coast."

"How do you guys hear that?" He threw his arms up. "But you can't tell the difference between an American and a Canadian?" said Simon, shaking his head.

"Every region has its own accent and inflections. If you were here long enough you would hear it," said Jeff. "These guys from up north sound a lot different from me and my proper British accent."

Tom leaned into Jeff, laughing as everyone dug into the fresh plate of chips and curry.

Tom's phone pinged. "Hey, guys, there's another crop circle about eighty miles away. They found it this morning. We could go tomorrow."

"What happened to going back to the one from today?" asked Simon.

"You've seen two, so use this one as a comparison. We can go back to the second one later," said Tom.

"Weird though, I don't remember there being this many in one area before," Al said.

"I can go in the morning. But this is it. I need to be looking for those kids," said Simon.

"Okay," said Tom.

"Tom, why don't you pick me up? Jeff, could we take your drone?"

"Sure. Tom knows how to use it. Remember, you need to get permission from the landowner. Don't..."

"Yes, yes, we know, Officer Jeff," mocked Tom.

"I'm not warning you, Simon. I am warning Tom. He's been known to push the limits of the law."

"Hey, maybe we can record a podcast on the way over? True crime one? Or better yet, we can just go on about anything. Keep it loose. It's a three-hour drive."

Looking at his watch, Simon bowed out of the conversation. "Okay, I should check in with my kids. I'll see you guys in the morning," Simon said, pushing back his chair.

The men at the bar followed him with their eyes as he left the pub. When the door closed, they slowly looked in the mirror at the others.

"They look like they want to leave, but know we're watching," said Jeff.

"I need to leave, anyway. We should all get up and go in different directions."

The trio left the pub together, each one glaring at the two men sitting at the bar. Tom sat in his car waiting to see if they immediately followed them out. After an hour of waiting, he drove home with no story to tell.

CHAPTER FIFTEEN

Jeff's phone played the Looney Tunes theme as he circled his cruiser, doing a safety check. He retrieved his phone from his pocket. The constable waiting for him to leave for their first call laughed.

"Hi, Norm," said Jeff into his phone. "Well, I can't, but I think Simon and Tom can. I'll call them."

• • •

Simon drove to Norm's farm. His confidence of driving *on the wrong side of the road* was improving. Tom rode shotgun, wanting to catch up on his social media because his latest podcast had exploded, with mostly good comments. But he had a few choice words about Simon's driving. "Mate, I'll drive us home. Socials aren't any good to me dead."

Norm stood at the barn, the dust from the car tires signaling he had guests. Simon was the first out of the car to approach Norm. He shook his hand and turned to see where Tom was.

"Sorry, Norm, I think he's in a bit of a comments battle with a couple of his so called fans."

"Oh aye, I listened to a few of his radio shows."

"Podcasts."

"Right. Well, my son hooked me up on my computer. Very entertaining. Six weeks ago, I would've listened to it and laughed. Now, well, here I am a contributor to the show and living the insanity."

"Morning, Norm. Sorry about that. Just having a chat with a fan."

"A fan? The cursing under your breath as we arrived didn't make it sound like a fan," said Simon.

"Okay, a hater. He thinks we should drop this whole thing. He warned us we could find ourselves in more trouble than we think."

"What was his name?" said Norm.

"Government sees you. Only it's spelled, GvrnmntcU."

"Interesting. I had some strange happenings last night."

"Oh boy, a comment like that never starts a pleasant conversation."

"No, no, it's okay. I just want you to know what's happened since your last visit."

"Did little green men visit you?"

Norm looked at him, confused. "One was little, but he sure wasn't green."

"What?"

"Get in my truck. We can talk on the way over. Is there anything you need to load into the truck before we go?"

"Just the drone and our backpacks," said Simon.

• • •

Norm told them how his fields were growing and how there was plenty of damage from trespassers wanting to see his crop circle. Tom stepped back into the truck after opening the gate to the third field.

"So, let's get to the heart of this. I'm glad you're back. A few things have happened since I found Ricky a week ago. Jeff, Al, and you Tom were the first to arrive, and since then I've had a lot of visitors. Some came to me to talk, others were out in my field doing some rituals or prayers, and others just trampled my fields to get a photo with the crop circle. But what concerns me is what happened last night."

Tom reached for his phone. "Can I record?"

"Yes, but I don't want my voice on your little show. You can use the information."

"Right. I'm okay with that."

"Yesterday, after I finished my chores and dinner, this group arrived. There were six of them standing in my driveway. They were all dressed in black, and some had balaclavas covering their faces. It scared me, to be honest. Then, one man in all white got out of a Jaguar."

"Jag?" asked Simon. "High rollers."

"He approached me on the porch. I asked him to stop, and he did. I asked what they wanted from me. He waved his arm, and one of his soldiers or monkeys approached with a duffle bag. He tossed it at my feet."

"Did they talk?" asked Tom.

"No, nothing. Just motions." Norm slowed the truck, and Tom jumped out to open the gate to the next field. "I bent and opened the bag. There was a piece of paper on top."

"What was under it?" asked Tom.

"Relax, Tom, I'm getting to it."

"Money," he turned to Simon. "Betcha' it was money," said Tom, holding his phone close to Norm.

"Yes, money, a lot of it, too. Five thousand pounds."

"What?" asked Simon.

"The note, the note, what did it say?" asked Tom.

"It was written in cursive. According to your older podcast, they use cursive because computers can't read it, and neither can most people under thirty."

"Hey, you listened to that episode?"

"Yes, I'll admit you have some very interesting topics."

"The note?"

"Right." He stopped the truck and leaned on the steering wheel. "It identified them as new order Druids. The note explained how it was a full moon and they wanted to worship the earth, the universe and power from within the crop circle, something like that. It also mentioned my circle was rare because there were four large circles."

"Last night was a lunar eclipse," said Tom. "They were worshipping the eclipse."

"The note explained about offering the money for the use of the field until nine the next morning, with no interruption or calls to the local authorities. When I mentioned unwelcomed people approach my fields at night, the man in white shrugged his shoulders and pointed to a few large men."

"Strange, but I guess we all know there are groups like them around," said Tom.

"Yes, so I agreed. No one thanked me, no one said anything. They all bowed their heads to me and left in their vehicles. I went to bed with my bag full of money. Around three in the morning I heard loud noises and a thumping of a beat. I looked out my bedroom window toward the field, and there were lights pulsing to this noise. I don't know how they thought all this was being discreet. Anyone could see it from the road as they passed."

"What the hell?" asked Simon. "Before you go on, it's a strange question, but did any of them have tattoos? The ones you met by your house."

"Yes, I think most of them did. One guy in black had Stonehenge on his inner forearm. He's the one who tossed me the bag. There were a few others with Celtic symbols on their forearms."

Simon scribbled on his notebook. "Go ahead, Norm."

"I took my bicycle and headed up the road with binoculars. It was perfect, a clear night, the eclipse was halfway through its cycle and gave me just enough light to bike on the road safely. I got myself in a position to see what was going on."

"So, you took the money and still went out to the field? Well done, mate," said Tom.

Norm stopped the truck. "Well, here we are. Wait, tattoos. The man in white had a strange one." He closed his eyes. "Yes, it was on his chest. His robe hung open just enough to expose it. There was a strange cross, some filled in red, the lower in gold. On the cross were Arabic or some strange markings or letters. I have no clue what they mean, and I can't even describe them."

"Was there an acorn below the markings?"

"Yes. How do you know?"

"I saw the same thing on a farmer at another, what I believe to be, a fake circle. If it's not fake—well, it isn't to the standard of yours."

"Let's get out so I can explain what I saw."

They followed Norm to the second circle. "So, right here, a group of twelve people stood in a circle. There were lights on the ground. I think, in the same holes that we found around the circles. Notice the stakes are gone? The lights flashed three colors—yellow, red, and blue. Over there, outside the circle, a man stood with a snare drum. He kept a beat of 1-2-3-4 roll and repeat. It eerily echoed across the fields. Oh, the lights changed to his beat. In this circle, they had built a cross and hung a naked woman to it. But not a cross like Jesus' but more like an *X*."

"They tied a woman to it?" asked Tom.

"She was alert and laughing. The whole time I watched, they didn't abuse her. It was more like they were worshipping her. She had a crown of black roses on her head. Those twelve people in red robes walked around her. I could hear the chants and mantra they spoke. It was, *'Mother of the universe, mother of creation, mother of all the children on Earth, your blood flows, your blood heals. Send us more of your pure blood.'* Then they repeated it. Over and over. Every other time, they added a timed hum. Always the same tone, they held the hum for around forty-five seconds, maybe a minute, they timed it to the drummer's beat. Then back to the words. And when they chanted, the drummer stopped his roll and just played the beat."

Simon and Tom were stunned into silence.

"Oh, it gets better."

"How?" Tom asked.

"Follow me." They walked to the third circle, stepping around the location of where Ricky was found. "In this circle here, you can still see where a second cross was placed." He showed them the holes that had not been filled in. "In this spot was a second smaller cross with, like I said to you before, a small person, just not green. At first, I thought it was a child. I was about to call the police. Then I realized it was a small man dressed or made up to look like a small child. Another group in black robes walked around this one."

Norm marched around the circle, demonstrating the process. He dragged his feet and paced around the hole to a beat he was calling out.

"They were silent, kneeling and facing the cross, until the other group stopped their chant. The first group kneeled and faced the woman, then this group started, *'Child of the golden sun, child of the golden moon, bleed your precious blood on us. Heal us, make us immortal.'* Same thing, they hummed after five chants, a different pitch than the other group, though. They repeated theirs seven times and kneeled while the others began again."

While Norm told his strange tale, Simon and Tom followed in step behind him, circling, circling. Abruptly, Simon stopped. "Stop, look as we're talking. We're marching around the circle in time to the beat Norm produced earlier. Weird. I feel, I don't know, but there..."

"It's almost trance like. Like we're being guided by others," said Tom. "I feel we are in a group. Like others are walking with us."

They looked at Norm. He continued pacing the outer circle.

"Norm!"

Norm's body jerked, and he turned to look at them, blinking wildly. "Okay, this is strange. I feel it too, like there's more than us here."

Simon looked around. He looked up at the sun. "What time is it?"

Norm checked his watch, then shook his wrist. "My watch has stopped," said Norm.

Tom pulled out his phone. "What? That's impossible. We've been here for an hour?" said Tom.

"No," replied Norm in disbelief.

"Yes, according to my phone." He turned and showed it to Simon.

"So, Norm, what happened after that?" asked Simon.

Norm paced the circle again. "There's something peaceful about this. Let's keep doing the circle, and I'll finish up the story."

"You're right. I feel like a teen again," said Simon. "I don't know, it's like we have an audience we can't see." He thought of Robin's call the day before.

"This went on till half past four. At that point, what I believe was the same man who wore white earlier approached the lady on the cross. He took a jar of what I hope was a thick red liquid and not blood, and splashed it on her stomach. Then the group that worshipped her approached her and placed their hands one at a time on her stomach. Like rubbing a bald man's head for luck."

"Okay, that's just weird," said Tom. "Did she look pregnant?"

"No, far from it. Then the same man moved to the other cross and the small man. He poured another jar of a thick golden fluid over the small man's head. The second group did the same thing. They walked to him, touched his head, did two more passes around the circle and kneeled facing the cross. Then, and I must say, this was crazy too, but the two groups began saying their mantras in unison. It was amazing, like the world's best gospel choir singing on the most perfect sound stage. It rang in my ears, especially when they both hit their tones. I'm not mystical or anything like that, but my body vibrated. I saw the lights change and felt my body change." He stopped walking and smiled. "I felt like a kid. I would love to feel like it again. All my pains and worries were gone only for a few minutes, but—well, it was magical."

"So, how did this whole thing wrap up?" asked Tom.

"Well, one man cut the two people down. They were wrapped in robes and left by car. By half-past six this morning, the entire group was gone with all their stuff. I went to the field and tried to find the fluid, but it looks like they turned it into the soil."

They entered the circle and looked around. No stain or any sign of moisture remained.

"Let me get the drone in the air and see what has changed," said Tom.

The drone buzzed around the fields. Tom sent it following the group's trail of footprints to the gate by the road, where he assumed the vehicles were parked.

Simon followed the drone, looking for anything that might have fallen from a pocket.

Leaning against his truck, Norm watched Tom work the drone. Norm breathed deeply, something he wasn't able to do before his visitors and their ceremony. "When you're ready to go, I have two more things to discuss."

"What, there's more? Norm, you have already blown my mind for today," Simon said with a big smile on his face.

"Norm, what else is there?" asked Tom. He landed the drone. "I see nothing out of the ordinary from the last flyover."

"Yeah, I followed the trail of footprints out to the gate. Nothing seems to have been dropped. They were all barefoot until they got to their cars," said Simon.

Norm helped Tom with the drone while Simon took more photos with his camera. They sat on the tailgate of the truck.

"What else do you have to tell us, Norm?" asked Simon.

"Well, I had a visit from a couple of fellas. They asked a lot of the same questions you did, only they weren't as nice. They also left a note for you boys."

"A note? For us? How did..."

"It's in the glove box." He lifted himself off the rear of the truck and walked to the passenger side. Simon looked at Tom, confused.

"Who wants to open it?"

Simon took the envelope and tore it open. He held it so both of them could read it.

Stop looking for the kids. Simon, go back to Canada. Tom, stop your podcasting and get an actual job. Jeff, worry about the criminals in your little area. Al, your girlfriend misses you. This is larger than all of you. If you continue, you might just find yourselves in a place no one wants to visit or stay. It was written in cursive.

Simon held the paper, his hands shaking. "Who are these guys?"

"They didn't say. They looked like military to me. Muscular, shaved heads, stood straight, and when they inspected the crop circle, they seemed to be a bit more systematic than you guys were."

"Okay, do we have military brats chasing us as we look for missing children?" asked Tom.

"Were they British?" asked Simon.

"Yes, I would say one had a Welch accent, and the other was London area."

Simon stopped. "Look."

"What?" said Tom.

Norm looked back at Simon. "What's wrong?"

"What are we doing?" asked Tom.

"Huh, when did we start to pace around the circle again?"

"Hey, yeah. There's something magical going on. But it feels right. Maybe there's something to this mystical ceremony," said Tom.

"Well, I need to head back to the house. Is there anything else you need today?"

"No, I think we have plenty here to think about," said Simon.

The three men drove in silence. Simon had the note folded in his pocket.

CHAPTER SIXTEEN

Two days after the visit with Norm; Simon, Jeff, and Al met at Tom's house. Simon had spent the previous morning searching tattoo designs on the internet with Tom before they recorded two podcasts. Al had to work, but on an extended lunch break, he investigated the soil and plants gathered from Norms. Nothing extraordinary came from his experiments. He compared his findings to other researchers of crop circles and their documents, not finding anything his experiments didn't show. Jeff found a report of another circle appearing, four hours away from Tom's house.

• • •

The group left in Al's car, hoping to investigate this new circle.

"I got my ass chewed out last night by Robin and Susan. They want results. They didn't expect me to join a *boy band*. I could hear their frustration. They're wondering if the twins are even in England. Then, because that call went so well, I called my ex. I guess with everything going on, I forgot to transfer her child support." Simon shook his head. "She threatened to bring her lawyer into it and, of course, jail time for being a deadbeat dad. I've only missed two payments since she left me. She actually said to me if I was on the run, to avoid paying support, she would have me extradited back to Canada. Then hung up without letting me chat with the boys."

"Harsh," said Tom.

"And for my third strike, work wants me back in a month now. I guess the bean counters saw how Terry arranged my time off, so now I am down to three weeks' vacation and a week of overtime. The clocks ticking. Oh, and one other thing. How do you guys live like this? The dampness makes my back feel like someone took a baseball bat to it," said Simon.

"Cricket."

"What?"

"Cricket bat is what we say here. And yes, I'm aching too. The rain yesterday will find its way into your bones," said Tom.

"Sorry about the rant. But what are we doing?"

"Simon, I feel the kids are just a small part of a larger organized issue," said Jeff.

"I don't disagree, but they're not funding me to chase circles. They have me here to find their kids. And I'm no closer to finding their twins than when I got here. I totally understand their frustration—I have it too."

. . .

They arrived at the farm where the newest circle popped up. The farmer, already upset that people had been on his property and stomped down his crops, refused to let them into the field.

"Can we ask you a few questions before we go?" asked Tom.

"You have two minutes." He looked at his watch.

"Did you look closely at the circles? Were there holes dug around the perimeter and in the center of the circle? How many circles were there?"

The farmer looked at Tom, then the others. Tom knew he had got the farmer's attention.

"I don't know. I didn't look that close."

"Was there anything found in the circles, by that I mean, bones, flesh, blood, clothing?" Jeff asked. He relaxed. The look on the farmer's face made him believe they would be granted permission to the field.

"Are you asking if there was a ritual killing on my property? Who are you guys?"

Simon sensed he was hiding something. "We're just some amateur investigators who love crop circles. In Hayfield, they found a body and, in another one, a bone. And we never mentioned anything about rituals or a killing."

"Right, nothing like that here. But…"

"Yes?"

"Your time is up. I need to tend to my farm and try to save some of my crops damaged from this prank."

"You were about to say something. If not, I have one last question. Did you see any men in black hoodies?" asked Tom. He said it with the confidence of already knowing the answer.

"Men in hoodies?"

Al looked at Simon and winked.

"Yes, maybe three or four men," said Jeff.

"What?" The farmer pulled out his cell phone. "I want you to leave. I'm calling the police."

"Sir, you obviously have seen things you want to talk about."

From behind, Simon heard footsteps. He looked around to see a man in his twenties approach them with a hunting rifle over his shoulder.

"You texted, Dad?"

"Son, these men don't want to leave our farm. Can you help me convince them?"

"Is this about the crop circles?"

"Yes, we came from Hayfield to see it," said Tom.

"Well, sorry to say, but you'll not be seeing it. We have our help out now, plowing the field. The barley was close enough to be cut."

"We asked your dad a couple of questions. He seems to have the answers, but is hesitant to tell us," said Tom.

The farmer shook his head. "Leave, I need you to leave."

His son pointed his gun at Jeff. "We would like you to leave."

"Fine, fine. Let's go lads. We aren't going to see anything here," said Jeff. He turned to the farmer's son. "I assume that has been registered?"

"What business is it of yours?"

"None of mine, but when you pull out a weapon on a person, there are criminal consequences," said Jeff. He knocked shoulders with the farmer's son as he walked past.

The rest followed Jeff to the car and climbed in. The farmer and his son stood in the laneway and watched the car leave.

Al drove to the next town and pulled into a petrol station. Tom filled the car while Simon sat and wrote in his notebook.

"What are you writing?" asked Al.

"Shh, give me a minute." He finished writing and flipped back through the pages, looking for the rough drawing he had made of the other crop circles. "There's a restaurant up there. Maybe we can get a bite and I can talk. You all missed something big at the farm."

"Oh, I think I got it too," said Tom, shaking his phone.

•   •   •

They sat in the restaurant and ordered the Farmer's breakfast.

When Simon's plate was placed in front of him, he grabbed his chest. "At what point do they come take my blood and replace it with pork grease?"

"It happens naturally through time, mate. It's part of the English charm," said Tom.

They dug into their plate of sausages, bacon, eggs, bread and fried tomatoes, all cooked with bacon grease.

"What's this?" asked Simon.

"Blood pudding. It balances the grease and blood in our bodies."

"Dare I ask?"

"Try it, you'll love it, and if you don't, I'll gladly take it," said Tom.

With their plates empty and removed, coffee mugs topped up, Simon whispered. "Listen, did anyone notice the tattoos they had? The father had one on his right arm and the son had his on his left arm. I noticed it when Jeff *bumped* into him."

"No, not particularly. Why?" asked Jeff.

"They both were the pillars of Stonehenge on the outside of their arms. But on the inside of both their arms they had the same tattoo. I saw it and so did Norm," said Simon. "How does so many people have the same thing? It's like they all belong to a gang."

"Yes, but this time I snapped a photo. Look." Tom passed his phone around the table. "We can now find out what those markings mean. When I saw the tattoo, and Jeff was talking with the son, I took the photo. It's a little blurry."

"Well done, Tom," said Al.

Tom opened his backpack and pulled out his notebook. "Look at this. I did some digging yesterday. The note we got from Norm mentioned four circles being rare. So I did some looking to see how often they appear. Boys, there is rare and then *rare*."

They looked at Tom. His smile grew as he flipped through his notebook, then his phone. "Here, look at these circles. Two, three, six, and five circles. I could show you hundreds of these. But here, a four circle. Not clover shaped like Norm's, but four large circles. A finger was found in this circle." He pointed to the circle at the top of the photo. "This appeared in June 2015. Remember the circle where a person was discovered in the sixties? Here's a photo, four circles."

Everyone looked at Tom.

"Say that again?"

"The report says they found a finger of a child in the circle, in 2015."

"Four circles?" Simon asked.

"Correct."

Simon glanced at Jeff and smiled. "What have we found now?"

"I'm not sure, but I feel like I need to find out if they matched the finger to a missing person. Tomorrow, when I'm back at work, I'll do some digging."

"Yeah, I couldn't find any follow-up in the news about a person being identified. It's as if someone scrubbed the story from the internet but they missed this small crop circle site," said Tom.

"Do we think these tattoos are part of the Druid upper level? Like the masons and their thirty-three levels?" asked Simon.

"I know we had a brief history in middle school about the Druids, but do any of us know the truth about them?" Al asked.

"Nothing, except aren't they connected to the mystery of King Arthur and a magical sword?" asked Tom.

"Lads, I'm here to find two missing kids, not solve the riddle of King Arthur to see if I'm worthy of pulling his sword from a rock."

"I'd like to go back to the farm, but we could just be asking for trouble," Al said.

"So, the Druids are like the Free Masons?" asked Simon.

"Not really, but similar. They were considered the elite elders of their societies—the priest, doctors, elders—things like that, back before the Romans found these islands." Al hesitated and produced a sheepish smile. "So yes, like the Masons in some ways, I guess," said Al.

Everyone finished their coffees as they surfed through pictures of crop circles on their phones.

"Look here, another four circle image. But it's a drawing from 1815," said Jeff. "We'll need to do more digging than on our phones in a restaurant. I work tomorrow. I'll try to get some time to see if there's any information on the finger. Tom, you and Simon can maybe visit the library and do some reading on the Druids, the tattoo and our mysterious four circle, crop circles?"

"Simon, I'm in if you are. We should call a bunch of the Druid society branches and see if we can interview anyone. Maybe we can record another podcast after we do our research?"

"I guess. These circles are the only leads I have. I'll admit, I thought I was wasting time and was ready to break away from you three. But the threatening letter, the tattoos, the rareness of four circles and the fact another body part was found in a circle just over a year ago makes me believe, well, there has to be some connection. I just need to convince Robin and Susan of this," said Simon. He shook his head. "Strangest thing, but I feel like the farmer's son just passed by the window."

Tom jumped out of his seat and ran to the door. He looked at Simon, who pointed to his left. Tom stepped outside and looked to his left. He moved along the sidewalk looking in store fronts. In a narrow alleyway, a figure pressed against a wall. Tom slipped into the alley. He hugged the bins and shadows. Behind the final bin, ready to step out, he identified the person by her name tag. A staff member from the ladies' clothing store leaning against the wall stealing a smoke on her break.

He looked around the alley, a strange feeling of being watched engulfed him, stronger than any other time in his life. He looked over his shoulder every few steps. As if an invisible person was beside him, just out of sight. He studied the stores through the large front windows as he returned to the pub.

After paying the bill, the others waited for Tom to return as they scanned the street.

"No luck on the farmer's son. I don't know fellas, but I have the strangest feeling we're under surveillance. But the weirdest part, it's as if the person is right beside me, only I can't see them," said Tom. "Right here." He reached his right arm out.

"I had that feeling in Norm's crop circle and honestly in the bed-and-breakfast some evenings," said Simon, approaching their car.

"Well, someone's handing out pamphlets," said Jeff. He took the piece of paper from under the wiper, folded it and put it in his pocket.

"Jeff, what does the paper say? Our car is the only one with a pamphlet," said Simon.

Jeff reached into his pocket. "Here read it, it's probably a sale on wool at the local market."

Al put the car in gear and backed out.

"Al, park the car." Simon said. His voice was quiet and monotone. "Put the car into the spot."

Tom took the paper from Simon and read it. Jeff looked over Tom's shoulder and read the note. "Al, park it."

He did as instructed. Tom handed him the paper. Al read the note out loud. "*The Canadian should go home before... The rest of you get back to your normal lives. Playing Sherlock Holmes is over.*"

"Well, we have someone's attention. I think you have proof, Simon. We're on the right path to finding the twins."

"Look at the penmanship of the writing—old school, like the one left for us at Norm's. The way it flows, and the cursive style is more early nineteenth century than present day," said Tom.

Everyone stared at him. He looked around the car. "I took a handwriting analyst course in college. It was more a history of writing. Trust me, that is not what they are teaching in the schools these days. The paper is old, incredibly superior quality to today's rubbish."

Simon sat back in his seat and stared through the front window. He rubbed his head and face with his hands. "Well, I'm not going anywhere," said Simon.

The defiance in his voice made Tom smile. He nodded in agreement.

Al turned in his seat. "Guys, I'm out."

"What?" said Jeff. "Al really? Now? A couple schoolyard threats are going to send you running?"

"Jeff, it's more than that. Maybe they see me as the weak one or the one not as involved. But the other day, under my office door was a note. Security doesn't know how it got there, but let me just say it scared me. And my girlfriend isn't happy about how much time I'm spending out at night. When she finds out about the threats, she'll *lose the plot*."

"Why is this the first we're hearing about your note?" asked Jeff.

"Because it also said not to tell you." He got out of the car and went to the trunk. From his bag, he took out a piece of paper and handed it to Tom.

Tom read the note aloud. "It says, *"Allen, you should pick a better class of people to socialize with. These friends will have you lying in a circle before the winter. But before then, you will lose your job, girlfriend and your flat."* It's not signed, but I would say the handwriting is the same as what's on the paper we just received."

"No matter." Al started his car. "I'm done."

CHAPTER SEVENTEEN

The next day, after they found the note on the car, things were quiet, just what they wanted. Jeff took an extra shift to help with coverage. On his breaks, he searched through old files looking for more crop circles with remains found in them.

Al, scared of his and his girlfriend's safety, wouldn't return any calls or texts.

Simon and Tom recorded and released podcasts. They started a new podcast dedicated to the crop circle phenomena and the search for missing children. After searching the web and the local library for information on circles, tattoos and the Druids, they agreed they would need to visit the larger library in Manchester for more information. Discouraged about not cracking the tattoo mystery, Tom sent his photo of the tattoo to an acquaintance at the University of Glasgow.

With pages full of the latest information, Simon spoke with Robin and Susan. He told them about the threatening notes, and how he felt they were getting into something bigger. Worried about his safety, they demanded he return home. He denied their request. An hour after he hung up from their call, Gary called asking him to return to Canada. Again, Simon refused.

•   •   •

Simon and Tom drove into town to pick up some groceries.

"I'm starving. How about we grab lunch while we're here?" asked Simon.

"I think we have a more immediate problem. We might have someone following us. How should we handle it?" asked Tom.

Simon glanced at the side mirror. "Huh, the blue two-door?"

"Yep," Tom said, looking through his rearview mirror.

"Just keep on this road. Make it look like we're heading back to your place." Simon pulled out his phone and texted Jeff, asking for police support. Jeff was three streets over, handing a teen a ticket for racing through a red light. He instructed Simon to stop at the chippy wagon on Hope Street. He'd be waiting in his cruiser to pull over the blue car.

Tom did as Simon instructed, and the car drove past. Jeff immediately pulled out and followed. When they rolled through a stop sign, he put on his lights and pulled the blue car over.

"Good afternoon. That was a full stop you needed to make when you turned left onto this street. If school wasn't letting out, I might have turned away. But look, the street is filling up with children. Can I see some identification, please?"

"Jeff, is it? Why don't you take a step back from the car? We did nothing wrong."

"Sir, again. Identification, please."

The driver looked at Jeff, then his passenger.

"Since there seems to be an issue, can I see a piece of photo ID from you too, please?" Jeff asked the passenger.

At that moment, Tom and Simon drove slowly past. After following Simon with their eyes, they begrudgingly handed over their driver's licenses.

"I'll be right back." Jeff walked back to his car and slid into the seat with the driver, watching him through his rearview mirror. After typing in the information, Jeff took a photo of each identification with his phone.

His computer returned the information he wanted. The men he pulled over had past government clearances. Their records were clean. He had nothing to hold them for.

He returned to the car and handed them their identifications. "What are two men from Cardiff doing up here? Looking for crop circles?"

The driver smiled at him.

"I don't want you guys running stop signs anymore, understand? This one's free, but your names are in the system now. So, the next one won't be. How long are you here for?"

"As long as we want. Last I checked, we didn't have to sign in to be here. If we're done, have a nice day, Officer Jeff. Maybe we'll see you and your friends around town."

Jeff stared at him. "Have a nice day. I don't want myself or one of my fellow officers to chat with you two again."

"Are you threatening us?"

Jeff turned and returned to his cruiser. Once inside, his body shook. He watched as the two men drove away. Resting his head on the headrest, he took in a full breath and exhaled. He fumbled through his pockets, looking for his phone, then texted Simon. *"We need to talk. Pub seven?"*

After a few minutes, Simon texted back, *"Perfect."*

• • •

Simon and Tom sat at their usual table, waiting for Jeff. While fingering a Coke, Simon wished for a split second he was holding something stronger, something to calm his nerves. Twenty minutes after the agreed upon time, Jeff arrived.

"Tardy, not a good sign. What happened?" asked Tom.

"I was on the phone with Al. He finally picked up. He yelled at me, called me foolish and looking for trouble. He says he hasn't been sleeping well, he's been having weird dreams about someone in his flat," said Jeff. "He wants to put this all behind him."

"Right, and a threatening letter has nothing to do with it?"

"He feels he's being followed. Someone was in his office at work last night and took the seeds, plants, and soil he gathered from Norm's farm."

"They took his samples? So, theft? That's a concern," said Simon. "And why take the samples? Go into the field and get your own."

Tom nodded and sipped his drink.

"Unless he missed something when he quickly examined the items," said Tom.

"Simon, you don't know Al too well, but honestly, I'm surprised he lasted this long. He's feared his own shadow since I met him," said Jeff.

"So, it's the three stooges," said Simon.

"Yes, but I need to be careful," said Jeff. "You know the politics of a police station, Simon."

"All too well," he replied, as he winked.

"I want to be involved, but you can't be using my name on the podcast or any other media you two are doing. Going forward, you need to be careful what you release on the show. Some of the information we discuss isn't public knowledge."

"Understand," said Tom. "But you're coming on the podcast tomorrow?"

"Yes, Tom, but with an alias and, if possible, one of those voice changers."

"It's called a distorter."

"Okay, so what have you got for us? Who were the guys following us? What do they want?" asked Simon.

"At the traffic stop, they didn't say much. They were rude, but well, most people are."

"Did they recognize you?"

"Yes, of course, but they weren't any of the three we've seen in the pub. I haven't seen them before. They're ex-military."

"What?"

"I did a background check before I left. British Army. We should be a bit more careful when we go to the farms too," said Jeff. "I've seen you two mentioned in reports now, as aggressively attempting to force your way onto farmer's fields."

"From the farmer and his son with tattoos?" asked Simon.

"Yes, when the officer at his local station returned to have a few follow-up questions answered, they brought us up."

"Interesting," said Simon. "As for those tattoos, the photo was a little pixilated when we zoomed in. Tom sent it off to a friend. Hopefully, we get something back."

"Also, as I was leaving, my sergeant called me into his office. He brought up the crop circle investigations and a complaint about a traffic stop this afternoon." He raised his eyebrows.

"So those guys got to your boss?" asked Simon.

"It appears they did. Their complaint was, I targeted them."

"Did you mention anything about us being followed or the letters we received?" asked Tom.

"No, I took my lumps and left."

An alarm went off on Tom's phone. He looked at it and tapped his forehead. "I have to go. I totally forgot, I have an appointment," said Tom. "A pre-screen for a podcast later this week. I'll get all our information together for the podcast in the morning."

"Simon, can you stay and talk?" asked Jeff.

"Sure, if you can drive me home."

Simon grabbed another pop and a beer for Jeff. "What's bothering you?"

"I think you are thinking the same thing, we're spinning our wheels. Honestly, if you were back in your job, would your boss approve of the time you have spent without coming to any conclusions, theories, or evidence?"

Simon dropped his head. "No, you're right. I was lying in bed last night thinking the same thing. We are sitting playing defense, waiting for something to drop in our laps. We need to knock on some doors, ask the right questions. Whoever left us the note last week isn't feeling any pressure from us now or we would be well—*threatened.*"

"Right. I feel we have some items we need to follow up on, but we—we are just casually working it. Tom's a bit of a distraction with his podcasts, but we need him, and I like him, too."

"I agree. What are you thinking?"

"Reviewing what we know, we should go interview a head of one of the local Druid Societies. Somehow, they're involved. The one farmer has a fake circle appear, with a threat for you. The second one won't let us on his property."

"What about Norm?"

"No, he's the odd one. No tattoos. I stopped in to see him while working the other day. He was in a tank top. Nothing there."

"I've no doubt Norm's circle was a surprise to him. And no harm to the library in town, but we need to go to a bigger one like Manchester's. There has to be more information about the circles, especially the four circles."

They sat quietly, finishing their drinks, watching people come and go.

CHAPTER EIGHTEEN

The next morning, Jeff picked Simon up at his bed-and-breakfast. Their ride to Tom's house and studio was quiet, with both of them looking over their shoulders and down side streets as they drove through town.

Tom answered their knock, scanning the street as he let them squeeze in. He ushered them up to the spare bedroom he used for his studio. Bottles of water were waiting on the table for them.

"Do we want to review your notes, Jeff? Or go straight to the podcast?"

"We can go straight to the podcast. Do you have a voice distorter for me? And I don't want to be on camera."

"Understood. Yes, you sit there by the water, and Simon, your usual spot is ready, too."

"Okay, let's jump into this. I'd like to do a couple of things this afternoon," said Simon. "Let's make some calls and set up appointments with a few Druid leaders."

"Yeah, my shift starts at two today. So, I need to be gone by noon," said Jeff.

"Okay, let's do one sound check and roll. Phones off, fellas, I try to run a professional show." He placed his headphones over his ears. Leaning into the microphone. "Jeff, give me a sentence or two."

"Tom, you need to dust around here," Jeff said, smiling.

"Okay, that works. The distorter is working. I believe it said, You have a great place around here." He laughed. "But seriously, I'll feed it through my headphone, I'll leave one ear piece out. You guys won't hear the distortion. Jeff, if I wave my arms, you stop talking immediately, just in case the distorter stops working. You don't need to say much, anyway."

"Got it."

Tom did the introduction to the show as everyone sat quietly. Then, with the introductions done, he introduced the panel.

"My co-host to the show is here, Simon Elliot, from the great white north, known as Canada. Welcome friend, and today we have a special guest, so special he can't be on camera or have his voice heard. From somewhere in this universe, welcome *Mata Hari* to the show."

"Hello, Tom, Simon," said Jeff.

"Hello," said Simon. "My back and knees hurt from the cold and damp, and my brain hurts from everything we need to talk about today."

"You'll learn to embrace the arthritic pain. It builds a stiff upper lip, British attitude," said Tom.

Simon and Tom reviewed the information the team had found leading up to Jeff's interview. Tom took a break and read a commercial for a chain of stores. As he concluded the ad, he looked to Jeff for the final segment. Simon was excited to hear the latest information Jeff had to reveal.

Simon nervously tapped his pen on the pad of paper in front of him. Tom looked at him and tapped his headphones. Simon placed his pen on the paper and smiled.

"Right, now, let me introduce my special guest. He comes from Europe. He believes he has information that will help Simon and I find Don and Doug, the missing twins from Canada. So, I hand the mic to you."

"Thank you. I'm nervous about revealing this, but it needs to be heard. I have a contact in London that revealed this to me. The same person told me to contact you, Tom, to discuss the information."

Simon gave Jeff a thumbs up for the fake background story.

"Go ahead," Tom encouraged him.

"A crop circle appeared early last week, east of London. The one I was told your group wasn't allowed to see."

"What of it?"

"They found a body inside the third large circle. There were four in total."

Simon looked at Jeff, then Tom. He mouthed. *"What?"*

Tom looked around his microphone at Jeff and flashed a piece of paper at him. *We should have talked first!!!*

"I have information which states it belonged to a fourteen-year-old girl. She's European and had been missing for eighteen years."

Dead air. Tom looked at Jeff, then Simon. Simon wrote in his notebook and turned it to Jeff. *You're saying age 14—missing 18 years?*

Jeff nodded his head.

"The police identified her by her prints. I know we're short on time, but let me run through this. On this podcast, you guys have brought up theories that the Druids might have something to do with the circles. I believe you're right. I just don't know how much. Forget the theories for now. Let's talk facts. The family of the girl had visited Stonehenge and a few other mounds and prehistory sites about three months before their daughter and younger two sons were taken. One day, the children never returned from school. They were with their friend at a park. After hanging out there, the children split up and headed towards their houses. The missing ones had a longer walk. One traffic camera identified a car with no plates on it. There were two men with short haircuts and sunglasses on..."

"Let me guess, dressed in black hoodies."

"Yes, what else?" replied Jeff. "As a side note, it was a very wet day."

"So, when this happened, there were no witnesses?" asked Tom.

"It's been eighteen years. No one is talking *now*."

"The other children?" asked Simon.

"Still missing."

"Well, that's..." said Tom.

"Tom, I'm not done yet. There was one witness," he paused. "The only witness was a cyclist."

Tom held up his notebook. *distorter works well, keep monotone if possible.*

"Sorry, can you repeat that? Simon was the only witness to..." said Tom.

"I know. The cyclist was killed two days later on his commute to work. A lorry swerved, hit him, then dragged him for fifty meters before stopping. The driver, a foreigner, spent time in jail."

"Are you telling me they killed him?" said Simon.

"Oh, it gets weirder."

"How?" said Tom, his voice rising.

"There were plenty of traffic cams around, but the hit happened in the twenty meters of road with no overlapping surveillance. The driver reported a car pulled alongside the lorry. One man jumped out of the car—he was in coveralls. He slid under the truck and removed a box and a series of wires. Not a large box. When he came from under the lorry, his coveralls had some blood from the cyclist on his back. He jumped back into the car, and they left."

"Remote control," said Tom.

"Yes, that's what it would seem. The driver stated he had no control of the vehicle. The steering wheel did its own thing. He swore in court the vehicle did not respond to anything he did."

"We've heard of this before, we know kill switches and overrides have been installed in the software of vehicles for a few years now," said Tom. "If the listeners want to go back, I believe it was around episode seventy-eight when I did a deep dive into it."

"Yes, and it seems the technology is beginning to be hacked or controlled," said Jeff.

Simon sat back in his chair, Jeff and Tom could see he was upset.

"Back to the body that was found, and I think I know your next question. No, I don't know if her blood was drained. I didn't think to ask."

"Was there anything special about these children?"

"Not that I was told."

Simon took his headset off and walked to the window. Looking out, he thought back to the day he witnessed Robin and Susan's children's kidnapping. In the distant background, he heard Tom wrapping up the show. The street below was quiet, not even the trees were moving.

A hand landed on his shoulder. "You okay, Simon?"

"We should record a second podcast. I can tell you of the attempt on my life a week after I witnessed the kids' kidnapping," said Simon.

"Simon, you never mentioned this. Yes, this is important information we should release."

"I know. I thought little about it until today and the news of the other cyclist that was killed."

"Are you okay to share it as a podcast?"

"I think it needs to be documented. We don't release it today or this week. But yes, it's all part of it, now."

"Simon, all right, mate?" asked Jeff.

"Wow. It would have been nice to have a heads up on that before the show," said Simon. "Any chance we can talk to the parents?"

"No, I tried. The father moved to America. He told me he has moved on."

"The mother?" asked Tom.

"She committed suicide ten years ago. From the kidnapping, she was unstable, in and out of hospitals."

"Oh, that's disappointing," said Simon. "So now we have evidence of a second family with three kids taken by men wearing black. The two youngest are still missing and the oldest was found in a crop circle."

"You guys set up. I'll run down the street and pick up some food. I need to eat before I head to work," said Jeff.

"Thanks Jeff," Simon said.

"Hey, Simon," Tom said, while putting a kettle on for tea. "How much are you spending on the B&B?"

"Thirty-five a night. Well, Robin is. Why?"

"Why not just move in here? I won't charge you."

"Well, the weekly contract ends on Saturday, anyway. I was going to talk to them tomorrow to renew for another week."

"I have three rooms upstairs. One is yours, mate. It might be better if we stay together."

"Thanks, Tom. We could make the move later today."

Jeff arrived with chicken sandwiches and crisps. They sat around the table and ate while Tom worked on his equipment, resetting for the next podcast. "Just checked our numbers. We have downloads of the last episode I released from every continent. Wait till they hear the one we just recorded and now this one. We had 855,000 downloads and 701,000 have fully listened to the episode. Those are some big numbers."

"We're celebrities," said Jeff, holding up his cup looking to be toasted.

"Right, let's just hope we don't become so popular we follow in the footsteps of John Lennon, JFK or Diana," said Simon.

"Exactly. Now, with this added information we just discussed and Simon revealing his story, we'll need to be more careful. I think we're beginning to rattle some cages. Simon's going to move in here, Jeff."

"Good idea. It'll save Robin and Susan some money, and I think the more time we spend together, the safer we'll be." He checked his watch. "I wish I could stay for this second one, but I need to run."

"Should we give Al a heads up too?" asked Simon.

"We could, but he's doing as he was told anyway, staying far away from us," said Tom.

"I'll call him on the way into the station, all the same."

Jeff left the house with his phone to his ear. After Tom cleaned up the wrappers and plates, he said, "Five minutes, Simon, and we can start."

. . .

Tom ran through the introduction of the podcast and reviewed some of the information again. A *reset* for the audience.

"Simon, our last podcast, was when we had a guest in the studio explaining his findings. When he discussed how a witness to a kidnapping, a cyclist, was killed, it hit home, you being a cyclist and a witness yourself. It also appears to have opened up a few memories."

"Yes, Tom. I haven't revealed any of this to anyone until today. Well, except for a police report." He swallowed some water and looked at Tom. "As we all know, I took leave from work after the kidnapping. That's why I'm here in jolly ol' England. But there is another reason too. A week after the kidnapping, I took a trip, just myself and my bike. I have a minivan, so I loaded it up and headed to my sister's cottage. It's north of where I live, just outside a town called Collingwood. So, that day I took a bike ride along the south shore of Lake Huron. Beautiful area, the lake to the north and ski hills to the south."

Tom pulled up a map on his computer screen. "For those watching the show, you can see what he means. It's lovely. I can only imagine it in the winter."

"So, when I got back from the ride, about one-hundred-twenty kilometers, I jumped in the lake to cool off. After an early supper, I thought I would try some fishing just off the coast. I usually catch fish most would call bait, but it's relaxing. So, it was an hour from sunset. I was sitting back in the boat. All the night lights on, pole in the water catching nothing."

"How big is this boat, Simon? I can try to find a photo for the listeners."

"I don't know. It's about twenty feet long, made by Tahoe, I think. Good little day boat."

After a few clicks on his keyboard, Tom put a photo of a boat on the screen.

"Yes, the boat on the right, that's the one, a different color, but that's the model. So, I was out in it. Legally, I still had enough light to be out. I wasn't too far from shore and was pulling the anchor when from my right I heard a motor, wide open, just humming along and getting closer. I looked over my shoulder and saw a boat heading in my direction. The wake it was making, I knew if it came too close, it would toss me. But I really thought nothing of it, though. I assumed it saw me and would veer away. I just kept pulling up the anchor. The water was about thirty feet deep."

"Nice depth for fishing."

"For most, I caught nothing, as usual. Well, I shouldn't say that. I caught my anchor in my line. Let me put it like this for you: when Jesus walked the shore calling fishermen to be disciples, he would have quietly passed me." They both laughed. Tom gave Simon a thumbs up.

"So fishing isn't a strong skill for you."

"No. As I pulled up the anchor, I hear this boat still full throttle coming in my direction. It's a larger boat, probably a fifty-footer. It's, I don't know, about one hundred meters away. I started my motor. I was muttering something under my breath about how drunk the asshole probably was and where was the OPP when you needed them."

"OPP?"

"Ontario Provincial Police. They do it all. In southern Ontario, they do a lot of traffic patrol on the larger highways. Further north, they patrol in between cities, waterways, and where towns don't have local police services. They would be in between a city cop, like me and the Mounties."

"Okay, sorry, so, you've started your engine, and this boat is barreling towards you."

"No, at that point, I had moved away. I didn't think the boat was coming at me. But then it turned and headed straight for me and my sister's boat again. It was about fifty meters away. I engaged the drive to the motor and moved my smaller boat out of the way at the last minute. It was so close to hitting me the wake from it almost tipped me out of the boat. If I had the boat turned, she would've tipped. It slowed, and I pursued it. From the back deck, I saw a bright light. By the time I registered what I was seeing, a flare was exploding in my boat. The other boat sped up. I kicked at the flare with my bare feet. After the third try, and by now with burns on my shins and feet, I kicked it off the side of the boat. I'm lucky it didn't ignite the fuel or catch the fiberglass on fire. That was their plan, I think. I radioed in the boat's name. Of course, it had been reported stolen."

"Of course."

"So, I gave the coordinates to the dispatcher, then headed for shore. Oh, and the only reason it didn't ignite the fuel was because I was so low on it. The crazy part of all this, I never saw a person on the boat. I didn't see anyone shoot the flare."

"Who was driving it?"

"I know the type of boat. It only has one set of controls, and no one was manning them, that I could see."

"You're saying remote controlled?"

"I'm saying there was no one standing at the controls where I know them to be, and I saw no one on the boat even when the flare was shot. But there had to be someone. I just can't confirm it."

"Right. So, a boat possibly driven remotely straight at you in your sister's boat a few days after you witnessed the kidnapping of three children. Nothing to see here, folks. Please go back to your regular programming."

Simon adjusted his headphones. "Exactly. I never thought about it until I heard what our guest told us during the last show. The police investigated the incident."

"Did they ever find the boat?"

"No, I called back to the office a few days later. They never found it. It's at the bottom of the lake, I assume."

"So, you believe this was an attempt on your life?"

"Why don't we leave it to the listeners to decide? I've presented the facts."

Tom did his wrap up of the show and ended the recording.

"Simon, that was crazy. I'd no idea. I'm sorry."

"Yeah, I filed it away as a crazy incident until what I heard this morning. Then those memories flooded back into my mind."

"So, what do we do now?"

"How about we move me over here? Safety in numbers? Isn't that the saying?"

"Yes, let me close up a few things and we can get your stuff."

"I'll take the front room upstairs."

Simon entered his new room and sat on the bed. He needed to check in with Robin.

• • •

Simon dialed Robin's number. There was no answer. He left a voicemail. He called Helen. Their conversation was emotionless. After two minutes, she handed the phone to the boys. He talked to them for twenty minutes about school, sports, and their exciting fun-filled lives in British Columbia. When the call ended, he sat and looked out the window. His mind swirled with thoughts of what he was missing with his boys as they grew up. He even detected a voice change in his oldest, Richard.

"Ready?" asked Tom.

"Huh, yes, let's go."

"Not that I was listening, but I heard some good laughs from you while you were on the phone."

"Yeah, it was a good call with my boys. Helen was distant and, well, just detached," said Simon. He followed Tom down the stairs. They drove in silence to the bed-and-breakfast.

CHAPTER NINETEEN

Simon opened the door to his unit.

Oh, you have to be kidding me!

The neat room he left was a mess. He stepped back and closed the door. Crouched down, he walked back to the car and knocked on Tom's window.

Tom looked up from his phone, confused by the look on Simon's face.

"What's wrong, mate?"

"Tom, my place is in ruins. Somebody got in and ransacked the place."

Tom sat forward in his seat. "What? How?" His head spun, looking around the property.

"Come look, grab the tire iron out of your trunk, you know, just in case."

Simon opened the door to his room slowly. Tom stood behind him with his tire iron raised beside his head.

"You can put your arm down. I don't think anyone's here."

Simon stood over the pile of clothes on the floor. Leaning against the wall was the mattress. The cabinets below the microwave and coffee maker were open, and what little food Simon had in his room was on the floor.

Tom bent down beside the bed. "They didn't take your watch," he said, picking it up from under the bed.

"Open the drawer. Is there an envelope in there?"

"There is, stuffed with money."

"Yeah, this wasn't a robbery. They knew the family was away and that today would be a good day to get in without witnesses. This is a warning of some kind. I don't see a note," said Simon.

"I'll call Jeff. He needs to know."

"Okay, but no police," He looked at Tom. "No official police. I don't think we need the attention right now."

"Right, I'll get my phone out of the car."

Simon lifted his clothes from the floor, tossing them on the box spring. Under all his clothes was his suitcase. He filled it with clothes.

Tom returned to the room. "... no, we're fine. No, it doesn't look like there's any damage. Yes, we're checking now. Yes, I know. I'm sure he knows. Jeff... Jeff, we are fine. Just come to my place when you're off shift. No report. Yes, bye."

Simon continued to pick items off the floor. "Looks like a few things are missing, mainly all my notes. Some photos we printed off from our phones are missing."

"Well, this just took a turn. So, who do we think did this? The kidnappers?" asked Tom.

"I assume someone in black clothes, likely hoodies," said Simon.

"Can this one go?" Tom lifted a closed suitcase.

"Yes, this too." Simon put the envelope and his passport into a satchel and handed it to Tom. He put the mattress back and cleaned the room.

Concerned about the owners' safety, he called and spoke to them about the break in. Thankfully, they were safe.

"We agreed I could just leave my key. So, I won't need to come back. They sounded upset," he said.

"Do you blame them? They thought they had a quiet author staying to finish his book."

"No. I understand." He left two hundred pounds with the key in the dresser drawer.

"All right. I'll see you back at your place," said Simon, closing the door behind him. He looked around. "Hey, do you feel like you're being watched?"

Tom looked at him. "Not watched, but like someone's close to me. I feel if I turn my head quick enough, I should see them." They both shuddered and hurried to their cars.

Tom drove away, and Simon sat in the driver's seat of his rental. Looking at his phone, he saw four missed calls from Robin.

. . .

Simon dialed Robin's number as his fingers shook. The phone rang and with the expectation of Robin's voicemail, he was ready to disconnect the call.

"Hello?"

"Robin?"

"Simon, thank God. Are you okay?"

"Yes, I was calling to check on you. I had an incident over here, and they took your information with other items."

"Yes, we know. We received a call about an hour ago."

"Oh?"

"Yes. It was a man with a gravelly voice, definitely British."

Simon tapped on the steering wheel. "What did he say?"

"He said I should get you back to Canada where you belong right away, or they'll send someone to shut you up."

"Did you get a number?"

"No, we even called our service provider. They wouldn't release anything. I called Gary. He is looking into it, but he wanted to wait until you called to see if you wanted to push the matter."

"Okay, I think I know who they are. We've seen them around town, so don't waste too much time on it. The phone was likely a burner, anyway. But I don't plan on leaving. I just left the B&B to stay with Tom. Someone broke into it while I was out."

"Simon, I think this is over. I think it's time to come home. That man was threatening to kill you. He said to tell you that you don't know what you're getting into. We don't want your death to be because of us."

"Robin, don't be ridiculous."

"Simon, we can't make you, but as your friends, we're asking you to consider this threat to be real."

"Robin, *it is real*, I know. Was there anything else?"

"Umm, well."

Simon could hear Susan in the background. "Just tell him, Robin."

"I'm not sure how they knew all this, but they told us our address, our family's addresses, and that if you didn't come home, they would hold us responsible. And then..." He paused and took a deep breath. "And then others that we love could go missing."

"Okay, you told Gary or Mark this, correct?"

"No, no, I didn't. They instructed me to only tell you. They said they would know if we went to the authorities."

"Okay. This makes it even more urgent for me to find these men."

"Move to my house, both of you. You have my spare key. Do it at night so you can see if you're being followed. The garage door code is 23998. Park in the garage, not the driveway. Just give me a few days. Today is Thursday. If I find nothing else, I'll put this behind me and fly home in fourteen days. Agreed? My leave at work will be done shortly after that."

"Fine. We'll move to your house tonight. Simon, be careful, please."

"One other thing. Do you still see the twins?"

There was silence on the line. "Robin?"

"Yes, we're still seeing them. They're alive, and Susan, this might sound crazy, she's communicating with them through sign language. But it's not the same as holding them, hugging them, or tucking them in at night. Simon, my logical brain is saying you need to come home. But my emotions want my children home. Simon—oh Simon." he paused.

"Give me the phone," Susan said. "Simon, listen to me. I'm not crazy, but the boys said to me this morning that you need to watch out for the men in black hoodies."

"Susan? What does that mean?"

"I don't know. I'm not sure I even got it right—I'm still trying to learn sign language. Just be careful. And bring my boys home. They're alive."

Simon thought of his own boys. He took a deep breath. "Take care of yourself. I'll keep looking for the kids. We have a bunch of small leads, but we need that one big one."

• • •

When Simon arrived at Tom's house, Jeff was already there. He placed three cups of tea around the kitchen table.

"Right fellas, what happened?"

Tom began, and Simon filled in the gaps. They sat for an hour talking. Jeff, unofficially working, asked the right police questions, probing more information from the two of them.

Tom stood suddenly from the table and darted to the back of the kitchen. He leaned over the sink, looking out the window into his backyard and the laneway beyond.

"What is it, Tom?"

"I thought I saw a light flash into the window. Strange."

He looked through the window, moving side to side. Simon joined him, peering out. Both men heard the front door open as Jeff ran out, and Simon raced to follow. He found Jeff standing in the street.

"Jeff? What's happening?"

Jeff looked at Simon in the door's threshold. "Three men in black just drove away. They came out of the alley in a blue car. I'm sure the same one I pulled over the other day." He walked back up the path towards Simon. "Strangest thing was, one looked at me. He had no face."

"Like a mask over his face?"

"I guess, but to me it looked like a void. Like nothing under the hood. Just blackness."

Jeff jumped when Tom appeared from behind the neighbor's hedges.

"My gate to my driveway was open. Did you see anything?"

"Let's get back inside, then talk."

• • •

"So, here we sit, your flat was broken into, the body count rises, even if it is over multiple years, and now strange men without faces are chasing us."

"Come over here, you two." Tom sat in front of his computer. "Look, Jeff, this is what you saw."

They watched a video play of a man in dull light pulling a full hood over his head and, as the video claimed, without camera tricks, his face disappeared into a void of light. He then pulled the hood off, and his head appeared.

"I saw this a while ago. It used to be top secret military equipment. Now the average hack magician uses it. It's a light absorbing material. Black, of course. But in a dim light, you disappear. From what I read, it was first used after 9-11 to hide military equipment and people. If you have a black, let's say runway or airfield, you can drape the material over a plane, and on the sunniest day, a satellite won't see it. Even a plane at low altitude would struggle to pick it out."

"What? So how would these guys get it or know about it?" asked Jeff.

"This is the first I'm hearing about it," said Simon.

"Yeah, me too. Pretty impressive, though," said Jeff.

"It isn't common knowledge, but it is available to the public."

"Okay, I have something to rock your worlds," said Simon. "It doesn't make any sense, but here goes." He told them how Robin, Susan, and her parents had all seen the twins since Simon arrived in England. He gave the details of waving, sign language and the fact that they must be alive.

"Do you think they're on another plane, beside us, but not quite here?" asked Tom. "Like, I don't know, like they're working in a different dimension. It would explain how a crop circle appears overnight, too."

"And that feeling we all have of being watched, or having people close to us? But how does that make any sense? We're looking for kids that aren't even on this planet, or in this dimension? It's not that I don't believe them, Simon. But could this be how they are coping? Their brain is making their children appear?"

"I guess? I thought the same thing but, they feel so sure of it," said Simon.

Jeff stood, tapping his wrist. "I have the early shift tomorrow."

Jeff said his goodbyes and left. Simon and Tom carried the luggage to his room.

"Well, there's a lot to sleep on tonight, Simon. Can you even fathom the inter-dimensional?" He shook his head and walked to his room.

CHAPTER TWENTY

Simon's phone rang. By the time he opened his eyes from the dreamworld he hid away in, he missed the call. He picked up his phone and heard Tom's ringing. He looked at the number. It was Jeff. The time on his phone said 5:15 am.

He dialed Jeff back, but stopped when he heard the heavy footsteps of Tom enter the hallway. Then a knock on his door.

"Simon, you awake?"

"Yes."

"Jeff just called. A new crop circle, with four circles, showed up outside Spalding. I have the address. Can you get up and be ready to roll in ten?"

"Make it five." Simon said. He hastily pulled the covers off himself and searched for clothes.

• • •

Tom was at the car loading a bag into the trunk when a police cruiser pulled alongside him.

"Tom, here, take my drone," said Jeff.

"Yep, I was going to call you back and ask about it."

"Morning, Simon."

"Early morning at that."

"First thing I saw when I got in this morning was the crop circle report. A farmer reported lights last night. The detachment sent a car to investigate and there was a crop circle. It had four large circles from the initial report and..."

"A body?" Simon said.

Jeff nodded.

"By the time you get there, the police reports should be done and maybe you can talk to the farmer. I'm not sure if that will help get you up close. Use the drone, but if there are any cops around, keep it off the property."

"Thanks, Jeff. We'll call you with any updates."

Four hours later, they arrived at the farm. A police car had the laneway blocked off, and by the house sat two more cruisers.

Tom continued driving around the property, passing a couple of cars until he was out of sight of the house.

"Tom, I don't agree with this. If they see the drone from the house, we could be in some legal trouble."

"I'll keep it low."

Simon shook his head. "Tom, by the time we get home, the news will have the images of the circle on every channel. It isn't worth the risk."

. . .

The drone's impellers increased RPM, and the machine rose, defying gravity. Simon stood by the car, watching the road for vehicles.

Tom sent the drone straight up over their heads. The fields of wheat looked untouched. Then the circles appeared.

"Wow, that's a big one. Like the grand finale for the season," said Tom.

"What was that?"

"Where?"

"Over there." Simon pointed further into the fields.

"I think I saw it too. I'll have the drone chase it."

"Chase what? I don't know, but it looked like a dog to me. One of those raccoon dogs?"

"Do you see it?"

"No. It looked like it went there. Further into the fields. Keep that thing low. It's too high. They might see it from the house."

Tom maneuvered the drone in the direction Simon pointed. The camera flashed white. Tom turned it. "The sun's at the perfect height, just low enough to cause the camera to white out. What is it?"

He moved the drone. The screen became static, and the drone wobbled. More static filled the screen, then communication with the drone ended. Simon watched it drop from the sky as Tom struggled with the controller.

"We better run in and get it," said Tom.

"We? You," replied Simon.

They looked around the field for any movement. Tom hopped the old stone wall and ran across the fields of wheat. He retrieved the drone. Trying to stay at the level of the tall wheat. He ran back to the car.

Simon waited by the fence, pacing, watching for Tom to stand up so he could locate him. A white van sped by Simon. He jumped when the bark of large dogs came from the back window. He turned back to see Tom a few meters away.

"Get the stuff in the car, Tom. We need to go. A commercial van almost hit me. It was loaded with dogs."

"I think we need to interview the farmer. Then get home and do a podcast."

They drove back to the farmer's house. The police vehicle blocking the entrance was gone. Looking up the laneway, Tom didn't see any police. He turned in and drove towards the house.

As they neared the barn, a man stepped out from a man door. They parked the car and climbed out.

"Can I help you?" asked the stranger.

"I hope so. Do you have a few minutes to talk?"

"About the body they found in my field? I already spoke to your uniformed officers. They said a couple of others would be here to ask me questions, but not till later."

"We are not... well, he is an officer of the law," said Tom, pointing at Simon.

"Come into the barn. I'm just feeding some of my young ones before I put them out."

Tom followed Simon into the barn.

"Sir..."

"Leon."

"Leon, just to clarify what my friend insinuated. I am a police officer, but not the one you are expecting. I'm Canadian and here investigating a missing child. My friend here is Tom, and he's—well, a conspiracy podcaster."

"So, why are you here?"

"We were told about the crop circle from a friend, and I wanted to see if there was any connection with my friends' missing kids."

"Tom, Tom, not from Hide the Truth, Find the Lies, podcast?" he snapped his fingers.

Tom stepped beside Simon. "The very one. You know my podcast?"

"Know it, I love it. This new series you're—oh wait, the new series and you are here." He dropped his head. "This must be serious."

Leon took a bag of feed and walked the length of the barn. He spilled feed into large bowls as lambs buried their heads into the full bowls.

"I don't mind talking to you, but I don't want to be named or my farm's location mentioned on the show. I love a good conspiracy, but I just bought this farm, and as you can tell from my accent, I wasn't born here. The locals, especially the older ones, aren't too happy about a *Kraut* buying their old friends' property."

"I understand. Can we have permission to see the circle up close?"

"Sure. But I can't go. I have chores to do, and the other officers are coming to ask questions."

"Why don't we ask ours first, and then we can get out of here before they arrive?"

"Yes, ask your questions."

"How did you find it?"

"Last night a lot of noises and lights woke me, around two in the morning. I called it in to the police. When they arrived, they told me it was the local reserves, army, I think? You would think someone would tell the owners of the property. My neighbor down the road said it happens, you learn to sleep through it. Well, they were doing night training and from what I was told, they saw some lights, headed this way, and flew over my property. With their night vision, they saw the outline of the crop circle and some hot spots around the perimeter. Then their chopper had some technical problems, they lost electronics, and the engine sputtered. The pilot pulled up and away."

"Strange," said Tom, remembering his compass and how it acted in Norm's circle.

"Yes. When they were pulling away, one of the cabin men thought he saw a body through his night vision."

"When they returned to their base last night at three, they reported it to their commanding officer. At five, there was a knock on my door. Military with the police who were out earlier. They asked me a few questions, including if I could drive them out to the field. By that time there was a crop circle in my field." He picked up another bag of feed and moved down the other side of the barn.

"So, what was found?"

"A teen was lying in the center of the third circle. Dead, blood drained and a possible bite mark. I don't know for sure. I'm only repeating what I overheard the police and the medic talking about. They haven't told me much. Just that I can't harvest my wheat until they do a full investigation."

The song "A Kind of Magic" by Queen played loud from Leon's pocket. "My phone."

Simon stepped to the side with Tom. "Well, that's interesting, the same thing that brought you to jolly ol' England."

Leon hung up his phone. "Sorry, the police are about five minutes away. They went to the back lot instead of here. You should leave. You were never here." He winked at them.

"Right. Can I get your number to call you later?"

"Yes." He gave Simon his number, who wrote it in his notebook.

• • •

They left the farm and headed to the small town, looking for somewhere to eat before heading home. Tom pulled into an open parking space on the main street. "We ought to find something close by."

"I should call Robin. You find a place and text me the directions."

"Okay. See you soon."

• • •

"Hello,"

"Robin it's Simon. More strange activity today. Another crop circle with a complete body in it. The circle had four large circles, keeping with our theory of bodies and four circles." Simon told him of the farm and activity from the night before.

A black van pulled out of its parking spot, and Simon watched as it drove away. Parked in front of it was a white van. He looked at it again. There were bars on the back windows.

"Simon, I don't have much more here. The boys are here with us. I wasn't sure if we would see them here at your house, but we do. The police are sending cruisers by our house and yours regularly. Susan is back to work, and we think—know the twins are still alive but..." he trailed off in his own thoughts.

"I do too. We know of one other kidnapping. It follows a similar pattern to yours—one but only one child was found dead. That should give us hope." He didn't add that the other children hadn't been found after 18 years. "Robin, I need to go. I see something I want to look at."

"Yeah, okay. Take care and call tomorrow."

"Bye."

Simon texted Tom, *"location?"* then stared at the van again. He left the car and crossed the street. He heard a dog bark, then a second one.

Big dogs.

The pedestrian walking beside the van shuddered and looked startled at the van as the dogs barked. Simon checked his phone for a response from Tom.

He leisurely approached the van, looking in all directions for anything out of the ordinary. An older lady with a walker jumped when she passed the van's door. Simon walked to the back doors and looked in. There were five cages. Inside each cage sat a massive German Shepherd. They all turned in their cages and looked at him. The middle one barked, then the others joined in, shaking the van as they thrust at him against their cages. On the floor of the van were six large plastic equipment cases, secured with padlocks. Beside the heavy duty cases were two shovels with dirt still stuck to the blades.

"Simon, get away."

Simon turned his head to the voice. An arm slid around his neck, and someone pulled his left wrist behind his back. He felt his right ankle being kicked, then he was on the ground.

• • •

A group of people stood around him, waiting for his eyes to open. His phone was buzzing in his pocket and his head throbbed.

"Young man, are you okay? You took a nasty fall."

"I saw a guy in a black hoodie throw him to the ground," said another witness.

"Yes, they jumped in the van and drove away. Did you know them?"

"You should be more careful," an older man said, leaning on his wooden cane.

"Their dogs scared me a couple minutes before all this happened, when I strolled past the van," an elderly lady said, shaking her fist at the vehicle.

A car pulled up. The owner put his window down. "Can I use this spot?"

Simon lay on the ground, holding his head, trying to get his phone out of his pocket.

"Sir, do you need an ambulance?" the driver asked. "Your head has a bump on it."

"He fell. He might need a minute. Take the spot up there." A man pointed further up the street. "Should we call the police?"

Simon sat up. A younger man pushed through the group of onlookers and helped Simon to his feet. The group from the retirement home lost interest in the event and continued along the sidewalk.

"Thank you," said Simon, looking at his phone. The directions to the restaurant were on his screen. "I'm still a bit shaky. Could you take me here? I have a friend waiting for me."

"Sure. I'm going that way. Are you sure you're okay? You have a large goose egg on your forehead."

"Yes, I'm find, I mean fine. My friend is meeting me there. I'm Simon, by the way."

"Jeremy," he said. "Nice to meet you. Canadian?"

"Yes, yes, I am."

They slowly made their way to the restaurant. Simon listened as Jeremy told him of his vacation years earlier to Niagara Falls.

·   ·   ·

Simon entered the small chip shop with Jeremy and quickly spotted Tom. As they neared him, Tom's face clouded.

"What happened to you?"

Simon told him what he saw, up to the sweep of his ankle. He then introduced Jeremy.

"I wasn't paying much attention, but when the one man yelled at Simon, he knew you, I assume, he used your name. Then I saw a second man grab Simon. He swept at Simon's feet, causing him to drop and bounce his head off the curb. They climbed into their van and drove away. Before you ask, there was no plate, so no number. But both were young, fit and in black hoodies."

Tom looked at Simon.

"Thanks for your help. Do you want to stay for a bite?"

"No, thank you. I need to keep moving. I have to pick my kids up from class. Here's my number if you have questions." He showed his phone's screen and Tom wrote the number on his notebook.

"Are you sure you can't stay?"

"No, but if you need anything, call me." He stood and left, waving as he passed by the large front window.

"What happened?" asked Tom.

"That covers it, what Jeremy said. I swear the one guy that called to me, I saw was from the car the other day. It was the same van that almost hit me when you were getting the drone. There were dogs, cases and shovels in the back."

"Do you think they have what is in the holes around the perimeter of the crop circles?"

"Tom, right now all I want is some water, a hand full of painkillers and to go home."

CHAPTER TWENTY-ONE

"Hello? Tom, Simon, are you guys here?" Jeff asked, entering Tom's place.

"Jeff upstairs," said Simon. His head ached with raising his voice. He sat up to a flurry of spots in front of his eyes.

Jeff met him at the top of the stairs. "Where's Tom? What—what happened to you? Never mind, you can tell me later. Where's Tom?"

"Where else?" Simon pointed to the studio door.

Jeff swung the door open with no concern for Tom or if he was recording.

"Sit, you two, sit," said Jeff.

Tom and Simon sat at the studio table. "What's going on, Jeff? You're like a kid at Christmas."

"I know it's late but, I have the name and address of the family of the child they found in the crop circle this morning. They're in France. I say we leave in the morning and go see them." He pumped his fist in the air. "I called them. Unlike the others, they're willing to talk with us."

"What? That's great news. France? How far is it from here?" asked Simon.

"Roughly a day's drive. We could leave early tomorrow and then meet them the next day," said Tom. "Well done, mate. Are you going to tell us how you found out, or is it better that we don't know?"

"There was a note on my desk. I'm not sure who placed it there, and I'm not asking. The timing is perfect because I have the next three days off. I called the number, and the father answered in French. I have enough French to be dangerous, but we could talk. He was noticeably upset from the news he was told earlier, but once I told him of you, Simon, he spoke to his wife. With two kids still missing, they agreed to meet with us."

"Does anyone speak French?" asked Simon. "It might help."

"Not me," said Tom.

"A little. We were able to communicate on the phone. He spoke a bit of English, too. I think we should be okay. So why does Simon have a golf ball growing on his head?"

They told Jeff of their day around Spalding.

•   •   •

The next morning, Jeff knocked on the door to Tom's house early.

Simon, a little groggy and now with a purple-colored goose egg above his right temple, answered the door.

"Wow, I wasn't expecting it to look like that, mate."

"Huh, I know, I know. I'll need to wear a hat for most of this."

"Morning Tom, quite the lump on his head."

"Yes, I'm a little concerned he didn't go to the hospital," said Tom. He tossed a bag at Jeff's feet. Then stepped around Simon with three more.

"Simon, are you sure you can travel? We can put this off a day or two if you need to. We could go to the Manchester Library today and leave you here to rest."

"No, I'll be fine. I took a couple of pills to help me sleep on the trip."

"Well, we have eight hours of driving, at least, so sit back and enjoy."

•   •   •

After a couple of unexpected stops, a delay at the France side of the Chunnel and Tom recording two hours of his podcast, the team arrived at their hotel in Le Havre. Once the group unloaded their bags, they headed out for a meal.

•   •   •

The following morning, Simon and Jeff approached the house of the family who had lost their children. As they passed the large bay window, Simon glanced in. A lady stood leaning over the island counter spreading jam on bread. Across from her, he watched a man hand her a plate.

"They're home," he whispered, questioning himself why he whispered it. "Ready?"

"Yes, I hope we can understand each other," said Jeff. "If they get emotional, I might struggle translating." He stood in front of the red door and knocked.

He knocked again.

The door slowly cracked open.

"Bonjour."

"Hello, English?"

"Who you are?" the man asked.

"Good morning, Andre. I'm Jeff. We spoke a couple of days ago. This is Simon."

"Ah, Jeff. I remember." The door opened a little further. "I am not—we are not prepared to talk right now. We are sorry—you come this far."

"Andre, open the door," said a voice in French from inside the house. "Don't be so rude."

Andre turned and mumbled a few words in French to a lady holding a drying cloth and wiping her hands on it. She reached for the door and pulled it open.

"Hello. I thought you were coming later. We were just heading out."

"Please, a few minutes. I represent a family from Canada who had their three children taken. Their oldest, like yours, was recovered in a crop circle in England a few weeks ago. I have some questions for you. If you don't have time now, we could meet later? I'm sorry, I thought this was all arranged." said Simon. He looked at Jeff to confirm their meeting.

"We have about half an hour before we need to leave. The child they found in Hayfield, you knew?"

"No, I witnessed him being taken. Strange story for later. I'm a police officer from Canada, but I'm not here on official business. The family hired me to investigate and hopefully bring their other children home," said Simon. hoping they understood. "Sorry, I don't speak French. Did you understand any of what I just said?"

"Yes, it's fine. Please come in. Both of you. My name is Adrianna. This is Andre."

"Are you American?" asked Simon.

"Yes, I'm from Baltimore," said Adrianna. "Andre is French. His English is improving, but I might need to interpret some things as we talk."

Simon stepped into the hallway. On a shelf by the door was a lit candle with three photos of children.

"Do you want a drink?" asked Adrianna.

"No, no, just some answers," said Jeff.

"Please sit," said Andre.

Simon looked at him and wondered how he missed the large butcher knife Andre hid behind his back. "I see you're nervous answering the door."

"Yes, well, when your children are taken over three years ago and then the oldest is found in a field in England, it makes you a little nervous. We have also had a few protests from a group blaming us for allowing our child to be scarified in a crop circle for the elitist. The police are supposed to be watching us, but as you can see, you made it to the door."

"So, you're here because they found our son. I assume the same way they found your friend's child."

"Yes, exactly. I, we are so sorry. I've been in England trying to find my friend's twins. They were younger and are still missing," said Simon. "Tell me how they took your children from you. Can we start there or is it too emotional to discuss?"

"No," said Andre. "We are able to talk about it."

"It's hard finding Benny's body that way. We had hoped..." She took several deep breaths before continuing. "We've never given up hope of finding them alive, and now we wonder about our other two. But, to answer your question, we don't know how they were taken," said Adrianna.

"What? You don't know or can't remember?"

"Well, that's just it. We were at a park with our children," said Adrianna.

"We think—we think we were at the park. Sorry continue," said Andre.

"We were sitting on a blanket and the kids were running around. There was another family from America sitting close to us. They were on vacation. I struck up a conversation with them. They were from Charlotte, North

Carolina. I noticed a man in a black hoodie, a little out of place, but nowadays, who isn't when it comes to fashion?"

Simon smiled and shrugged his shoulders.

"The other family packed up and left, as the sun was going down. I noticed the man in black again across the park. He was coming back in the direction he had walked away from earlier. Then, from behind, someone covered my face. I struggled for a second. Then I woke with a couple of teens standing over me. It confused me why they were there. They told us they had seen what happened and wanted to know if we were okay. I jumped up, looking for our kids. Andre was already on his feet, running across the field. The teens didn't notice the kidnapping. They thought they robbed us."

"Were you?" asked Simon.

"Only of the life we knew and our three beautiful children. My purse was beside me when I woke."

"But no one saw the kids being taken?"

"The medical report said they gave us a cocktail of chemicals to knock us out. Apparently, it also causes memory loss," said Andre.

"What about the kids?"

"Nothing. The police canvased the area. There were no witnesses. That was three years ago. Since then, we've been hoping for some information, even a ransom note. The police keep telling us not to lose faith, but then the call came yesterday. Who would do that to my boy?"

"Let's back up a little. I'm sure you've been asked all these questions before. The man in the hoodie. What did he look like?"

"The hood was up over his head, but at one point the wind kicked up and blew it back. He was bald."

Simon looked at Jeff, who was writing notes and flipping pages, trying to keep up with the conversation. He looked up and nodded to Simon.

"What—what was that look for?" Simon asked.

Jeff tapped his watch.

"Oh, the time. Can we come back?" asked Simon.

"We don't have an appointment. I lied about that," said Adrianna.

"Huh, you just used the appointment excuse until..."

"We've had a few strange visitors over the last few years," said Andre.

"Simon, tell us how the children were taken in Canada."

Simon explained how he was on his bike when he saw the kidnapping happen. He told them how he ended up in England and meeting Tom and Jeff, then finally arriving on their doorstep. "I'm not sure if you want to, but I'd like to connect you with Robin and Susan. It might be some support for each of you. Plus, and this is a long shot, if you all talk, you might find something in common with your kids. Something alone you aren't thinking of. You never know what might come out of a conversation."

"Yes, I think you're right. We would like to talk to them," said Adrianna.

Simon tore a piece of paper out of his notebook and wrote their number on it. "I'll call them later and tell them to expect a call. I'll tell them the same thing, try to find something in common. There must be a reason both families were targeted."

"Thank you. What about the man in the hoodie?"

"Right, him. I think a couple of those men are watching Tom, Jeff and I. With the reports on the crop circles, some have included men in hoodies. The other day, after visiting a crop circle, I was knocked over by what I think was one of them when Tom and I went into town to grab a bite." He removed his hat to show the lump on his head. "Now, if I were to see them here in France, then I'd really be concerned for my safety."

"We'll keep an eye out for them, too. Do you think there's a chance we'll see our other two children here, with us again?"

"I don't want to get your hopes up, and I can't say either way. But we have to try. There's something strange going on. Why only one child? What's different about your other children, anything medical, intelligence wise, special abilities?"

They shook their heads.

"When you talk to Robin and Susan, those are the things you guys need to discuss. Please be honest with them."

"Are you asking if my kids have ESP or psychic powers?" asked Andre.

"Right now, yes, anything like that, a sixth toe, an extra tooth? Maybe left handed. Don't close your mind off to anything when you're talking to them. Open your mind to anything right now."

"Okay, I see what you're asking. The police never asked us to think like that. But yes, think outside the box," said Adrianna.

"I don't even want you to think there is a box," said Simon. "Leave nothing on the table."

Andre looked puzzled. Adrianna spoke to him in French. "Ah," he said, nodding. "Now it makes sense."

"Is there anything else? Since the kids were taken, has anything strange happened? Anything else I need to know?" asked Simon.

Andre and Adrianna looked at each other. Andre shook his head. Adrianna nodded. Andre grabbed her hand and pulled her to him. He whispered into her ear.

"Andre doesn't want you to think we're crazy. But..."

"It's okay. I don't. I feel it too sometimes, like there are people right beside me. Have you seen them? Like ghosts in the house? Or like they are behind a dirty window. That's one way Robin describes it."

Andre sat forward. Adrianna buried her face in her hands. Her shoulders bobbed as she took in breaths. Andre placed his arms around her and pulled her into his chest.

"You're not crazy. That's the stuff you need to talk to Susan and Robin about. They have been through the same thing, seeing their kids. It's the strangest thing." Simon pulled out some tissues and handed them to Adrianna. "Here, you're okay. You both are."

Once the tears had dried, they sat around for an additional hour talking about how she ended up in France. With the conversation beginning to repeat itself, Simon stood and offered to return the next day to see the park where the kids were playing.

• • •

The next day, Simon, Tom, and Jeff met the couple at the park. Jeff introduced Tom to Adrianna and Andre. The couple showed them where they were seated and where the kids were playing the day of the kidnapping. Jeff wandered off towards the street. Tom and Simon sat with the couple on a park bench. They looked over the field to the ocean just beyond.

"It really is a beautiful view and park," said Tom. A few people walked their dogs or ran through the park. "How busy was it that day?"

Adrianna bent forward and wiped her eyes. Andre put his arm around her. He whispered a few words into her ear.

"Sorry, Adrianna. If you need to leave, we all would understand," said Tom.

"No, this is my first time back since—back since that day."

"Where was the man with the hoodie before it happened?" asked Simon.

Andre stood up and turned. "He was on that street there."

"You were sitting here?" Simon pointed across the field to the edge, where a swing set and slide stood. "A couple of teens witnessed it? Did the police interrogate them?"

"What are you saying, Simon?"

Simon looked at Andre and could see anger building in his eyes.

"Nothing. It's just clear they waited for this part of the park to empty before moving on your family. It's just like in Canada—they had other areas to stop the family, but except for me, the area they chose was vacant of people."

"Are you saying that we were involved?" asked Andre.

"*No, not at all.* I'm saying your family was targeted, just like in Canada. This was planned, and they possibly followed you. I'm saying this wasn't random. It was a targeted attack. That's all," said Simon.

"But why us?" asked Andre.

"That's why you need to talk to Robin and Susan. Right now, we can't answer that, but hopefully, the four of you can."

Jeff rejoined the group. "I didn't find any cameras. But what strikes me is how strange this setting is. So open, you would think it would be easier to do a home invasion and take them that way. I have nothing else to look at. You guys done?"

"Andre, Adrianna, please call my friends in Canada. Discuss your kids and see if the four of you can find anything in common that would help find your children. There must be something we're all missing."

"We can do a group call too, where we ask you questions," said Tom.

"We will, Simon. I'll call them this afternoon to set up a proper call. Thank you for coming to see us."

The group shook hands and hugged. Simon sat back down on the park bench and looked around. Tom sat beside him. "What are you thinking?"

"We know there are others. We just need them to talk. The more we get talking together, the easier it'll be to find why these families are targeted. Why don't we call out the Druid society on the next show? Put some pressure on them. If none of them want to talk to us, then let's make it public."

"Do we have enough evidence to do so?"

"Let's find it," said Simon. "I think the tattoos have something to do with it. Has your friend called back yet?"

"No, remind me to call him when we get back home. What makes these families so special?"

CHAPTER TWENTY-TWO

At the police station, Jeff sat in front of his computer. The search engine was looking for unresolved kidnappings. It revealed an extensive list, so he tightened up his search looking for strange reports of families not recalling how their kids disappeared. The results showed a few in the United States, one in Germany, two more in Vietnam and one in New Zealand. He scanned the reports. One American report listed the mother as the suspect. She had severe postpartum depression and potentially buried her children at the bottom of a lake. The report noted she didn't remember it, but her neighbors were witnesses.

An older case from 2002 in Wisconsin was never closed. A few young men attacked the parents and took the kids. Jeff continued to read the news report and pulled a notebook from his desk. A few constables walked by greeting him. He didn't look up or acknowledge them. The more he read, the quicker he wrote. He moved to the next case, reviewed it, and closed the web page. He found more information about a family in Germany and finally New Zealand.

"Are you going to get in your cruiser today and see the public, or just review cold cases all day?"

Jeff spun in his chair. His sergeant stood with her hands on her hips. "Sorry, Christine, I got caught up searching for some evidence."

"Jeff, I know you're working with Tom and that Simon from Canada. I've been listening to the podcast. I think most of us are. Honestly, we're all rooting for you guys, but I can't let you use our computers and secure servers to do your research. Especially when you have calls to do."

"Sorry, Christine, time got away from me." He turned back in his chair and logged off the computer. He took his notes, put on his cap, and headed towards the elevator.

"Jeff, this can't interfere with your work. I think you know this, but you better not be using your badge off shift to help with the investigation."

"I haven't been. But if we crack this, would it actually matter?"

She turned, moved past the line of desks to her office. "Jeff, come with me."

He entered her office and stood by her desk. She raised her hand and motioned for him to close the door.

"Listen, we all want this to end well with the children returned to their families. If you need support when you're off duty, call it in. Your mate's podcast is being played on every phone in the area, I think. You three have our support, but please don't overstep your powers. If you need to do research, do it on a computer in one of the empty offices. If you need to see files, let me know, I'll grant access. Your mates are doing a good job."

Jeff stared at her, stunned. "So, you're okay with this?"

"Just be careful what you say on the podcast. You have a pleasant baritone voice. Get rid of the scrambler. You're not foolin' anyone. But be careful not to release anything that is not public knowledge. The *friend of a friend left a note for me,* will not work."

He smiled at her. "Right, Christine. Not sure why I thought it would."

· · ·

Jeff called Simon and arranged to meet at their favorite pub after his shift.

Arriving first, Tom and Simon settled in and talked about the guest they had just interviewed on the podcast and his theories on interdimensional energy manipulation. Simon's phone rang. Robin quickly confirmed they had arranged to talk with Andre and Adrianna in a couple of days.

Jeff entered the pub and waved, stopping at the bar to pick up a Guinness. The bartender poured his drink as Jeff looked back at the table.

With his facial expression, he asked if they needed drinks. They both shook their heads. Simon picked up his mostly full glass of pop, wishing to have it mixed with something harder.

"Hello, fellas. Good day?"

"Interesting day, for sure," said Simon. "How about you? Did you find time to do some digging on the computer?"

"I did, and I found some interesting items." Jeff sipped his beer. "Can we order some food first? I'm famished?"

Tom went to the bar and ordered for the group. Simon used the men's room.

When Simon and Tom returned, Jeff had papers and two notebooks spread on the table. Tom placed the plate of chips and fish fingers on the table moments before Jeff snatched a handful of fish fingers.

"Have we forgotten table manners? Who just drops their hand into a plate of food like some big Caterpillar high hoe," asked Simon.

"Sorry, mate, my stomach is screaming for food. Every break I spent on a computer trying to find information."

"Well, stuff your face, then talk. With the smile you've had on your face since you came in, I assume this will be good," said Tom.

As Jeff ate, Simon told him how the two families had scheduled a time to talk. Tom told him of their podcast guest.

Jeff rapidly emptied the plate of food, listening to their stories. With the crumbs wiped from his mouth and hands, Jeff opened his orange notebook. "Okay, so I have a lot of information for you two. How about a high-level review for now, then when I finalize some of it, we can get to the nuts and bolts?"

"Sounds good to me," said Tom. He twirled his pen in his fingers.

"Okay, case one. Germany, over the last six years, they've had at least three crop circles in the southeastern part of the country annually. Nothing too exciting except at one two years ago, a farmer found a stuffed teddy in the field, not in the circle itself."

"How many circles?"

"That was the only one with four circles." He flipped through a couple of pages of the notebook. "The teddy belonged to a four-year-old child. She was the youngest of four siblings, again all the kids were taken, but the only evidence ever found was the stuffed animal. Authorities searched the field, but they found nothing else. No body, or belongings."

"How were they taken?"

"Carjacking. Downtown Cairo."

"What?"

"The children were kidnapped six years earlier. The teddy appeared the same time as the crop circle. At least that's the theory. They questioned the farmer, but he said he saw nothing."

"Has there been any updates since then?" asked Simon.

"Nothing, and the family refuse to talk about any of it. Next case, Mexico. This one is strange. Over three nights back in 1999, six small crop circles appeared on the grounds of an ancient ruin." He flipped through his blue notebook. "Sorry, eight appeared in Chichén Itzá."

"Don't tell me eight children appeared?"

"No, just one, adult, rough age eighty, but looked like he was forty. They didn't find him in any of the crop circles—they found him on the pyramid named El Castillo. I quickly looked up the location on Google. The Aztecs sacrificed people to their gods, but mostly children. So, our history books tell us. One circle had four, well, circles."

"I wish I hadn't eaten. I'm feeling sick," said Tom.

"There was an investigation. After the first night, they set cameras up. They found nothing, just more crop circles the next morning. The third night, two teens hid on the property with recording devices. No one knew they were there."

"Did they find anything?"

"They found themselves in shallow graves. That was the night the body appeared. One teen borrowed his parents' camcorder and recorded a video. Security found it two days later. The clip released was only six seconds long, and it showed three men grabbing the boys. They were—they were in the same black hoodies we are looking for."

"Black hoodies," said Simon.

"The video showed nothing else. They scrubbed the internet of the video about a week after it became viral. I had to find it buried on a government site." He took a drink. "But get this, my computer crashed about twenty minutes after I downloaded it. I watched it once. My IT department told me a virus hit the computer I was using. She told me I was lucky it didn't take down our station's network."

"You find this video on a secure site and your computer crashes?" asked Tom.

"Huh, I would think the network you were on would have been very secure," said Simon.

"Thus, all the handwritten notes," said Jeff. "I don't trust computers or the internet right now."

"Next, two New Zealand children were taken from their mom at a supermarket parking lot. The kids climbed in the van while she loaded the back with food. She turned to grab a bag from the cart. Next thing she knows, she's sitting on a seat outside the store. Her van and groceries were gone. She didn't remember any of it. Twelve years later, her oldest was found in a field outside a town in Missouri. Four circles."

"How many more of these do you have?"

"I'm not done with this one. So, when the child was taken, he was fifteen, the oldest. Meaning he should be twenty-seven when they found him. But when they found him, remember twelve years later, he had *not* aged. Looked the same as the last photo they took of him."

"How?" said Simon.

"Autopsy stated his time of death was within forty-eight hours of finding the body."

Tom and Simon sat in silence, trying to absorb what Jeff had just revealed.

"I found a few more. We need to head to a library and go through some old newspapers."

"I'm still hungry. Another plate of chips?" asked Simon.

"Yes, and grab a few more drinks, too. I have two more tales to tell. These are strange."

Simon returned with a plate of chips and a bowl of curry. He went back to the bar and returned with three drinks and a pitcher of water. He studied the patrons in the pub, mostly groups of friends, laughing and talking about their day. His gut said someone had eyes on him, like they were sitting beside him, listening to their conversation.

"Okay Jeff, next story."

"Right, this one gets strange. No one ever claimed the body. I don't remember this being in the news honestly. Maybe you will, Tom."

"I won't know until you tell it, Jeff."

"It happened Dec 21, 2012." Jeff sat back in his chair and took a drink. "Honestly, I don't remember this at all. That morning, security did their patrol of Stonehenge. At 4 a.m. everything was secure, same as at 5 a.m. But by 6 a.m., two bodies appeared in the center of the monument." Jeff lowered his voice. "Both were dead. Drained of their blood."

"Okay, the blood again. But by drained, do you mean spilled out or, like before, mechanically removed?"

"Mechanically removed. But these people weren't children. According to forensics, they were in their early sixties, male and female. Both were lying on their backs. One was pointed to the Orion cluster and the other to the stones highlighted during the winter solstice."

"Who were these people?" asked Tom.

"They were never identified, from what I read. They now lie in an unmarked grave in London. One very thin thread said the woman could have been Hazel Adams."

"Okay, that's promising," said Tom.

"She was born in 1866."

"Strange," said Simon.

"One more thing—they had tattoos. Not new ones either. Each was a series of numbers."

"From a Jewish concentration camp during the war?" asked Simon.

"No. They were marked with numbers on their necks just above their shoulders. Not just numbers either, but symbols."

"Did you get a photo of the symbols?" asked Tom

Jeff took a big swig of his drink. "I emailed the photos to myself before my sergeant interrupted. Here."

He pulled his phone out and showed the photos. First to Simon. His eyes bulged out and his mouth dropped at the third photo. Jeff then turned his phone to Tom.

After the second photo, he smiled. "That's more than a few numbers."

"Show him the third photo," Simon said.

"Are you kidding me? Is that what I think it is?" Pointing to the ones they identified on the farmer's arm, נפילים. "With all these other markings too, they marked these people as slaves?"

"Maybe, with the series of numbers across their neck, and a 33 inside of a five-sided star just below them. What's that about? Then the other markings are the same, I am sure of it. Just no cross."

"It's strange to have a pentagon and a cross on the same body," said Jeff.

Tom pulled his phone out and compared the farmer's tattoo in his photos to the one Jeff had.

"Huh, close enough for me," said Simon. "Has your friend called back yet, Tom?"

"No. Maybe I will send him these photos because the letters are clearer."

"And that is definitely the Eye of Horus on their left shoulder. Jeff, send those to us."

"Yes, I will. Better than that. I have copies here for you." He handed them papers with a scanned copy of the photos.

"Back to what you said. You are right, I don't remember any of this in the news," said Tom.

"Exactly. You two need to do some research on all of this," said Jeff. "Not on the internet, but with newspapers and books."

"If nothing else, this would make for a great podcast."

"Okay, what is the last case?" asked Simon.

"A strange one, too. This happened in Castlerea, Ireland on Christmas Day 2009. This I remember seeing in the news. My mom was crying, and my dad was blaming the Protestants. So, the official report shows midnight mass, at the local Catholic church, had no issues. At 3 a.m. a security alarm sounded. There was a quick check of the building. Neither the police nor the priest found anything. At 5 a.m. a call went out to the fire brigade. The building was on fire. Two days later, when the investigations began, authorities found five bodies."

"What? I remember this. The news didn't mention arson, and there were no fatalities," said Tom. "The news said it was an electrical fire from a heater."

"Tom, I'm just reporting what I have here from the police blotter. As you always say, *'you can choose for yourself what to believe.'* Two bodies were burned to where only bones and teeth were found. They wrapped one body in an asbestos blanket, like it was supposed to be found. The fourth, severely burned, was identified as a boy kidnapped in 1999, on Christmas day. Exactly ten years earlier."

"What about the individual in the asbestos blanket?"

Jeff smiled. "I'll get to it. They found the priest of the church tied to the cross at the front of the sanctuary." He picked up some chips. "He had two holes in his head, 22 cal. holes, to be exact."

"What are we getting involved in? This started as a kidnapping of three Canadian kids. Now we're investigating a torched church, ancient rituals in Mexico and Stonehenge? Threats and attacks. I didn't sign up for this," said Tom.

"What about the body in the asbestos blanket?" asked Simon.

"Oh, the one wrapped in asbestos? He had the same tattoos, same place, same ink as the others from Stonehenge. The difference? They identified him as a man who went missing." Jeff moved in his seat. He stared at both Simon then Tom. "William Fields, a British soldier who went missing when his division was attacked outside of Somme, France, in 1916. He was eighteen, at the time."

Jeff showed them a photo. "That's impossible, he doesn't look a day over thirty. Like the other ones you mentioned."

"I know what you're saying. I'm just presenting the facts, mate."

"We've a lot of work to do. How is this even possible?"

"I don't know whether any of this is tied together or not. I just did a quick search for bodies found in crop circles or ancient sites. Now I understand what those threatening letters mean when they say, *bigger than we can imagine.*"

They sat silently as Jeff flipped through his notes. He tapped on a page. "One more. A couple were on vacation in Mexico. They were on a tour with a group of people heading into a town in a ten-person van. Everyone's statement was the same. Three motorcycles cut the van off and directed it to the shoulder of the road. Six men in black got off the bikes and walked towards the van. Six hours later, the van was on the road, pointed in the opposite direction. Everyone woke at the same time. The only things taken were three children. From three different families. This time, the teens were not taken. The oldest taken was nine. A twelve-year-old was left behind."

"Hold on, they turned the van around? What about wallets, jewelry, stuff like that?"

"All still there. Just the kids. Three of them. From the age of six to nine."

"Is it some form of a pedophile ring? And why does three seem to be a common number with these kidnappings?"

"I don't know," said Jeff.

They finished their food and drinks. Simon looked at his watch. "It's ten. We should head home. It looks like we'll have a busy couple of days. Should we drive into Manchester to their library? Or even head to London for a few days? I wonder if we'll get much more off the internet on some of this stuff."

"I agree. We can decide in the morning."

"Okay, what are you working tomorrow, Jeff?"

"Same as today."

"Right, we'll call you around noon and fill you in," said Tom.

They stepped out onto the street. A car started across the road. Simon bent and examined the driver and passenger. "I recognize that couple. They left the pub ten minutes ago." They pulled into the street and drove away.

Simon shook his head. "I don't know if that means anything or not. I feel like this whole thing has made me a bit paranoid."

Neither of the others responded. The trio walked in silence towards their cars. Jeff pulled away.

"Jeff," Tom yelled. He waved his arms, hoping to catch Jeff's eye in the mirror.

"What's the matter?" asked Simon.

"He has all the documents. He'll need to email us all the information."

CHAPTER TWENTY-THREE

Jeff drove the windy, narrow road to his residence, listening to Tom's last podcast. His headlights reflected the moisture of the fog rolling in, causing him to slow as he approached a crossroads. At the intersection, he stopped and looked through both side windows, peering into the fog for headlights. He looked forward as he lifted his foot from the brake, then pressed it hard. Two men in black hoodies stood before him, the muzzles of M-16 rifles aimed at his head. He put the transmission in reverse and spun the tires, trying to get away. A shot from a rifle passed over the roof of his car.

He stopped.

Each man approached the sides of his car with their guns pointed at him.

"Out," the man at his door commanded. "Out now, Jeff."

He opened his door and stepped out, his arms in the surrender position.

"Back of the car. Now," said the other man.

He trudged to the back of his car, followed by the man from the driver's side with his gun pressed into Jeff's back.

The other man opened the passenger door. He bent in and reached to the back seat and took Jeff's shoulder bag. Then, opening the glove box, he emptied the contents and searched the floors before he stood. "Found it."

"Don't move for five minutes. Understand, Jeff?"

He nodded. "Wait, how do you know my name?"

"Jeff, we know all about you and your friends. Stop what you are doing. This is bigger than you. Unless you want to be the next person found in a crop circle."

"Will you drain my blood first? Or keep me around but not allow me to age? We are getting close, right? Why not kill me here and now? All you have is idle threats."

The person behind Jeff spun him around and drove his M-16's butt into Jeff's midsection, causing him to fold over then fall to his knees. "There'll be no more warnings, no more notes, *and no more idle threats*. Understand?"

"How do…"

A single shot passed by Jeff's ear, close enough to feel the air move.

From behind, headlights broke through the fog. The two men disappeared into the darkness. Jeff stepped to the side of the road, shaking as the car stopped behind him. Simon was the first one out.

"Jeff, did your car break down?" He grabbed Jeff's arm. He could feel the tension in his forearm.

Struggling to breathe, Jeff said, "They got our notes. They took my bag and everything I showed you tonight."

"What? Who did?" Simon helped Jeff to stand. "Are you okay?"

Still in shock and pain, he explained what had happened moments before they pulled up to him.

"Jeff, your phone. Pull up the pictures. Quick," said Tom.

Jeff, startled and still upset by the robbery, searched for his phone. "It was on the passenger seat."

"It's not here Jeff. They took it."

"We should move, drive together until we get back home. Jeff, are you okay with driving?"

"Yeah, I'm fine now. I'm glad you guys got here. They took everything. My wallet, badge, all those documents were in my shoulder bag."

• • •

Jeff arrived at the station to start his day shift. Leaving the locker room, Christine approached him.

"I'm not sure what you've done, but HR, Inspector Watson and the president of your union want to meet you in the interrogation room right away."

"Oh, good morning to you, too. Do you know why?" asked Jeff.

"They didn't say, and, Jeff, with that much fire power waiting for you, I didn't ask. Are you okay?"

"I was robbed last night."

"Oh, are you..."

"Fine, just fine."

∙ ∙ ∙

Jeff gently opened the door to the interrogation room and entered. He knew where he was to sit—the lone chair in the middle of the room across from the formidable looking group.

"Jeff, come in," said Peter, his union representative.

"Hello, what's this all about?" Jeff asked, taking his seat.

"Jeff, we have some concerns about your behavior lately," said the inspector.

Jeff looked at his union president. "Shouldn't you be sitting beside me and not with them?"

"Jeff, I'm concerned about you," said Peter.

"Am I getting fired?"

"No, no, Jeff. But that brings us to why you're here. Yesterday you were looking up cold cases, using the police system to do personal research, maybe for a certain podcast with your friend and the cop from Canada," said Inspector Watson.

"What? No, I was looking up cases to see if anything ties in with the events at Norm's farm."

"Jeff, we have concerns about your mental health. We feel you need to take some time off. Maybe a month to learn how to manage your stress. You are young, and finding a body in a field can be traumatic," said Jan, his Human Resources member.

"Is this because of the files I was investigating? Can we not fight this, Peter?"

"Jeff, take the time. Maybe take a holiday down south. Let this pass," said Peter.

"Am I being disciplined?"

"No, no, no, Jeff. We've seen you change in the last couple of weeks and feel you need some time to deal with finding the body in the crop circle. We have a therapist for you to talk to," said Jan.

"So, I'm getting a month off work, paid, to help me deal with the body we found at the farm?"

"Yes, Jeff, anytime a child's body is found, we offer this to our staff if we see a change in their personality. It's difficult to be the first on scene sometimes," said Inspector Watson.

"But it doesn't feel like this is being offered to me as much as forced on me. And why now? Where was this a few weeks ago?"

"Jeff, we saw your search history on the computer. It's full of crop circle questions. That's the first flag. Then there's your friend who's running a podcast. A podcast all about conspiracies and now with a heavy touch of crop circles. Then what about Simon Elliot? Shouldn't he be back in Canada by now?" asked Peter.

"Wait, so my personal life and friends are part of this too?"

"Jeff, take the break, please—this discussion is over. We've all agreed. Change back into your civilian clothes and head out. Here is the card of the staff psychologist. It will help," said Jan.

"I haven't agreed to any of this. Peter, what about my union rights?"

"Jeff, take the time. I don't think any of us want to investigate this matter further."

"One last thing. You left your bag at a pub last night. The owner brought it here. Sandy has it at the front desk. Pick it up on your way out," said his Inspector.

"I didn't leave..."

"Jeff, *you left it at a pub*." Peter said, nodding his head.

Jeff shook his head. He stood and stomped out the door, slamming it behind him. At his desk, he opened the top drawer. Looking around, he grabbed a USB stick and placed it in his shirt pocket. Passing by his sergeant's office, he found it strange the door was shut. In or out, that door never closed. He looked through the small window. Sitting in front of the desk were two men, well built with short hair.

"Jeff, to the locker room, please," said Peter. Jeff could hear the nervousness in his voice. "No one said to go to your desk."

"Yes, I'm going."

• • •

"A month off, lucky you," said Peter, leaning against a locker. "Get yourself sorted. Everyone has issues with their first body. I still remember mine, a suicide. Eighteen-year-old boy hung himself. It took me months of therapy to get myself back. Don't forget your bag with Sandy."

"I'll go see her once I'm changed." He emptied his locker and headed to the front desk.

"Sandy, where did this come from?"

"Inspector Watson gave it to me. He said you forgot it at a pub. I guess the owner returned it. That was nice of him."

"Or it was *stolen* from me," he yelled, looking back at the offices. He opened the bag. His identification, phone and wallet sat in the bottom of the empty bag.

"Jeff, what's gotten into you?"

He turned to return to the secure area. He swiped his card. The light didn't change from red. He swiped again, slower. The light stayed red. "Sandy, can you buzz me through?"

"Umm, Jeff, they asked me to take your access card."

He tossed it on her desk.

Peter opened the secure door. "Jeff, I need you to leave."

Jeff threw his arms in the air and rushed out the door.

In his car, shaking, he tried to dial Tom's number when there was a tap on his window.

Christine stood looking in at him. "Mate, are you okay?"

"How would you feel if you were told to leave for a month?"

"Listen to me, Jeff. There's more to this. A lot more top-level government stuff. I don't know what kind of tree you're barking up, but you seem to have something up there that wants down. I didn't hear much, but the podcast you and your friend Simon were on was brought up several times, mostly in anger. The men that were here, I'm not sure who they were, but I am sure there's an MI on their business cards. I'm just not sure of the number following it."

"Are you serious?"

"Just passing it on. We all know what happens when people fly too close to the sun. Take care, Jeff, and tell your friends to be vigilant. I want you back in a month, safe. Also, tell Simon to be prepared to be escorted back to Canada. He's rattled some cages, too. The government might revoke his passport."

"Can I ask if you hear anything, you update me?"

"Of course. I think we're all listening to the podcast. Well, maybe not the upper brass, but we all are." She tapped on her sergeant stripes. "I'm sure if we uncover anything, it'll take you an hour to drive through town with all the cruisers pulling you over to talk." She laughed at her own comment.

"Thanks. Hopefully, we wrap this up shortly. With no more issues."

"Jeff, I'm serious. Those men did not seem pleased with your behavior. Watch yourself and your friends."

"Thanks, Christine."

Jeff rolled up his window and drove out of the parking lot.

CHAPTER TWENTY-FOUR

Tom and Simon heard the doorbell ring while recording the newest podcast. The microphones picked up the noise, causing Tom to stop the recording and look at Simon.

"I guess people can't read anymore. You put the sign on the door not to ring the bell?"

"Yep, let me go."

Simon opened the door. Jeff stood with a tray of coffees and a brown paper bag. "Brought some thinking food."

"We're recording the next podcast."

"Oh, sorry."

"Why are you here?"

"If you let me in the house, we can discuss it on the podcast, too. This episode might go long, very long. But we should talk first. They have put me on leave."

"We agreed that you..."

"Wasn't my choice to be on leave."

"What? Oh, sorry." Simon walked into the kitchen and yelled. "Tom, we need to see you here. Pause everything. We need to talk before we record anything else."

After a few minutes, Tom appeared in the kitchen. "What's going on, Simon? *Jeff?*"

"I brought coffee and some treats. We need to talk."

Jeff recalled his morning at the station and the conversation in the parking lot. Simon and Tom sat in silence. Simon's only question was about him being sent back to Canada and if they could prevent it.

Tom said. "I think we should get this recorded now when the emotions are still raw. Jeff, this just proves we're on to something, something big. But what?"

"We need to find those men and interview them," said Jeff.

"I really don't think it will be that easy. If they're MI something, then they have more training than all of us at hiding in plain sight."

"Well, we'll need to be smarter than they are. We know we have over eight hundred thousand downloads, a lot of them right here in this area."

"No, no, *no*. I don't think that's what we want to do. You can't identify these guys on the show. They could charge us with causing mass hysteria. It's like calling fire in a movie theater. Next thing you know, we'll have all kinds of people dropping off fit men with shaved heads and black hoodies at our house," said Simon.

"Yes, good point," said Tom. "Are we wrapping up the podcast?"

"Yes, let's get ours done. Jeff, do you want to head to Manchester's library? Once we wrap up the show, we'll meet you there. We can get a couple of hotel rooms for the night and keep going in the morning."

"Why don't I just sit here and wait? Toss me a couple of notebooks, and I'll start writing what I can remember. Safety in numbers?"

• • •

Simon and Tom dropped Jeff at the library in Manchester before looking for a parking spot.

Jeff looked around at the architecture. The building was less than one hundred years old, but looked like the Romans had built it two thousand years earlier.

With his shoulder bag stuffed with notes to research, he stopped at the main desk. Waiting in line, he looked up at the ceiling and then down the long hallways, admiring the craftsmanship. With his turn next, he looked back over his shoulder. Standing at the entrance were two men.

I've seen them before.

Jeff turned and looked away.

"Sir, I can help you here." The pleasant lady with gray flecks in her hair offered.

Jeff approached her terminal. "Good day, sir. What can I help you find?"

"If I was looking for newspaper articles from the nineties or older, where would I go?"

"We have a web-based program to search ninety percent of the world's newspapers."

"Web based?"

"Yes, it's what most libraries use now. Do you have an account here?"

"I did a few years back." Jeff gave her his name and address. Two minutes later, he was walking towards a bank of computers to research his notes. He took out his phone and turned on his camera. Standing it up against his bag and, with the screen camera on, he watched behind him. His camera showed him the long gothic hallway he had just passed through as he entered his username and password into the computer. His peripheral vision picked up movement on his camera. He looked down to see one man he believed to be following him enter the room.

Jeff texted to Tom and Simon, *"I have company. What's your ETA?"*

"Just parked the car. Will text when there."

"KK," Jeff replied. He snapped a photo of the man behind him and sent it to Tom and Simon.

"Familiar face, pub one night?" Simon texted. *"Maybe the first night we met???"*

Through his phone's screen, Jeff watched as the man wandered in and out of the area he was in. Jeff surfed through articles, taking notes and finding plenty of information to confirm they were barking up the right tree.

Looking at his camera again, Jeff watched Tom approach and let out a breath.

"So, what's happening?" Tom asked, sitting at the computer beside Jeff.

"One of them is somewhere in the library. The other one is two or three aisles over, looking through books. Where's Simon?"

"He's in the history section looking up the tattoo letters or symbols. What do you need me to research?"

"Work on the Druids. See if you can get more contact names and numbers for the local groups. I'm still looking through old circles and men in hoodies."

Tom wandered through the library picking out books on the Druids. After a few hours, he returned to Jeff. "Did you see Simon?"

"Yes, he was speaking to a man, so I didn't interrupt."

"I found a wealth of information on local Druid groups."

Jeff looked at his phone. "One man following us is just behind us down the second aisle. I'm done here too. If we quickly jump up and you go down there to that wall, I'll go down the center aisle. We should be able to contain him."

"On three we jump. One—two—three," said Tom. The chair didn't slide back but tipped. His leg tangled with the chairs, and they both spilled onto the floor.

Smooth Tom, real smooth.

Jeff was up and rushing to the center aisle while Tom collected himself and headed to his assigned wall. They both made eye contact at the first opening, then the second and third. At the fourth row, Tom slowed and shrugged his shoulders. They continued along the aisles to the last row of books. Except for an elderly lady and two kids in school uniforms, there was no one. Tom moved to the last aisle towards Jeff.

"Were you sure?"

"Yes, one of them was here. There must be an additional exit."

They walked the perimeter of the room, looking for a door. Tom's pocket vibrated.

"Following one of them now, could use help." A map of the city appeared on the text page.

"Grab your stuff. Simon is following one now. I'll head out and send you my location."

Tom rushed through the hallways to the main doors. He looked at his phone and followed Simon.

• • •

Simon ran towards the man Jeff identified as he left the library. He surveyed the street. It was busy, but he didn't see a tram coming, so he sprinted across the road. He followed the man as he ran to Dickinson Street, keeping his eyes peeled for a second person. Once on Dickinson Street, the man looked over his shoulder, and seeing Simon running towards him, he turned left. He wove through pedestrians and streets. Simon arrived at the mouth of Faulkner. The man he was chasing was gone. The street was a typical British street, narrow with parking on the one side and old buildings casting shadows everywhere.

Jeff tapped Simon on the shoulder. "All right, mate?"

"I lost him," Simon said, pulling in as much air as his lungs would allow. "You take the right side. I'll take the left. Wait, let's check the parking lot first. We could get lucky. Where's Tom?"

"He's coming. Too much time sitting in a chair. His body isn't moving like ours."

Simon smiled at Jeff as they crossed the street. They entered the mouth of the parking lot. Two cars were parked in the small area. Both had tinted windows. Simon pointed to the one further back in the lot and then to Jeff.

Jeff ran to the car and stood in front of it. The car jerked forward. He jumped on the hood. It accelerated, then braked hard, and Jeff slid off the hood, taking both windshield wipers with him.

Simon ran to the side of the car. He tried the door handle.

Locked.

He pounded on the window, trying to break it. The car stopped with Jeff's leg trapped under the front bumper.

"Hey! Stop the car!" Tom yelled as he entered the lot, sprinting to Jeff. He pulled a knife from his inside coat pocket. "Stop!" He swung hard at the driver's window with the butt of his knife. The tempered glass fractured and collapsed on the driver. "Turn the car off, mate. Don't make me do something I *will* regret. My friend's under your bumper, and I'll do what I need to keep him safe."

The driver, with pieces of glass over his shoulder and in his lap, put his hands up. He reached down and turned the engine off.

"Where's your friend?" Simon demanded. When he was met with silence, he ran to the entrance of the lot and right into the second man. Both fell on their backs, but Simon was quicker, rolling over and climbing on the person. He sat on his chest and cocked his arm, poised to drive his fist down. "Just try to get up. I welcome it," threatened Simon.

The man turned his head and closed his eyes, waiting for the impact of Simon's fist. He slowly opened one eye and looked up at Simon. He spread his arms out and turned his head back. "No, no fight from me, Simon."

•   •   •

Simon took the man back to the car, his arm bent securely behind his back. Tom had already rolled the car back to help Jeff free his leg. Except for a few scratches and a tear in the leg of his pants, Jeff was fine. A small crowd had gathered on the sidewalk.

"Okay, I'll drive. You two and Simon in the back. Tom take the passenger seat. There are too many eyes here now. One false move and we'll do to you what you've been doing to the children. Understand?" said Jeff.

The one man opened his mouth to say something.

"It wasn't a question, and I don't want a response," said Jeff.

The five got into the car, and Jeff pulled out. Tom gave him directions to a nearby parking garage.

Jeff pulled into a spot at the top level of the parking garage. Only one other car was there.

"Right, everyone out. You two. Go to the back of the car, slowly," commanded Simon.

Jeff, Simon, and Tom stood around the two men.

"Tom, can you watch these two? I need to talk to Simon." Jeff tugged on Simon's arm. "Simon, we have a problem. Those two look a little like the men at the pub, but they aren't."

"What do you mean?" Simon looked back at the car. "I'm sure they're the same guys from one night at the pub."

"No, close. I'm not certain who they are, but they're not the guys we're after."

"Well, let's go figure this out. They know who we are. The one used my name as I picked him off the ground."

They returned to the car.

"Who wants to go first? Let's start with names," said Simon. He nodded to the man that still had glass in the folds of his sleeves.

"Hi, I'm Matt. It is such a thrill to meet you. Tom, Simon, Jeff, I'm a huge fan, maybe your biggest. How cool is this, kidnapped by my podcast heroes? I mean, this is beyond anything I've dreamed of. Tom, can I shake your hand? Will you sign my car?"

Jeff laughed as Tom looked at the ground.

"And you?" asked Tom.

"Noah. It's nice to meet you. Sorry about running into you, Jeff. I didn't know what to do. I freaked out. What's the saying? *Never meet your hero.*" He bounced and smiled. "Well, I just *did.* Jeff, you are okay, aren't you?"

Jeff rolled his eyes, but nodded. Simon grinned and tried not to laugh.

"Right, so who wants to talk?" said Jeff.

"I guess I will," said Noah. "I got you into this, Matt. I'm sorry."

Simon glanced at Tom. Tom shrugged his shoulders and shook his head.

"Okay, so—I am a super fan of Tom's, well, all of your podcasts. I don't miss an episode—I take notes, repeat episodes, hang on every word. So, I researched crop circles to see if I could help."

"Wait, wait, are you two, *theflood#1* and *walkonmetom*?" asked Tom.

Jeff and Simon broke out in a fit of laughter,

"Noah and Matt, brilliant," said Simon.

They both smiled, then laughed at the tears running down Simon's cheeks.

He grabbed his back. "I might have thrown my back out—amazing," said Simon.

"Are you two done?" Tom asked sternly. Simon leaned on the car. He wobbled side to side, then front to back. "I really did hurt my back."

"We both love the show. We're computer engineers. Total geeks. When I realized how close this was all happening to where I lived, I looked you guys up on the internet. From there, we followed you around. It's not every day we get to track a celebrity."

"Huh, we're not celebrities. We're a couple of cops and a podcaster looking for answers to a kidnapping, or multiple kidnappings," said Simon.

"To me, us, you're celebs," said Noah.

"Okay, so we're celebs," said Tom. His smile grew.

"We have followed you guys and listened and re-listened to the shows. We've done our own research, too. Taken notes and come to some conclusions you might have overlooked. We also found a few other cases that might interest you once you crack this one."

"Hold on, why are you following us?"

"Extra eyes. We know others are doing the same. We've seen them a few times. I'm not sure who they are, but they look a bit like us. Same shaved heads and build. We went out and bought some black hoodies to blend in. Only..."

"We've seen them too. We thought you were them. I'm sure none of us were expecting super fans when we began the chase today."

"We can help. Can I open the trunk?"

"Sure," said Jeff. "Slowly."

Matt opened the trunk and pulled out a backpack. He unzipped it and removed three folders. "See, this is our documentation. I would be honored if you each signed a copy."

"Matt, can we see the documents?"

"Really, you guys want to see my research? Do you think it will help? Some of it might. Noah did a deep dive into the history of crop circles. There isn't much evidence or connection to aliens."

"How would you know these days?" asked Simon.

"How about we get off the roof? You drive us back to our car and we meet at the pub tonight in Hayfield? We can talk about all this then," said Tom.

"You're inviting us to dinner? To talk about..."

"Oh, this is so cool," Noah said, clapping his hands.

"One condition. This all stays just between us now. And the whole super fan act needs to go. We'll review what you have and move on from there," said Tom.

With the distraction of the super fans, they headed home.

CHAPTER TWENTY-FIVE

Jeff was at the bar picking up drinks when Noah and Matt entered the pub. He smiled at them and pointed to a table at the back corner of the pub. They nodded, but Jeff sensed an issue. The glow in their eyes was gone. He gathered his drinks from the counter. "Can I get you two something?"

"No, we can't stay. We shouldn't be here," said Matt.

"What?" asked Simon.

"Two men, you know who, stopped us after we split up this afternoon. These guys are hardcore. Military, or James Bond type, not sure which. They threatened us, told us to go home and forget this whole thing. They took all our papers," said Noah.

"Who? What?" asked Tom.

"They were obviously following us, maybe all day," said Matt.

"The same guys that went after me," said Jeff. "What's happening? What are we uncovering? Do you want to go to my place or a different location?"

"No, I think we should stay in the public eye, just in case," said Noah.

"With your support, we will help you. They took all the papers, but not my tablet. I had everything scanned on it yesterday," said Matt. He looked around the pub, noticing the families eating, the couples laughing over a drink and the old men sitting watching sports on the television. He took his shoulder bag and opened it. From inside, he removed a few torn pages and a tablet. He lay it on the table and opened the home screen. A picture of him and a young lady popped up.

"Girlfriend?" asked Simon.

"Yep, she thinks I'm crazy for chasing this, but well, I'm trying to help her family get some answers," said Matt.

"I thought you were super fans?" asked Tom.

Noah looked at Matt and smiled. "We are, but we also have, like you, a close connection to these crop circles and a body found on one."

"Sorry, so the talk we had..."

"All truthful, but once we picked up on your podcast, we figured we could follow your show and, if possible, fill some holes you missed."

"They took my girlfriend's cousins back in 2001, two little girls, and like the other parents, they have no memory of the kidnapping. At the time, they lived in Germany. Then in 2014, they get a phone call. Police in Kansas had identified one kid, Melody."

"Crop circle?"

"Yes."

"Did you see the circle?"

"How many large circles?" asked Tom.

"Four like the—you guys made the connection, too?"

"So, what did they find?"

"This farmer owns over two thousand acres. His dogs were running the fields when one didn't come back. He could hear it fighting. He took his gun from the rack in his truck and headed towards the sound. His dog came to him, cut and scratched. It had been in a fight, a bad one. The dog survived. It also had half a hand in its mouth."

"A hand?" asked Tom.

"A child's hand, to be exact, Melody's right hand. There was a thumb, the meaty part of the palm, the index and middle finger. Police used the fingerprints for identification. Then the phone calls began. We flew to America to see what was up."

"So, here I'm from Canada flying to England and you guys were going the other way. I wasn't aware of crop circles in the States."

"Did they ever find the second child?" asked Jeff.

"No, just the one—hand," said Matt.

"What we've found is the circles show up everywhere around the world. Not just in fields of wheat, corn or barley. Some happen on grass or in forests. But the ones we're talking about are man made. And an offering to the gods and the planet," said Matt. "With the four circles."

"They show up around celestial happenings. Like the eclipse the other day, or the great planet alignment earlier in the year. We thought the circles were random, but we found a pattern tied to the phases of the moon, planetary alignments, religious holy days and even turns of the season," said Noah. "In a way, the circles become predictable. Unfortunately, the four circles are not. They show up randomly, but in the last three months, there have been more than we can find documented over the last fifty years."

"The religious holidays could be Jewish, Christian, Babylonian, you name it, but we think mostly the ancient religions," said Matt.

"Wait, how do you know this?" asked Simon. "How do you know they're man-made?"

"We believe this is some kind of ancient Druid technology or something. It's definitely a ritual of some sort. Why else would they drain the blood?" said Noah. "Plus, we snuck onto a field. There were holes around the outside of the circles. We interviewed one farmer from an older circle. He had video of men in black hoodies digging holes. It wasn't the best video. Two days later, his house was broken into, and the video was taken."

"We all enjoy a good alien story, but honestly, do you truly believe that theory?" asked Matt.

Tom smirked at the question.

"Have you ever seen this tattoo?" Tom showed them a photo from his phone.

"Oh, with all this going on, I forgot to tell you guys, I know what the letters mean," said Simon.

"What?"

"Yeah, I was sitting at the table with a series of books open. One of the staff asked if I needed any help, so I showed her the text I was researching. She studied it, then told me to sit and wait. I did. Five minutes later, she returns with an elderly man. He looks at it. *Nephilim,*' he said to me. Then he left. I packed up the books and came looking for you two when I started to chase Noah."

Noah and Jeff both laughed.

"Nephilim, for real? About three weeks ago, I found a document where it talked about the Nephilim and a connection to crop circles. In old times, it was how they marked their territory, or something like that. It's on the tablet," said Matt.

Simon watched two men enter the pub. They looked around the room and found an empty table.

"Not the men we're looking for, I assume?" asked Simon.

"I wouldn't know. I don't think any of us have seen their faces yet. They're always hidden under their hoods," said Tom.

"I know the one had ice-blue eyes," said Noah.

"Was there anything special about the child who wasn't returned?" asked Simon.

"No, the only thing I can think of, after asking my girlfriend's family, was she was born with two different colored eyes, blue and green. By the time she turned five, they were both gray. Other than that, nothing."

"When we went to France, we asked those parents to call my contacts in Canada. Do you think you could get your girlfriend's family to call and talk to them too? There has to be a common theme with why these kids, why these families, just why?"

"I will ask them. I promised to update them tomorrow after telling them about tonight's meeting."

"Maybe the eyes?" said Noah.

Simon raised his eyebrow. Let's find out. He dialed Robin's cell. After asking Robin, he shook his head. He gave Robin a brief update before disconnecting the call.

"There has to be something—this can't just be random," said Simon.

"I agree. This doesn't seem random to me," said Matt.

"If it was, we wouldn't be sitting here discussing all these common facts. I've seen enough cold cases just sit on desks, going nowhere. But then again, none of those have bodies showing up in crop circles," said Simon.

"We should go. We just wanted you to take the tablet for safekeeping."

"How about doing the podcast with us tomorrow? We can get one out quick. It might just save your lives. I think it's the only thing keeping us alive," said Tom.

"Right, your disclaimer at the top of the show. '*If we don't put out a show every three days, call the police because those discussed in the show have murdered or taken us. It's not just kids who get kidnapped! None of us hosts have any suicidal urges.*' I think it might just be working."

"Hey, so far we're still doing shows," said Simon.

Noah looked at Matt. "Dude, we just got invited onto the mother ship. It makes sense. They can't get us if we're public figures."

"I'm in. When?" asked Noah.

"Come to my house at nine. I assume you know where it is?" said Tom.

They looked down at the table. "Yes," Noah said.

Simon could hear the shame in his voice.

"Take the tablet." Matt motioned like he placed the tablet back in his backpack, but slipped it onto Simon's thighs.

• • •

Noah offered to drive so Matt could call his girlfriend. When she didn't answer, he left her a voicemail and then texted. "*Call me.*"

Heading out of town, Matt noticed a car close up on them quickly. Noah slowed to let the car pass. The car pulled out around them and sped past. Now in front of them, its brake lights glowed. Noah panicked, pulled to the other lane, slamming on his brakes.

"Hello," said Matt, answering his phone.

A van approached and swerved as Noah pulled hard on the wheel to avoid the oncoming van and the one braking in front of him. The car tires squealed. Matt dropped his phone by his feet as the sudden movement threw him against the door. The grass and dirt gripped the tires and pulled the car hard to the left. It rolled down into a gully, coming to rest on its side with the air bags discharged. Noah, strapped to his seat, lay unconscious, and blood dripped from Matt's chin. From his phone, lying in the back, his girlfriend screamed his name. The engine sputtered and died.

•   •   •

Noah lay lifeless, his arms dangling in Matt's limited field of vision.

"Noah, Noah." He shook his friend's body. He looked out the front window.

Who are you?

A man stood looking through the cracked front window, his black hoodie pulled over his head. He took a phone out of his pocket and left with the phone to his ear.

Matt closed his eyes, he took a deep breath, he heard gurgling from his chest and a copper, metallic taste on his tongue. "Call the police, Michelle. Use find my phone, *Michelle*." He hoped she was still connected to his phone. "Send an ambulance to us. Please hurry, we're both injured."

•   •   •

Jeff called Tom's cell phone early the next morning.

"Tom, our super fans, they were in a terrible accident last night. Matt's in critical condition in Manchester; he might not survive. Noah passed away in the air ambulance from internal injuries."

"Jeff, where did this happen?"

"On the main road out of town."

"How did you find out?"

"I had Rodney run the names for me yesterday after we met them. He was one of the two responding officers to the call."

"Was that wise?"

"Yeah, I can trust him not to spread this around the station. I'm coming over. This is messed up."

CHAPTER TWENTY-SIX

Forty-five minutes later, Jeff knocked on Tom's door. He tried the handle, unlocked. Stepping into the front hallway, he called out to Tom. There was no answer. He entered the kitchen and placed the coffees he brought on the counter before searching for his friends. Climbing the stairs, he surveyed the long hallway with the bedroom doors closed. He was sure there was someone else in the hallway with him. Slowly, he opened the studio and looked inside. Two lights were on, illuminating both Tom and Simon.

Tom looked up and placed his finger to his mouth. Simon turned and smiled at him.

Tom brought the microphone closer to his mouth. "So, you're saying, with magnetic fields, you can change shapes, bend materials and possibly even flatten crops to a special shape?"

While Tom asked, Simon wrote on a blank pad, *interviewing a physicist all about magnetic fields and crop circles. Grab those cans to listen. It's fascinating!*

Jeff nodded and put his finger up. He stepped backwards into the hallway.

He returned with the tray of coffees. After placing a coffee with Tom and Simon, he put on his headphones. The sound caused him to lift them off his head. Tom reached to the mixer in front of him and turned a dial. He tapped his temple and smiled. Jeff placed the headphones over his ears, sat back, and listened.

• • •

An hour later, the interview ended. They sat quietly, looking at each other. The distraction of the podcast was gone, and the reality of what happened to Matt and Noah sunk in.

"Noah was killed trying to help us," said Tom. "Is there any update on Matt?"

"Tom, don't jump to conclusions. There is no update on Matt. The whole incident could've been an accident. We don't know anything."

"What does your gut tell you, Jeff?" Tom snapped back.

Jeff lowered his head and quietly said, "They were run off the road. A witness stated that."

"They had a couple of beers while they were with us," said Simon.

"Noah was driving, and he had one beer. He cradled it the whole time. I think he had more water than beer," said Jeff. "So, what do we do?"

"What are our options? I go home to Canada. Or we keep pushing for the truth—we must be close. They're becoming more aggressive. We know of at least nine to twelve kids who are still missing. They might not be dead."

"We need to talk to one of those guys in black. They keep showing up when the crop circles do. They must also have eyes on us constantly."

"So why not kill us if we're such a problem?" asked Jeff.

"Look around. What we produce here is what's keeping us alive, for now. I'm sure if we miss releasing one podcast, there will be hundreds—thousands of amateur sleuths running around the countryside. But this will only last so long," said Tom.

"I'll step outside and call Robin and Gary. See what's happening over there."

Jeff flipped open his laptop and checked the podcast's emails.

"Hey listen to this. *'Good morning, gents. I'm Landon, a farmer in the Middles Brook area. Yesterday, I noticed three men in one of my fields, all in black, like you've described on your podcast. I waited for them to leave before I approached the field. When I arrived, I noticed they disturbed the soil in a few locations. I'm not sure what this means, but it was my wheat field. If you want to come and investigate, I would welcome the company. I'm going to set up cameras today around the field just in case I find a crop circle tonight.'* Well, that's interesting."

"So, this guy has seen our men in his field?"

"Hold on, there's a follow up email. *I woke this morning to a crop circle and a young male dead in my wheat field. If you want to come see the circle, let me know, the police are wrapping up the investigation. But either way, you need to come to my farm. Hopefully, within the next day or two.'* He included his address and name at the bottom."

"How far away is he?"

Jeff looked at the screen. "I would guess that's about four to five hours from here. Are you thinking of a road trip to the farm?"

"I guess we could. Maybe he caught something on his cameras. If nothing else, maybe you can poke around and get a name of the victim."

Simon entered the kitchen. "Well, that was interesting."

"We have something too," said Jeff. "You go first."

"What do you have for us, Simon?" asked Tom.

"Susan's happy. She's accepting the arrangement with her kids of being around sometimes. She figures it's better than not knowing if they are alive or dead. They're happy and she knows it. They signed to her, she is still learning but thinks it was for us not to give up, we're getting close. If we continue with the investigation we will be, at that point she couldn't follow what they were signing. She's going to ask them tomorrow what they were signing."

"She still sees them?" asked Tom. "And can communicate with them?"

"Yes. Better yet, they've become friends with Andre and Adrianna. They have the same viewings or visions. I don't know what to call them. She wishes she could find something in common with their children. It's bugging all of them."

"I asked her to communicate with the kids asking for a location, names or anything they can do to help us find them. She already asked."

"What did they say?"

"When she asks questions like that, they wave bye and leave. Here's the strange thing and even Susan believes she read the signing wrong, but she thinks Don signed, *'I have to go to watch the opening of King Tut's tomb with my class.'* She signed, *'on video,'* and he responded, *'no in person.'*"

Tom and Jeff looked at Simon, waiting for the punch line. After a few seconds of silence, Jeff asked. "Wasn't that opened in 1920 or so?"

"Around then. But hear me out, why wouldn't that be possible? They can appear daily in their house. Why not time travel?" asked Simon.

"There've been rumors of scientists with the ability to do that, mostly military labs," said Tom.

Everyone sat silent, distant in their own thoughts.

Simon broke the silence. "With the information we have gathered, how does this make us any closer to finding the kids? And how does Susan's kids know we are getting closer? What are we missing or what are the parents missing? I still think it has to do with the Druids, somehow."

"The fact that not one of their groups will talk to us makes me wonder what they are hiding," said Jeff.

"Do we just go to one and walk in?" asked Tom. "We need to talk about the tattoos, too."

"No time like the present," said Simon.

"The Nephilim are Biblical, all the way back to Genesis, and they are mentioned in most civilizations' written works. The story goes they came from the heavens, or a dimension, possibly? They mated with the women of Earth and created giants. But they were against God and wanted to break the bond man had with God."

"By tainting the blood of man, the reason for the flood," said Jeff. "The Old Testament is based on the pure bloodline history of Christ."

"Exactly. The tattoo has the cross's circle filled in with a blood red color then the word Nephilim."

They were all writing notes on their notebooks.

"What does that all mean? The Druids are part of a..." said Simon.

"GMO's, they say it changes our DNA, and so far, the people with tattoos have been farmers," said Tom.

"Yes, experiments gone wrong. The polite thing to do is return the body to the family."

"We never saw all their fields. Maybe they have some Frankenstein crops growing out of sight."

"Do we believe they can manipulate dimensions? Really?" asked Jeff.

"There's only one way to find out. We visit Landon and see what he has. But if we are right about this, and as the kids say, *we are getting closer,* we could—I hate to say this—but we need to be ready to fight for our lives. Look what they did to Matt and Noah."

"Hold on, who is Landon?" asked Simon.

They showed Simon the emails and gave him time to read them. "He has a circle with a body? Another question I can't understand, why are there so many bodies appearing?"

"I think we are sniffing up the right tree now. I'm ready, Simon," said Jeff. "Time to make those men in black hoodies uncomfortable."

"Let's do this, lads," said Tom. He eyeballed the room and ceiling. "You hear me? We're coming for you. You *will* be exposed."

"I would like to see my kids and tell Helen I'm sorry for what I didn't do but should have. Let me call her, and then when I come back into this room, I am fully pledged to finding these kids, no matter the cost." He walked outside. Tom and Jeff sat in silence, waiting for him to return.

Twenty minutes later, Simon entered the kitchen. His eyes were puffy, his cheeks red, and his nose running. He smiled at his partners. "Okay, what's the plan?"

"Let's go meet Landon," said Tom.

CHAPTER TWENTY-SEVEN

The next morning, they pulled into Landon's farm. The long shadows of the barns and house extended across the laneway and into the first field. Tom pulled his car beside the Vauxhall parked in front of the house. A man in his thirties walked out with a small child in his arms. Behind him, a child slightly older walked behind him. They all shook hands, and with the pleasantries completed, Landon put his kids back into the house.

"I couldn't imagine having them disappear," he said. "What is wrong with this world?"

"We know of three families who have been through it. It's not easy. And to be honest, we *are* trying to find out what is wrong with this world," said Tom.

"We drove the perimeter of your property. We saw nothing suspicious," said Simon.

"I hope you didn't drive down here for nothing. I just thought it was strange. You have mentioned the Druids during your podcasts and I know there is a Druid society in this area. They've been around for years. Let's head over to the crop circle."

"You're young to be running a farm," said Jeff.

"Fourth generation. I was born in this house. Dad's car broke down the day Mom went into labor. By the time the doctor got here, Mom was washing me in the bath. I grew up playing in these fields. When I was ten, our neighbor over there had a crop circle appear overnight." He pointed down the valley to a series of barns. A helicopter flew over their heads. "I don't believe there was a body found in it."

"So, what did you see the other night?"

"Oh, mate, that's a story." The wheat rubbed their legs and arms as they passed through the first field.

"I had just put the kids to bed. My wife was washing dishes, and I was in my office cleaning up the endless paperwork the government needs for a farm this size. She was sure she saw lights out in the field we're heading to. This field is only an acre. You can see how it dips. From the kitchen, it almost disappears."

Simon and Jeff turned to locate the house.

"After looking out the kitchen window with my lady watching the lights, I went back to my office and took my night vision goggles off the shelf. I use them to check the fields for animals. Against her wishes, I headed to the field." He stopped and looked around. "About here, I put the night vision on. There were three men in the field. They were moving around, pointing, and looking at the sky. Dogs were with them. They sat together. I watched as one beast raised his nose and sniffed the air as I approached. I assumed he had me on his radar, so I stopped here."

"King shepherds?" asked Simon.

"I would say yes to that."

Simon looked at Tom, his mouth ajar. He pointed to his temple where a large goose egg had once sat.

Landon led them towards the circle. "How did you know about the Shepherds?"

"Oh, I had a run in with them and their owners a week ago."

"Yeah, they left him on the ground with a giant goose egg on his head," said Tom.

"I quietly moved through this field, knowing the beasts were waiting for me. I felt an electric charge in the air. It's the best I can describe it. Low and behold, three more men stood in the field beside the dogs. They just appeared."

"What time was this?"

"Half-past eleven or around there." He climbed over a small stone wall, followed by the others. "This is the field." He leaned against the wall. "Everyone scurried around the field, working like bees in a hive. One dog walked away on patrol, I assume. When he got here, he stopped, jumped on the wall, looking at me and howled. The other dogs came to him. They stood in silence, staring me down. One man who had just appeared, I assume he was a man, called the beast's back. Then, a few minutes before midnight, everyone stopped working. The winds changed, and there was a feeling of, I don't know, like there was a weight to the air. Two more men appeared. Again, I'm assuming men, I couldn't see their faces or even if they had faces. They were all in black, hoods pulled up. These men were carrying the body that was found in my field." He stopped and crossed himself.

"Where did they come from?"

"I don't know. You can see where I first saw them. I should have been able to see them if they came from the road. But let me finish my story first. As they entered the circle, everyone stopped what they were doing and hummed. It was beautiful. I found myself humming the same tone. My body vibrated and, mate, this might sound made up, but I hurt my hip as a teen, had a limp from then on."

"You weren't limping today," said Tom.

"I know. I feel like a teen again. At midnight, the hum got louder. The ground was electrified, or so it felt. My night vision shut down, my smart watch stopped working and this ring with my finger was pulled." He raised his hand like someone was helping him stand. "I could hear the fields move. There was no wind, but the fields shifted."

"Like they created a magnetic field," said Tom.

"After a few minutes, my night vision rebooted. The field was empty, except for a body." He stood and walked twenty meters. Here the ground was glowing, red hot in my night vision. But yet when I took off my goggles, there was nothing except the ground was disturbed. So, I kicked at the dirt with my foot, like this.

"The holes we keep finding," said Simon. Landon's story mesmerized them.

"My foot hit something hard. With my hands, I dug around it. Look, you can see the burn marks on my hands from touching it." He held his hands up, his wrist still had fluid-filled blisters. He turned his hand to show the redness of his palm. "I took my shirt off and..."

"You took one? Please, *oh please,* tell me you still have it," pleaded Tom.

Landon nodded. Simon looked at Jeff and then Tom, the expression of a child on Christmas morning.

Jeff clapped his hands. "Well done, mate."

"One last thing and then you can explore the circle. At quarter-past-two, a vehicle pulled up. Three men exited a van and rushed to the middle of the circle. They had flashlights, bright ones. After crawling back to the wall, I rolled myself over. I lay in the field watching them. I can't be sure, but I think one man is the lead of the Druid society in town. They got in trouble back in the eighties for faking a crop circle. The police caught them red-handed. Then six months later there were three real ones in the area, so my grandfather would tell me. It was weird they walked the circles, stood over the body for a few minutes, then put the sheet over it and left."

Simon stood at the edge of the circle and looked across the field. "Another four large circle complex one."

"Do we care? I want to see the device he pulled from the soil," said Tom.

"I agree," said Jeff. He checked his watch. "Hey, look at the time."

Simon pulled out his phone, Tom and Landon looked at their watches. "Can't be right," said Tom.

"We've been out here for two hours? Impossible," said Simon.

"We should head back to the house. You can have the device I found. My donation to the show and hopefully finding those poor children."

• • •

The barn was dark as they followed Landon. He reached the first support post and pushed a button. With a buzz and a flash, the lights turned on and the old barn, now a workshop, housing farm equipment and work benches, appeared before them.

"Back here," said Landon. He wove his way through the tractors and harvesting equipment. Simon led the group as they followed behind. An old nail protruding from a post snagged Tom's shirt, tearing a hole in the shoulder and scratching him.

"Careful, this place is full of surprises," said Landon. "Including this one." He bent and lifted a worn wood board, then a second. Below was an opening big enough to hide a person. Simon looked into the opening. Tom and Jeff stood beside him. The expressions on their faces told their story and amused Landon.

He lowered himself into the hole and struggled to lift the device onto the floor. "That's her. Not too big, but it has a lot of energy, from what I saw."

"How dense is it?" asked Tom.

"Well, you carry it to the car and see. It's not big, but it has a weight behind it. I'm not sure what the material is," said Landon. Jeff extended his hand to help him out of the hole.

Tom picked up the device with both arms, and with a bend in his back, carried it to the car.

"Put it in the back seat. We don't want it rolling around in the trunk," said Jeff.

Landon hung back, checking his phone. When he exited the barn, his smile was beaming, and his shoulders were back. "I have one more piece of information for the team. But I need a favor for it," he said.

"Huh, here comes the catch," whispered Simon to Tom.

"The farm isn't making the money I had hoped it would. We're struggling, to be honest. I gave you the device I recovered, and this will also help in the investigation of finding your kids." He shook his phone before them. "All I'm asking in return is you mention my farm on the podcast, mention tours of the circles and the market we have open on Fridays and weekends. Help drive some listeners here to hopefully get some money into the bank for the winter. Would you do that?" asked Landon.

"You've given us a piece of technology likely unknown to a common man, and you're asking for free advertising on the podcast?" Tom shook his head. "Mate, you are welcome on the show to advertise for yourself, and of course, I'll push all that for you. Email me the details, and we'll have it on tomorrow's show. I hope it makes you enough money to stuff the hole in the barn."

"Thank you, fellas, thank you. So, here's what I have too. They identified the body. He was Australian, South Wales." He was reading off his phone. "They took him and his sister in 2010. I have the family's contact information. You just can't contact them until the police get hold of the family. I can add all this to the email."

"Can I ask how you are receiving this information?" asked Simon.

"My cousin. He works at the local coroner's office and is a huge fan of the podcast. We should keep the information I gave you hush-hush."

"Of course," said Simon.

"Okay. Thank you for all your help. And don't worry, we'll get your farm's name on the next series of podcasts, multiple times," said Tom, reaching to shake Landon's hand.

Jeff and Simon said their farewells to Landon and loaded into the car.

"I'll text Susan and Robin and Andre and Adrianna to tell them there might be another family to join into their group," said Simon. "Can we stop in town for a bite to eat?"

•   •   •

They arrived at the city center and parked. They placed the device on the floor and under Simon's shoulder bag.

"You guys grab a table in there. That way, we can watch the car. I'm going to head back down the road. There was a Druid Society sign hanging on that building over there. I might, as a lone Canadian on vacation, get more information than a couple of locals."

"Just be careful. We'll give you an hour," said Tom.

The door was ajar, and the labeling above said *The new Druid society*.

He pushed on the door. It swung open on its squeaky hinges. The reception area had worn tiles on the floor. They were a pale green with assorted colors imbedded in them to depict an acorn. Two large wooden double doors towards the back hid the rest of the building. The walls were covered with drawings of oak trees, sunrises and people covered in brown and black hooded robes tied at the waist by yellow rope. A table to the right held pamphlets and a group of acorns in a bowl. Above the double doors, a photo of a group of Druids hung.

"Hello?" Simon called out. "Hello, is there anyone here?"

He heard a door open, and then the double doors swung open. An older version of one man in the photo above the doors appeared.

"Can I help you?" he asked.

"Hello, I was just walking by and saw the door open, and being Canadian, I had to stop in and see what this was. I've only heard about the mystical history of the Druids—I didn't know they still existed," said Simon.

"Ah, well we do. Come in. My name is Freddie," he said in a soft voice. "Canadian? Are you here on business or pleasure?"

"Pleasure, visiting where my great grandfather was born."

"Uh-huh."

Simon followed him through the heavy wood doors to a hallway. On the wall was a drawing of Stonehenge. Another had hooded men standing around fires. As they moved further into the building, photos and drawings of four circle, crop circles hung on the wall. Simon stopped and looked at an old painting of one. "When was this drawing commissioned?"

"I believe it comes from an artist in 1640."

"What's this place in the drawing? And all these circles have four large circles? Do you have drawings of crop circles with three or five circles?"

"We can talk in my office."

Simon followed him up a set of stairs to a modernized area of the building. He held a door open for Simon and invited him to take a seat at a round glass table with an acorn etched into it.

"I assume you are here to ask me about the latest crop circle and what the Druids have to do with it?"

Simon sat forward in the chair.

"It's okay, Simon. Who isn't listening to your podcast? So, please, don't play the innocent tourist with me. You were checking out Landon's crop circle. And now you're here. I can assure you I have no secrets. So, why don't we start here then? Do you have any knowledge of the Druids? Besides the misinformation on the podcast."

"No, enlighten me," Simon said. "Maybe you can start by showing me your arms and chest. I would like to see your tattoo."

"I don't have any tattoos."

"No? Nothing with a drop of blood and the word *Nephilim* written in Hebrew?"

Freddie adjusted his shirts neck.

"There's your tell. Tugging on your shirt. It's hidden under your shirt. I assume on your left chest. Is it true you were at the circle the other night? You and a few friends? Only a few hours after it appeared? What were you doing? Draining the victim's blood? Do you finish the ritual by praying over the body and placing the sheet over it? Where did the body come from Freddie, and who were the men that made the circle?"

"Simon, I will not sit here and listen to these accusations. We believe the Earth is a live being, and we need to live in harmony with it. We are a peaceful group. The last thing we would do is take a life to sacrifice in a crop circle. I've no idea what you are talking about, walking around a circle in the middle of the night. I am home sleeping by ten most nights."

"Can you prove that to me?"

"How? This is ridiculous."

"What do you do for a living?"

"I'm a—why? What business is it to yours?"

"Just answer the question, Freddie."

"No."

"Easy enough to look up on the internet."

"I think you should leave." He looked behind Simon.

Simon turned, expecting to see a person in the doorway. "Are you looking for support? Maybe a few men in black hoodies to help remove me? Or take me away to a different dimension."

"What?"

"Freddie never play poker. You can't keep up with the pace of the game. I think you answered all my questions." Simon relaxed in his chair, watching Freddie.

After a minute of awkward silence, Freddie cleared his throat and looked at Simon. "I have a book you can take, plus we have pamphlets and literature by the door."

"Okay, and what's your involvement in the crop circles?"

"We have nothing to do with them."

"How are the circles made?"

"Simon, I can't be sure, but in our past, we had a relationship with the Earth. At certain times of the year, the ancients manipulated her lay lines, magnetic forces, and weather to entertain those in our clans. But that was many moons ago. Today, I have heard rumors that magnets are used. Scientists playing with Mother Earth. We still try to go to the circles to show the Earth some people still have respect for her."

"That's quite the story."

"Please take the book and pamphlet. It explains our history, present and future."

"Thank you," said Simon. He placed the stack of papers on his lap.

"My group in town is small. We have many more across the country. If you think we hold some secret knowledge or power, *we do not*. We, unlike most people these days, have a respect for the planet. We find peace from within and by connecting to the earth's many fields of power. You're not here to hear that. Like most old religions, we believe in inner awareness, inner peace and a god, creator, or greater one."

"Huh, you look tired. I don't deny we all need to get tuned to the Earth, but sacrificing children taken from their families or worshipping the circle that the body appeared in is not being in tune with the Earth or anything good."

"Simon, you need to leave."

Simon stood and leaned on the table. "I have a few more questions to ask you."

"Please, I have others waiting to see me. I will show you out."

Simon followed him. He had the feeling of being watched as he walked down the hallway. To his right, in a darkened corner of the hallway, three men in black watched him leave. The door closed behind Simon when he stepped on the sidewalk.

• • •

Simon arrived at the restaurant and found the others sitting at a table.

"Huh, I risk doing some investigative research, and you guys decide, instead of waiting for me, to load up on grease and fat. Well, thank you very much."

"Mate, you've been gone over an hour."

"What happened to giving me an hour?"

"We were just waiting to settle the bill, then like a couple of superheroes, we were coming to rescue you."

"That's impossible. It didn't feel like I was with him that long. I rattled his cage, though. We need to watch our backs after that conversation. I *really* rattled his cage. I asked to see his tattoo, why he was in the field overnight, stuff like that. He was very uncomfortable and out of sorts. I assume he's making some calls right now."

Simon ordered a plate of food. They flipped through the pamphlets and book he was given as he ate. Once finished, they returned to the Druid society.

Simon tried the door. "Locked." He knocked on the door and then called the number on the back of one pamphlet. The call went to a voicemail that had not been set up to receive messages. "Strange, he didn't seem to be in any rush to leave when I was here. He said he had other appointments."

"Maybe he has a job to get to. We have a long drive home and a metallic device to have a look at."

• • •

Jeff drove, and Tom called Al. He was the only one with a lab and the equipment to investigate the device, at least the only one they trusted. Tom told him what they found and described it to him. Al was hesitant and concerned for his safety, but his curiosity won over, and he agreed to take the device to work and see what it could do.

Simon sat in the back seat, studying the object. It was the size and shape of a large can of vegetables. With no visible welded seams, the object weighed enough that Simon had to hold it with both hands and struggle to lift it off his legs where it rested. It had the texture of a cat's tongue but without the visual spines covering it. Using a lot of upper arm and shoulder strength in the action, he raised the device to his ear and shook it. He detected no interior movement.

"I would think this is lead because of the weight, but it's not. At least the outer shell isn't. Maybe one of those exotic metals on the periodic table. All I know is it weighs a lot more than it should by looking at it."

Using everything he had in his shoulders, he raised the item towards the roof of the car. Six inches from the interior fabric, the item lifted from his hands, levitating, and then attaching itself to the roof of the car. Jeff swerved the car, watching the feat in the mirror.

Tom reached up and tried to remove it from the roof. He turned and kneeled backwards, using both hands to pull on it. The car roof flexed with his effort, but the device held its position. He looked at Simon.

"You need to go to the gym more, Tom. You're getting weak sitting in the studio." Simon reached with both hands, rolled it, and lowered it into his hands. Slowly, he brought it down from the roof with little effort until it was six inches above his lap. Then the full weight of the object forced him to drop it to his legs, pinning his hands underneath.

• • •

Al met them at the front door of his lab's building. With security clearances hung around their necks, they headed to the third floor.

He led them into a large, bright lab and to a bench made of epoxy. The fume hoods around the perimeter caused a draft in the room, sucking air through their lowered sashes.

"Show me what you have," said Al.

From his backpack, Tom removed the metallic item. He placed it on the bench. It rolled towards the middle where a gas faucet protruded through the countertop. Simon reached and pulled it back before it hit the faucet.

"Interesting. The weight of it is incredible. This was in the field at Landon's farm, I guess? In those holes? I'm still not sure how this and a series of others can make a crop circle appear. It could be programmable, so I'll need to run some tests with it. And if it's magnetic, it would need a source of power and some form of communication to coordinate with the others. Can you leave this with me? Remember Mark? Simon, you won't, but Tom and Jeff should."

"I do. We met him at a party, and then he came out to a crop circle a year ago," said Tom. "What of him?"

"He's going to help me with this tomorrow. Metals are his specialty. He has an awfully expensive machine in his lab that should tell us what this is." Al continued to examine it from all sides. "Wow, look at it. Not a seam or mark on it. Do you care if he puts it in the saw and takes a section of it? He has other equipment to see the inside, but worst-case scenario, he might need to open it. I don't see how else he can get into it."

Tom looked at the others. Jeff shrugged his shoulders.

"If that's the case, we need to get some more photos of it," said Simon.

"Agreed." Tom pulled out his phone and took photos. Al weighed it for them.

"Thirty-point three five kilos," said Al, as Tom took a photo of the scale.

"Okay, I think we're fine with the photos. Al don't lose it. Can you lock it up somewhere safe? Or should we keep it and bring it back tomorrow?" said Tom.

"I have a safe in my lab. It's not metallic, but it's made to resist bullets, sledgehammers, things like that, and it's bolted right into the floor. They would have to cut through the concrete to take it. It's even alarmed right to the security desk. It'll be a lot more secure in there than if you were to take it."

"Okay," said Simon.

"Give us a couple of days to play with it to see what it is. We'll run it through a couple of machines to see inside and process what it's made of. By the weight of it, I think... no, it wouldn't be that color. Never mind, I have to go. It was good to see you guys."

"I'll call you tomorrow, Al," said Jeff.

Handing in their security passes, they returned to their car.

"I have to ask," said Jeff. "But did anyone else feel like we were being watched?"

"Of course, Jeff, cameras were mounted every twenty feet in the hallways. The elevator had three. Where we stood in the lab was a blind spot, I believe, but there wasn't a square inch of floor that wasn't under surveillance," said Simon.

"Yes, I saw it—I don't know. I felt like people were in the lab leaning on the bench watching us."

"Well, it wouldn't be the first time we've felt that. I think the closer we get to solving this, the more we'll have those feelings and people looking over our shoulders. It was like when I did my drug bust. For the last three or four days, I was sure we would fail. I thought I was followed. I was worried my team was talking to the wrong people—we were missing something. I think it's normal. Consider it your subconscious telling you we're close. Another thing, I don't think we should mention the object on the podcast. They, whoever *they* are, likely know it's missing," said Simon.

They returned to Tom's house. He put the kettle on for a coffee. "I'll call the hospital and check on Mark," said Simon.

"Yeah, good idea. We should go see him if he's allowed visitors," said Tom.

"I agree."

A few minutes later, Tom carried a tray with three cups and a handful of cookies to the table. Simon was looking out the window, and Jeff stared aimlessly at the wall.

"Lads, what's with the..." He looked at Simon, then Jeff. "He's dead, right?"

"Died this afternoon. His ventilator malfunctioned, and he suffocated," said Simon.

"How does a ventilator malfunction?" asked Tom. "Really, with all the technology and staff in a hospital, he suffocated?"

"The way things are going, what if these men in black appeared in his room, did the deed and disappeared?" said Jeff.

"It could have happened just like that Jeff, after these last few weeks, that's a believable theory."

"What evidence would the police have? They could do the same to us. Just appear and set it up as a murder suicide, I guess."

"Are we safe?" said Jeff, grabbing a cookie and a mug.

"I don't know anymore," said Simon. "We believe the kids are still alive. My job is to bring those kids home. I need to call Robin. I'll meet you in the studio after."

CHAPTER TWENTY-EIGHT

The next day, Jeff received a text. *"Family has been informed. Call this number to talk to them."* A phone number appeared on his screen four seconds later. He drove to Tom's house, where the curtains were closed and the house was dark. Jeff opened the door and walked in. "Hey hello? You guys here?"

He flipped on a light in the living room, stopped, and took a step back. The room was ransacked. The intruders threw the couch cushions on the floor and a lamp lay under the window. He moved to the kitchen. Most of the cupboard doors were open, and cups, plates, and cutlery were scattered on the countertop. The oven door was open.

"Hello?"

No response. He checked the other rooms on the main floor. There was no Simon or Tom, just rooms ripped apart. He ran up the stairs and opened Simon's door. Clothes were thrown on the floor. The bed mattress was leaning against the wall. He opened the bathroom door and then went into Tom's room. It was in the same state as Simon's. The last door to open was the podcast studio.

What has happened?

He swung the door open and reached for the light. The room brightened. Everything was in its place, including Tom and Simon, tied to their chairs with duct tape placed over their mouths. They squirmed in their chairs and squinted as their eyes adjusted to the light.

Jeff reached Simon first and pulled the tape off his mouth. Simon took in three deep breaths. Jeff went to Tom and did the same.

"What happened to you guys?"

"Untie us. No—call Al. Tell him to be careful if they haven't gotten to him already. Then untie us."

∙ ∙ ∙

They huddled in the podcast studio. Jeff retrieved a couple of bottles of water and a wet cloth with ice for Simon's carpet rash on his shoulder.

"Al's not answering his phone. Should we call the police or go to his house? I called his office—no answer there either. I talked to security, they're now aware of the threat, even though they seemed very casual about it," said Simon.

"Can you track his phone?" asked Tom.

"Yes. It looks like he's at a coffee shop. I'll text him. What happened here? Someone has ripped apart your house," Jeff said, texting Al.

"We were in here last night recording a show when the door burst open. Three men, of course, dressed in their finest black hoodies and this time with balaclavas over their faces, stepped inside the studio. They pointed guns at us and told me to shut down the podcast. I turned everything off as they asked. Then they tied us up and gagged us. They told us our little show and investigation needed to end. Simon called them out on their idle threats."

"I was thrown on the floor, and one placed his gun on my temple. I told him to pull the trigger, but he didn't, the cowards," said Simon.

"They ran a large magnet over my computers. It likely ruined thousands of dollars of equipment. I'll need to run tests all morning."

"Did they ask for anything? Say what they were looking for, anything like that?"

"What do you think?"

"The device we gave Al," said Jeff.

"Then they told us to stop our investigation or else. Same threats as the letters. I don't know if they'll make the connection or not, but he's in danger."

"I texted him—he hasn't responded. Not a good sign," said Tom. "We should get over to his lab."

"Here's a thought. Why didn't they kill us last night? Or earlier? It's a bit of a stretch, but what if they know by threatening us we'll dig in deeper?" asked Simon.

"What?"

"Yeah, even when buddy held the gun to my head, he wasn't pressing hard. He had no intention of pulling the trigger."

"What if, and this is a stretch, but what if they want us to continue because they're searching for the same thing?" said Jeff.

Jeff continued to text and call Al's phone. "Guys, what about Al?"

"Keep trying him, but listen too. We might be on to something," said Simon.

"Think about it, all their threats have been boy scout level. Why not throw us in the trunk of a car, rough us up and put some fear in us," said Simon. "When I was working on a mob case there was no, *please stop what you are doing,* it was more likely they mailed a part of your body to your family."

"Right, we're doing all their work? Maybe they've tried but—but we're closer than they ever got?" said Tom. "Are we patsies?"

"Wait, wait." Jeff held his hands up. "Why? They are the ones who make the circles and bring the kids to the circle."

"No, think about it. The guys last night, I believe, were the real hoodie guys, but what if some are imposters, dressing like the real men in hoodies, trying to intimidate us to think they are all the same? But they are trying to find the hooded men from the circles or the missing kids. Just like we are," said Tom.

"If they're looking for kids too, why not work with us? Why the bully tactics?"

Jeff and Simon stared at Tom—they all felt the lightbulb click on together.

"You could be onto something there, Tom. Yep. Why not kill us or stop us? Look what happened to Noah and Matt. Did the real men in hoodies do them in? Or was it imposters going too far?" said Jeff.

"Maybe, but we can't confirm there are imposters. Let's not complicate an already confound situation," said Simon.

"I'm going out on a limb here. Maybe we're onto something big, some big government coverup and those guys are agents, but for who? Could they be the men in black? Could they be Russian or some foreign intelligence trying to find—what? And we are, well, we're doing the work they can't? Is this why they are hidden all the time? What farmer is going to talk to a foreigner about their circle? What, oh wow, what if we are searching for children but they, they are searching for what they need the kids for? Some secret—what government project. Aliens?"

"It goes back to what do the children have in common."

"We can now contact the Australian family. Maybe they can help," said Jeff. "When the men spoke, did they have an accent of any kind?"

"You know, only the one spoke. The others didn't say a word. The one who spoke, spoke gruffly. I don't think I could have recognized an accent if he had one."

"Simon's right. I couldn't tell you anything about his voice. No wait, it was too plain like when a British actor attempts to do an American accent, it's close but never right. There was something off with his inflection of certain words."

The implications of what they were contemplating hung heavy and silent in the air.

Simon finally broke the silence. "What are we missing?"

"What would a few kidnappings have in common that the parents aren't aware of? We need to put some pressure on the parents. We need to have a talk with them, press them hard with questions."

"That's it. If the parents can't even figure out what could be the reason, how would anyone else know?" said Jeff. "Yes, let's get them together, hopefully with this new family and work them over."

"Just throwing this out there. What if a government tagged them as babies? Some extra vaccine or something, some extra time alone with the babies, micro-chipping them? Injecting them with something that takes a few years to incubate in their bodies? Then another group takes all the kids for research. They don't need the one, for some reason, so they make it look like a ritual killing. Or maybe the one they don't want they sell to the highest bidder," said Simon.

"By highest bidder, you could mean aliens. Then they make their crop circles to return the bodies to earth. Look at the ones that didn't age right, for an example," said Tom. "It's farfetched, but that's the new world we are in now."

"What about Al?" asked Jeff.

"Keep trying him," said Tom. "It's weird that he's not answering. Has his location moved?"

"No."

"Do we need to prepare questions for the Australian family?" asked Simon.

"What time is it there?"

"Good question." Simon reached for his phone. It was dead.

Jeff looked up the information on his phone. "It's seven in the evening. We could call."

"Before we call, we need to figure out what we want to ask. I think it can wait a day. I need to get my house cleaned, my computers replaced, and we need to contact Al."

•   •   •

They walked through the house, looking at the mess left behind by the intruders. Mostly superficial, like when too many children show up to a kids' birthday party.

Jeff called Al's phone and left another voicemail. He tried his office phone and, again, left a voicemail.

Simon and Tom entered the living room. Jeff had put the cushions back on the chairs, righted the lamps, and put most of the items back in drawers.

"I think they stole your remote for the television," said Jeff.

"Say that again, my remote?" asked Tom

"Right, I couldn't find it."

Tom searched around the room. Under the couch, he found two socks.

"They have a sense of humor, I guess. I don't see it."

"They also took my driver's license, passport and wallet, but left my cards and money. I see nothing else missing," said Simon. "It doesn't look like they want me to leave town after all."

"Same here. All my identification is gone, but my cash was lying on my bed."

"They want us to know they aren't a local gang looking for drug money," said Jeff.

Simon left the room and ran upstairs. He yelled, "They took my remote up here too. What's that about?"

Jeff's phone vibrated in his pocket, making him jump. He looked at the screen. "Al!" he said, looking at Tom.

"Al, are you okay? Hold on, let me put you on speaker."

"Al, are you right?" asked Tom.

"I had some visitors last night. They pulled me and my girlfriend out of bed. They tied her up and demanded I give them '*what belonged to them.*'"

"Is Cindy okay?" asked Tom.

"Yes, she's fine, just pretty shaken up. They dragged me to the office. I told them there was no way I could sneak them in with security at night. Well, they took care of that."

"I'm sorry, Al," said Jeff.

"No, no, they didn't kill them. They had these guns. The best I can explain, they emitted a pulse or wave. It knocked the guards out. Then they had me hold a device of some kind and looking at the guards and the monitors, it made us invisible. We went to my office, and I gave them the device. Outside of the building—and stick with me here, please, it gets weird. We walked towards my car. Three men and two women appeared, I would like to say, from a car or from behind the building, but I can't—*I can't.* They appeared from nothing, dressed in blue tunics. One woman grabbed me and pulled me away from my captors while the others engaged them. Weapons were pulled, but everyone was too close. So, it turned into a rock'em-sock'em fist fight. During the melee, there was a flash of light, and a man appeared. I swear he was dressed in a black priest uniform with a purple chasuble lined with gold and crosses. He called out, *'revertere ad me.'* There was a pause, and by pause, I mean like there was a vacuum of time and space. In that instant, I felt motion sickness, but ageless. Then the men in black were gone."

"Like they ran away?" asked Jeff.

"No, gone. The ones in blue were left punching or kicking only air. When you told me the men in the field had disappeared, I thought you were crazy. But I saw it, *I saw it with my own eyes.*"

"Then what happened?"

"The lady holding me said, *'We're watching you and your friends. Thank you for this little piece of technology.'* I hadn't realized they'd taken it from my attackers. I asked her what it was, and she just said, *'Technology that is both ancient and futuristic.'* It sounds light years ahead of our understanding."

"Sounds military to me," said Tom.

"Yes, it does," said Jeff.

"She went to her group and helped them up. They waved at me and walked away, yelling, *'Not on our watch, Allen.'* I sat on the curb and watched them. Half my brain said to follow them, the other side was saying go home, have a cup of tea and call in sick. That's what I did."

"Cindy will be waking up. She took some sleeping pills last night. I need to get home. I'll talk to you later."

Jeff and Tom sat in silence, looking at each other.

"Aliens, it's the only thing that makes sense," said Tom. "The kids are aliens, bred and raised here on Earth to a certain age, then taken home."

"After that conversation, I'm thinking aliens, too. People don't just disappear," said Jeff. "And a Catholic priest appeared? I don't even know how to react to that."

"Well, we definitely know we're dealing with two separate groups now—what we think are the bad guys, the black hoodies, and, I guess, possibly the good guys, blue tunics."

"I guess the blue tunics are helping us? Like the lady I saw in the studio. And the black hoodies are the ones chasing us? What are we saying? This isn't a comic book—it's our lives."

"Let's clean up the rest of the house. I need some time to—I don't even know," said Tom.

Simon returned to the room and looked at the shock on Tom and Jeff's faces. "Hey, they took my toothbrush too."

"DNA sample, I would think," said Jeff.

"What's wrong? You two look like you have seen a ghost."

"Let's clean up and we'll fill you in on our call with Al. Not ghosts, but a priest and I don't know how to explain the rest," said Tom.

Jeff called his station to report the break-in. Two officers arrived an hour later and took down the details of what happened. Satisfied the only things stolen were two television remotes, a toothbrush and identification. The police left. The damage to the computers and a few glass items would need to go through Tom's home insurance.

Simon called the Canadian Embassy in London and reported his missing passport.

"I was just thinking about what those guys said when they were leaving last night."

"Idle threats Tom."

"Maybe, but you and I both know they had the addresses and names, right?"

"I know. They should be our next call. I don't think my ex is going to be happy some international kidnapping organization is well aware of her address and my kids' schedules."

"No, and my two sisters will not be any happier to hear the news, either. We need to end this, Simon."

"Or figure it out."

"I guess we should hit some stores and get me some new computers. Insurance told me to buy what I lost," said Tom.

CHAPTER TWENTY-NINE

Jeff arrived the next morning just before nine with his usual tray of coffees. Simon dialed the number for the Australian family and waited. The phone rang four times. He looked at Tom and Jeff sitting across the table and shook his head. He hung up and called again.

The phone rang three times. "Hello? Who is this?" said a voice with a thick accent.

"Hello, is this..." Simon said as he switched the phone to speaker.

"Who is this? What do you want?"

"Sir, please hear me out before hanging up. I'm here with a couple of friends. We have other families that have been through what you're dealing with. We're trying to help. I only have a couple of questions for you. Do you have time to talk? Five minutes tops, I promise. Then you can either work with us or hang up," said Simon. "But please give me a few minutes."

"You're not a reporter, are you?"

"No, sir. I, we are hoping to help you get some answers about your child. The one they found in a crop circle."

"Ask your questions and my wife and I will decide if we choose to answer them or not."

"Thank you. Is it true both your children were taken?"

"Yes."

"Okay, we have identified at least three other families where their children were found in crop circles. Two of them are talking to us about it. Would you mind talking with them? We're trying to find something in common that we can work with. We believe you and the others were targeted."

"There are others like us?" his tone lowered.

"Yes, we have contacted two families, but we know of more. That's how I got involved in this unofficial investigation. I witnessed a kidnapping in Canada," said Simon.

"Are you calling to ask for a ransom?"

"No, sir. Nothing at all. I assume the police tapped your phone, and I am perfectly fine with that. The police can trace this phone call to England. My name is Simon Elliot, and I'm a police officer from Guelph, Ontario, in Canada. I'm willing to talk to you while the officers on the line or in the room make the calls to confirm my identity. Let me know if they would like my station's phone number." Simon revealed some of the information they had found and researched. As he talked, he could hear noise from the other end of the phone, the police listening and instructing the family how to answer and to keep him talking. "So, if you would help, I would like to introduce you to the other parents."

"You can call me Greg. I don't know if..." There was a pause while a female voice spoke in the background. "Yes, we, Melissa, is my wife's name, would like to talk with the others. We still believe we have one child alive. We'll do whatever it takes to get her home."

"You say you still believe you have one child alive. Now this is going to sound strange—have you seen your missing child?"

Tom waved his hands, trying to get Simon's attention. He shook his head and mouthed. *"Not yet."*

"If Barb was missing, how would we see her?" asked Greg. Another whisper to Greg. "Why would you ask that?"

"The other parents have seen their children, and still do," said Simon.

"But she's behind a veil, like beside us but behind a dirty window or a wall of haze or like the blur of rain on a window. We think she can even hear us. She looks happy," said Melissa.

From behind Greg, they could hear a loud male voice. "Greg, Melissa, stop talking. You don't know who they are. Hang up the phone."

STEPHEN W. BRIGGS   213

"I do, Officer West. I'm not sure how, but they know parts we've kept secret. I trust them," said Greg. "These men will have answers for us."

"I can locate the family in Guelph and contact them on your behalf," said the voice in the background.

"No, thank you. We'll let—umm, Simon arrange it."

"Okay, thank you for your time. Do you see my number on your phone? Again, I have nothing to hide. I would have thought the police around you would have called my superiors in Guelph by now."

"Hold on, Simon. Yes. They have given me the nod. You are who you say."

"Impressive."

"It is, isn't it? Will you find Barb?"

"That's our goal. This is the only number we'll ever call you with. We're being watched and followed and could be in danger. So, if anyone calls saying it's us, don't trust them. We won't call from another number. Remember my voice, too."

"Understood."

"Thank you for the time. We'll get back to you tomorrow with a time to talk with the other families."

Simon disconnected his phone.

• • •

Two days later, Tom worked in his studio, setting up the phone lines for the group call. The Canadian and French families had talked, but this would be the first call with the Australians. Everyone anticipated the call, hoping they could make a connection.

Jeff and Simon wrote questions in the kitchen to help jog memories or trigger a thought that might lead to any common denominator.

Tom stepped into the kitchen and opened the fridge. "I'm nervous about this, fellas."

"What for? If we drop a call, we call back."

"No, not that." He took a pop out of the fridge. Sitting at the table across from Jeff, he rolled a small black metal object out of his hand onto the table.

"Look what I found. Tucked under the table, hidden behind some cables. I ran to keep them off the floor. How long has it been here?"

"A bug?" asked Simon.

"Looks that way. If there's one, what's the likelihood there is more?"

"Do we have time before the call to even search?" asked Jeff.

"I swept the studio. I think we should be okay in there."

Simon glanced at the clock hanging on the wall. "We have a half hour before the call. Let's make the best of it, see if we can find more."

"You and Jeff do that. I have a few more things to do to get ready," said Tom.

Simon searched the kitchen while Jeff did the living room. They both ascended the stairs together, each with a bug in their hands. After checking the bedrooms and bathroom, they added to their collection of electronic listening devices. They entered the studio and placed their bugs on the desk.

"Found this in the opening where the wire for the coffee maker can be stored," said Simon.

"Found mine in the soil of your hanging plant by the kitchen window. These three were in the bedrooms and bathroom," said Jeff. He lifted one to his face. "Hello, I assume you have more around here, and *we will find them*. I'm going to keep one to insert up..."

"Robin's calling in," said Tom.

"What do we want to do with them?" asked Jeff.

"Flush them," said Simon.

Jeff gathered the devices and took them to the washroom. He dropped them in the toilet and pushed the handle down. They swirled, then disappeared through the trap way at the bottom of the toilet.

When Jeff returned, both Simon and Tom had their headphones on and were having a casual chat with Robin. Jeff joined them, placing headphones over his ears.

"... and then they drove off," said Robin.

"Robin, Jeff is back and with us now. Hold on, I have the family from Australia calling," said Tom. "Hello?"

"Good-day mate. How are you today?" Greg said. His voice wavered.

"Fine, we already have Robin and Susan on the line. We're just waiting for Andre and Adrianna," said Tom.

"Roger that. Hello Robin and Susan," Tom, Jeff and Simon sat back and let the families become familiar with each other.

"I'm Greg."

"And I'm Melissa. I'm sorry to hear about your sons, but I hope we can help find a connection today."

"Hey guys, I'm patching in Andre and Adrianna now," said Tom.

"Hello, can you hear me clearly?" asked Andre.

"We can," said Robin.

"Us too," said Greg.

"Okay, we can do this two ways. We can ask a series of questions for you each to answer or you can just talk, get to know each other, and talk about your experiences and children. We can jump in if we hear anything we want to follow up on," said Tom. "I'm recording it. I'll send a file to all of you to review and hopefully, continue the conversation."

"Can I just say a big thank you to the three of you for this? Our law enforcement teams didn't see the point of linking the kidnappings. So, thank you for your private investigation," said Greg.

The families decided the second approach might be a good place to start. They talked about how their children were taken and how the kidnappings were investigated. Each believed at least one child was still alive, somewhere on the planet. After a half hour of letting them talk and heal, Tom jumped into the conversation.

"Would it be appropriate to throw out some questions for you to think about and discuss?"

"Please, I almost forgot you three were still on the line," said Andre.

"First question. Were all your children taken and what were their ages?"

"They took all three of our boys. Ages eight for the twins, Doug and Don, who are still missing and ten for Ricky, who was found in the crop circle," said Susan.

"We had two children taken, Mike, seven, they found him in a crop circle, and Barb, nine," said Greg. "I have an older son from my first marriage, he's twenty-two now, and still with us."

"All three of our kids were stolen from us. They found our youngest, Matty. The twins, Deb and Ken, are still out there somewhere," said Adrianna.

"Okay, the twins, anything in common there?"

"Not that we've found. Ours are fraternal while Robin's and Susan's are identical," said Andre.

"Our theory of it being the younger ones is out the window now," said Simon.

"Yes, or the twin theory," said Tom.

"Is there anything in your family history that might have been a trigger for them to be taken?"

"From talking with Robin and Susan, our great-grandfathers fought in World War Two," said Adrianna. "They stormed the shores on D-Day. Greg and Melissa, what about you?"

"Yes, yes. Same here!" Greg said, but his voice deflated as he added, "But I suppose that's not that uncommon."

"Who knows," Simon said. "Anything we learn is helpful. You never know when we're going to hit on the right thing."

They talked for a half hour, answering questions. The frustration of the group grew as each question ended in a dead end. Tom had all but given up and wound down the meeting.

"Okay, so here's the weird one. You've all seen your missing kids after they were taken," said Tom. "Please tell us how many times and what happened."

Robin and Susan went first, telling of the many visits from the twins, how they interact with sign language. Andre and Adrianna told their stories and finally, Greg and Melissa told of the few visits they had and how Barb looked older.

"The way you each describe your kids, it's as if they're in another dimension looking in on you. You all mentioned a dirty window. Robin also used the analogy of rabbit ear antenna for an old television, and Andre, you described it as if looking through water. All the same things, just your unique life experiences. It could be dimensional. Here's something to think about for another time. Why would the people let the kids see you and you them?"

"Better question is, how are they doing it?" said Greg.

"Oh, wait, one day Ken had a cotton ball on his left arm inside his elbow," said Adrianna.

"I can't believe this! How could I be so stupid? Greg, it's like we forgot after they took them from us. How did we forget this? *There is one thing*," said Melissa, she took a breath. "This is a long shot, but have any of you heard about golden blood, or as our doctor called it..."

"RHnull, yes, *yes,*" said Susan. "Yes, of course." It was like the memory of the golden blood was turned on in her head. "I forgot how we spent so much time making sure the twins didn't get hurt. Guys, I forgot about that." Her sobs echoed through the phones.

"Wow! No, no, we did too," said Adrianna. "When you said it, it was like a slap on the cheek. Both twins have it. Of course, less than forty people on the planet have that blood, according to our doctor. We all have children with it?"

"Is it possible when they took the kids and blew powder at us, they turned off those memories? I still can't remember the kidnapping," said Robin.

"I think that's it, the powder. What else could have caused us to forget we had some of the rarest children on the planet?" asked Melissa.

"Guys, just give us a minute. Susan needs a break," said Robin.

"Robin, we'll take a quick one. Everyone, this is great, *just great.* Get some water or use the washroom—we're going into overtime," said Tom, trying to hide his excitement. He looked at Jeff and Simon, nodding his head.

"I could use another coffee," said Greg. "But I think we've cracked it."

"Let's take a few minutes to let it settle in," said Tom. He muted their microphones.

"Simon..." said Tom.

"Already searching the web. We did it, fellas, *we did it!*" said Simon.

"I'll run down and get some waters. I think we've found what we need. Now, what do we do with it? Are we off aliens and on to vampires?" said Jeff.

• • •

"Everyone back on the line?" asked Tom.

"Yes," everyone said with enthusiasm.

"We were told our children had the blood of the gods," said Greg.

"Our doctor said the blood was so rare—the blood was so rare, people would kill to have—to have a supply of it," said Susan. "How are we sitting here as parents to the rarest children in the world?"

"That's it. I would think Tom, that's what you guys need, right?" asked Adrianna.

The discussion turned to how they didn't do enough to protect the rare commodity their children had coursing through their veins. Everyone went silent. The only sound being picked up on the microphones was the clicking of Simon's keyboard as he continued to search for information on golden blood.

"Is everyone okay?" asked Tom.

"Sorry, Tom. Reality just set in for us," said Melissa. "Our kids are still missing."

"Us too," said Andre.

"Same here," said Susan. "I just had a vision of my twins in a medical room. It's all white, and they're strapped to beds, scared, and crying, but can't move. There's a crimson red tube coming from their left arms, pulling blood from them slowly. Men and women in white lab coats with hoods on and clipboards cradled in their arms are watching the machines as they steal my child's blood and life," said Susan. The last few words crackled out of her as she broke down again. Others cried over the phone lines.

"Do you all want to go? Should we try again in a couple of days?" asked Tom.

"No, I don't. I think I need to stay talking for a bit. I just need a minute," said Adrianna.

"No, I think we need each other more now that we know why our children were taken," said Susan.

"I have one more question when you guys are ready to answer," said Simon. "Did your children, who were found in the circles, have golden blood?"

"Ricky had a rare blood, but not golden," said Robin.

"No, ours didn't. But I wonder if the people who took them kidnapped all our kids because they didn't know who had it," said Andre.

"Or it was easier to grab all of them to see why the others didn't," said Jeff.

"Back to the image of white coats and labs," said Greg.

"Golden blood. No one made that connection. I had never even heard of it before this conversation. I guess we have our research to do," said Simon. "When were they found with it?"

"We had complications after they were born. They did some blood work and then told us of this disorder, as they called it," said Robin. "Disorder is what our doctor called it because it's so rare."

"Same with us," said Adrianna.

"Us too," said Melissa. "I found it strange—the doctor came back to me minutes after Barb was born, but we hadn't authorized a blood test. He was excited, like he'd won the lottery when he saw the blood test. Then he told us we couldn't vaccinate her. He was very clear. We could never vaccinate her."

"Susan, Adrianna, did you have your kids vaccinated?"

"No, no vaccinations for them. We had a big fight with our doctor. We wanted them vaccinated, but he refused," said Susan. "Just like Melissa."

"Same here. No vaccines. Our doctor told us not to. Wait, Andre, do you remember what he said? Wasn't it something like, *'You don't want to taint that perfect blood, others will want it left pure.'* Then he—he winked."

"Interesting. And what about the other kids?"

"Ricky was."

"The two older ones were," said Greg.

"We didn't vaccinate any of our kids," said Andre.

"So, what I'm getting here is we all have kids with the rarest of rare blood who were not vaccinated. We were obviously targeted by what seemed to me as an elite group of men who seemed to have some form of military training.

I'm convinced more than ever, this is not a random kidnapping. This is about our kids' *blood*," said Greg.

"Yes, we were targeted, maybe from the time our children were born," said Robin.

"Agreed," said Andre.

"I think we've made some amazing progress here today. I think we need to spend some time researching what you've told us," said Simon. "I agree. This seems to be a very precise targeted group. The crop circles are some form of a sacrifice for the ones who didn't have the golden blood. Sorry, maybe I should have kept that to myself."

"No, you're right. They didn't need all our kids, so they lay them in the center of a crop circle. How many of them are made in a year? Are they all sacrifices?"

"There has been an increase over the last few years, but most of them do not have bodies in them. We have a theory that the ones with four large circles have a body. We believe it is ancient ceremonies and the placement of the planets and moons. But we believe this has happened way back in the past, too," said Simon.

"Not to sound crazy, but is our children's blood being harvested and sold to the highest bidder? Keeping the rich and elite alive?" asked Melissa.

"Google says there are thirty-three known people with this blood alive today," said Simon.

"I don't think they counted our kids in that statistic," said Greg.

"I agree," said Jeff.

"Oh, one interesting fact. Some people with this blood are walking the streets. So what makes them different, besides their age?"

"Vaccine?" said Greg.

"Could be," said Jeff.

"Okay, we should let you all go," said Tom. "This is a very rare elite club. Can we do this again in a few days? Hopefully, we'll have more details for you. And please, if you need to talk, support each other. If this podcast gets any bigger, you'll all be here for a visit. My treat."

"Thank you everyone. Please keep in touch with each other for support and to help us with the investigation," said Simon.

"Not to be a bearer of bad news, especially after this productive talk, but be very careful, please. They likely know of this meeting and that we just took some giant steps. We don't know what they could do. Honestly, we still don't know who *they* are. So far, I think we are only alive because of the podcast. It might be wise to identify the three families for your own protection."

"Can we talk in a couple of days to the families again?" asked Greg.

The families agreed to meet two days later and let Simon know if they had any further updates.

Tom looked at Jeff and Simon. They all had huge smiles covering their faces.

"Now what?" said Tom.

CHAPTER THIRTY

The trio spent the next day with their heads buried in books from the library and on pages of websites, learning about the benefits of golden blood or RHnull. They searched the internet for people with RHnull blood but only discovered two names. Tom was sure someone had scrubbed the others from the internet. One lived in India and one in Italy. With the help of interpreters, they called both people. Neither wanted to speak to them. Or, as Jeff suspected, were allowed to talk to them.

Tom found one news article from a small German newspaper. He took notes from the article. The incident happened in 2006. The news article revealed a man, Charles Hampton, attacked two men outside his house. He claimed they were following him. Police investigated the incident and detained Charles and two men. Charles insisted he had spent his life running from the men in black hoodies moving from Australia to hide from them. He told police, they would take him and draw blood from him. He had a rare form of blood, RHnull. All charges were dropped and the men from Italy, left town. Charles Hampton moved to Berlin in the 1980s.

Tom decided it was worth the expense of a trip to knock on his door. Once he revealed the information he had found, Simon and Jeff agreed.

• • •

They walked up the walkway of the row house on the outskirts of Berlin.

"This better work or we wasted a lot of time and money," said Simon.

"Yeah, plus I just saw a report of a new crop circle in Wales. We could research that too," said Jeff.

"Don't worry, I feel we'll get something for our time," Tom said, knocking on the door.

"Yes, can I help you?" a voice from the other side of the door said in German, the Australian accent faint.

"English?"

"A little, not well," came the response.

"Umm, can we speak to you for a few minutes? We won't take long. We have a few questions about your past."

The door opened wider. "If this is about my blood, I just want to be left alone. You have taken enough of it. If you want more, then take it all." He held his arm out.

Simon noticed the scars from many puncture holes in the bend of his elbow and inside his wrist. "Your English improved quickly. No, we are not here to take it. We want to learn about it. You might be able to save the lives of a bunch of kids."

Jeff watched as a car slowly drove by them and parked further along the street. He tapped Simon on the shoulder and motioned with his head for him to look at the vehicle. Simon turned and watched as the driver and passenger sat motionless in the car.

He whispered into Tom's ear. "Get in the house. We'll be back in a minute."

Jeff rushed down the path to the sidewalk, followed by Simon. They sprinted towards the car, watching the men inside. A plume of exhaust floated behind the car, and it rolled away.

"I don't think they stopped for a conversation. They followed us here. But *who* is what we need to find out," said Simon.

"I think we all know the why," said Jeff.

When they returned to the house, Tom was inside. They knocked, and the door opened. Tom stood in the hallway with a man who looked to be in his late forties or early fifties. He was thin and short. His hair was thick and black, and his eyes were ice blue.

"Come in, you two. We saw the car. Who was it?" asked Tom.

"Not sure. They drove away before we could identify them. But I think we know the answer. The same people who broke into your house and killed Matt and Noah," said Jeff.

"Son, many have died by that group," said Charles.

Tom introduced the two of them to Charles Hampton, the oldest man alive with golden blood, at least freely walking the streets.

He invited them to sit at his kitchen table. After small talk about each other, Tom asked, "Can we interview you for the podcast?"

He agreed.

"Hold on. Let me check the street," Jeff said as he stood and left the room. "They're back," said Jeff when he returned to the kitchen.

"We're going to deal with them," said Simon.

"Blue or black clothes?" asked Tom.

"Black," said Jeff.

"I've been dealing with them my whole life. They chased me here. And with all our medical information now in clouds and digitized, I can't hide. We're all tagged. Our blood is so precious." He sipped his coffee.

"Were you kidnapped?"

"No, not like the children you're looking for. Under the pretense that I was a special kid, they took me from my parents. I was one of the first to be found with this blood disorder in this modern era. But by the time they found it in me, my mom had allowed the hospital to vaccinate me. When I was two, all my regular doctors stopped seeing me, and new doctors arrived in Australia. They were not as nice or professional as the first batch. Italian, I believe. They took me away from my family on and off for years. They did all kinds of things to me. All kinds of crazy tests, none of them I understood. The documents I stole years later showed they could clean me of all the vaccines except the one for polio. They took so much blood from me, but they could never clean it to its original pure state. Because of me, now doctors check the blood before vaccinating in the hospital."

"Well, that explains what Melissa said about Barb's blood being tested even though she hadn't authorized it," Simon said.

The others nodded.

"Sorry, please continue, Charles," said Simon.

"Most of my youth, they would come get me and take me away for months at a time and then return me to my family and watch. Then one day, most of the medical team left, but one doctor stayed behind. As I aged, we became closer. I would ask him questions. When I asked where the other doctors went, he told me they found a child who hadn't been vaccinated. I had the blood of the gods and if I wasn't vaccinated, I could help people live to Biblical ages. My blood is the same blood as in Genesis before the sons of gods came down to taint it."

"The Nephilim," said Tom, looking at Simon.

"What? What about them? Noah had my blood, or I have his. That was back when the Nephilim were said to walk beside us."

"We've encountered a few people who we believe are associated with the Druids. They have an Ankh cross with a drop of blood, the word Nephilim written in Hebrew, and an acorn below the word tattooed on them."

"Interesting. I remember back when I was a teen seeing that same style of tattoo. It was on a priest who came to visit me at a lab. It only stood out because tattoos weren't popular back then, unless it was military or gang related, and then seeing a priest with one shocked me. Those medical visits lasted until I was sixteen. But they always watched me," he ruminated. "Each time they returned me to my family, they warned my parents to keep me safe. There were no blood transfusions in my future."

"What year was that?" asked Tom.

"Early to mid-fifties."

"But the internet says we discovered golden blood in," said Tom, flipping through his notes. "1961."

"True. That's when the world discovered it, but others have known about it for centuries. Like I said, it's talked about in the Bible, right from day one."

They sat holding their cups, staring at Charles.

"Who do the men in black hoodies work for?" asked Jeff.

"The church, I assume."

They exchanged glances with raised eyebrows. Jeff said, "Al said in the parking lot he thought a priest appeared and called them back."

"So we should investigate the catholic church? With what Al saw and now a priest visiting Charles," said Tom.

"They're all connected. All these secret and not so secret societies," said Charles. "Who are the people in blue? I never saw them before. Fresh players in the game?"

Tom told him about Al and his encounter with them. Charles sat hanging on every word. Jeff looked out the front window, surveying the street and identifying the parked car.

"Hold on, I think we're all thinking it. How old are you?" said Simon.

"I was born in 1941. I'm seventy-five."

"No way," said Jeff.

"We've done our digging on the web about this. I'm not sure what the big deal is about this blood."

"Right, the web, the holder of all truths, or the truths you need to believe. The truth is, this is a curse. My blood is so rare. If I bleed, you can't help me. I can help *you*, all of you. I've never been sick in my life, not even a runny nose. I've never had an ache or pain. I eat what I want and have no issues with my blood levels. My weight hasn't changed since I was twenty-three and look at this hair." He took hold of it. "Thicker and stronger than any teen I know. But I'm watched. I have scars I see every morning in the mirror, bringing back the horrors of my childhood. And then there is the scars hidden away in my mind. The ones that keep me awake at night, or have me looking over my shoulder as I run errands. Now those characters in my nightmares are parked in front of my house, again. You three must be annoying them."

"Oh, I think they are fed up with us," said Tom.

"Huh, your blood is special, not just rare?" asked Simon.

"Yes, there's less than one hundred of us on the planet. At some points less than twenty. I know of three others walking freely."

"How?" asked Simon.

"They paid a doctor to inject them with every vaccine known to man. It was in the seventies before they changed the cocktail to the polio vaccine."

"If your blood's so precious, why are you free? Why are you not hidden away like the children we're searching for?"

"Simple, from what I was told years ago. They monitor me, but I'm not important to them."

"Why, because of a vaccine?" asked Simon.

"Exactly. My blood is tainted to them. They can't use it."

"For what?" asked Jeff.

Charles shrugged his shoulders. "I doubt for the good of mankind."

"Did you ever meet others when you were under the care of the doctors?" asked Simon.

"At one time, there were three of us in the lab being tested. We weren't allowed to speak to each other. One was from Mexico and the other from India, so I was told. I was the only one vaccinated. The last time I saw my doctor, the special one who spent time with me as a kid, I was in his lab keeping him company when the phone rang. I could tell the call wasn't going well. It escalated, and he ended the call by yelling, *You didn't have to kill them.*"

"By them, I'm assuming children like you. But who killed them?"

"Yes, others like me. And I asked him who *they* were. He called them '*Custodio.*' I assume the men parked outside are members of Custodio. It means the guards in English."

"Custodio," echoed Simon.

"Yes, the men who have been following you around, probably since you guys started the podcast. You know, I think it's the church behind it all. I can't prove it, but one time a high level bishop talked to me back home. It's why I moved here."

"The church," said Jeff.

"Just a wild theory, but my whole life is based on wild theories. I'm not completely sure. But ninety-nine percent sure it's the church. Not the side the public sees, the hidden side. Just something I overheard when I was seven, so take it with a grain of salt. But I heard the doctors talking to men in black robes, and one in a bright red robe. The men in hoodies stood around them. The head doctor was nervous that day. They threatened him to find a remedy for the live polio vaccine. He recommended a blood test be given to all babies around the world. The one thing I remember him saying was, *The church has its claws around the world. Use it to make all doctors give this test before they administer any vaccine.'* He showed them the quick test that could be done minutes after childbirth without a mother knowing. If you're wondering how I can remember that? Photographic mind, another curse. I can pull up my entire life like it's one big directory."

"So—vampires run the church?" asked Tom, a smile growing on his face. "The little I know is they aren't run by an elderly man who wears funny hats and sits on a large throne. At best, he is the PR man for the organization."

"It's strange how in the eighties," Charles continued, "our population dropped to less than twenty with golden blood and now the numbers are rising again. My friend is a doctor here in Berlin. They tell doctors if they identify a person with RHnull not to vaccinate them, it could be deadly. It's in medical books and taught at medical schools around the world. That's how much power *they* have. He has a number to call if he identifies one of us. Now this only worked with kids born in hospitals. In the sixties, in all third world countries, through a bunch of churches, they found people with the RHnull blood. So, they expanded the program."

"You keep saying, 'they.' Who are *they*?" asked Jeff.

"The men in hoodies, people within the church walls who hide in the shadows," he said. "Nephilim, as you mentioned earlier."

The room went silent. No one moved.

"Sons of gods?" asked Tom.

"The very ones. They work within the church. Where do you think the kids you're looking for are? They're in some lab with white walls and people in white jackets bleeding them alive. They only take enough daily to keep the kids alive. Then they take the blood to use for eternal life for themselves and others who know about the program."

"Hold on. How do you know this? How is this possible? It all seems a little far fetched."

"You introduced yourself as a man who runs a conspiracy podcast, and you're questioning me about this? Throughout my life, they've taken me for check-ups. With my photographic memory, I read as much of the documents in the lab as I could. This goes beyond a few kids being kidnapped. They are using the blood to extend lives of select people, and I might be wrong with this, but they believe they can prevent Christ's return by controlling the bloodline he had. Just like they have tried from the beginning of time."

Tom shook his head.

"Come on, mate. You came here to learn the truth. Well, I'm giving you the truth, and like most things, it's likely not what you wanted or expected to hear. My whole life has been a conspiracy—my parents died because of my blood. Other parents are walking around like zombies wondering what happened to their kids, and you question me?"

"Slow down, don't get upset. It's not that we don't believe you, but Christ's blood?" said Tom.

"No, they take our blood, not mine, but they take the blood and have it intravenously put into themselves, and others. Maybe by now modern medicine has improved the process. What I have coursing through my veins is the real fountain of youth. Look at me, I'm seventy-five. Do I look it? Again, I never, ever got a sniffle. I will live to the original ages of the Biblical people, none of this average life expectancy of eighty, or so, and out. If you had cancer, three to five vials of my blood, well, RHnull pure, would cure you and not just of the cancer either. All aches, pains, sprains—it would reset you to birth, good as new, maybe even a little better. That's why they milk those kids." He laughed at the confused looks on their faces.

"I have an appointment to get to, and the look on your faces says your brain is overflowing with information. Boys, this isn't your dad's JFK conspiracy. You're in up to your necks in something that will probably kill you before you find the children you're looking for."

Simon looked up at him as Charles stood. "How is any of this possible? Do you, please forgive me, but do you have the blood of Christ in you?"

"Yes, if you know your Bible, it's all based on blood and the purity of the original blood. The flood was to destroy those who were impure. Christ was part of that bloodline. I'm part of it too. It had branches, but it's all the same *golden blood.*"

"Can we just have a minute before we leave? I'm not sure I can stand right now," said Simon. "It all seems so surreal, but at the same time it feels like the most truthful thing I've ever heard."

"Oh, it's real, and when you walk out that door, reality is going to be slapping you in the face or pointing a gun at your chest. So, please leave by my back door. I'll give you five minutes, then I'll leave through my front door. They'll likely take me away knowing I told my story to you. But that's okay, there's not much they can do to me they didn't do as a kid."

"Sorry, one last question. Why did you tell three strangers all this?"

"When I saw the car pass with the black hoodies, I knew you were the real deal. And that my time is likely up. I hope what I told you can take you to the next step in your investigation. Just be careful. They can appear from anywhere." He looked out his front window. "You need to leave."

Jeff stood beside Charles. "There are two cars there now. Same make and color."

"He's right, they're waiting for us. They're sitting in their cars waiting."

"Use the back door. Quickly. Give me your number. I'll call you tomorrow. If I don't, you know why. Maybe you'll find me in a crop circle."

. . .

They followed each other out the back door and across his lawn to a narrow road. They waited for the five minutes Charles needed. Then from the front side of the houses they heard tires squeal, men yelling and then tires squealing again.

They lowered themselves behind a white car and waited. A few minutes later, a man in a black hoodie appeared at the mouth of the street.

"What do we do? Are we fighting or going with them?" asked Simon.

"We need to fight to get out of here. I don't think they're the type that are going to take us to the park for ice cream. You two crawl up along the cars. I'll stand up and let him see me, and you take him from behind," said Tom. He stood and raised his hands. "Looking for me, mate?"

"The very one. Where are your friends?" he replied.

"We split up. I guess I should have gone with them."

From behind the stranger, Jeff and Simon appeared. Simon grabbed him, wrapping his arm around the man's neck. Before Simon knew what was happening, the man flipped Simon over his shoulder. He landed on his back, knocking the wind out of him.

Jeff hit the stranger around the waist with his shoulder. But the man twisted away, sending Jeff falling forward on top of Simon. Tom charged, kicking the man in the ribs. At the same instant, Jeff rolled over and kicked their assailant in the groin. The man crumpled with his hands covering his crotch. Simon stood over him, and Jeff reached under the hoodie and felt for a gun.

"Hey what's going on?" From fifty meters away, two men in blue tunics sprinted towards them.

Tom grabbed Simon's arm and pulled. "We need to go. Jeff, let's go."

They ran towards a pathway, bringing them to a street with stores. Once in an empty parking lot, they stopped. Bent over trying to catch their breath, they looked to see if they were followed.

"We—got away," Simon said, trying to suck in as much air as he could.

CHAPTER THIRTY-ONE

They safely arrived in England and booked into a hotel in Salisbury. The goal was to see the new crop circle reported in Wales the next day.

Outside the hotel, two men in a black car sat watching as the trio talked in Tom's hotel room. Simon came into view, leaning against the ledge of the window. He was irritated and angry, his arms waving through the air. Jeff joined him and put his hand on Simon's shoulder, but Simon shrugged it off, shook his head, and left the sight of the window. He returned to the window, pointed at Jeff and Tom then, closed the curtains.

"Things are not going well in their room tonight, are they?" said the passenger in the car.

"There he is," said the driver, noticing Simon's form in a room to the left of Tom's room.

Jeff opened the curtains and sat on the ledge of the window where he had just argued with Simon. They watched as he had a heated conversation with Tom. He disappeared from sight, but soon the lights three windows down turned on. Jeff closed his curtains in his room and turned off his lights.

· · ·

Simon woke at two in the morning. Without turning on any lights, he dressed and left his room. The stairwell opened to the back parking lot, protected by bushes and a large storage shed. Keeping in the shadow of the bushes, he ran to the property's edge. Bending down, he checked the road for any vehicles. Seeing none, he slipped into the night.

• • •

Tom woke to his alarm set for 8 a.m. He texted Jeff to get moving. Jeff knocked on his door twenty minutes later.

"It looks like Simon got away. I just hope he knows what he's doing."

"We won't know if we don't get on the road."

They loaded the car, looked up to Simon's window a couple times for dramatic effect for the men watching them, then left the parking lot.

• • •

"You stay here and follow Simon. Their brief argument last night might have just broken up the group," said the driver, pulling his hoodie over his head.

"Yes, sir, I'll wait for an hour, then go to his room if he doesn't come out."

"Call for a pickup. I believe Carson's team is in the area."

The passenger exited the car, grabbed his shoulder bag from the back seat, and entered the hotel lobby. He took a complimentary newspaper and sat on a couch in the reception area.

• • •

Jeff drove the windy roads from England into Wales. At eleven, he found a small roadside restaurant and stopped. They ate lunch, watching out the window for their tail.

Tom texted Simon, "*Right on cue.*"

"*Kk*" appeared on Tom's screen a minute later.

With the meal eaten, Tom and Jeff drove for another sixty miles. Jeff slowed the car. He watched his rearview mirror, and a vehicle appeared over the last hill. He slowed his speed, then took a sharp right turn. The tree line hid their car. Jeff turned his car and stopped it, blocking the road. Within a minute, headlights brightened the bark on the trees and a vehicle made the turn. The car's nose dipped as the driver slammed on the brakes. Tom ran to the car, waving his arms. The vehicle reversed away, but stopped as a third car blocked it from behind. Simon got out of the passenger side. He opened the back door and pulled out a hunting rifle.

The driver of the car, trapped and blocked on the road, looked over his shoulder. His head spun, looking for a place to move. Giving up, he stopped his car.

A man in a blue tunic stepped out.

Simon glanced at Tom and Jeff. He mouthed, *"Blue tunic?"*

Tom shrugged his shoulders.

"Let's keep those hands where we all can see them. Get them up over your head," Simon commanded. He raised the rifle towards their captive.

"Please, turn around and place your hands on the roof of your car."

Jeff patted him down. He pulled a Browning pistol from his chest holster and a knife from under the sleeve on his left forearm.

"Are you MI6? Isn't this the pistol they use as standard issue?"

"Who are you?" Tom said, looking at him from across the roof of the car.

"My name's Nigel. That's not important right now. The men in hoodies will arrive soon. They'll kill me and, probably this time, you too."

"Simon, did you get the ties?" asked Tom.

"In the back of the car."

Jeff quickly retrieved them and approached their prisoner. "I'm going to lower your left arm then your right," said Jeff. He took Nigel's arms and brought them behind his back and pulled the ties tight around his wrists. Simon opened the back door of Nigel's car and Jeff placed him inside.

Simon's driver finally stepped out. "Tom, this is my cousin Carl," said Jeff.

"Nice to meet you," said Tom.

"Jeff, I wasn't expecting all this. I'd like to leave? Even with everything Simon told me on the way here, I still can't believe I just witnessed a kidnapping."

"Thanks for all your help. Yes, you can go. But not a word to anyone about this," said Jeff.

"Don't worry, no one would believe me, anyway."

"So, what do we do now?" asked Tom.

"First thing is, we need to move these cars. We've been lucky no one has shown up."

Jeff drove his car, followed by Tom driving Nigel's, with Simon and Nigel in the backseat. They drove a mile up the road and pulled over.

They gathered behind the cars. "So, what's the plan now? I didn't think it would be so easy."

"I know," Tom said, smiling.

"It was too easy, I think. And he has a blue tunic. Didn't they help Al? I was expecting black hoodies," said Jeff.

"And when they appeared in Germany, it looked like they were there to help?" said Jeff.

"Who knows how many people are after us? Just because they helped Al and then us in Germany doesn't make them allies," said Simon. "Maybe they need us too."

"No, you're right. It only means they aren't working with the black hoodies," said Tom.

A car approached, slowed, and passed.

They searched Nigel's car, finding his wallet and phone.

"You guys should look at this," said Tom.

They gathered behind Tom. "I'm fairly sure none of them are legal here." They looked in the trunk. Three M-16 rifles were under a blanket Tom had removed.

"I wouldn't think they would be legal in too many places, certainly not Canada," said Simon.

Tom looked around, checking for cars, before lifting out a rifle.

"Put it back before someone comes around the corner," said Simon. "Look, two tunics too, and other clothes in this bag." He searched through the bag. "No hoodies."

"So, what are we going to do with him?" asked Simon. He closed the trunk and looked at Tom.

"His wallet has a driver's license and a credit card. Nothing else," said Jeff.

"Give me his phone," said Tom.

Jeff tossed it to Tom. He caught it, fumbled with it, and dropped it on the road. He shook his head and picked up the phone.

Leaning Nigel forward, he held the phone to Nigel's thumb. It unlocked. "Let's see what we have here. First, I need to change the password so we can look into it later." He worked on the password, then pulled out the SIM card.

With the phone secure, he opened the photo app and scrolled through photos of the three of them in farmers' fields, at multiple pubs and around town.

"We need these photos. It's like our vacation photos. He's been following us since you arrived, Simon," said Tom. "Okay, let me check his emails. Nothing but emails from a CM. I'll forward them all to the podcast's email later."

"Forward them to Al. They know who he is, but he can also print them as he receives them. I've a feeling they'll never make it to your email," said Jeff.

"Good call." He replaced the SIM card and forwarded the emails to Al as Jeff texted Al to print them immediately.

Next, Tom scrolled through the text messages. "A lot of code words and coordinates."

Simon pulled out his phone and snapped photos of the screens. "I think they could be where the crop circles are appearing, or where the kids are coming from."

Tom continued to open apps.

"We need to move. I have a bad feeling about standing on the side of the road. He wasn't the guy who was watching us last night," said Simon. "The black hoodies could appear at any moment."

"What are we doing with this guy? I can't and I don't think either of you has the stomach to take him into a field and pop one in his head," said Jeff.

"Not me," said Tom.

"Me either," said Simon. "Do we let him go?"

"I guess we can keep his wallet and his phone," said Jeff.

"No, we need to question him. Let's get in the car and ask him some questions."

Simon and Jeff climbed in the back with Nigel.

Jeff opened Nigel's tunic and pulled it down to his wrists.

"What are you doing, Jeff?" asked Tom.

"No tattoos. No markings at all. I thought maybe he would have the same tattoo as some others." He pulled the tunic back over Nigel's shoulders.

"Okay, so here we sit. You have been following us around for over a month. What's your story?"

"I have no story."

"Huh, we think you do. You're kidnapping kids from their families and killing some in a sacrifice to your god. You have destroyed families and ruined property. I think there's a story," said Simon.

"You have no evidence of that. We have saved those kids. We have only one God to serve, the Creator." He sat up straight and looked all three men in their eyes. "You have no clue what you have opened by your podcast and investigation. This was not intended for the world to learn about. Now that it's exposed, you might have started the end times."

"Enlighten us, please," said Tom.

Nigel turned and looked out the window. "That field of sheep. Say that's the population of the planet. Most live a long life not knowing what is on the other side of the fence. They are fed, comforted and live an uneventful life as long as they do as they are told. They have walls, but always with a false sense of security. Then there are sheep that will push the limit and try to fight the farmer on when to eat and how to live, not wanting to be in the system. But with a little force from the farmer and other sheep, they turn away from the fence and give up. Every once in a while, the farmer comes and takes a couple of sheep away. It's noticed, but the other sheep let it happen because it's not them. They go on with life, all the while quietly worrying that they could be next. They look around and can see more of the world but choose not to, only wanting to see what is inside their fenced field. Then there's you three, you push against the wall. Trying to get to the other side of it. I suggest you go back to the herd and mingle. Live your lives, put the blinders back on. It's an easier life. I know a few that have made it over the fence—they lose their security, food and place to sleep because the predators wait by the fence for the brave. The brave inside the walls become the vulnerable outside the wall."

Simon shook his head and tapped his watch.

"You all are on the fence right now. Today, you will have to decide to go back or take that leap off into the unknown."

"Let me guess, you're the farmer?" said Tom.

"No, no," he laughed, "I'm an old sheep. I escaped the field a long time ago. I'm here to help you guys, protect you from the predators on this side of the wall. Take you to the others that made it over the fence a long time ago."

"You're taking us somewhere? Huh. You're the one with his hands tied," said Simon. "What if we want to see the farmer?"

"Oh, you don't. Once you leave the field, the farmer has no way of getting you back. Unlike the parable Jesus told of the lost sheep, no one's coming to bring you to safety."

"Can we stop talking about sheep and farmers? You're wasting time. I assume you have colleagues on their way. What are you involved in?" asked Tom.

"I'm, we're all involved now. It's an ancient practice going back to the beginning of time. It's all about the blood and who controls it. Untie me. You know I'm not the bad guy. You know we helped your friend Al. I'm one of the good guys," said Nigel. "I'm here to protect you and get you to safety. If you want to see what you have been searching for, untie me and I will take you there. Or you can go back to your jobs, and frankly, boring lives. Untie me and we go our separate ways."

"Really?" said Simon.

"I'm just trying to give you some understanding without revealing more than I can right now. Until you are at..."

The back window shattered, covering them in pieces of glass. Nigel slumped over, falling onto Simon's lap.

A black sedan sped away from them.

Tom and Jeff jumped out of the vehicle, but the car was already hidden behind a turn.

Looking down at his blood covered shirt, Simon gasped for breath. Then his eyes settled on Nigel's head in his lap. Blood ran from a small hole at the base of his skull.

Tom opened Simon's door and pulled him from the vehicle. He fell on his back on the gravel and grass. Simon's hands searched for a bullet wound. He looked up at Jeff and Tom standing at his head.

"Simon, you're all right. It's Nigel's blood over you. Simon, take a breath."

"I was shot."

"No, Simon. They shot Nigel. You're covered in his blood."

"No, I felt the bullet hit me. *It hit me.*"

Jeff leaned into the car. He looked on the seat, then the floorboard. The blood from Nigel was pooling on the floor. He picked up the bullet and held it over Simon's head. "Here, it must have bounced off you after passing through Nigel."

Simon sat up and looked into the car. "He died on my lap. What are we doing here? I think we should get back in with the other sheep."

"I think we just landed on the wrong side of the fence. There's no going back. Only now we don't have him to protect us from the predators."

"What about the car and him? Our fingerprints are all over this car. And now you're holding the bullet," said Simon. he was on his feet pacing beside the car.

"First, we need to clean you up. You can't be seen like this," said Tom.

"I have a first aid kit. It should have some wipes," said Jeff.

"I can change my clothes, despite that, what will we do with this car and him?"

Simon wiped the blood off his face, neck, and arms. He changed his clothes and leaned on the trunk of Jeff's car.

"What do we do? Where do we go now and what are we doing with all this stuff?" said Simon.

• • •

They moved Nigel from the back seat into the trunk. Standing around, they noticed a farmer in the distance bouncing through his field. He drove to them and waved. Tom waved back and Simon pointed and kicked the front tire of Nigel's car, then gave him a thumbs up. Simon thought about knocking him out and stealing his tractor to pull the car and its passenger into the valley in the distance. He kept the suggestion to himself, assuming Tom might think it was a good idea.

They watched as the farmer drove away. "I think we burn it to the ground. There was a petrol station back about five kilometers. We could get a couple of jerry cans and light this car up," said Jeff.

"The right thing to do is to report it. But I think we are too far down this rabbit hole. I hate to say it, but Jeff might be right," said Simon.

"Can't we just leave it off the side here? Let someone drive by and report it?"

Simon leaned on the car. "Tom, think about it, we've all been in the car. Forensics will find our prints, hair, something. We have a car with rifles in the trunk, a guy in a blue tunic dead with a bullet hole in his head. Looking at the bullet, it's close to what his M-16s shoot. We have no way of wiping the car down, cleaning off any evidence of ourselves. I vote burn it."

Tom looked over the fields of green.

"Honestly, Tom, unless you have a better idea, I think it's our only option," said Simon.

"Why don't we drive it over to that pull out? It seems like a place you would stop to look over the valley. We could park it behind the hedges."

"Okay, you two move the car. I'll get the petrol. We need to seriously look at what we're doing when we get home. Now we're breaking laws and not just speeding or running reds," said Jeff.

Simon laughed at him. "Little late for that, I would think."

"I'll be right back," said Jeff.

• • •

Tom sat in the passenger seat and searched through Nigel's phone. His browser history had searches for restaurants in several cities they had all visited.

Simon looked over the valley of green grass and stone walls, thinking. The mountains beyond glowed in the sunshine.

"I think we need to get home. I don't think I need to see another circle right now. Plus, getting out of Wales and away from this little crime scene may benefit us."

"I fully agree," said Tom, working through Nigel's phone. "Simon, Simon, I might have something. I'm going to need to connect his phone to my computer, but I think I can download information from here to his past locations."

Jeff pulled up to the car. "Got it. Follow me. I found a more secluded area to do the deed."

Simon drove Nigel's car, following Jeff along a dirt road hidden by a hill and trees. They stopped the cars and Jeff lifted out two jerry cans. Simon took one from him and splashed its contents on the seats, dashboard, and floor of Nigel's car. Jeff opened the trunk and doused it in fuel.

"Do you have enough?" asked Tom.

"Yeah, use the rest in the engine compartment and on the paint."

They emptied their cans and tossed them into the car.

"Well, this is the craziest thing I've ever done in my life," said Jeff.

"It's up there," said Tom.

"Who has a match?" asked Simon.

They looked at each other.

"No way."

"I've got a flare in the trunk. I'm sure that will help," said Jeff.

CHAPTER THIRTY-TWO

Tom sat at his desk, with his computer connected to Nigel's phone. Using a software program, he downloaded the information from the phone to his hard drive. As the photos flashed on his screen, he thought about how many places Nigel had been and if his bosses knew he had recorded so much of his travels. He spent the day working through files, photos, and apps. Many had tracked and saved the locations Nigel had been in the last month. Tom used the information to follow him as he shadowed them to France and then Germany. He had been to the restaurants and hotels they had visited. After three hours of digging, he found what he was looking for. A location Nigel had visited three times between chasing them around.

He disconnected the phone and sat back in his chair. Five minutes later, he dozed off.

Simon entered the room and looked at Tom. He was leaning back in his office chair. His head had rolled to his left with his mouth wide open.

Deciding to let him sleep, Simon exited the room. Out of the corner of his eye, he was sure he saw a figure by his bedroom door.

Veiled, they're still watching.

He went to the kitchen, looking behind himself periodically. He made a meal for supper. Peeling a potato, he heard a thud from upstairs. Then footsteps running down the stairs.

"Simon?" called out Tom.

"Kitchen."

"Look, look at this." Tom tossed Nigel's phone to him. "Check out the text message and then email."

Simon looked down at the phone.

"We need you back to base. Michael will replace you. You have been compromised," Simon said out loud.

"Now read the email."

"How do I get to it?"

Tom took the phone back and swiped his finger over it.

"This one, with the subject line: *Tom, Simon, Jeff.*"

"What?"

Simon looked at the phone, then back at Tom.

"Read it."

Simon took the phone.

Hello Gents, It seems you just won't go away that easily. I can assure you, the children are safe and happy and, as you know, they get to spend time with their families. It's unfortunate they have the blood of the gods, but we are all burdened from the day we are born to the day we return home. Please understand when you see a blue tunic, we are there to help, not hurt. If you can help us take one of the black hoodies, I would forever be indebted to you three.

Simon, I know your past haunts you with your family and drinking, but we all live with our decisions daily. Being the hero now will not change the past. So the children need to stay with me. Nigel was there to help you meet with me. Did he not tell you about the sheep? Now you are on the outside, with no guidance.

"Call Jeff. I'm reading that letter as a threat," said Simon. "We need to release a podcast."

Simon handed the phone back to Tom. He ran his hand through his hair. "What do we do now? I'm more curious than ever to know what's on this side of the fence."

"I called Jeff. We all need to talk. I have more information."

•   •   •

Jeff arrived a half hour later. Simon had a small meal ready for their talk. Everyone sat at the kitchen table, and as Simon brought the food to the table, Jeff read the text and email.

By the time he finished the email, he had lost all the color in his face, and his hands were shaking.

"Like sheep in the field," said Jeff. He looked out the window. A shadow passed over it.

"If you're out, we understand, but remember, we have three families who are looking to us to find their kids," said Simon.

"But like the email said, the kids are happy and get to see their families," said Jeff.

"Come off it. Do you think signing to your kids in another dimension or something is the same as touching them, holding them and being with them?" said Tom.

Jeff shrugged his shoulders.

"It's not Jeff, *it's not*. Take it from someone with experience," said Simon. "Whether it's a different dimension or a video call, *it's not the same.*"

Jeff sat and looked at the food in front of him—mashed potatoes and sausages with baked beans. He smiled at the food, then looked up. "My Nan made this for me every Saturday night for supper. She passed last year from cancer in her blood." He chuckled to himself. "I think this meal is a sign from her to keep searching. According to Charles, this golden blood would have saved her."

"Jeff, it was all we had in the fridge," said Simon.

"Let it be, Simon, let it be," Tom said.

They talked about the email and text. Tom was the first to finish his food. He wiped his mouth and stood. "Be right back."

He returned with his laptop and a photo.

"Can you both see this?"

They nodded as they chewed. "This photo was taken two years ago. It's Nigel. I can't identify the man in the white lab coat. The building behind them is a manor located close to Stonehenge. It's privately owned. I searched for the property on Google Earth. It shows nothing there, just a low-resolution image of fields."

"What do you mean by that?" Simon asked.

"It shows fields and trees, no house, no fence line, just untouched land," said Tom.

"Nigel visited this property three times in the last month. He just stopped there for a picnic?"

"Not at all," said Simon, sitting forward. "What about an underground bunker?"

"The text message makes it sound like he's part of a security detail or team. So follow me here." He moved his screen to Google Maps. "Here's the street view."

"It's just a laneway."

"Publicly owned though. As we move towards the property, we are in high resolution, but watch. See it?"

"There's nothing there."

"Better than that. I did some digging, and Google reported a glitch with the camera on this one taken in 2015. But if you go back to 2012, they also did a drive by, and that time there's nothing but fields and trees."

"I guess we're leaving early tomorrow?" asked Jeff.

"No, we need to plan and prepare for this," said Simon. "We're not strolling up to this place and knocking on the door trying to sell girl guide cookies."

Tom looked at him quizzically.

"Figure of speech from Canada, I guess."

They sat quietly at the table. Jeff scrolled through his news feed and gasped. "Well, lads, it looks like we can add to our death count, again. Talking to us can be bad for your health. I was checking the news in Germany since we hadn't heard from Charles. Looks like he passed from a car accident yesterday. The news article says his front tire ripped open on debris on the road. He lost control of the vehicle and hit a bridge support. Dead on the scene."

•   •   •

Tom connected to the live stream the next morning and welcomed his listeners to a special advance release of the news they brought back from Germany. They spoke of all the things that happened in Germany. There was no mention of the trip to Wales, or the body and car they burned. He wrapped up the podcast with a note of a delay in the next release because of other work the team had.

He spent an hour cleaning up the live podcast for advertising and sent it out to the internet. Checking the numbers for the downloads from the last two releases, it astonished him that the numbers had tripled.

• • •

While Tom worked on the podcast, Jeff and Simon headed to the library in Manchester to research the estate. They arrived and parked in the lot where, just a couple of weeks ago, they met their biggest fans. Simon walked directly to the library, and Jeff looped around, stopping at a coffee shop, watching where Simon entered. After ten minutes, he entered the library, meeting Simon in the history section.

"No one followed you in," said Jeff. "But who knows, I might have been."

"No, it didn't feel like I had people watching me. I'm sure they know where we are."

They looked through books and documents, searching for any known history of the large estate.

Simon approached Jeff with a thick book under his arm. "Jeff," he whispered. "Come look at this. I think this is what we're looking for."

They found a table in a corner away from other library patrons. He opened the book to the middle.

"This is it—I believe." He pointed to a black-and-white photo of a large brick building. The chimneys were billowing smoke, and a group of eight people stood by the main door, dressed in late eighteen-century clothes. He turned the page, revealing a color photo of the same building. The landscaping had changed and twelve people posed in front of the door. Jeff leaned in for a closer look.

"Turn the page back." Simon turned back to the black-and-white photo. "Back again."

"What is it?"

"I know the black-and-white photo is a little grainy, but is that not the same man in both photos?"

Simon flipped the pages back and forth. "It can't be."

"Oh, I think we both know it can't be, but my eyes are saying it can. Look closely. He's the same height and build, hair is the same too."

"These photos were taken," he glanced at the notes under the photo, "eighty years apart. How can it be? His son, or grandson?"

"We now have photos of the place and, if we do more reading, we'll have a history too. Built in the late 1400s and early 1500s. Named after the original owner, it's called Chapwilk Manor."

"Well, let's hit the computers and see what else is available for this. There must be maps of the area," said Jeff.

They searched the library and internet. The library had four books mentioning the manor. Jeff hunted them down while Simon continued searching the computer for details on the manor. He sent a text to Tom, *"Will be here for the day. We have found some good information. If you have time, look up Chapwilk Manor, see what you can find."*

Simon went back into the wing of the library, looking for Jeff. In the third aisle, Jeff was chatting with a young lady. Bent over, he was picking up papers scattered on the floor. Simon stepped away and gave him space. After ten minutes, the lady appeared with her arms full of papers and an innocent smile on her face. Jeff followed her, hugging three comprehensive books. "I'll call you tomorrow. Good luck with your thesis." He looked at Simon as his cheeks reddened. A smile appeared on his face as he raised and lowered his eyebrows.

Simon shook his head and chuckled.

"What? I bumped into her in the aisle. I backed into her."

"Uh-huh."

"Hey, it was fate."

Simon rolled his eyes and laughed. "Oh, to be young again."

"Listen, in a way, it was fate. They lock this book in the rare book area." He picked up a large ancient book. "This is a copy, but I saw the original. We can use the original once we review this and find what pages we need to view. She, Bethany, got me into the room. And yes, I got her number. So, win—win."

"Win—win. Let's see what we find. Right now, it's a win for you."

They opened the books and looked for Chapwilk Manor. The first book had a couple of pictures of the well-kept grounds, fountains, and flower gardens. It showed the wooded area. *"The men would cut wood and hunted for foxes."* The note under the photo stated.

Two pages after the photos was a drawing of the building with Gus Chapwilk. They completed construction in 1501, and he commissioned the piece during the summer of 1502.

"Simon, is it me or..."

"I see it too. It looks like the same man in the other two photos. It could be the family resemblance?"

"Let's keep digging. Look at this. In 1508, a crop circle appeared in the gardens. That's an artist's rendition. Looks familiar, four circles."

"It does. It looks like the one that brought you here."

They opened the rare book and searched through it. Jeff found a section of the manor's history, up to 1850.

"I'll read through this. Can you run your fingers through the last book?" said Jeff.

Simon checked his phone, looking for a response from Tom. There was nothing. He found three pages of information on the manor. He scribbled notes in his notebook. The more he read, the messier his handwriting appeared.

"Simon, what are you finding?"

"Some strange things happened at that place and in the area. Sightings of strange lights at night, before electricity. Crops ruined by circles and dead people found in them. Oh, and to top it off, here's a photo of an oil painting from 1698 of the owner who looks a lot like the man in all the photos we've seen. It says the original owner had twelve children with his second wife. Only four survived to the age of eighteen. All history ends in 1850, in this book."

"This book gives the family line who owned the house. It stayed in the family except for a thirty-year span in the 1700s when the king took ownership of it. At his death, a questionable one to be sure, the new monarch quickly returned the manor to the family. It says here the original owner's uncle was Vlad the Impaler, or as we call him, Dracula."

"What? Where does it say that?" Simon read it to himself, his lips moving with the words he read.

"This family has some strange notes on history. Their and the manor's history seems to end, at least here, in 1850. All I can find is the odd photo, and they are odd. The maps show rolling hills and a small forest on the property," said Simon.

He pulled his phone out. "Nothing from Tom. I texted him two hours ago."

CHAPTER THIRTY-THREE

The text alert on Nigel's phone chirped. Tom opened it and read the email from undisclosed, "*Tom, you and your friends have done well. It's been years, forty or more, since we've had guests. We look forward to your visit. But be careful, the men in black hoodies can't follow you.*"

Tom replied, "*We're coming for you and the kids.*"

Sitting in his living room, the sun warmed the room and brightened the couch. He heard a knock on his back door. He stood to answer the door when the sound of glass shattering came from the back of his house. The sound of boots crunching on glass and men talking came from his rear room. He sat back on the couch and waited. The door to his living room opened, and a large man in a black hoodie, holding a rifle, entered the room.

"Found him!" he yelled over his shoulder. Two men appeared behind him.

They stepped into the living room. Two of them lowered their guns and the small ginger haired man sat in the chair across from Tom.

"Here," Tom tossed the cell phone at him. "I guess this is what you're looking for?"

"What? No, I don't want your cell phone." He tossed it back.

"We're looking for so much more."

"Are you pulling the trigger today? Or, as we believe, you need us alive and well to find what you've been looking for long before we started looking for it," said Tom.

They looked at him. "Here's the deal I have. Checks for you and your friends, a million pounds each. All you need to do is tell us everything you've found and the location of Gus," said the ginger.

"Who is Gus?" Tom asked. "We're so close, your bosses will throw money at us. Add a zero to each check, and I'll present it to my colleagues. Your bosses steal children from their families because of their blood. They kill the ones who don't have the golden blood. How many children have you taken? What country are you working for? *Is it the church?*"

"Last offer, Tom. Work with us to end this kidnapping ring. We're the good guys here."

Tom looked out the window. Men in blue tunics were running up his pathway. "Well, here comes a group in blue tunics that believe they are the good guys. Since we're all here now, let's discuss it, unless there are more good guys that wear tartan patterns?"

"We have company," said a large bald man, entering the living room. Tom looked behind him. Two men in blue tunics were in his hallway, hidden, watching from behind a veil. They watched as the men in hoodies ran out of the living room.

There was a knock at the front door. Tom could hear the people on the outside work the lock.

"Hold the front door closed," the ginger said to the large bald man. "Tom," he yelled from the hallway. "This little game of cat and mouse is going to get a lot worse for you and your friends. These men in blue tunics are the ones you should fear. We'll try to protect you, but we need to know you'll cooperate with us."

"So, you say. It seems these other good guys are here now," said Tom. "I don't think I'm ready to pick sides just yet."

Without another word, a man in black tied Tom's hands behind his back. Then, as Tom tried to kick him, he tied Tom's feet to his radiator in the corner. Tom listened as the men in hoodies ascended the stairs to his studio.

Finally, the group in blue tunics entered the room. One retrieved Nigel's phone as the other bearded man watched the hallway.

"Hey, aren't you going to untie me? Wait. You're the good guys, I thought. So, help me." He heard the front door close and footsteps moving around his studio. "Hello? If you're the good guys, why tie me up and ruin thousands of dollars of equipment? Are we going to discuss the money again?" There was silence. He listened for footsteps or doors closing—nothing.

Where did they go?

• • •

The panicked voice of Jeff snapped Tom out of his daydream, calling his name. The living room door opened, and Jeff stepped in. He dropped to his knees and pulled out his pocketknife, attempting to slice through the plastic ties. The plastic had a metal band his knife couldn't cut through. "Do you have a metal cutter?"

"In the shed out back. The key is on the hook by the door."

Jeff left the room, brushing shoulders with Simon as he entered.

"All right, Tom?"

"Sure, this is how I planned on spending my day. The guys in black offered us each a million pounds to work with them. I told the guy no—we wanted ten million."

"We can't be bought," said Simon.

"Then the guys in blue showed up. They're supposed to be helping us. Sure. They came in, took Nigel's phone, and left. *Left me tied up.* That's teamwork."

"Now the guys in black are saying they're the good guys and the ones in blue are not," said Tom.

Jeff returned with large bolt cutters. "What do you need this for? We've nothing as nice as this at the station."

"Used it in a past life," said Tom.

"What did you do before we met?" Jeff asked, cutting the ties.

After shaking his hands, Tom moved to the more comfortable couch. He twisted and stretched his back before sitting.

"I spent three years in our government intelligence sectors before I moved to an IT job. Before they fired me for, well, stuff."

"White collar stuff?" asked Simon.

"Yeah, that's it. White collar stuff. The odd hacking of a system, cutting of locks, and maybe you could say I hacked into a small government system. Moved some money around and released some documents. Let's just say from where I came and the career I had, maybe a lot of what I talk about on my podcast isn't so much conspiracy as hidden truths." Tom shook his phone in the air. "These devices are going to be the end to freedom. All conversations, locations and thoughts are on here. Anyone can take them without a reason. Look how easy it was to track Nigel."

"That explains the computers upstairs," said Simon.

"Has anyone been up there?"

Both Simon and Jeff shook their heads.

"Let's go. Give me the bolt cutters."

They followed Tom up the stairs. He checked each room before entering the studio.

"What are you looking for?" asked Jeff.

"So, let me tell you what happened, then you can tell me what you found." They sat in the studio while Tom explained his day—ending it with, "The hoodies all came up here, but no one came back down the stairs, not that I can remember."

Tom motioned Simon and Jeff to the hallway. "Don't mention what you found," he whispered. "Would you guys mind cleaning up downstairs, and I can see what damage they did in here?" he said with a normal volume. Then he whispered, "I'll run my bug finder over the house, and I would suggest once we sit down to talk, we put our phones away and go with no form of electronics."

"Yes, they're following us in person, but I think also electronically," whispered Simon.

Jeff and Simon cleaned up the broken glass from the back door window and cut a piece of plywood Tom had in the shed to fit into the opening. Jeff moved the cars into the back laneway and locked them. Simon cleaned the kitchen. He wondered why they would spill cereal on the counter and mash all the bananas.

Why not?

. . .

Tom turned on his computers. The lessons he learned from the last break-in saved him this time. He moved his hard drives into secure cases, preventing magnets, water, or any other force from damaging them. Microphones were damaged, and they broke two keyboards in half. Hidden in the back of the closet, he retrieved a couple of spare keyboards and turned on his computers. The extra thousand pounds he spent on the boxes paid for themselves. With the computers working, he took his bug finder from a cupboard hidden behind boxes. He walked through the upstairs, searching. Hidden in the bathroom closet under a stack of towels, he found a microphone. Examining the small bug, he assumed it had to be very sensitive if they believed it could pick up a conversation from under a stack of towels in a closet.

Finishing the sweep upstairs, he searched the main floor. He found two devices—one in the kitchen, in a box of crackers, and the other in a coat pocket.

. . .

They decided it would not be wise to stay at Tom's house to discuss their next move. They gathered their notes and laptops before heading to the pub.

The table in the corner where they could see everything, not only the pub and its patrons, but out the large window to the street, was available.

With a few drinks and Simon's new favorite snack, chips and curry, they reviewed the information they had gathered at the library. With his laptop opened, Simon spun it around to face Jeff and Tom. He showed Tom some photos from the library. He deliberately flipped back and forth through the shots.

"Anything look familiar, Tom?" asked Simon.

"No way, how's that possible?" asked Tom.

"See that person there?" Simon tapped the screen with his pen. "He's the one we said has been in every photo. I mean, every photo where there's a picture of people standing by the front door. Even pieces of art had him in it. Logically, it can't be the same person. The images are spread over hundreds of years."

"Could it be, though? We've seen some strange things since the three of us began this investigation," Tom asked, still flipping between the photos.

"That would make this man, well, five hundred and something years old. Yes, we've seen some strange stuff, but that's impossible. Charles looked maybe twenty years younger than his actual age. But this just makes little sense. Now we *are* going back to Biblical times where they lived to be almost a thousand years old."

"*The blood*," said Tom.

"Why don't we head to London to the library there and see what new information we can find?" said Jeff.

"We can research all we want. But we know where the actual answers are," said Simon.

"We go knock on his door," said Tom.

"I agree. I don't see any other way to what's actually happening on the property. We'll have one shot at it, and if we fail, I believe we'll be buried somewhere on the property, so we need to be sure it's what we want," said Simon.

"But the email you received, you said, almost welcomed us," said Jeff, looking at Tom.

"If it isn't a trap," said Tom.

"We know of at least two parties interested in what we are investigating," Simon said. "The way I see it right now, we don't know who to trust. But what we know is we have a location where the people in tunics seem to be based."

"I assume the place will be secure, too. All kinds of toys to prevent people from getting on the property. Especially if the black hoodies can't access it," said Tom.

"Yeah, dogs and guns are the two toys that worry me," Jeff said, as he grabbed some chips.

Tom shuffled papers and placed an aerial drawing of the property and adjoining properties. He gave Jeff and Simon a copy to review. "As you can see, the back of the property is landlocked with other farmers' fields. The only piece open to the public is a road at the front of the property. We could just drive up and knock on the front door? It's a small road. I assume it has cameras up and down it." He tapped on the map. "There's only one way onto that road and one way out. You could say it's their private laneway from this point where the neighboring farm has access to its fields. It doesn't look wide enough to turn a car around. If we were to use it, I would suggest we walk to the manor."

"Do we want to talk to the neighboring farmers? See if they have any information on the manor?" asked Jeff.

"We could, but that would reveal that we're in the area. I think we need to be invisible, if possible. To do that, instead of the road, I think the best way to get on the property is from this farmer's field. Look at this here. The stream that runs through the manor's property loops back around to here. The land between the two properties looks to be split by the curve of the stream. That little peninsula of land is split right down the middle. It's a strange agreement. The stream flows through both properties. We could use it to get in," said Tom. "I think we start our adventure here at this castle ruin that's open to the public. We can make our way through the gardens to the back of the property, then travel through these fields. If we make it to the woods here." He tapped on the map. "I believe we are on the manor's property. Then it's a quick skip, hop and jump to the building."

"If only it would be that simple," said Simon. They heard the concern in his voice.

"If this place is as secure as we think, you would assume they have the woods, stream and fields monitored." Jeff pointed to the stream.

"Possibly, but I feel they prefer to stay low key. I don't believe they have ten-foot barbed wire fences around the place or armed guards every fifty feet," said Simon.

"I agree, but they likely have technology we might not be aware of."

"True. We've seen plenty of it," said Simon.

Jeff went back to the bar and brought three more drinks back. He placed them in front of Simon and Tom.

Simon stared at Tom's glass of beer. "Tom, could I..."

"NO! I know what you are thinking. There's no chance Simon, I'll be the one letting you drink."

Jeff looked at Simon. "Simon, stay strong, we are about to crack this investigation. Stay strong for the kids. We can get rid of these and drink pop too, if it will help you."

Simon hung his head and nodded. "Moment of weakness. Thank you both for the support."

"When I was at the bar, I'm not sure, but I think just out of sight of us is a car with two people sitting in it. I'm sure they were there when I picked up the plate of chips, too."

"We're very popular, aren't we?" Simon said, smiling.

"Black hoodies or blue tunics?" asked Tom, as he gathered up his notes and maps.

"I couldn't see."

"Let's see how many of them are following us. We all leave at different times, and I'll leave out the back," suggested Simon.

"I think tomorrow we pack up and move towards the manor. We can spend two nights in different hotels on our way to the property. That allows us to see what kind of detail is on us. We might have to take them out on the way," said Tom. "I know this can be expensive, but we should take rental cars and go three different directions. The podcast is making money now. I'll fund it."

"There's a rental place in Manchester that a sister of one officer I work with owns. We could get cars from her. She could let us know if anyone asked about us and, if so, feed them some false information."

"Okay, in the morning, book three cars. Each of you, take the map—we can meet here in three days." He pointed to a hotel close to the manor. "We should buy new, call as you go phones. Leave our phones at my place," said Tom.

"I'll pick up the phones and leave them for you two at the rental place," said Jeff. "I'll be on the road by eleven in the morning." He picked up his phone and called about the rentals.

"Okay, so tonight we leave as we normally would. I know we talked of splitting up, but there's no point anymore. We don't want to alert them to anything out of the ordinary."

"Now we need to discuss the hoodies versus the tunics. The tunics are helping us. I've seen them veiled a few times," said Simon. "As if they are observing us."

"Definitely, so we are involved in some fashion gang fight?" asked Tom. "Look at me. Unless there is a third group out there for the super casual ill-fitted fashion, I'm not sure I'm being recruited."

Jeff placed his phone on the table. "He's going to let me know by nine tonight about the cars," said Jeff.

"Okay, here's a theory. Follow me," said Tom. "The hoodie guys can't find the manor. Look at the trouble we're having."

"Could the technology surrounding the manor make it invisible?" asked Simon. He wrote a note in his book.

"Possibly. That's why the guys in the hoodies need us. For some reason, the tunics are protecting—helping or I don't know," said Tom. "They aren't working with the hoodies."

"I guess if we believe Nigel, he was prepared to take us to the manor. So why not send someone else to escort us?" said Jeff. "Is it now a test to see if we are truly willing to give up everything for this group?"

"Like a chivalry test?" asked Simon. "Or the lonely sheep lost to their shepherd?"

"I'm open to anything right now," said Tom. "I think if it comes down to it, we need to side with the tunics. None of us have seen them wandering around crop circles or kidnapping kids."

"Agreed," said Jeff. "But we should be careful. If Nigel was one of them, they could be seeking revenge."

Simon and Tom took their papers and laptops while Jeff went to the bar to settle the tab and survey the street.

They met at the bar. "Car's still there. When we leave, it's across the street, behind the moped." His phone chirped. "Looks like three cars are reserved."

"Perfect," said Simon. He looked out the window of the pub. "We could rush it and see what they're up to."

"I'm in."

"Yep, let's do it."

"Okay, I'll go to the driver's door. Jeff, you take the passenger side and Tom, you watch the street and back seat."

Simon held the door for the others to leave. They walked across the street. Simon made a sharp right turn and ran to the driver's door. He bent down and tapped on the window. The driver turned and looked at him with shock and confusion. Simon tapped again, then tried the door handle. The door opened. Reaching in, he grabbed the man by the shoulder. Jeff opened the passenger door and slid into the car. Behind the car, Tom took his post and surveyed the street. He tapped on the trunk, warning of two young lovers holding hands strolling along the sidewalk.

"What's the deal, mate?" Simon asked. He leaned into the stranger with his hand on the driver's chest. The man sat silent. His tall, slender build, plaid shirt and blue jeans differed from the others who had followed them.

"I think my friend asked you a question," said Jeff.

"What? I was just—just watching."

"We know you were just watching, watching us. Why?"

"No, no not you. Why would I watch you?"

"Look, you need to tell us why you've been sitting in your car in front of the pub we attend regularly."

"Who are you guys? Is one of you the guy she's cheating on me with?"

Simon looked across the car at Jeff. Jeff looked back at Simon and mouthed, "Oops." Simon released the handful of shirt he had in his hand.

"I think we made a mistake. Sorry, we thought you were someone else."

Jeff pulled himself out of the car, and Simon stood up and stepped back. "Sorry, mate. Honest mistake."

The driver was distracted as a lady, his lady, left the pub, hanging off the arm of another man. Jeff closed the door and moved back to Tom. "Let's go."

They headed to their car, passing a black four-door. Two men sat low in the back seat, watching as they passed.

CHAPTER THIRTY-FOUR

Jeff realized halfway through his trip to the hotel, he was being followed. In Oxbridge, he stopped and stayed with his cousin. Being the same build and height, they switched cars the next morning.

Corey, Jeff's cousin, pulled into his office complex. A car followed him to the lot. He stepped out of the rental car and waved, watching the driver hit the steering wheel and the passenger lift a phone to his ear. They pulled over and moved towards Corey on foot. Seeing the men rush towards him, he turned and ran to the front door of his building. He entered the main doors and showed identification to the security team, looking over his shoulder. The men who followed him had broken off their pursuit and walked back to their car. The passenger held his phone and was waving his free hand in the air.

· · ·

Jeff sped along the road to the rendezvous point to meet his friends. Being the youngest, he had to stop and check a paper map for directions. He grew up with a pleasant voice giving him directions through his phone's GPS app. Without it, he made a few wrong turns and backtracked twice, adding three hours to his drive.

· · ·

Tom and Simon sat on a park bench outside the hotel. "I forgot how dependent I've become on my phone for information and connection to others," said Tom.

"I know. I've reached into my pocket three times, thinking I could just text Jeff to see if he's okay. Going with the pay as you go phone was a smart decision."

They sat waiting. Then, with a honk and a wave, Jeff drove by them. A confused expression from Simon and Tom welcomed him. It wasn't the car they were expecting. Tom and Simon met him in the parking lot.

He stood by a silver Vauxhall and smiled. "You guys made it, okay? I had to pull a switch-a-roo this morning. They followed me."

"Are you okay?"

"Yeah, I just hope Corey is." He told them his story as he unloaded the car.

• • •

Simon parked his rental car in the visitor lot of the ruins of the ancient castle early the next morning. They took out their backpacks, Nigel's pistol, and a map. Each man put on their bags and looked at each other.

"All the phones stay in the cars," said Tom. He hesitated. "All in?"

Simon nodded. "All in."

"Yes, all in," Jeff said, hiding the gun under his coat.

They all embraced. Confident that what they were doing was right, they steeled themselves for what lay ahead. But without saying it, they each felt this could be the last time they would be together as one group. They were now heading to a manor, hidden from the public, to meet a man potentially five hundred years old.

"The next twenty-four hours will probably be the hardest of our lives." Simon pulled his baseball hat down on his head and took the first step. Tom patted Jeff on his shoulder and the three of them were off.

The castle greens had trails that snaked over the enormous property. They took the blue trail. The weather was cool with a threat of rain, keeping the trail light for use. They hiked through the trees and flower gardens in silence.

Simon pulled a map out of his coat pocket and confirmed their location. He pointed to an overgrown trail to their left. Checking the area, they turned off to the unused trail. Walking in single file, they pushed overgrown branches of trees and brush out of the way. They were quiet, each in their own thoughts.

After a kilometer's hike, they arrived at a fence. Simon pointed to their location on the map. They climbed over the wooden three-foot-high barrier. Simon sat on it. "Okay, three large fields to cross and then we hit the manor's property."

Jeff took the gun from inside his coat. "Locked and loaded."

"Okay there, *Rambo*," said Tom.

Tom took off his coat and sipped the water. "Let's go. We're a few hours away from finding the truth and, hopefully, a bunch of children."

Simon led, following the fence and then the stone wall dividing fields. The dark clouds and the light mist helped give them cover. Tom in the rear repeatedly looked around, feeling they were being followed. They hopped over another stone wall and walked up and down two rolling hills. The mist lifted, and the day brightened, exposing them in an open field.

Simon stopped and dropped to his knees. He put the map on the ground and looked at it, then up to the horizon. "Okay, we have this field to pass through, and then we'll be at the property. Tom, get your electronic finder out. I know it's a pointless question, but who else feels like we are being watched or have more in our travel party than the three of us?"

They both nodded at Simon.

Tom rummaged through his pack and pulled out a detector as dark clouds filled in above them. "I'm not convinced it'll work, but they said it should detect any electromagnetic fields within a few meters of us."

Simon paused and surveyed the dark clouds—visions of his kids played in his mind.

Love you, boys.

He questioned himself and what he was asking his friends to do for him and a couple of children they had never met. He breathed in and stood. "For the truth," he said. He looked at Jeff and Tom, then followed the stone wall. The sun poked through the clouds as they arrived at the manor's property.

Simon looked at the map, then at the property.

"Are you sure we're in the right spot?" asked Tom.

Simon looked back at where they had come, then across the field.

"How long was it since you used a map?" asked Jeff.

Simon studied the horizon. "No, this is it. This is the property. Look, the road is here on the map." He dug into his backpack and pulled out a piece of paper. "See, I printed this off Google Maps. We are roughly here. Look, there is the fence we walked along. Trace it back to the castle parking lot."

He ran his finger along the page.

"What are we getting into? The photo can't be that old, and it shows a small forest right here. All I see is a field of cut wheat. And a rolling hill."

"Well, we climb the hill and see what's waiting for us. Do you think..." Tom said.

"Do I think they can manipulate what we are seeing? An hour ago, I would say no. Now I'm not too sure."

Tom waved his electronic device in front of them as they hiked through the field. Exposed to anyone watching, they made their way up the hill.

"We walked all that? It didn't seem that far," said Jeff, looking over his shoulder. The castle ruins just a speck on the horizon. He was the first to reach the top. He stopped and crouched. "I found our forest," he said.

Tom and Simon sat beside him, winded. "Okay, the trees will hide us. I feel we should sprint to it from here. Are we worried about any detection devices picking us up?" asked Simon.

"Look at the field we're running through. To me, it looks like a minefield. No one has farmed it in years. It's not that big, but it definitely divides the properties," said Tom.

"You should lead, Tom," said Simon.

"Why should I lead?"

"You have the device," said Simon.

Tom looked at the field he would need to cross to access the woods. He waved his device. The digital numbers rose, then dropped. He pointed it to the forest area again. "There's something out there. It must be powerful if this is picking it up here."

"Mines?"

"I doubt it. Motion or vibration detectors. But you'd think wild animals would trigger those items. Just stay low and get to the woods quickly," said Tom. He crouched and sprinted to the tree line, listening for a gunshot and then an impact that would knock him over, but nothing came. Arriving at the tree line, he stood tight to a tree. Peering into the forest, there was no noise or motion. With his monitor held before him, a faint signal came from deeper in the trees. Checking again for any motion in the trees, he turned to Simon and Jeff and waved them over.

Simon sprinted to the woods, holding his hands up around his head, ready to deflect a punch, but thankfully, one never came. Once Simon arrived at the trees, Jeff left his location and darted to Simon and Tom. He tripped in a hole and, like a runner stealing second base, arrived at the tree line sliding on his belly.

"Safe," Simon called out.

Jeff looked up at him. Blood dripped off the tip of his nose.

"Graceful, Jeff, very graceful. Your nose is bleeding," said Tom.

He stood and wiped it on his sleeve. "Hopefully, this is the worst injury we incur on this little adventure."

• • •

Stepping deeper into the woods, they sensed the air change. It was heavier and humid. They cut their way through the small brush and old trees.

Simon checked the compass to keep them moving as straight as he could.

"Do we trust the compass?" asked Jeff. "It wasn't too reliable in some of the crop circles. They could use the same technology here to have us pace around in circles."

"You're right. I'm also trying to follow the sun when we have breaks in the tree canopy," said Simon.

After a half hour of struggling through the woods, they stumbled upon an opening. It was circular, with three rows of stones equally spaced. Tom whispered, "It looks like a giant target."

"What do you suppose they use this for?" asked Jeff.

Tom ran his hands along one stone, forming the outer circle. "Smooth, it's been worn down from years of wear."

Simon stood in the middle of the formation. He kicked at the pebbles in the center. "I would say a meeting place, maybe a Druid sanctuary? And sorry fellas, but it looks like this tricked the compass. We're off course, as whatever this formation is was pulling the compass needle to it." He abruptly stumbled backward and grabbed his head. Tom ran to him, grabbing his arm, slowly he helped Simon out of the circle.

Simon dropped to his knees. He looked around. "What happened? How am I here?"

Jeff looked at Tom, the concern on his face was mirrored on Tom's.

"Simon, take a minute," said Tom.

Simon took some water, then slowly got to his feet. "Maybe we go around this."

"There are two trails leaving here," said Jeff. He wanted to leave the area. He felt uncomfortable and sensed they were being watched.

"We should keep moving. We're already behind our schedule. It's like the maps aren't scaled right. We're covering more land than they show and it's taking more time," said Simon.

"Let me get a couple of photos first." Tom pulled out his instant camera and snapped some shots. His third picture called for the flash to help brighten the area.

"Did you see that?" Simon pointed and stopped just outside the circle. "Something reflected off your flash." He looked up into the trees. "Take the same photo again."

Tom snapped another photo.

Simon pointed into a tree. It had a dense cover of leaves, but one little opening was pruned to reveal a camera. "Smile lads, we're on camera," said Simon, waving at the camera.

"Great, so much for the element of surprise. Do we turn around?" asked Jeff.

"No, we continue and march into whatever is waiting for us. I've come too far to stop now."

"I agree. They want us to come to them, or else there would be an army of heavily armed men standing in front of us right now. *I guess this little adventure is entertaining you*?" Tom yelled, looking towards the camera.

"Let's get moving. It's after noon and we still have a ways to go." After a check of the map, Simon decided the trail to the right would be the most direct route.

$$\bullet \quad \bullet \quad \bullet$$

Within fifteen minutes, the trail widened. Birds sang and a cool breeze through the trees reminded Simon of the trails at Guelph Lake where he hiked with his kids when they were young. They would run ahead of him, laughing and chasing squirrels or chipmunks. In his own world for a moment, he stumbled into the back of Tom, who had suddenly stopped.

Tom lowered himself. "Quiet."

"What is it?" Jeff whispered, straining to see what got Tom's attention.

"I'm not sure. Stay here and..."

The brush ahead of them moved.

"Deer," Simon said. He stood watching deer cross ten meters in front of them. "You had me convinced we were getting shot."

Tom turned to Simon. "Roe deer, to be exact."

"I know it sounds crazy, but I feel with each bit of progress we make to the manor more people are watching us," said Jeff. "Like we are on some crazy survival show.

They began their trek again. "I feel it too," said Simon.

"What's that over there?" Tom asked. He pointed to his left. Through the trees was a dark area. The wind picked up, and the leaves rustled. Tom bent to see if he could get a better look. "Do we stay on the trail or divert to it?"

"I'm curious. It can't be thick dense trees, and look, the sky is blue, so it's not a dark cloud," said Simon.

Jeff took the first step—the others followed. The closer they got, the more curious they became as the area darkened.

"It's like when you play a video game and a couple pieces of the background don't load," said Jeff.

"Yeah, it's like someone didn't draw a part of the forest. I feel it's moving away from us as we walk towards it." Simon turned to see how far they had come off the trail. They had been walking for ten minutes, according to his watch. They arrived at the blackness—a large building covered with a paint that did not reflect any light. Tom stepped back and examined the roof. It was the same blackness. They moved around the building. Made of stone, likely dating to the same time they built the manor. It had no windows and a single door, made of steel on the opposite side of their approach. Simon could not see any trails leading away from the building. It was just a black box, ten meters square, randomly erected in the woods.

"Okay, this is strange. Does anyone have any idea what this is?" asked Jeff.

"My guess would be a safe house for the family. I bet if we could get inside, we would find a tunnel to the manor," said Simon.

"That's still seven kilometers or more away," said Tom, as he rubbed his hand on the stone covered with the black material.

"Do we try to get in or continue with the original plan?" asked Jeff.

"Or what if this is the cloaking device that hides the property from those men in black hoodies and the rest of the world?" said Tom.

While contemplating what to do, Simon took a bottle of water from his pack, took a drink, and offered it to Jeff. He gladly accepted the water and finished the bottle. Simon offered Tom another water bottle, but he brushed it aside. His attention drawn to the building and the door.

"Look, it must have a basement of some sort. The stones go into the ground," said Tom. "There's no door handle. There is no access to the building from the outside." He ran his hand around the frame of the door and across it. He pushed on a couple of stones to see if they would release the door.

Simon walked around the building again. He ran his hand over the stone wall. When he circled back to the door, Jeff had pulled himself up into a tree and was looking at the roof.

"The roof is black, too. I don't see a hatch or any form of access. The roof is newer than the walls," said Jeff. He jumped down. "Did anyone push on the door?" He pushed on it. Nothing moved. He tried with his shoulder. "It probably opens out. But the door is fit so well into its frame you can't grip it anywhere."

"Simon, where's your compass?" asked Tom.

He pulled it from his pant pocket and held it out. "Well, that's strange." They gathered around Simon's hand. The compass spun rapidly.

"Different from the circles. Keep it out and see where or when it returns to normal," said Tom. "We should go back to the trail and get through these woods before dark." Looking at his watch "It's already three? What?"

"No way. Tom, your watch..." Simon looked at his watch, then at the two men in front of him. "How?"

"I don't know. But let's get back to the trail to get out of the trees," said Jeff.

Returning to the trail, Simon was sure it took longer than the walk to the building.

Once back on the trail, Simon checked the compass. "It's stopped spinning, but the needle is still pointing back to the building."

They headed towards the manor quietly, each man in his own thoughts of what could be waiting for them.

· · ·

The shadows of the woods lightened ahead of them, and they hiked towards it. Simon, leading the group, increased his pace, looking at the light ahead. The group could see the edge of the forest. The tree canopy was thicker, and the songs of birds increased.

"Do you think people will be waiting for us when we step out from the protection of the trees?" asked Jeff.

"It wouldn't surprise me. I saw a couple of devices hanging from the trees as we walked the trail," said Tom.

Ten meters from the tree line, Simon stopped, took his pack off his back, and pulled out a pair of binoculars. Moving off the trail, he moved between the trees to the edge. He raised his binoculars and surveyed the property before him. Fields of wheat swayed in the western wind, and a stream separated the wheat fields from manicured grass and gardens that hid the manor over a rolling hill. In the distance, he saw the roof and chimneys of the manor. Smoke rose from several chimneys. Between them and the manor was the stream. A man stood with a fishing pole in his hand, his line connected to a bobber. It drifted with the stream's current. He reeled in his line and cast out again to his left, upstream.

"What do you see?" asked Jeff.

"I see a place I could retire at. From here, it looks peaceful. There's a guy fishing in the stream. He looks content."

"Do we approach him?"

"We could try, but he'll see us the minute we step out of the trees. We have the high ground here. The minute we step into the field, we'll stick out."

Simon waved his hand behind him. "Quiet."

"Why?"

Simon whispered, "A man in a blue tunic just appeared over the hill. He's heading towards the person fishing."

"That's a long stretch of fields to get across. Must be at least a kilometer to the stream alone," said Tom.

"Well, I would say we're at the right manor. Who else dresses in blue tunics to collect a person fishing?" said Jeff.

Simon watched as the two men interacted. The fisherman held up his hand and flashed an open palm with his fingers spread out. "Something is going on. I wonder if this guy was trespassing."

The man in the tunic shook his head and tapped his wrist. He picked up the white pail. The fisherman reeled in his line and quickly cast again. He was grabbed by his arm and pulled away from the stream's edge.

"I'm not sure, but these two look like they're going to fight in a second," said Simon.

The fisherman threw down his pole and stormed away from the other man. He followed the worn grass trail up the hill. Simon swung the binoculars back at the man in the tunic. He was talking into a small radio. When his conversation ended, he picked up the pole, reeled in the line, and with the pail in his other hand, followed the same trail over the hill.

"What was that all about?" asked Tom.

"Was that person—do you think he's a prisoner in the manor?" asked Jeff.

"That was just strange. It certainly wasn't a person trespassing. They knew each other," said Simon.

"Look at the time—he was getting the person for dinner. That could be it," said Tom.

They walked back to the trail and sat with their backs against trees. Jeff opened his pack and tossed everyone a bottle of water and a sandwich. "Do we wait for dusk before we cross the fields? I didn't expect to be out here at night."

"It's too late to go back now," said Tom. "I would rather face the manor than the forest and trails behind us."

"So, I guess we can wait till the sun goes down further and cross the fields. I'm curious to see what's hidden behind that hill."

•   •   •

The forest canopy made it look darker than out in the fields. They watched as a groundhog scurried beside the wheat field, looking for a meal. Simon stood and moved to the edge of the trees. "Well, let's get moving. I wouldn't mind seeing the manor with a bit of daylight."

They walked down the gentle slope of the first wheat field and reached the first wall. Simon climbed over it. He felt a loose stone move under his foot. "Watch the wall, it's not stable."

"I saw the stone move," Jeff said as he sat on the wall and swung his legs to the other side.

Tom took his pack off and pulled out his electronic finder. He waved it over the wall. The meter came to life. "That wasn't a loose stone. It's some form of security. Either to keep us out or the others in."

"Okay, well, let's just keep moving to the manor. There's no point in running," said Simon.

They proceeded through the field. Halfway through the second field, Jeff stopped and turned around. The noise of the wheat blowing in the wind had increased and a feeling of energy was in the air. "Look." He pointed to the first field they had just been through.

The smell of ozone filled the air, and a blue ball of light hovered over a small section of the field. The wheat swayed and moved in different directions. Then, as the blue light grew, blinding them for a second, a large smiling face and the word *WELCOME* appeared in the light. The standing wheat returned to swaying with the wind and the light disappeared.

They all stared at the field. Tom spun on his heals and looked towards the manor, now hidden behind the hill they had yet to climb. In the dim light, he saw no movement, expecting an army's division of men charging at them.

"Well, I guess we go to them?" said Simon. "A golf cart or some vehicle would be nice. I don't think they know how far we've come today."

"A golf cart with some snacks. We might as well have just marched up to the front door and knocked," said Jeff.

They headed towards the stream.

•   •   •

With wet feet and pants, they sat on the bank of the stream and put their shoes back on.

"Well, here we go, the final push, I guess," said Tom.

"I thought they would have been out to meet us by now," said Jeff.

"Why come to us when they know we're coming to them?" said Simon.

"I guess, they know we aren't turning around and running. What are the chances they have a meal prepared for us? I'm starving," said Tom.

They walked up the hill, and when they crested the top of it, the manor was in full view for them to see. The twilight made the grassy field tough to see, but the land around the manor was lit up with security lights mounted on tall poles and on the manor walls.

"Wow, I wasn't expecting that."

The lights showed a large pool, an even larger play area with swings, slides, jungle gyms and soccer fields. Separated by a tall row of cedar trees was a second pool and a large deck area with loungers and tables.

"Is that a driving range?" asked Tom.

"Yes, I believe so. And a small go-cart track."

"Did we misjudge this whole thing?"

"No, look there. See our friendly men in tunics patrolling?" said Simon.

"Is that a projection screen?" Jeff pointed to the side of the Manor.

"What is this place?" asked Simon.

Between them lay a large, manicured garden with paths and walkways. Simon looked through his binoculars. He spotted all kinds of exotic plants and multiple rows of vegetables and herbs. A German shepherd wandered through the paths. Simon focused his view of the house, looking into the windows. Most had the curtains pulled, but the glow of lights shone around the perimeter of them like a halo.

He found a window with the curtains still opened. A man stood with binoculars, looking back at him. On the first floor, he could see a large dining table and staff moving around it, placing plates and utensils at each setting. He lowered the binoculars. "We're being watched."

"Of course we are. We have been since you arrived in England," said Tom.

"I find it strange there's no one outside except a couple of men in tunics. If there was one kid we could identify, then we could turn around and get the police here. I wish we had brought a phone."

"Wouldn't have mattered. See those boxes beside the lights under the eavestrough? They're scramblers. I thought I saw a couple in the woods, too. Our phones would've been useless. They wouldn't have even taken a photo," said Tom.

They lay on the grass watching the activity outside. Tables were wiped, and they moved cushions from the chairs into a shed. Two men in white lab coats stepped out from the manor and sat at a table, lighting cigarettes. A man in a tunic walked to them. He pointed at the hill. They looked up, put out their smokes and returned to the building.

"What was that about?" asked Jeff.

"Lab coats. They're running some kind of medical experiments on the kids?" said Tom.

Simon lifted his binoculars again. He looked through the door the men used. It was a hallway. He surveyed the windows again. The one where he saw the man watching him was empty, and the curtains were closed.

"What are we waiting for?" asked Tom.

"I say we stand straight, head level and march right onto the deck and sit at a table. Who knows, they might even feed us some dinner. I would assume there is a chef somewhere in the building," said Simon.

They stood, put their packs on, and headed down the hill.

CHAPTER THIRTY-FIVE

They arrived at the edge of the gardens to sounds of dogs barking. Their paws kicking up the small stones on the pathway as they rushed towards the trio. Jeff froze. Simon jumped into a raised bed of carrots. Tom stepped out of the garden, back onto the grass. The first dog turned onto their pathway and charged at them, barking and growling. Then a second sprinted towards the three men. Behind Simon, another shepherd was in full sprint.

"We came this far to be attacked by dogs?" Simon yelled.

Each dog stopped in front of one man. Simon could see the large teeth of his dog as its tongue hung from its mouth. The dogs didn't move, they just sat looking at Simon, Jeff, and Tom.

A whistle blew three times. The dogs retreated to a lady in a blue tunic.

Simon jumped off the carrot garden. "Quite the welcome, wouldn't you say?" he called out to the house.

Tom looked towards the manor. Five men in blue tunics approached. "Do we run?"

"I have seen you run bud, you can't outrun a turtle, so I doubt you'll get away from the dogs or the men," said Jeff.

"Good evening. We are a little lost. We were visiting the castle and took an unmarked trail. Could you show us to the road, and we'll be on our way?" said Tom.

"Smooth," Simon said under his breath.

"Good evening, Tom, Jeff, Simon. I don't believe you're lost."

"If you would take your packs off, we will deliver them to your room, and, Jeff, please hand over the firearm."

Jeff looked at Simon with raised eyebrows.

· · ·

They released the dogs to patrol the gardens. Simon followed two of the men in tunics, with Jeff and Tom in line behind him. Three guards followed them. Simon was astonished—they had no visible weapons, just a few dogs. The group made their way across the deck to the same door the men in white lab coats used.

"Hey, are those King Shepherds?" asked Simon.

"You'll be our guests tonight. We have a room ready for you," the lead man said, entering the building. "My name is Kenny. I was a friend of Nigel's. And yes, they are King Shepherds."

Simon glanced at Tom, then at Jeff. Tom shook his head and attempted a smile at Simon.

The hallway lights turned on once they stepped inside the building. The walls were painted a bluish gray hue. Oil paintings and photographs populated the walls, some of which Simon thought were very well done, while others looked like a five-year-old had drawn them. At the end of the hallway, they stopped in front of an elevator door. With a press of the call button, the single door slid open. Simon followed Kenny and the others onto the elevator. Jeff hesitated and was pushed into the opening, bumping into Tom. Their host pressed the 3 button. The door engaged, and the elevator rose. They stepped out to a plush brown and gold carpeted hallway. A man and woman in blue tunics were in the foyer, carrying towels. They stopped and backed against the wall as the group passed. They handed the towels to the trailing guard. On the walls hung pictures of waves and animals, each one with a motivational saying under it.

Simon broke the silence. "What are we doing here? Are we getting a tour of the manor or being locked up like prisoners?" No one answered. Instead, they continued to lead them down the hallway. A few of the doors they passed leaked the sound of a radio or television playing behind it.

"Hey, what's the game? I assume you have called the police by now to have us charged with trespassing," said Tom.

Jeff turned to Tom and frowned.

"*Now, boys,*" said Tom. He stopped and turned to the guard behind him and swung his fist. Simon turned to see what the commotion was.

Tom's punch missed as the guard sidestepped it. But Tom's momentum spun him, and with a push from the guard, he was lying on the ground.

"There is no need for that. What have we done to deserve that treatment?" asked Kenny. "You can leave if you wish, but I assume with what you three have been up to in the last month or so, you won't want to. Do this, get some sleep tonight. You had a long day getting here, and in the morning, Gus will meet with you to answer your questions. You impressed him and all of us with your sleuthing to get to this point."

"Then what?" asked Tom, lifting himself to his feet.

"That depends on you." He walked to the next door and opened it. "Your chambers for the night."

•   •   •

They stepped inside a room furnished from the 1800s. The beds had canopies over them. On a dresser, a hand basin had a jug of water beside it. Electric lights were the only modern convenience in the room.

"I'll be back in the morning to collect you. Does eight seem reasonable?" asked Kenny.

"Yes, thank you," said Simon.

The door closed, and a key turned from the hallway.

"First, this room is bigger than my flat," said Jeff, ignoring the door closing.

Simon stood at a writing desk in between two large windows. There was a pad of paper and several pens. Beside the pens were three sandwiches and a variety of cookies. Steam rose from the pot of tea wrapped in a cozy. "Hey, our supper's over here." He pointed at the desk. Through the window, the sun had set, and he strained to see the forest.

Tom noticed the floral patterned bedspread. "What is this? This all looks to be at least one-hundred-year-old furniture if not two hundred. How many people have slept in this room who are now dead? This is crazy, but I will risk eating the sandwich," he said.

"What was with the *'now, boys'* and attempted punch?" asked Simon. "This isn't some TV show. I would assume someone trained those guys in multiple hand-to-hand disciplines."

Jeff laughed. "When I turned, you looked like you were moving in slow motion, Tom."

"That's the weird thing. I could feel myself slow down like they had a force field around them, or someone had hold of my arm. I felt I had to try something."

"Now that you say it, I felt nothing once we met them. Not like I had no thoughts, but I wasn't scared or angry. Like I knew them," said Simon.

"Yeah, before they came to us, I thought we could overtake them. Then the thought just left. Like my mind accepted the situation we were in. How come none of us is upset that the door to the hallway was closed and then locked? We just inspected the room."

"Right, like they drugged us, but how? I don't think they actually touched us. Like you said, Simon, I feel I know them."

"Not one of them touched us except for you being pushed into the elevator and me, well, landing on the floor," said Tom.

Jeff tried the door. "It's locked."

"Where does that go?" Tom opened the large wooden door. "Another bedroom, not as big, but just as old. I guess this would be the nursing room? We all have our own beds, so that's nice."

"What do we do to get out of here?" asked Jeff.

"I don't think that's an option right now. These are stone walls, and the windows don't open. I think we try to get some sleep, like they said. We can each take a watch if you guys feel it's needed. But tomorrow we'll need to have our wits about us, and staying up all night will not make it any easier. Since we're here, we need to remember our mission is to rescue the children. Or at least have an answer for the parents," said Simon.

"I agree. We should sleep. Then we'll be rested for when we meet Gus," said Jeff.

"Okay, so just to clarify, do you guys think we are meeting a man who could be five hundred year's old tomorrow?" asked Simon.

"Simon, I wouldn't be surprised if we do, and he has little green men with him. With all we have been through, I think anything is possible now," said Tom.

They sat on chairs and ate the food left for them. When their teacups were empty, they each took a bed. Simon slept in the nursing room while Tom took the bed with the floral bedspread. "Can I just say one thing before we all get to bed?" asked Tom.

Simon stopped in the doorway.

"If we don't make it through tomorrow, it's been good to meet you, Simon, and you know how I feel about you, Jeff. This has been the highlight of my life," Tom said, lying on the bed. "Wow, what a mattress and these sheets. So thick and soft."

"Don't talk like that. We'll get out of this," said Simon. "Hopefully dragging a group of kids behind us."

"Whatever happens tomorrow," said Jeff, sitting on his bed, smiling as he lay back, "at least my last night on earth will be very comfortable."

"If they were planning on killing us, we would've been dead weeks ago. No, I think they need us or want us. I guess we'll find out tomorrow. They've kept the black hoodies from killing us multiple times," said Simon. He turned and walked to his bed, not sure if this would be his last sleep or if he would see new things not previously known to the world outside the manor.

He looked out the window as he lay on the bed. The moon shone on his face.

Good night, kids. Don't forget your ol' man loves you.

He fell asleep quickly with memories of his kids at a water park in Kitchener.

CHAPTER THIRTY-SIX

The door to the bedroom swung open, startling Jeff, whose bed was the closest to it. He sat up on his elbows. He looked around the room, confused about where he was.

Tom jumped out of bed and stood in his green boxer shorts. "You can't knock?" he asked.

"Time to go," Kenny said.

"Go where? Where are you taking us? I'm not going anywhere until you give me an answer," said Jeff, getting out of bed.

"Where's Simon?" Kenny looked at the door to the adjoining room and pointed to the man flanking him.

He swung the door open. Simon lay in his bed, motionless. The guard approached and shook his shoulder. Simon grabbed his arm and pulled him onto, then over the bed. He wrapped his arm around the guard's neck and strained to keep him from fighting.

Tom stood in front of Kenny. "Who are you? What do you know of this place? Did you kill our friends a couple of weeks ago?"

"What? Step away from me," said Kenny.

Tom stood nose to nose with him. He grabbed Kenny's shoulders and swept his leg, dropping him to the floor. Jeff ran to the door and closed it. The sound echoed in the room and down the hallway.

Jeff ran to help Simon. He was on the chest of the guard, his forearm pressed into his neck, as he leaned in. "What's your name? Name?" demanded Simon.

"Noel."

Jeff spun around to check on Tom. Kenny was standing from his kneeling position. Jeff dove at him, hitting him with his shoulder and knocking him over. Tom climbed on him, but Kenny's body was stiff, out cold.

Jeff reached out his hand to help Tom up. They joined Simon, carrying Kenny to the adjoining room. Simon stood over Noel.

"Is he dead?" asked Jeff.

"No, but we need to get him tied up. How did you guys make out?" said Simon.

"He's out cold. But same thing, we need to tie him up."

Simon took the corded ropes from the drapes in his room. He tossed one to Jeff, who tied Kenny up. Tom tore stripes off the bedsheet. He stuffed one in each of their prisoner's mouths.

"Right then, what are we doing? Do two of us dress up in the uniforms and escort the third out?"

"Whatever we do, we need to decide now. If we don't show up shortly, they'll send more guards."

"Option one. We tie them up," said Simon. "Then we get to the main floor, run out the front door, and hope we make it out. Option two. We tie them up and explore for as long as we are able. We get suited up in the blue tunic and see what happens. Tom, you're the same build as Kenny. I might squeeze into Noel's tunic."

"Run, run fast and run far," said Jeff.

"I vote to explore," said Tom. "We came this far. Either way, we need to get them tied up."

"I'll stay and explore too," said Simon. "Jeff, we have to take a chance and look for the kids."

"Fine, all for one," said Jeff.

Both guards woke from their unexpected slumbers. "We need to borrow your uniform, Kenny," said Tom. "We have to untie you, but no funny business."

Jeff and Tom undressed the guards. Once Kenny was in his underwear and socks, Simon re-tied him to the bedpost. With Noel seated and his pants and tunic on the bed, he was re-tied to another bedpost. They found pass cards and tasers in the pockets.

Simon raised his fingers to his lips and motioned his head for his friends to follow him. They went to the main bedroom and closed the door.

Whispering, Simon said. "Do we want to interrogate one of them? Ask questions? We can threaten them with their own tasers."

"We need to hurry. I'm sure there must be someone wondering where they are," said Tom.

"Right, two minutes, then we go," said Jeff.

Simon entered the room and stood before Kenny. "We have a few questions for you. Answer them and we won't hurt you, Kenny. If you don't, I *will* use your taser to help you. Understand?"

He nodded.

Simon reached down and removed the ball of linen from his mouth.

He looked up at Simon. "We had breakfast for you. Gus was looking forward to meeting you three," said Kenny. "We let you in. Things are ramping up, and we need some help."

"Who is Gus?" asked Simon.

Kenny lowered his head. Simon grabbed his jaw and raised his head. "Kenny, who is Gus? What is this place? And most importantly, where are the kids?" Simon asked through his gritted teeth.

Tom reached in with the taser.

"Mate, careful with that. It's not a toy. Gus owns the house. I can't explain what this place is. The kids aren't here right now."

"When will the kids be back?"

"I don't know their schedule, sorry."

Simon pushed the linen back into his mouth.

Discouraged by the answers and aware of how much time they had wasted, Simon opened the bedroom door and surveyed the hallway.

•　•　•

They stood hidden from the elevator door, waiting for it to open. Jeff's stomach was cramping, and Tom shook with adrenaline.

"Here it comes. Be ready," said Jeff.

The door slowly opened. Tom leaned in. "Empty."

Simon stepped in. "Where to?"

"Here, what will this do?" Tom waved the ID card in front of the dull red light under the *1* button.

A lady's voice filled the elevator. "Hello, Kenneth. Level, please?"

"We have the three men caught last night," Jeff said, trying to impersonate Kenny's Welsh accent.

Tom looked at him surprised, then gave him a thumbs up.

"UG1." The door closed and for a second, they felt a sense of lightness as the elevator dropped. The buttons lit up as they passed the second and first floor. Then the sudden stop caused Tom's knees to bend.

• • •

The door opened to a blinding white light. Tom pushed himself against the back of the elevator. Simon threw his arms over his face. Three arms broke through the light and grabbed Jeff by the shoulders and arm. He disappeared into the light. Tom took two steps and jumped towards the light, leading with his right leg, like Bruce Lee kicked in the movies he watched as a child.

Simon reached for the floor buttons on the elevator. He ran his palm down them all. The door slowly moved across the white light. Two arms grabbed his shoulders, and he was pulled through the door and forced to the ground on his stomach in a hallway. A knee pressed between his shoulder blades. The bright light used to blind them was extinguished, and Simon struggled to adjust his eyes to the dull walls and low light. He lay on the floor of a large hallway with passages heading out like a giant T.

He looked up. Jeff and Tom stood facing a wall made of tile. Three men stood behind them. The military issued boots and thick legs around his head showed him there was no getting away.

That didn't go well.

"Get up, Simon," a voice came from over his head.

Two sets of arms grabbed him under his shoulders and lifted him to his feet. They forced him against the wall beside Tom.

"How did that kick work for you?" he asked Tom.

"Landed on my backside. Nothing but air. Maybe I should just give up fighting."

"Right."

He turned his head to the far left. "Huh, what now?"

"Simon, you guys have been very persistent with your attempts to find the children. Maybe it's because of the internet and technology making the world smaller, but no one has ever gotten this far investigating a missing child. Bravo. I'm Paul Bridge, by the way."

Tom shook his shoulders, trying to break the grip of the man behind him.

"Gus is impressed with you three. Extremely impressed."

"Who is this, Gus? We have heard his name many times," said Tom.

"Oh, you will meet him and plenty others. But for now, we are your hosts. We had breakfast prepared for you. But with the excitement you created this morning, we'll have to skip it."

"We broke in here, and you're making us breakfast?" asked Jeff.

"You didn't break in. We let you in. The old building you found in the woods?"

"What about it?" said Tom.

"That has the ability to... Not my story to tell. Frankly, I don't fully understand it," said Paul, pacing behind them.

The three were forced back into the elevator, accompanied by the security team.

"Gwen, first floor, please."

"First floor," the voice replied.

Slowly, the elevator rose. The door opened to a large entrance with twelve-foot-high doors reflecting the sun through stained-glass murals of large rolling fields and vials of a red golden liquid. The ceiling had a large chandelier hanging from the second floor. Gold leaf accented the wooden railing, curling with the stairs as it rose to the second floor. The large marble tiles, white with red and black streaks, accented the wood trimmed walls and stairs.

"I assume this elevator was not original to the house?" asked Tom.

"It was, in a way, just a manual form of it. We had staff use ropes and pulleys back then," said Paul.

Tom looked at Simon, then at Jeff. "You had staff? Son, you look to be about thirty. Elevators don't need people. As long as I've been alive, they had motors."

"Of course, and thank you for the compliment."

They walked down a hallway with wooden floors and wood framed walls. At the end, they stopped in front of double wooden doors with medieval door handles and images of books etched into the wood.

Jeff looked around the hallway. His gaze froze on the portrait to his left. It was the largest one on the wall.

"Hey," he whispered, "doesn't this guy look familiar?"

Simon turned and looked. His eyes widened and his mouth dropped open. The painting was of the same man they saw in all the old pictures standing in front of his house. Only this portrait was commissioned in 1995, according to the signature in the bottom right corner.

Tom looked at the painting. "Gus," he said, his voice shaking.

"Yes Gus. Who else?" Paul said. He stepped around them and pushed open the right door.

Tom stepped through the door first. He stopped. Simon bumped into him, knocking Tom further into the room. Jeff stepped around both of them and took three steps in before he stopped. The room was larger than they could have imagined. All three heads spun on their necks.

The large windows, seven meters tall, looked out on the fields of grass, wheat, and barley. Inside the room sat a large, ancient desk. The chair behind it was just as old, hand carved with images of a long ago battle and the victory flag carved as the headrest. On the desk sat papers, two laptops, and vials of blood, standing in a six-vial holder. The walls were made of walnut, and around the room hung photos and portraits of the same man shaking hands with Einstein, Hitler, Shakespeare, Churchill, Napoleon and many others with royal bloodlines. Oil portraits of all the British kings and queens, going back to the 1500s, showed the same man. Their dates were pressed into gold plates attached to the frames. Simon spun on his heels and looked behind him. More photos, newer ones of the Clintons, Margaret Thatcher and the Kennedy brothers all hung on the walls between oil painted portraits.

Jeff looked up at the high ceiling. Small children playing in fields of grass graced the mural spread across his field of vision. He dropped his eyes to the floor. A large polar bear rug almost glowed on top of the dark wood.

To their right was a sitting area. The furniture looked like set pieces made for a television documentary from the 1700s. The gold frames and red pillows welcomed them. A door beyond the sitting area stood open.

The three men stood with their mouths wide opened. They watched as shadows moved in the light beyond the doorway. Then, with a burst of energy and a childish laugh, two children ran into the room. Dressed in white golf shirts and blue sport shorts, they stopped and studied the three men staring at them. Two men in tunics followed them.

"Hey, aren't they the two..." said Jeff.

"Yes, they are, the reason we're here," said Simon. His head felt light, and the room was closing in on him. "I need to sit."

"Hello," Simon said, sitting on a chair.

"Hello," said one twin, in the first Canadian accent Simon heard since he landed in England.

"Are you Doug or Don?" asked Simon.

"I'm Doug. Who are you?"

"I know you," said Don. He pointed at Simon. "Who are your friends?"

A figure stepped through the door.

"*Gus,*" the trio said in unison.

"Children, classes start in five minutes. Please get prepared. You can meet these men later," Gus said, the smile on his face carried from the children to Simon, Tom, and Jeff.

The twins turned and looked at Gus. "Yes, sir. Nice to meet you," said Doug, as he followed his brother out the door.

All they could do was nod. Their minds frozen.

CHAPTER THIRTY-SEVEN

"Well, here we are, finally," said Gus. "It's been a bit of work to get you into this room, I hear. We're not the enemy here. If you must know, we've saved you three and your friend Al multiple times. Robin and Susan would be grateful to my team, if they only knew what could've happened to their children and themselves two nights after the children were taken."

Tom moved his mouth, but nothing came out.

"Who are you? And what do you want from us?" Simon asked, his body struggling to get the words out.

"I am Gus Chapwilk. I own the manor. I want nothing from you, well maybe a few small things. But I have many things to give you. Remember, this is my house, and you came here. Your little quest ends here, gentlemen. Come sit. I don't bite." He smiled. "That's just a Hollywood myth." He looked at Simon and Tom. "Would you like something more comfortable than Kenny and Noel's tunic's?"

They looked at the tunics and pants, then nodded to Gus.

Simon moved to the desk and examined the vials. "This is blood, isn't it? Golden blood." His legs struggled to support him.

"No, it's even more valuable than golden blood. That's ancient blood, the last of it. If I said Christ's blood, would you believe me? Have any of you read the Bible?"

They nodded.

"When Christ was crucified, they collected his blood during the torture he went through and then finally, when the guard pierced his side as he hung on the cross. That guard was looking to make money not to confirm his death." He looked at Tom and Jeff, then at Simon. "You all look like your minds have already been..." He moved his hands from his scalp outward and made a *"puffff,"* sound.

Simon glanced at the papers on the desk. Some were printed from a computer, but most were handwritten with a fountain pen in cursive. He picked up a vial and gently shook it. "You expect us to believe this was taken from a man two thousand years ago?"

"Yes, and over the next few days, if you let me, I'll show you even more impressive things. Please, come and sit over here, Simon." Gus smiled at him. "Oh wait, with all the fuss this morning, you still haven't eaten. How rude of me. Please follow me. I'll get you clothes to fit and show you the dining hall. We can begin our talk while you eat."

"Hey, how old are you?" Jeff burst out his question. The surprised look on his face made Tom think his mouth said it before checking with his brain. He laughed at Jeff's surprised look.

"Son, that's an excellent question. But not one I will answer just yet. Even though I believe you already know the answer. Come, follow me."

They used the door the children had left through. The hallway was well lit and modern. Photos of landscapes from around the world, sunrises, beaches, and sunsets hung on the walls.

A photo from on top of a mountain with three men made Jeff stop. "Everest?"

"The very one. That photo is from the first time I climbed it. Before it became a vacation hot spot and full of humans and their waste."

Jeff looked over his shoulder at Tom and Simon and raised an eyebrow.

"Tour de France? With Lance Armstrong?" asked Simon.

"Yes, great kid. Was open to my help when he beat cancer, then won seven tours."

Simon looked at Tom. "What *is* this place?"

"Sorry, it's a big house. This is the dining room, not as formal as it once was. Please, sit at a table, I'll have your food brought to you."

The room they entered had hosted meals for years. Kings, queens, dignitaries, and all those that supported the hierarchy had sat around the large redwood table. The room looked like the others, with photos and art hanging from the walls. Simon walked the perimeter of the room. Noting famous artists' signatures, some going back to the 1100s.

He sat beside Tom, across from Jeff. The table was so large he felt miles away from them. Gus excused himself, promising to return shortly.

"There has to be millions of dollars' worth of art in this room alone. Some of it is as old as England. I think that one," he pointed over Jeff's shoulder, "was taken during World War Two by the NAZI party. I'm sure I've seen a replica on one of those *History Channel* shows."

"So, do we think this guy is a vampire?" asked Jeff.

"Honestly, I have no clue. But one portrait on the wall on the way to his room was of Vlad the Impaler. That I'm sure of. Or as Gus might call him, Uncle Vlad."

"Real smooth, Jeff, blurting out, *'How old are you?'* Any other situation I would have been on the floor laughing," said Tom.

"Okay, what about the blood he said was Jesus' blood? Really, how is that even possible?" asked Tom.

Two ladies, dressed in blue skirts and white golf shirts, entered the room. They held silver serving trays. A third lady followed with a stack of folded clothes. Behind her, Gus followed with his infectious smile.

"You can change in the bathroom, out the door and to your left. Enjoy your food. I need a few more minutes to deal with a situation out on the grounds. But when you are done, Tina here will bring you to me, and then we can talk. I'm so sorry about this. I was hoping to chat while you ate, but we have an unexpected security issue I need to tend to."

The smell of bacon caught Jeff's nose. His stomach rumbled, begging for a piece.

"Thank you for your hospitality. We look forward to our talk. I was looking at the time. We need to be back home by seven tonight or," Simon chuckled, "or people will come here looking for us. It was a security measure we took. Not knowing what to expect."

"Yes, I would've done the same. But we both know that's a false statement. No one knows you're here. Jeff, you're single and an orphan. Tom and Simon, do you think your ex-wives will put up much of a search?

The best anyone will do is find the hotel you stayed in. After that, there's no trace of you three, including the rental cars or phones. Just like you planned it. And Allen, well, he's just happy not to hear from you three after what he saw the other night. Your podcast fans? You'll be putting out a show soon enough." He smiled and winked.

Jeff looked at Tom. He tried to hide his fear.

"Enjoy your meal, gentlemen."

They lifted the lids to the serving platters and steam escaped, rising with the lids. As promised, full plates of bacon, eggs, waffles, and potatoes were served. The smell filled their noses. The ladies served them their food. They placed a carafe of coffee and a jug of freshly squeezed orange juice on the table.

They sat in silence, not realizing how hungry they were.

•   •   •

Silencing his burp behind the linen serviette, Jeff looked at Simon and Tom. "I couldn't eat another bite. I hope we don't have to fight our way out, because I'll be no help." He drank the last of his coffee. "I have never in my life had such a satisfying meal. If this was my last…" He caught himself, the reality of the situation coming back to the front of mind.

Simon leaned into the table. "We saw the kids. We need to get them and run. I need to find a phone and call Robin. Let him know what we have seen and where we are. Maybe he can send the police."

"I don't know, Simon. They're watching us closely. The only phone I have seen was beside Gus' desk. We'll have to be careful," said Jeff. "I want to see more of this operation first. Maybe the kids will sign to them that we are here."

"Yes, we need a few answers," said Tom. "The blood, the hoodies, crop circles and I think the one question that answers everything, *why?*"

"All done, gents?" asked Tina, one of their servers.

"Yes. Could I have a glass of water, please?" asked Simon.

"We can do better than that," she replied.

She went to the kitchen and returned with three one-liter glass bottles of water. "Straight from the fountain of youth. Drink up."

Simon smiled at her when he took the bottle. "Perfect, I need some parts fixed."

She laughed. "We all used to."

"Excuse me?" Tom asked, thinking back to Charles' comment in Germany.

She leaned into Tom and Simon. "You have no idea what's in this house, no idea. I think you three are the first ones he has let in, the first three without golden blood, since the sixties. You men must be special." She was a short lady with a medium build. Her hair was golden red.

Tom looked her in the eyes.

An old soul.

"Tell us," said Tom.

"I can't, but I will leave this with you. I was born the same year as Napoleon marched recklessly into Russia." She smiled.

Simon rolled his eyes up as if the answer was on the ceiling. "You're two hundred years old?"

"Not yet," she said, with a twinkle in her eye. "Follow me. Gus is waiting for you."

"Hold on. You all work here. This is almost like a dream. People all dressed in blue. Some of the craziest artwork and photos I could ever imagine, and then to top it off, the children I'm looking for, run into a room, greet me, and then leave for a class?"

"Simon, listen. There is so much for you to understand. Believe me, we are the good guys. Just remember that," said Tina. "Go change, and then I'll take you to Gus."

"Will we ever leave this place?" asked Jeff.

"Yes," she replied.

"Alive?" asked Tom.

She hesitated. "Yes, if you stop fighting us. You upset a lot of the fellas when you tied up Kenny and Noel. We are still mourning Nigel and how you handled that situation. That day—well, that day he was to bring you here. Before his untimely death. Listen, learn, and ask questions, yes. But stop the violence and the threats. We're not here to hurt you. With all you've seen, were you ever hurt by a person in a blue tunic, or was it men in black hoodies?" She paused, letting them recall their memories. "But, Tom, if you want to entertain us again playing Bruce Lee, we all enjoy a good laugh. Remember, you three came to us."

Tom and Simon had a lot to mull over as they changed their clothes.

• • •

They retraced their steps back to Gus' office. He was waiting on the couch with a young lady. She was in a pencil skirt covered by a white lab coat. Her dirty blonde hair was pulled back in a ponytail.

Simon, Jeff, and Tom sat on the couch across from them. Tom tried but couldn't help himself and had to run his hand across the cushions and then the couch's frame. When he lifted his hand from the frame, a static charge shocked him. He shook his hand in the air.

"Yes, it's ivory with gold inlay. Made in what we now call Iran, back in the 1600s."

"Huh, the only thing I see made in this century is those two laptops, the phone and a few photos," said Simon.

"Yes, you might be right," said Gus. "This is April. She's one of my lead researchers. She'll monitor you while you stay here."

"Stay here? Monitor us? I'm not sure what your plans are Gus, maybe the best thing you can do is start from the beginning?" said Simon.

"Oh, even I wasn't around for that." He laughed. "But I can review what is going on here and why we have your friend's twins staying with us. I see you all have your water. You should start feeling better soon. Finish those bottles. I have more for you."

"Why? What did you spike it with?" asked Tom.

"Nothing. Did they not tell you when they gave you a bottle?"

"She mentioned '*the fountain of youth*,'" said Jeff.

Tom turned to Simon. "Didn't Charles say at one point he had the fountain of youth flowing in him? We're drinking blood."

Simon placed his bottle on the floor. Tom wiped his mouth on the sleeve of his shirt.

"What are you doing, Gus? Please tell me the food we ate was pork bacon," said Simon.

"Please, settle down. Yes, you had pork bacon. All the food you ate was as it seemed, no tricks. I don't want to hide anything from you. We purify the water. It is distilled." He paused and took in a deep breath. "You imagine a drop or visible amount of blood placed into your water. I need you to think smaller. There are some nano-sized particles of the spun blood in the water. We isolate *the fountain of youth* bits to add them to this purified water. Just like we reintroduce minerals into it. If you want a more scientific description, April here can do it while we tour the manor later. You have no issues drinking a cola or coffee from beans that are heavily sprayed with poison to kill bugs and parasites. Trust me, trust all of us and drink the water."

Simon looked at the bottle of half-drunk water. "I thought she was joking."

"Oh, we don't joke about those things here," said Gus.

Simon looked at Tom, then at Jeff. "He has a point. Like they say, when in Rome... Bottoms up." He took a mouthful of water and swallowed. "Okay, so you're trying to come off as this nice man. Meanwhile, there are photos of you with Hitler and Stalin. Your uncle was Vlad the Impaler, and I thought I saw a portrait of you and Napoleon standing by the great pyramid. Then there's the fact you kidnap children, lots of them and possibly from the beginning of time? Oh, and the ones without golden blood you drop off in crop circles. You are taking blood and using it to live for eternity like a vampire."

Gus and April laughed. They looked at each other and continued laughing. "Vampires? No, not in England," said April.

"What? Okay, so they *are* real?" asked Tom.

"No, well, yes, but no, not like Hollywood vampires. I've had a few family members who were killed for being accused of being vampires. But look at my teeth." He opened his mouth. "They're all capped, no fangs. Plus, how could that ever work? But that's not why we are here, unless you want to keep going down that rabbit hole and wasting time. I can assure you no one in this manor has ever bitten into a person and drunk their blood. Revolting."

"Okay, again start from the beginning," said Tom. "We will try to be quiet and listen to your story."

"How about I start here as you finish your bottle of water? Then, if you want, we can go through the building, show you what we do, why we do it and I guess if your mind is still functioning, how we do it."

"Gus, later today or tomorrow would be better. We are scheduled for a—milking of some and a..." she coughed. "A transfer of Jacob."

Simon looked at Jeff, then Tom.

Gus brushed April's comment aside and began. "Let me start with the children and the battle we are in. April, please keep me on the subject." He looked at Simon. "I can get off on different subjects."

"Okay, the kids," said Simon.

"As you have researched, there is an incredibly special ancient blood that is very rare, golden blood. Most people you see here have it. I have gathered them over the centuries. I, myself, do not have it."

"Okay, so why not skip ahead to where you kidnap children?" said Simon.

"I, we don't kidnap children, from their families. Here is where I need to change the subject." Gus stood and walked to his desk. He took a bottle of water and returned. "Keep drinking your water. Gents, we are in a battle for souls. We are in a war of all time." He paused and looked at Tom, then Jeff.

"What Gus is trying to say is, those men in black hoodies work for the church or a group associated with it."

"I'm sorry. It's been years since we had new people in. I'm not doing a decent job at any of this," said Gus. "Back in the day we brought people from around the world into my manor. I had the introductions down to a science, but now I'm all over the place. April, help me get this back on track."

"How much do you know about the Bible?" she asked.

"I was raised Baptist," said Tom.

"Catholic," said Simon.

"Salvation Army," said Jeff.

"Oh, old Willy Booth's organization. He was a good man, could grab a congregation's attention and then play with their emotions, firing them up to *fight the good fight*. He visited here many times. We had many good theological talks right here on these couches." He paused and smiled, thinking back to their talks. "So, you all have a foundation of the Bible. Good. I am not here to say it is lies or wrong, but there are parts of it the church overlooks or calls stories," said Gus.

"This all starts with Adam and Eve?" asked Jeff.

"Golden blood is rare and powerful. In Genesis, they talk of the Nephilim and how sons of gods came to Earth and mated with the beautiful women of Earth," said April.

"We met men with the word Nephilim tattooed on them. It was written in Hebrew. Can I see yours Gus? April, do you have the same tattoo?" asked Simon. "Does everyone here?"

"No, heavens no. I know who you are referring to. That's later in the story. Can I stick with the timeline, please?" asked Gus.

"These fallen ones, the sons of gods, they created giants when they had intercourse with the women of the Earth," said Tom. "I did a podcast about it a couple of years ago."

"Right, well, before that time, all humans and even some animals had what we now call golden blood. I don't know how well you know your Bible stories, but in the beginning, people lived into their thousands. That was taken away, but not from all. The Nephilim tried to ruin the blood, knowing it was given to the originals by our Creator God. They, the sons of gods, believed by spoiling the blood it would break the connection between man and God, making Earth a playhouse for themselves."

"But those are just ancient stories in the Bible," said Jeff. "Like many other ancient texts."

"Are they? The story of Noah wasn't about saving animals from a flood, it was about resetting the planet and removing those with the tainted blood and the world they were ruining. When Noah stepped off the ark, with his family, he was the new Adam and so were the animals he had gathered, the ones with original blood. During the flood, many of the sons of gods, or fallen ones, left and returned to another dimension or, as the Bible calls it, the heavens. But some stayed, determined to ruin the world created for mankind and spoil the pure blood given to us by God. The golden blood went from all mankind to only a handful through generations, but always a few remained pure. God watched over his chosen tribe, the Israelites, trying to keep them pure. Back in those days, there were no less than twelve people with the Creator's blood."

"The twelve tribes of the Israelites," said Tom.

"Those twelve tribes were scattered around the world. To the Americas and throughout Europe and Asia. The golden blood was around the world at that time. Hidden from those beings."

"Through history, civilizations were taught of the golden blood and were tasked to find it and control it, by those *mighty men of old*. Fast forward to after Christ's life. The Romans knew of the blood from other civilizations and ancient texts. Some men were tasked to search the known world to find all scripts and texts about the original blood and how it can be used for long life. As we know, the Roman Empire morphed into the Catholic church spreading around the world. Over the years, they have searched for and found those with the Creator's blood, taking them from their families to experiment on and then kill. The Knight's Templars learned of all this history through documents found under the Temple Mount. For years, they took the power from the church, not just controlling the blood but understanding how to use it. The reason? They found a portal. That I will explain later. You know of the power of the Ark of the Covenant?"

"Yes," said Simon.

"Well, they believed the blood had as much, if not more, power to rule the masses."

Simon looked at April. "Could I borrow your pen and a piece of paper?"

She took a few pages off her clipboard and handed it to Simon. At the top of his page he wrote, *portal?*

"On that fateful day, Friday the 13th 1307, the church, with the help of royal families, took back their power and, to their surprise, a portal. They moved the documents and the portal to Rome. Records show many men died as they transferred it. But finally, it was moved from one powerful city to another."

"You are in a fight that started in Genesis? Or before? With the Catholic church?" asked Simon.

"We are in that battle. We must save this realm, the Creator's realm. All other dimensions feed from it and back to it."

"Dimensions? This is all about blood for real? The blood of Christ, the pure ancient blood of mankind?" asked Tom.

"Please, let me continue. I'll explain the portal, dimensions and so much more. April, help me stay on track."

"Sorry, Gus. It's just that this is like a Sunday school class on steroids," said Tom.

"Okay, David had the pure blood, Samson, Daniel, Buddha, and many other prominent leaders through history, not just Biblical figures. Remember, the tribes spread the blood around the world," said April.

"Hold on, I'm so confused. God chooses these people with golden blood?" asked Simon.

"Well—possibly. We don't have that knowledge," said April.

Gus spoke as April drank some water. "By studying genealogy, they could predict a family line where and when the blood could appear. They would test people until they found it."

"How would they know? I assume it's not actually a golden color," said Simon.

"No, but by tracing ancestry lines, they figured it out. And even back then, before the knowledge of the portal, they had the ancient knowledge to test and identify the blood. We can still use it today. Pure copper dust mixed with the blood turns it golden. If it's regular blood, nothing."

"Alchemy," said Tom, leaning forward.

"Where did this ancient knowledge come from?" asked Simon.

"The fallen ones, the Nephilim," said Gus with a smile.

Tom looked at Simon, then at Jeff. The bewildered look on his face assured the others they were all thinking the same thing.

"Now the blood. We need it to keep this realm open. The others, the church, want to close this realm, preventing Christ's return. Well, really our bond with God. I only use Christ because of your religious background. Understand they are trying to break the connection with our Creator God. Then they can live for eternity, with no fear of their actions."

"Wasn't that part of the Nephilim's motives back then too? To taint the blood so there was no bloodline for Christ to be born into?"

"Yes, Tom, you are correct. They, parts of the church, had a taste of the power after taking out the Templars. They ruled over Europe, controlling the masses through fear and guilt."

"Hold on, how does the blood prevent that? The church, well, all religions still hold some power around the world. And I would think any Christian church would want the return of Christ. Unless I misheard in Sunday school, we, as Christians, were waiting for his return."

"No, the church or small groups within the church want to prevent Christ's return and the wrath that will fall on them. We call them *the Fallen*. Remember, this goes back to the beginning of Genesis when the fallen ones wanted to spoil all the original blood. Destroying what God created. They are the ones who have infiltrated the church."

"Throughout history, there have been small sects within the larger church. The Cather's, Dominicans, and the Jesuits, to name a few," said April.

Simon scribbled on his paper. "Okay, that is hard to absorb but, okay. So, what about the black hoodie people and you still need to explain the dimensions, missing kids and this portal thing?"

"The hoodies are members of those sects I mentioned. They believe what they are doing is the right thing. They work within the church and associated group, but are hidden away."

"Secret societies," Tom said, his eyes widened.

"So, they are part of the church, but not the public part?" asked Simon, scribbling on the notebook.

"Correct," said April. They work behind the scenes, around the world and within the Vatican, manipulating and working policies from the shadows. They work with other groups and religions around the world. You met some of the Druids, who work in the shadows as they do. Have you ever heard the saying, "*everything goes through Rome?*" Well, when it comes to this matter, we believe it to be true.

"This is all fascinating," said Tom. "But also, a lot to take in."

"Does that help answer some questions about the blood and the church?" asked Gus. "Obviously, if you decide to stay with us and help, we can reveal even more. Wait till I tell you the truth about Adam and Eve, the forbidden fruit, and Cain and Abel."

"It's a start," said Jeff. With Simon and Tom, nodding in agreement. "You are in a war of both the flesh and spirit."

"Essentially," said April.

"Okay. Let's talk about the present day. These days, we have funded ourselves and help mankind. We are a leading research group the world knows nothing about. What we learn here, we sell around the world. Anti-aging cream, vitamins, you name it, we have our hand in all the health care sectors. We are trying to help the general population live longer, healthier lives. We hide behind multiple companies, and like the manor, we hide our research team from any public interest," said Gus.

"This blood will cure cancer, Alzheimer's and every other ailment known to man," said April.

"So why aren't you helping where society needs it the most?" asked Jeff.

"Unfortunately, we can't, and it's not from a lack of trying. I could say more, but I think Tom covered it on his pharmaceutical coverup podcast."

"I was right?"

Gus winked at him.

"So, this water is part of your research work?" asked Tom.

"Yes, like this water. Only it's for those within these walls," said April. "It doesn't get sold in any form."

"You have all finished your first bottle. How do you feel? Tom? Move your shoulder around. Any pain?" asked Gus.

Tom grabbed his left shoulder with his right hand and raised his arm. He moved it in a circular motion forward and back and up and down. He increased the range of motion and the speed. The quizzical look on his face was contagious. Both Simon and Jeff watched him.

"No popping, no pain. Weird. What's in the water? You *have* drugged us."

"Tom, I can assure you there is not a pharmaceutical drug on this property. We don't need it. We have water. Water and the blood of the Creator. It works as a healer. Of course, we have stronger cocktails too. This is just a supplement."

Simon looked at his empty bottle. He stood and bent forward, then straightened, and bent at the waist to his right side. A smile grew on his face. He twisted at the hips and then he bent forward again, laughing. Looking at his right hand, he made a fist, watching his hand close, then open. His laugh grew into a deep belly laugh—tears ran from his eyes. He looked at Tom and Jeff. They looked at him, convinced he had mentally broken down.

"Simon, what is it?" asked Jeff.

He couldn't get a breath to answer. Tears ran down his face, and his chest heaved as he struggled for air.

"What Simon wants to say is when he was a teen, he was on his bike when a car struck him. The accident cracked four vertebrae, compressed his spine, and herniated three disks. Those disks, until now, have caused him chronic pain and suffering, especially on rainy or damp days. He also broke two fingers five years ago when he fell off his bike at Guelph Lake on a trail. Now all those injuries are healing. Gone is his pain, temporarily, gone is his lack of mobility. Simon, one other thing, you had a partial blockage in an artery. I'll get you a second bottle. When it's drank, the blockage will dissolve."

Simon stopped laughing and looked Gus straight in the eyes. He saw deep into his eyes and the age behind them.

"Wait, I want my pain back. I didn't agree with this—this witchcraft."

"Simon, we both know it's not witchcraft. If you stop drinking the water, all your aches and pains will return," said April.

"The water does other things too, but it's easier to show you later," said Gus. "Now for me. I see how you look at me. And yes, you are right. I'm the same man in all those photos you saw. We keep the internet scrubbed of information about me, the manor and what we do. It's not always easy. I sit here before you, a youthful five hundred-and-fifty-six-years young. I know, I know, I don't look a day over three hundred." He laughed at his joke. "April is only about two hundred years old. Go ahead, say it, that's impossible."

"Well..."

"Tom, look at Simon. Simon, look at Tom. Sorry, Jeff, you are a bit too young to enjoy this discovery. Think back a week ago. You two have spent a lot of time together. Simon, where are the wrinkles around Tom's eyes? Tom, where is the scar Simon had above his right eye, the one he got when he was twelve during a fight in the back of the schoolyard?"

Tom raised his hands and grabbed Simon's face. He moved the skin and his head. Simon grabbed Tom's arms and pushed them away. "What are you doing?"

"It's true. The scar is gone. I feel younger too." He looked at Gus and April. "You must be God or Satan. I'm assuming Satan."

"No, no. Neither. I am just a man who received ancient knowledge."

"How did you know about my scar?"

"Simon, before I let any of you in here, my team had to do background research on you three. So, we dug in our own unique way. We liked what we saw and the fact you made it here, well done. All three of you will have some extremely challenging decisions to make over the next three days. At the conclusion of these three days, you will be free to return to your old life or stay and take the roles we have prepared for you."

"What about the children you have taken from their families? The ones you have killed and left in a crop circle or who knows where else."

"Yes, that part is a little dark." Gus looked at April. "And not something any of us enjoy, but it's a failure on our part. I have never taken a child from their family. We rescue most of them from the Fallen who take them. But as hard as we try, we can't get them all."

"I guess we can get into it now. Then you will need a break." April left the room.

"We'll wait until she returns gents," said Gus.

After a few minutes of awkward silence, April returned with a tray of water bottles. "Second bottle. Drink up, I need you to finish three of these today," she said.

"The kids?" asked Simon.

Gus sat back and looked at April.

She nodded.

"As you know, their blood is rare. To complicate it even more, the blood is only at its best during the ages of eight and twenty, depending on the person."

"That's why the twins were taken at age eight," said Simon.

"Yes, we try to protect them, but we don't always do a good job, as you can tell. The Fallen take the children and milk them to twenty or when their blood weakens, then usually keep them for experiments. They're locked in a building and treated like a cow on a farm. Eat, milk, eat, milk."

"They still have some?"

"Yes, once we started to attack and retrieve the children, they moved their operation and continue to do so. They have many monasteries, churches and convents that have hidden buildings or areas. How we find out about that will be revealed later," said Gus.

"What we do is if we identify a child with golden blood, early enough, we place them in a boarding school, free to their parents. We tell a few fibs to put the parents' mind at rest, but there we can protect them, educate them, and use their blood. Then at twenty, we discuss with them the truth of why they have been separated from their family and protected, until then, they haven't been told about the others. I give them the option of staying and teaching or moving here and working. Most mix up where they stay."

"So why not do that with the ones you rescue?" asked Simon.

"They're tagged somehow. We can't figure it out." He shook his head. "Maybe one of you can figure it out for us. The tagged one's need to stay close to the energy of the portal for protection. If they leave, the Fallen will get them, guaranteed."

"So, we raise them here, protected," said April. "You will see tomorrow how well we treat them. We have special powers you common blood people don't."

"We met a Charles in Germany. He had vaccinated golden blood. Why not vaccinate them?"

"Oh, we thought about it. But the second vaccine they give a baby will ruin the blood and going back to earlier, we need the blood to keep this realm open. Remember our friends, the Nephilim," Gus said sarcastically.

"We have tried every scenario to help these kids. This is the best of what we have. Believe me, we have tried other ways, to no avail, and at a cost," said April.

"So, when they turn twenty, why not release them? You said their blood isn't as powerful."

"It's not as powerful as when they are younger, but it doesn't lose anything. It's the volume that changes for our purposes. As for releasing the ones we have at twenty? No, unfortunately we tried that years ago. The three we thought would be safe because of their age were captured and killed by the Fallen. They left their bodies on a street in Rome for us to find. Since then, we keep everyone here to live out their lives, hundreds of years here."

Tom smiled. "Gus, this is quite the battle you are in."

"I am fighting factions within the church. And another smaller group we call *the Scientists*."

"What? So, who are the scientists? Do they also wear hoodies?" asked Jeff.

"No, they have labs set up in Antarctica. They have a few samples they stole from the Fallen years ago. Back when the Ratlines were moving prominent people from Germany to South America. At one of their stops, they found a lab, it was in a Spanish monastery. I think they just want to synthesize the blood to help, actually I have no clue what they are up to. Maybe if you three stick around, you can find out for me."

"Do they have a portal like you and the church have?" asked Tom.

"No, they want one, that I can assure you. They believe there is one hidden in Antarctica, within the ruins of Atlantis, so they believe. As Tom knows, it's a restricted continent. Anyone that works, or visits, has a comprehensive background check done months before their scheduled arrival."

Jeff dropped his bottle—his body was going into shock. The bang of the bottle hitting the wood floor brought him out of his self-induced trance.

"I'm sorry." He leaned over to see his bottle on the floor. A little water had spilled, but the bottle remained intact.

"Do we have time to learn about the crop circles?" asked Simon.

"Yes, we can wrap it up with them for now. Okay, the crop circles." Gus put his hand on Tom's knee. "First, aliens don't make them and neither do the mole people from inside the Earth. Sorry Tom. They are all man-made. Some real, and some fake."

"If they're all man-made, how can there be fake ones?" asked Tom.

"You saw one Simon. The Fallen had the farm owner and his church friends make it. It was to leave a bone with a threat on it. You noticed the broken stems and how things were trampled and disorganized? Those are what *we* define as fake. The others without damage are real. Only circles with four larger outer rings have a body placed in them."

Jeff looked at Simon and Tom. "We got that right, too."

"How are they made?" asked Tom.

"You guys were on the right track with a lot of things. Magnets and the Earth's magnetic field. They program those magnets you had for a brief period. Then, working with either lunar gravity, solar flares or ley lines, they set off their magnets. It makes beautiful patterns in all the dimensions. Back when the technology was new, it was hit and miss on what would appear. Back then, they used it more for respect to the body being returned to the family for burial. Not many of them were identified. But with the invention of flight, the circles were the new craze. People would search for them around the world. We don't make any, it's all the Fallen. They started making more of them for entertainment and confusion. We all get a chuckle when we hear people talking about alien technology and the planet sending us signs of distress. All those theories divert from what is actually happening in the world to those who look for it."

"Conspiracy theorist," said Tom, his smile growing.

"Lately the Fallen has been off their game, and taking entire families. I found it started in the nineties for some reason unknown to me or anyone here. Before that, they would only take the children with golden blood. After 1991, they took all the children. There was a rise in the number of crop circles around that time, too."

"Like Ricky, Don and Doug's brother," said Simon.

"Simon, I'm sorry they killed him just before we took the twins. Our team always tries to recover all the stolen people, golden blood or not, but—they are ruthless, at times." Gus stopped and bowed his head. "We were lucky to find their lab with those twins. They hid in an old church in Ethiopia. Our team rushed to get the boys, but the Fallen sacrificed Ricky hours before we arrived. Then, for some reason, instead of having a circle appear close to Guelph, Ricky appeared in your friend Norm's field. So that is why there have been so many four main circle, crop circles. They're dumping inventory, to put it crudely."

"I have so many questions, but yet my mind can't seem to process the information enough to get any of them out," said Tom.

Jeff nodded in agreement. Tom stood and moved around the room. He looked at photos of historical leaders, scientists, and business leaders.

"How do you know all these people? This portrait of you and King Edward the Eighth. How is that possible?"

"Let's go for a walk. It will be easier to show you the different sections of the manor and what we're doing. I promise we will save the best for last."

"It's just past noon. Shall we do one wing then eat? You can meet some of the staff and guests."

Tom turned to the desk and looked at the clock. It was 12:19 p.m. "Where did the morning go? You did drug us."

"No, all part of the charm, time moves differently here."

"Okay, Gus, I only have one question I need answered. How about you tell us how you were selected for this—monster task? Start there before we go for lunch."

"Okay, but this is it. Last topic for a bit. Keep drinking," said April.

They all sat back on the couch. They sipped their waters and waited for a response.

"You've had a quick history of the blood, now for the strange part," said Gus.

"Huh, I am intrigued because, how can it get any stranger," said Simon.

"When I dug the foundation to this manor, I found an energy source, a portal. I didn't know what to think of it. Paul Bridge stepped through it first. He risked his life."

"Paul, the thirty-year-old that we met earlier is the same age as you?"

"Give or take a few years. Yes. When he returned, I stepped into the portal and was given knowledge—so much knowledge. It is still here today. The Elders tasked me as the guardian of this realm. At first, I saw it as a curse. The fighting, deaths, and pressure to build a team of loyal partners to protect this world. But the source of energy grew and expanded. As I mentioned, it has a twin in this realm—the one the Templars found under the temple—that now hides in the bowels of the Vatican. I'm going to stop there. Some things are better seen than discussed. You men need to eat, and I think you need time to absorb what we have discussed."

Simon emptied his second bottle. Jeff sat on the couch in awe.

"April, please take these men to the dining hall. They need some nourishment. We can get into deeper details as I give you a tour of the premises."

The room was quiet. The three men sat on the couch—in their minds, they each had hundreds of questions but didn't know how to express them. With all those thoughts swirling, they numbly followed April out of Gus' office.

CHAPTER THIRTY-EIGHT

In the dining hall, salads and strips of beef, turkey and pork waited for them. They sat in silence with April. People stopped and introduced themselves as they finished their meals.

Simon placed more beef on his plate.

"I'm astonished how, in the real world, we try to make things we don't understand so complicated, but yet you in a few sentences can simplify it for us," said Tom. "Amazing. Hard to believe it all, but amazing."

Jeff nodded as he slipped a piece of chocolate cake onto his plate. "Is the food always served like this?"

"Yes, why?" asked April.

"I feel if I stay, I'm going to gain some weight quickly," he said, grabbing his belly.

•   •   •

With another satisfying meal in their stomachs and a fresh bottle of water in their hands, they returned to Gus' office.

Simon broke the silence. "I have to say, you look pretty good for two hundred."

She smiled at him. "That's what all you newbies say. Wait till you look in a mirror tonight. You'll see a difference too."

Gus took his seat across from them. "Don't I get a compliment on my looks, too?" He ran his hand over his cheek. "You can buy all the anti-aging cream you want. This is the real thing." He shook his bottle of water.

"I don't know where to start. I'm here to take those kids home," said Simon. "But what you and April have revealed makes me want to stay and learn more."

Gus looked at April. She wrote on her pad of paper.

"Okay, where are your waters?" asked Gus.

"I finished mine," said Tom.

"Me too," said Simon.

"I had a bit left and forgot it on the table. I can run back and get it," said Jeff. He jumped up and left the room. Two minutes later, he returned with an empty bottle.

"Good, here is your next one. Start drinking," said April.

Jeff held the bottle up and chuckled. "I feel like I'll drown if I drink it."

"Jeff, it's not a sprint, but a marathon. Sip at it throughout the afternoon," said Gus. "This is your last one of these for the day. Any other bottles should have a red label."

Tom slumped down and wiped his hands over his face. "This is too much."

"I warned you. April, check his BP, please. After that, you can go out on the deck or go back to your room. Relax, talk, or take a nap. I or one of us will collect you for dinner," said Gus.

"His BP is a little low." She left the room and returned with a leaf. "Here, Tom, place this between your cheek and teeth. Don't chew it or swallow it, just hold it there. Go out to the deck and relax."

• • •

Sitting on the deck, the trio napped. Waking, Tom tried to speak about their morning.

Simon wanted to process what they had been told. With his clipboard on his lap, he reviewed the pages of questions he had. The first one on each page was: *How do we get the kids home?*

"Can I see those notes, Simon?" asked Tom. He sat flipping through the pages. "You're all over the place with your questions. We need to get organized. I feel Gus and April are trying to overload us with information. That way, we forget some of this."

"You feel like they are hiding more than we have been told."

"Yes, I feel like they're purposely trying to overwhelm us and confuse us at the same time. Really, a portal to the heavens? This is right out of the book of Enoch. But on the other hand, a lot of ancient civilizations have the same stories written in their texts, too."

"Jeff, what do you think?"

"I think this place is where I belong. I don't know, there is just..."

"Jeff, focus on what is happening here. Children torn from their parents are wandering around and going to classes? A portal of some kind and fighting factions within the church? It's more like we stepped into a movie."

"Everyone seems happy here, Simon. Even the kids when we saw them, I didn't see any fear or distress with them."

From the manor, April strolled across the deck.

"Dinner time lads."

. . .

April escorted them to the dining room. It buzzed with activity. Twenty people sat at the large table, all at various stages of their meals and most dressed in blue tunics. Scattered through the tunics were a few in white lab coats and a handful of children.

April invited them to sit where they had breakfast.

Did I sit here earlier today or a century ago?

"Are you okay, Simon?" asked Jeff.

"When were we here? It feels so much longer than earlier today. It feels like, I don't know, a lifetime ago."

"I was thinking the same thing. Feels like two lifetimes ago," said Tom,

"If everyone could just give me their attention, please." April paused and waited for people to stop chewing and turn to her. "Children, please, where are your manners? Forks down."

They put their forks and spoons down. "Sorry, ma'am," said a child with a long dark hair straight as a ruler.

"Tonight, we have guests. Some of you met them earlier, some of you have watched and protected them as they found their way to us. This is Simon, Tom, and Jeff." She pointed to each one while stating their names.

Tom stood and waved.

"They have had some time with Gus, and you know what that means. Please welcome them. They'll be here for the usual three days. If you find them lost in the manor or elsewhere, make sure you help them."

Simon flashed a glance of concern to Jeff and Tom.

She nodded and everyone went back to their conversations and meals.

"Your plates will be out shortly. Enjoy. I have a few things to do." She surveyed the table. "Ian and Ivan, when you two are done, can you help our guests to their rooms or outside to the deck? The house is theirs to explore if they have the energy." She looked at Simon.

He nodded.

Tom realized he was now starving. "What's going on? A while ago, I felt queasy. Now all I want to do is take a plate of food and devour it."

"Me too," said Jeff.

"I've never felt so young, so loose and pain free," said Simon. "But look around, everyone is drinking water. Everyone is smiling and calm. Is this the fountain of youth or drugged water that turns people into numb obedient slaves? They remind us they are the good guys but—think about, in every movie you have seen, every war or conflict—doesn't both sides believe they are working for the good of the people? With all his storytelling, he still has a bunch of missing people here. We need to be careful and figure out a way of getting ourselves and possibly them out."

Three ladies approached with heaping plates of food. A plate of salad was placed before them and in between them were plates of roasted potatoes, carrots, baked beans, and slices of roast beef.

"Is there anything you need?"

"Could I have some water, please?" asked Simon.

"You had a bottle earlier, I believe?"

"Yes, we all did," replied Tom.

"How many bottles have you had today?" she asked.

"We've all had three," Simon said.

She returned with new bottles with red labels.

"Why are these different?" asked Simon.

"You had three of the other. That's the limit for today."

"Thank you," Jeff said.

"There, doesn't that sound like we don't want you to overdose?" asked Simon.

Neither Jeff nor Tom responded. They were too busy digging into the plates of food. They ate as people completed their meals, then left the room. Some touched them on the shoulder or arm and welcomed them to the manor.

"They all seem happy and very healthy," Tom said, lowering his head and keeping his voice low.

"I don't know what we have stepped into, a cult or some kind of other dimension, but this is not what I expected."

"No, crazy as it seems, this all seems real. I think we get Ian and Ivan to give us a quick tour, then we go sit outside," said Simon. "I could follow him with the Biblical stuff, but then what is this energy portal thing he walked through? A gateway to the heavens? Jacob's Ladder?" asked Simon.

"I think tomorrow might be the last time we look at this world as we did yesterday. I have a feeling with all this Biblical talk and historical knowledge, they will make us choose a side. We didn't find this place, it found us," said Tom.

•   •   •

The *two I's,* as they called themselves, invited the trio to follow them once they had eaten dessert. Tom asked to see the kitchen to start. They brought them through the kitchen quickly as the staff cleaned from the supper time rush. Tom lagged behind, and once he confirmed no one was watching him, he took a chef's utility knife and stuck it under his shirt.

"How many people live in the manor?" asked Simon.

"Oh, I would say about fifty to sixty."

"Fifty people live in this building?" asked Jeff.

"Yes, at one time we had over one hundred."

"And what time was that?" asked Tom.

"Back in the 1800s," said Ivan.

Simon looked at Jeff, who mouthed, *"How old are these guys?"*

They walked past the door to the large dining area. "You have seen the main dining room. Here on the right is the library. It overlooks the yard and fields where you came from." Ian ushered them into the room.

Simon looked around the library. Just like on television and in movies, the dark wood shelves held books of all sizes, colors, and ages. The ceiling had murals of children reading in fields and adults eating meals of raw meat.

The room had six tables with four chairs. Tom ran his hand over a chair. The design on the back was of wolves carrying human babies away.

From floor to ceiling, wooden shelves held thousands of books. At a glance, Tom noticed none of them were published recently. "So, has anyone read all these books?"

"I believe Gus has read most of them. We all have access to it, but why read it when you can live it?" said Ivan.

"Who is Gus?" asked Simon.

"That's not for us to tell and even if we could, he is too hard to explain with the vocabulary we use," said Ian.

"Huh, that seems to make sense," said Simon.

Ian continued. "Some books in here are originals from hundreds of years ago. But they are yours to read."

"I don't think we'll be around long enough to be reading ancient texts," said Tom.

Simon walked along the shelves, glancing at the books.

"Shall we continue the tour?" asked Ian. "Or would you like time to explore the room?"

"I would like to see the children in the manor. Where are they?" asked Simon.

"In time, Simon. We were told to give you a quick tour of the building," said Ian. "That's what we're doing."

They passed through Gus' office and study to the grand entranceway. From there, they entered the ballroom. The artwork, again, was from the Middle Ages. Pottery and ancient artifacts sat on pedestals. Ivan explained how the floor was an old wood that no longer exists and was discovered in Brazil's rainforests in the 1700s. Large windows looked to the front of the house and the laneway hidden through the trees. The gardens and fountains were trim and neat. Old single paned windows were spotless, without a smear or spot of dirt.

"I can only imagine who danced in this room. Or who met in this room," said Jeff.

"Oh yes, we have hosted all kinds of people. You wouldn't believe me if I told you. It was an extremely popular spot during the early 1860s."

Simon looked at him, confused. "Ian, you don't look to be any older than thirty, but as I am figuring out, what you look like and how old you are, don't always jive. I assume you were here dancing up a storm in the 1820s."

"The general rule is we all stop aging or reset to thirty-three. It was the age Christ died at and, from what we understand, is the optimal age to be. When you see others that look older, they have begun the journey to pass to the hidden dimension. They decide when they are ready."

"This is too much to take in," said Tom, rubbing his head. "It all makes perfect sense but—wow."

Ian just smiled at them and raised his arm, inviting them back to the main entrance.

"We have two elevators. One here, which is the one you used last night, and a service one at the far end of the south wing." He opened a door across from the main stairway.

"This is our observatory." The room had telescopes ranging in all sizes and ages. Drawings on the walls showed ancient maps of Earth and the planets. A blackboard had notes scratched on it.

Simon studied the blackboard. "How old are these notes?"

"Older than you, Simon. Older than me too," said Ivan. "They are outdated but we keep them for the nostalgia. A simpler time."

Looking over Simon's shoulder, Jeff pointed to a photo. "This is crazy. Look at this photo. What's not right?"

"They all turned and looked at the photo, a color photo of men standing on the moon, looking at the camera, with Earth, small and blue, glowing in the background."

"I see it now. A structure behind them. Like the frame of a greenhouse," said Tom. "How is that…"

"Can we sit for a minute? I feel lightheaded," said Simon. "Tell me, are we being drugged through the water?"

"Yes, and no. No, not drugged with a hallucinogenic drug or anything like that. Yes, because we are cleaning your body, making it pure and ready for tomorrow. In case Gus didn't mention it, your urine and stool will have unusual colors and odors over the next few days. Don't be alarmed."

Jeff buried his head in his hands.

· · ·

From the observatory, they brought them through eight large rooms and twelve smaller ones, all with a theme or purpose.

They climbed the stairs to the second floor. "There's not much on this floor, just bedrooms, washrooms, and study rooms. That goes the same for your floor. Unless you want to see more, you can go to your room."

"What time is it?" asked Tom, looking at his watch.

"Ten past ten," said Ivan.

"I would like to see the lower levels of the building, the grounds, and the children. Take me there, please," said Simon. "I'm not ready for bed."

"It's a lovely night. We can let you sit on the back deck and wait for Gus. No running away," said Ian, smiling.

"We wouldn't think of it. You have us intrigued, to say the least," said Tom. "I always said, if an alien invited me into its UFO to travel the universe, I would run up the ramp. Well, this place is my UFO."

They walked down the stairs. In the distance, they could hear children laughing. Ian's back tightened at the sound, looking back at Simon. He stopped and opened a large door. Taking three woolen blankets from a shelf, he handed one to each man. "It can get a little cool." He led them down a hallway. Simon looked at the old photos of Gus with more dignitaries and groups of children.

At the end of the hallway, a wooden door, with scratches on the lower part and a stained-glass window on the upper half, opened to the outside. The cedar deck had wooden loungers, umbrellas, tables and chairs. The wind blew through the hallway, chilling Jeff.

"Please relax, move the furniture to a sheltered area and enjoy the stars. I'll turn the outside lights off so you can see God's creations. We'll let Gus know you're out here."

"Thank you, Ian, Ivan. Could I get another bottle of water? Preferably the one I was given first?" asked Simon.

"You can have a water, but it won't be one of those. You feel better, don't you? Your mind is a little clearer. Aches are gone. You feel younger?" He smiled and winked at them, and followed Ian into the house.

They moved a table beside a wall to protect them from the wind. Its supports were wood, and the round top, solid marble. "Should we have been able to move the table?" asked Jeff.

Tom smiled. "I was thinking the same thing."

They carried chairs to the table. When they sat, a young lady in a blue dress set their bottles of water on the table. "Gentlemen, if there is anything else you require, please come to the kitchen. Down the hallway and to your left." She leaned closer to the table. "I wouldn't suggest you try to go anywhere but to the kitchen or washroom. Same hallway." She looked at Simon. "No funny business, Simon."

They stared her in the eyes. Tom tapped his right temple and winked at her.

"Thank you," said Simon.

• • •

They opened their bottles and drank, looking over the fields of grass and cereal plants. Simon moved away from the house to the edge of the grass and looked back at the manor. He noticed two children looking out the window at him. They waved. He smiled at them and waved back. In the distance, he could hear dogs barking.

Tom joined him. "I don't think we're leaving here, Simon. But honestly, I feel we won't want to."

Simon motioned him back to the table.

"Say that again, so Jeff can hear."

"I don't think we're leaving here..."

"But I don't think we'll want to," said Jeff.

They both looked at Jeff. "You heard us?" they said in unison.

"No, it's how I feel. You guys too, I guess. There's something about this place. It feels like home, like I belong here. We'll be shown secrets, but nothing we can share if we leave. I feel like all these people know us, and, in a way, we have some connection with them. They need us, I think. I know this sounds crazy, but I think these people know the meaning of life and the purpose of why we're here. Plus, I've seen some of them. One was behind the dirty glass, or maybe in the pub. They've been watching and protecting us."

"But why? Why are we so special?" asked Tom. "We know it's not our blood."

"Two days ago, we were asking why the kids were so special. Now we are here asking why we are," said Simon.

"I don't know, but Jeff, I couldn't put it better myself," said Simon. "Take the water, for instance. I love feeling young again. My back, my legs, my mind."

"Yes, I feel the same. And I thought by now I would be raging about the kidnappings. But for some reason, I feel the kids want to be here. The story he told us makes sense when you look at the big picture. The people seem to want to be here. What are we missing?" asked Tom. "Yesterday when we stepped out of the car to come here feels like a lifetime ago."

"Actually, a different life," said Jeff.

"Okay, so we know Gus somehow is hundreds of years old, as is the manor. I assume the people in blue tunics are his security and staff and also hundreds of years old? But I haven't seen anyone come or go," said Tom.

"Huh, and one more thing. The fact we have three days to decide. Like the resurrection," said Simon.

The house door opened, and three men in tunics appeared, with Gus trailing behind. His charming smile was infectious to Simon, Tom, and Jeff. They involuntarily smiled back at him.

"How are you enjoying yourselves, gents?" Gus asked.

"We're fine. It's incredibly quiet here. What have you planned for us now?" asked Tom. "We had a tour of the main floor and the upper ones. How about you take us underground?"

"I can answer questions for you," said Gus. "About our discussions earlier. Then it will be bedtime. We have some work to do tonight because of a setback today. But I will be here when you rise in the morning. Tomorrow, I'll reveal more. Simon, you can meet the children, talk to them, see how they feel about being here. Tom, you can go to the basement." He turned to one man. "Can you get me a blanket and a drink? Is there anything you gentlemen need?"

"I could use the washroom before we begin," said Jeff.

Jeff stood and followed the others into the house. He stepped into the washroom, a room big enough to live in. Gold leaf accents covered the burgundy painted walls. Cradled in a counter, the hand sink was made of a rusty red marble. The mirror's frame was made of gold. To the side was a bathtub. At first, he thought it was stainless steel, but after touching it, it convinced him it was a pure silver tub. He looked around. There was no toilet. He went to the back of the room and opened a door. Inside was a smaller room. It housed a toilet, bidet and hand sink with a jug of water warmed by a ceramic tile under it. The toilet's tank hung six feet in the air, connected to the bowl by a brass pipe. A gold chain and handle hung from the tank. The bidet, with painted flowers outside, had a gold faucet. A basin made of fine china had a drawing of a Sabre-Tooth Tiger attacking a Wooly Mammoth, its blood weaving its way to the drain. The hand carved gold handles were in the shape of a swan's wings, with the body of the swan etched into the spout.

•   •   •

After returning to the table, he said, "Listen, you both need to go see the bathroom. I mean, the house is beautiful, but I have seen nothing like it."

Gus smiled at Jeff's enthusiasm. "Shall we talk?"

"The kids, I want to take them home," Simon said.

"Simon, I told you the consequences of taking them from the manor," said Gus. "How about I talk? Again, later you will see everything. Let's talk about you three. I will start with you, Tom. Your podcast is a hit around here. We all enjoy it. Some people are not happy with the way you speak of them, but we don't take it personally. As you meet them and work with them, seeing what they do, you'll like them."

"So how right are we with our little show?"

Gus rolled his head around. "Closer than anyone else who has tried to crack this mystery, including the Fallen. That's why you three are here. You all work very well together. Jeff, I have a role for you. I think you will find fulfilling and rewarding. Simon, Simon, you have so much potential, so much hidden talent. You know you can do better. Look at what you have done to be sitting here. You don't want to go back to the mundane life in Canada, do you? I can offer you so much more. Look how you put all the puzzle pieces together to find me. The three of you are a team. It's like you have been a team since childhood."

"What are you offering, Gus? Eternal life? We can bathe in the fountain of youth and then go collect children for you?" Simon questioned.

"Can you please *stop* with the kidnapping of children?" Gus asked, frustrated with the accusations. "I have already told you I do not do that. I rescue them. *Enough already.*" The color rose in his cheeks. He took a deep breath and leaned back in his chair. "Stop judging the book by its cover. There is so much in there for you to see."

"Huh, if we decide to leave, will we show up in a crop circle?" asked Simon.

"No, we will give you an injection, and drop you off at Tom's house."

"Forgetting everything we saw here," said Simon.

"Yes, of course. I took a risk letting you onto the property. It has already been costly."

"Costly?"

"Yes, my team works hard to keep this place off the internet and out of books, invisible to the world. When Nigel was killed in the back of his car, he was there to bring you to me. When we saw how you dealt with his body after being killed, well, some of my staff wanted the three of you disposed of. But I decided to set up a security detail around you at that point. The men in hoodies, as you know, work for the Fallen. All those threatening letters and break-ins were to keep you motivated, to keep you searching. Believe me, if they wanted to, they would have killed you all right after the investigation at Norm's crop circle. But—well, that little issue I had to excuse myself for earlier. Three of them followed you onto the property, somehow. We don't know how they snuck through, likely when we shut down the shed in the woods to let you pass. Frankly, I don't know how you didn't pick up on them tracking you. You were, as you said the other day, Tom, *their patsies*."

"Hold on, they followed us? The men in hoodies?" asked Tom.

"My whole life's work was compromised earlier and still might be. They have never found my manor until you three arrived yesterday, at least in this realm. I don't blame you. We let our defenses down, and three snuck in. Last night, I lost a good man defending the grounds."

"Jacob?" asked Jeff.

"Yes, Jacob. We returned him to his family today in 1765."

"What—how? Impossible," said Tom, looking around for confirmation he wasn't the only doubting the date.

"Just like the Fallen, we have our way of returning people to their timeline. We just don't use fancy crop circles." He lowered his head and took a deep breath. "Last night, while you slept, we scrambled here, and on the other dimensions, war was waged. Now, after hundreds of years, I've been exposed. I believe we contained the situation."

"How did they get through?"

"We had to turn off our security, to let you through. The building in the woods, when it's fully functioning, as it is now, it scrambles electronics and brains in a way. It confuses the brain, causing anyone close to it to lose their sense of direction and head back the way they came. Our problem is it takes a bit to fire back up. Between the time you passed it and us starting it up they got through. Luckily, they tripped a few other detectors, and we stopped them. They had tracking devices on, so others will know roughly where we are."

"Gus, we're..."

"No, I don't want to hear it." He raised his index finger and pointed to each one of them sitting around the table. "Be prepared. As adults, all this can be even harder to comprehend. Tonight, prepare your minds to be open to things you have been told your whole life didn't exist. Finish your waters," he spoke as a principal of a school, giving the last warning before expelling a child.

Simon and Tom moved away from Jeff and Gus. Standing on the grass, they looked at the fields of wheat swaying in the wind, lit by the full moon.

"I don't know what to expect now, but we need to be ready. I swear he has already lulled Jeff into a trance."

"Aye, be on your toes. Despite that, I feel like we are the bad ones here."

"I know. You do what you need to, but I'm sticking with my original goal." Simon looked over his shoulder.

Jeff and Gus stood listening to his conversation. "Please, follow me and be ready, as Tom said, *'stay on your toes.'*" Gus smiled at Tom and turned. He took them to their room and left them for the night.

•   •   •

"Okay, we need to discuss a few things," said Simon. He came from his room. Jeff was in his bed, already sleeping.

Tom looked at him. "I agree, but not tonight. I can't keep my eyes open, and Jeff's already passed out."

Simon shook his head and returned to his room.

CHAPTER THIRTY-NINE

A powerful knock on their door pulled them from their sleep. Once ready, they followed the *two I's* down the long hallway to the elevator.

When the doors opened, Gus' mesmerizing smile welcomed them. "Good morning, all. Here are your waters for the morning tour."

"Blue label," said Simon, holding up the bottle. "We're back to the original."

"You'll need to drink three again today," said Gus.

The elevator door closed. *"Lower level one,"* the voice said.

Gus stepped out into a hallway once the door opened. Tiles covered the walls from the floor to four feet up, then lathe and sheeting continued the wall to the ceiling. The lights were bright and reflected off the highly polished concrete floor.

"Come out, gentlemen. Our tour begins here. Like you have been requesting."

They followed Gus down the hallway, passing doors and rooms with observation windows in them.

"You could drive a car down this hallway. It's so big," said Tom.

"You could, but why would you?" asked Gus.

Simon shrugged his shoulders and continued to look through the windows. "What are these rooms used for?"

"Mostly storage and documents. Years ago, it was the bunks for my team. But that just didn't seem right. No one is greater than anyone else."

He opened a door. "Okay, through here."

They stepped into a room with lockers, shelves, and benches. "Anything you have that is metal or magnetic stays here. Nothing can pass beyond this door that is magnetic. You will pass through a highly sensitive metal detector first, so don't try to hide anything, on or in you."

Tom pulled out the knife he had taken from the kitchen.

"Not sure what you planned on doing with that, Tom. Unless you were going to slice some carrots, it's useless," said Gus.

Tom placed it in a locker.

Jeff took his shoes off. "Do you have something else I can wear? My shoes have metal eyelets."

"There are tunics in these lockers. We placed them there for you gents. But only if you want to wear them. You will also find shoes, Jeff."

Jeff opened a locker, found his size, and changed into a tunic. He was the first through the detector. The large machine hummed as he stepped through. A green light appeared on the door in front of him. Simon walked through and smiled when the green light appeared. Tom hesitated, then stepped through. A chirp and a red light appeared. Simon heard a latch slide into place within the door ahead of him.

"Tom, what have you got on that would set off the detector?" asked Gus.

He patted his body. "Nothing. I have…"

"Your shoes have metal eyelets I would think," said Gus. "Put on a pair of these." He tossed Tom a pair of shoes. "If they don't fit, we have plenty of other sizes."

Tom changed his shoes, then stepped through the machine, receiving his green light. The latch slid back. Finally, Gus walked through, receiving a green light. Simon raised his eyebrows at him.

"All must pass through it," he said.

Jeff's heart raced with anticipation. Simon and Tom stood shoulder to shoulder behind him.

"Push the door, Jeff, and welcome to the manor."

•   •   •

Jeff pushed on the door. He stepped to the threshold and stopped. Tom stood behind him on his toes, looking over his shoulder. Simon did the same.

They gazed into a large room with multiple doors. Everything in the room was a brilliant white. The walls to their left and right stretched straight for eight meters, where they met a curved wall that connected them. Each of the straight walls had two doors. The curved wall held six large doors, all white, including the handles.

"What is this, Gus?" asked Simon.

"This is our white room. Step in." Immediately, they sensed an energy in the room. Their skin tingled like one thousand feathers were brushing against them all at once. Jeff couldn't help himself and started laughing. It started off as a titter, then erupted into a full belly laugh with tears running down his face. He held his sides and bent over.

Tom tried to step back out. Gus pushed him further into the room. "You'll get used to it."

"A little underwhelming, Gus. Well, except for the tickling. How does it stop?" asked Simon.

"You become accustomed to it. Give it ten minutes or so."

"Do we have to choose a door? Is this the game we need to play?" asked Tom.

"No, no. No games. I will choose the door. We will, through time, be entering each one. But let's start with this one."

He stepped ahead of them and opened the door in the middle of the curved wall. Inside was a set of stairs spiraling down. They followed him as he descended.

"How far below the main floor are we?" asked Jeff.

"Twenty meters."

"Really? Why so deep?" asked Tom.

"The soil hides what is here."

The bottom of the staircase emptied into a large room with chairs, televisions, and medical supplies. Around the perimeter of the main room were smaller rooms, each with a bed and more stainless-steel medical supplies. All the rooms had large windows instead of walls dividing them. Simon counted eight people with lab coats and three children laying on beds.

Gus opened his arms. "This is our *milking room*."

Simon moved away from the group. Not looking at where he was going, he bumped into a lady in a lab coat. She caught her balance before spilling onto the floor. He apologized and continued to cross the room, not taking his eyes off the one child. Placing his hands on the glass window, he watched as they drew blood from him. He knocked on the window.

Don raised his arm and waved. Gus and his friends caught up to him. Gus lay his hand on Simon's shoulder.

"What are you doing to him? Stop it! *Stop it now!* You can't drain his blood. You, you bloody vampire!" said Simon, outraged.

All the others in the room stopped and looked at the group.

"Simon, we don't like that word here. Please don't use it. We are not those people. I explained it to you yesterday. This is a bit much for you at the moment. I told you to be prepared."

Simon looked at Jeff and Tom. He swung his arm behind him, pointing at the kids. "You see this, and you have no reaction? There are innocent kids being drained of their blood, one I am here to take home. Kidnapped kids taken from their parents. Their families at home are blaming themselves. You're just going to stand there? This can't continue. Tom, Jeff, *we have to stop this.*"

Tom watched as they disconnected each child from the tubes. They placed a cotton ball over the injection point and then a piece of sticky white tape. The children jumped off the beds and entered the room where the group stood watching.

"Children, come here for a minute," said Gus.

"Gus, hello, we don't want to miss our turn on the rides," said Don.

Gus smiled. "You won't."

"What rides?" Simon said to the group.

"I'm showing them around the manor. They watched you donate some blood. Thank you for that. Tell them what we do here."

The oldest stepped forward as he shook the trio's hands. "Hello and welcome. My name is Trevor. I hope to see you around. I have golden blood, or the blood of the gods. This is a privilege that I'm blessed with. In return for my donation, I get an education through eternity, I travel and learn from the greatest minds. One day, if I continue with my studies, they will know me as one of those great minds." He turned to Gus. "May I go?"

"Thank you, Trevor. Yes, you are all dismissed. Enjoy your day." He turned to the trio as they watched the three children exit. Their faces registered their confusion.

"Come, we can talk in another area. Let these people finish their work so they, too, can enjoy the rest of their day."

They stepped through a door and followed Gus down a hallway. He opened a door to a large waiting room. "Here, we can sit in this room for a minute," Gus said, his outreached hand inviting them to sit on a leather couch against the wall. "You lads need to let your minds catch up with your eyes and ears again."

He left and returned with a tray of sandwiches and three bottles of water. "I'm sorry. We missed breakfast, but I was able to find this."

"What did he mean by eternity? And being educated by the greatest minds. I swear I took it as he could time travel."

"They have taught you to look at eternity as a time in the future, like it is something we can look forward to getting to. But what if eternity meant all time, past and future, running parallel to us? No past, no future, just moments to pop in and out of. No time. Always remember, time is man made. Eternity isn't a time or a place, it just *is.*"

Simon fell back onto the couch. He drew a deep breath and scanned at the ceiling.

"What are you selling here, Gus? What's really going on? This sounds like a sci-fi movie."

"Can I show you a couple more things? Then you will have seen enough to understand what we do, I think. Keep your minds open. But eat, your body needs nourishment."

Tom shook his head. "I don't know if I can take much more of this. It's like a dream."

"This is no dream. It's real, I assure you."

They ate like they hadn't seen food in a month.

"What about time? It seems off here. Seems to almost slow down. I swear yesterday felt like a month."

"Yes, with what you are about to see, it distorts time. You are right, it slows down here. Again, time is a man-made way to count our sojourns on

Earth. There are two places on Earth where time is different—here and at the Vatican, where the other portal resides. Drink up, and we will get to the next part of the tour."

They carried their bottles of water and followed Gus back into the white room.

. . .

Gus selected a different door. They stepped through it and into an elevator.

After dropping for several seconds, the elevator slowed, and the doors opened. The room before them had couches, plants, and light. Natural light. Simon stepped under one of the bright spots of natural light. The heat felt like he was sitting on a beach in the Bahamas, his skin cooking under the sun.

"Can you explain this, Gus?" asked Simon.

"Tubes drilled from above. They are reflective, bringing down sunlight. We are out away from the manor, under the wheat fields."

A more modern childish décor replaced the old, distinguished decor of the main manor. Jeff could hear children laughing and playing behind a door to his right. Then a roar of metal on metal.

"Gus, I think you finally broke me. I could have sworn I just heard a roller coaster pass on the other side of that door."

"Sit, gents. Sit there." He pointed to three leather chairs. Simon supposed they could be the oldest pieces of furniture in the room. Gus sauntered to the door and opened it, exposing darkness. Jeff felt he had never seen a blacker black, like the building in the woods. They peered into the darkness. Gus stepped into the blackness. His foot, leg and then body disappeared. The trio's jaws dropped, and their eyes bulged. He stepped back, appearing from nothingness. His playful smile growing. He placed his hands out in front of his chest and flipped them up and down. He pulled on his sleeves. "Nothing up my sleeves, nothing in my hands." He stepped back into the blackness.

Simon and Tom stared at each other. The only sound was the growing rumble of another pass of a rollercoaster. Gus appeared and approached them with a bag of cotton candy. The scream of people grew as the roller coaster passed.

"What?" Tom said. It sounded more like a squeak.

"I see, again, your minds can't keep up with your senses. It's okay. I love that look on people's faces. And I haven't seen it in years."

"What?" None of them had taken their eyes off the blackness behind the door. Squeals of enjoyment echoed in the room.

"Gents, it's a dimensional port. It's how the kids see their parents, how we watched you behind—what did you call it, Tom? A dirty window."

"We have countless numbers of them. Many more if you have golden blood. This is what the portal has created for us. My team, over the years, has created and held these ports open, like this one. When we created the first dimensional port, it was hard to manage, but through education and testing, we now have many, many ports for the kids and staff to use. What did Jesus say? '*My Father's house has many rooms?*' Well, it's the same as this manor."

"What, what, is it?" asked Tom.

"Okay, this is usually easier with children. Are you okay?"

"Can we leave?" asked Tom.

"Leave here or the entire premises?"

"I just need to leave. I don't feel well," said Tom.

"Keep drinking your water. It helps to counteract the effects of being down here." He walked to a set of cabinets and opened the lower door. Retrieving three bottles, he spun on his heels. "Get going on this bottle. You'll all feel better."

"Gus, how does it work?" asked Simon.

Before Gus could answer, Simon jumped, and Jeff screamed as three kids appeared from the blackness. One was Don Easton. Seeing him helped Simon snap back to reality.

"Don? Can you come here?" Simon asked.

The child looked at Gus, who nodded to him.

"Hello, Simon. How are you?" said Don.

"I'm fine. Where did you come from?"

"An amusement park in Texas. It has one of my favorite coasters."

Simon looked at Gus, who was nodding.

"Gus, does he know about the ports?" asked Don.

"Just a little Don. I'll fill him in later," said Gus. "he's still trying to understand this one."

"I came here to bring you and Doug back to your parents in Canada. Would you like that?" asked Simon.

"Yes, but if you do, the evil men will get me, and they don't let us play. They just take our blood and lock us in dark rooms. Ricky didn't have golden blood, so they killed him. They made me and Doug watch. It was very scary. They walked around him holding crosses and singing a sad song. Ricky pulled on his straps. Then a lady came in. She stood over him and prayed to God. Then she took a shiny knife and cut him. Blood sprayed on her, and she smiled. She pushed two tubes into the hole on Ricky. Then one of the tall men turned on a machine. I was tied to the bed beside him when they did it. Doug was beside me." His eyes watered. "We couldn't save him." He looked at the floor. "Gus' men got us shortly after they killed him. Two of them died saving us. Ricky's on another plane now, one we can't see. There's no door to where he is now. But he's happy." He smiled at Simon, then looked at Gus. "I have to go. I have a class now. I hope you stick around long enough to talk again. Maybe tomorrow you can come visit Mom and Dad with me and Doug."

Simon reached for him, but was too slow. He left the room with his friends, laughing and skipping.

Simon looked down at his feet. "I came here to bring them home, Gus. It's still my goal."

Tom looked at Gus. "What is this all about?"

Gus smiled at him.

"We have been through this. As you can see, the kids are happy, and we let them see their parents safely. It gives them closure, and I know it gives the parents a sense of peace."

The port door mesmerized Jeff. "How do we cross through the door? None of us have golden blood."

"How many bottles of water have you drunk, the water with the blue labels? Like the ones you are holding?"

"This will be six since I arrived," said Jeff.

"Yeah, six," said Tom.

"I'm finishing my fifth. The one you gave me is my sixth," said Simon.

"Okay, the water is special, as you can tell. You need to have seven bottles to use these doors with common blood. That's why we have you stay for three days. If you do it too quickly, you will not survive the crossover. Once your blood reaches the acceptable level, two bottles a day will be enough, not just to travel, but to keep you young and vibrant. We can run a quick blood test to see what blood you have and how the water is interacting with it. You also need to make your choice tomorrow. By then, you should have enough water to gain access to this and many other places."

"What do you mean, use these doors?" asked Tom.

"We have them set up as ports to this time and age. This one, as you can tell, goes to an amusement park. It actually rotates through all the parks on the planet. Each day has a fresh experience. It's a reward for their blood and studies. The staff uses it too. What's the saying all work makes..."

"Is this the portal you keep talking about?" asked Jeff.

"No, these are *ports,* not *the portal.* The ports will transfer you to anywhere on this dimension and many others. But only at this time. Those with golden blood can use other ports to travel through eternity. Unfortunately, you and I cannot use those doors. But the entire world is available to us."

"What do you do with their blood?" asked Simon.

"It balances this world and is used to help people. Through our shell companies, we help athletes, who can't give up the game, movie stars, with all their fears and insecurities of their looks and, of course, like we discussed, we market it."

"Unreal," said Tom. "Everything you tell us just proves one of my conspiracy theories. You're putting me out of business, Gus." His smile turned to a laugh.

"No, I'm just going to give you new ones to talk about. I have one more room to show you, then it will be dinner."

"Dinner?" said Jeff. "We haven't had lunch."

"Time travels differently down here. Remember that if you are here alone and especially if you travel through a door. But I'll have to delay that by tomorrow now. I thought you had more water. That's my mistake. I need you fellas to complete the hydration numbers, though, before we can have that conversation." He raised his arms to a door at the back of the room. "This way."

They followed him down a long hallway. Jeff looked around. The walls were stone, the lighting was the worst he had seen on the property and a buzzing feeling on his skin intensified as they moved along the corridor, like being stung by bees.

Gus waited for them at the end. "Ready?"

"For what?" asked Simon. He wasn't sure how many more surprises his mind could handle.

Gus held his thumb to a red light. The light turned green, and the door opened. A large room stood before them.

. . .

The room had a blue hue to it. They stepped in. The smell of ozone filled their noses. One small blue ball floated in the corner.

"This is it. This started it all. I found it when we were digging the first foundation for the manor. This is the power source to all this. When I stepped through it, it transported me to heaven, another universe, or a planet we aren't aware of. I have never figured it out. I could only pass seven times. Each time was like a lifetime over there, but only a few days here. They told me the secrets of the universe and how to control it all within my manor. I believe Enoch called them the Watchers. They also told me of the battles I had to fight. They appointed me and those around me to protect mankind and this realm."

"The Watchers, it can't be," Tom whispered.

Simon felt lightheaded. He leaned on the wall. Jeff sat on the floor and Tom approached the ball.

"Tom, not too close."

"Can I step into it, like you did?"

"No, the elders on the other side locked it to prevent any bleeding through of our world. They told me there would be a time in the future, 2020, when the two portals on Earth will be unlocked again. It won't be a good day for mankind or the planet. Once that day arrives, I am to step through one last time. I believe it is to start the end times."

"So, you said the Vatican has one," said Tom. "Have you ever tried to get to their portal?"

"No, see, I was told to use the energy to help mankind. Let's leave the room. I see it's affecting each of you." Gus directed them back through the hallway. He held Tom's shoulders when Tom lost his balance.

Collapsing in chairs, their bodies felt like they had a bad flu. Jeff threw up, and Simon slumped to the floor.

"A couple minutes and it will pass," said Gus.

"When will this all end? Showing us stuff that makes no sense, and when will you tell us what you want us for?"

"You can decide tomorrow morning when this all ends."

"Sorry, Gus, I meant all the surprises. So, that portal powers all the ports you talk about?" asked Tom.

"Yes, don't ask me how. As they say, *it's above my pay grade.*" He smiled at them.

Tom slid out of his chair onto the floor. Jeff dropped beside him, checking for a pulse. He slapped Tom on the cheek. "Tom, Tom, it's okay. It's a lot to take on. I know. We're all struggling."

Tom's eyes fluttered as he took in a deep breath. He sat up and pulled his legs into his chest.

"That's enough for the day. Let's head back for some food. You guys can spend the evening with the others, reading or strolling through the gardens. I have shown you enough for today."

"One more question, Gus," Simon said, following him back through the rooms and stairs. "Why?"

"Because they asked me to."

CHAPTER FORTY

Jeff's eyes opened. The room was dark except for the glow around his door. He could hear a knocking behind it. He rolled over and pulled the covers up. His body froze as the bedroom door rattled with the force of someone knocking. He turned on the light and looked at the clock. 3:20 a.m., according to the direction of the hands. Jeff stood beside his bed. His mind couldn't decide whether he was in reality or dreaming. The knock was louder. He looked at Tom, who had not stirred. Slowly, he turned the handle. From the other side, the door swung open with a force, knocking him to the floor. He looked up at a dark figure standing before him. A black hood covered his head, and a cape hung from his shoulders.

"Jeff, friend, come with me. I want to show you something."

"What about the others?"

"Let them sleep. This is for you to see."

Jeff looked over his shoulder. Simon's door was closed, and Tom still lay with his mouth open, and the covers pulled up to his neck. Jeff turned and followed the figure down the hallway into another bedroom.

"Lay here, Jeff." The figured patted the mattress on the first bed.

"No, I'm fine."

The door slammed closed. Jeff spun to see who was behind him. Seeing no one, he turned around. Suddenly, the man knocked him on his back.

"I told you to lie down. Jeff, Gus says he can show you things, but I will show you so much more. Come with me. Let me take you away."

Jeff pulled back. The figure leaned into him, his four fangs dripping with saliva. Suddenly, Jeff watched as the black hoodie and cape were replaced with a white gown and a papal hat.

He screamed and kicked.

•   •   •

Jeff woke in a cold sweat, kicking the sheets and punching at the air.

"Bad dream, mate?" Tom asked, standing at the side of his bed. "Time to get up, anyway."

Jeff lay back on his pillow, his heart racing in his chest. He reached for his neck, searching for bite marks. "What time is it?"

"Ten to seven. We should get ready."

Jeff lay on his bed, looking at the canopy above his head, recalling his dream.

Don't tell them.

•   •   •

Simon opened the door to the hallway. Kenny and a Noel strolled along the hallway.

"Well timed—we were coming to see you." Kenny said, smiling. "Are we going to wrestle again today?"

"No, not today. Sorry to disappoint everyone, but there will be no Bruce Lee demonstration today." The group laughed at Tom's comment.

"Gus is ready to see you. Can you drink these bottles of water on the way to his study?"

"I swear all I have done the last couple days is drink water and piss," said Simon.

"Get used to it. It gets better as the water fills your cells. You won't need as much," said Kenny.

They took their bottles of water and cracked the lids open as they walked down the hallway.

"I assume your clothes fit?" asked Noel.

"Not just fit, but they are so soft," said Jeff.

They stepped onto the elevator and rode it down to the main floor. Gus stood in the hallway, his contagious smile welcoming them.

"I have it from here. Thank you, Kenny."

The trio stepped out and followed Gus. "How did everyone sleep last night?"

"Fine I think," said Tom.

"No strange dreams?"

Simon looked at Jeff and Tom.

"I had one that woke me this morning, Gus," said Jeff.

"Good, good, let me guess, a man in black tried to take you with him. He then turned into a religious vampire. You woke just before he bit your neck."

Jeff rubbed his hand around his neck. "Yes, sir."

"Ah, the young always get them. But you are here, so you have decided to stay with me. Thank you, Jeff."

"What about us?" asked Simon.

"We will need to do a quick blood test. Just a prick."

"For what?" asked Simon.

"It's an antigen test. Like I said yesterday, you can't cross without being tested."

They entered Gus' study. "Sit, gentlemen. I'll get April to do the test." He waved them to the couch as he seated himself behind his desk.

Simon, instead of sitting, stood over Gus' desk and leaned on it. "Gus, I was wondering, is the water changing our DNA?"

"No, heavens no. I'm not like the others."

"You mean the ones that have the same setup as you in the Vatican and the small setup in Antarctica?"

"Yes, through GMO foods, polluting the air, and many other ways, you have been changed since you were born. The water has been scrubbing that from your cells. Today is the day you decide to stay or leave."

"Gus, I came here to save those twins and return them to their parents. It's still the plan. This is all great, but you can't keep kids from their families. I'm not staying here to be one of your soldiers."

"Simon, settle. I wouldn't ask you to do that. You're not soldier material, quite frankly."

Simon glared at him. "What am I, some kind of sacrificial lamb for your cause?"

"You have this all wrong. We are the good guys—we wear the white cowboy hats. I, we didn't change your DNA, the world has. We're just bringing it back to where it should be. Simon, you can live older than seventy with our water. It scrubbed your blood, your cells are resetting. Dig deep, no pain, clearer thoughts, and your hair is growing back. Here is a picture of you three days ago. Come, gents, I have one of each of you." He placed five-by-seven photos on his desk. They each took their own and stepped in front of the mirror on the wall beside Gus's desk.

"This is a trick mirror or edited pictures."

"Neither." Gus stood before the mirror. His reflection did not change. Simon looked carefully into the mirror, then at Gus.

"Who thought if I walked before this mirror, I wouldn't have a reflection? Come on, it crossed through one of your minds. No? Didn't you watch horror movies when you were young?"

"Honestly, it crossed my mind," said Simon. He chuckled at the thought.

"You see the difference, right?"

He pointed to Tom and himself. "Yes, we look different for sure. Jeff, well, he's young, so I wouldn't expect too much change."

April entered the room. She held a silver tray with test tubes partially filled with a yellow chemical and needles still in their wrappers. She placed the tray on the table by the couch and chairs.

"Only Tom and Simon need to be tested. Jeff had the dream," said Gus.

She smiled at Jeff. "Welcome."

"To what?"

"You'll see."

"I thought you said just a prick. Why are there needles on this tray?" asked Tom.

"That's for later. It's a prick, just like a diabetic test. Can I have your finger, please?" asked April.

Tom stuck his finger out. She pressed the small collector into his index finger. A drop of blood gathered on the collection sheet. She took it and dropped it into a test tube, then gently shook the tube and watched. The color turned to a faint blue. "Two more bottles before noon should do it."

"What? Two more? I'll drown," said Tom. "Gus, with all this drinking, you need to add a bathroom or two."

April looked at Tom and smiled. She repeated the process for Simon. His was darker. "One bottle, Simon. Before noon, once you finish the one you have."

Simon nodded. He wanted to see what Gus had left to show him and find a weakness in the manor to steal the twins.

Gus sat on a burgundy leather chair and looked at each man, then wrote notes on the pad. He raised his head and took a breath. Before he spoke, April returned with her prescribed bottles of water. She handed Jeff a bottle. "Drink this one. It won't hurt. The first trip is always a little harder on the body."

Tom and Simon turned to look at her.

She smiled at Gus and left the room.

•   •   •

"Let's start with the children," said Gus.

"Yes, can I speak to the twins again? There is also a few other kids we would be interested in seeing. You must know, we have families in France and Australia looking for their children," said Simon.

"Yes, I'm well aware. But for now, here are the Eason twins." Gus turned. "Kids, come in, please."

The twins entered the room. They acknowledged Gus and sat beside Simon.

"Tell them what it's like here," said Gus.

"Simon, it's great here. We have fun learning and playing," said Don. "We can travel wherever we want and whenever we want. There is an older kid who saw his own birth. Gus is so nice to us. Gus and his staff treat us very well, and we have lots of fun." He paused. "I don't like the needle, but I know I'm special, and my blood is incredibly special. It helps keep the realm alive. I told Mom and Dad you were here with your friends. They were happy you're okay. They had tried to call you a few times."

"Don't forget about the daily trips to the amusement parks or beach and the go-carts and the ice cream," said Gus.

"Can I ask them questions?"

"Yes, that's why they're here."

"Don't you want to go home? See Mom and Dad? Your friends?"

"No, we're safer here," said Doug. "We would rather be here than risk Mom and Dad's life."

"We get to see Mommy and Daddy every day. We know Mom and Dad are sad, but when we visit, they smile. Then they're happy for a little while," said Don.

"How does that work?" asked Tom.

"I can explain it later. Or better yet, show you," said Gus.

"What about growing up with them? Hugging them and playing games?" asked Simon.

"Simon, it's okay. We have stuff to do here. We travel back in time. It's not the same time, I think, but it's so close," said Doug.

"Like right beside here," said Don. He stretched his arm out.

"Yeah here," said Doug. He placed his hand on his side. "Plus, we have a lot of friends here we travel with."

"So, you're happy here?"

"We don't want to leave. We can't right now," Doug said. "What if the Fallen gets us again?"

"Yeah, that would be bad," said Don. "I remember what they did to Ricky."

"Yes, very bad," said Gus.

Simon looked at them. He studied their expressions, the way they sat, and how they answered the questions. His training from when he was the lead interrogator in Guelph, a lifetime ago, didn't show any *tells* from them. They were not lying or being forced to say anything. All he saw were two cheerful children on a special mission.

"Okay, can we talk again later?"

"I would like that," said Doug. "Thank you for helping Mom and Dad since the wicked men took us. You were there that day on your bike. I remember seeing you. I saw you as they closed the van door. You were blurry through my tears."

"Can we go? I have music with Chopin," said Don.

"Yeah, I have a history class on World War One. I need to get to France and Flanders Field. Tomorrow, well a hundred years ago tomorrow, is a big day."

"Simon, do you have anything else?" Gus looked at him. His smile said *told you so*.

"Not right now," said Simon.

"You are dismissed."

Doug and Don ran out the door.

"Satisfied?" Gus asked Simon.

Simon studied Gus for a second. "Yes—no, what? I don't know what to think, Gus. How would I ever tell their parents they are happier here than with them?" asked Simon.

"You won't. You don't need to. They see them, not as often or how they would like. But Simon, I can't stress this enough. They can't leave the property in this realm. I need you to understand. Please."

"Huh, because the boogeyman will get them?"

Gus looked at the others and lowered his head. "Talk to him, please."

"Drink these bottles and go grab some breakfast and talk to people. Come see me when you get the water done. No cheating either. It's important, very important for your safety."

•   •   •

They sat in the dining hall. The table had more people than usual around it. Trays of pancakes, fruit, waffles, sausages, bacon, and bread were brought out, replacing empty trays.

"Excuse me, is this every breakfast?" asked Jeff.

"Yes, usually, you can't go wrong with bacon and eggs," said the lady seated beside him.

"Do people die young of heart attacks, all this grease and fatty food?" asked Simon. "Or do you just drink another bottle of water?"

"Son, no. This is pure food, no preserves, no chemicals, all grown with our own animals and fields. We make it all. Just like in the old days, well, it is the old days where we raise these pigs. It's the preservatives and chemicals that kill people, not the food."

Simon smiled. "Thank you."

"Another conspiracy confirmed. I should've brought a check sheet of conspiracies. I feel we are closing a lot of them off," said Tom.

"Drink your water. It's the purest thing in this realm," said the man beside Tom.

"I have never drunk so much water," said Tom.

"Yeah, but you feel good, right? I'm Bill." He stood and shook their hands.

"That I do, we all do. My back hasn't felt this good since I was a kid," said Simon. "What do you two do here?"

"I'm Martha." The lady said, seated across from Bill. "We work in the stables and help in the barns."

"This might be rude, but when were you two born?"

"Not rude at all. 1859," said Bill.

"He's a kid. I was born in 1798. We work in 1839. That's where most of our food comes from. Before the industrial age ruined the soil and air."

"What? You have golden blood?" asked Jeff.

"Yes, most of us do. You don't?" asked Bill.

"No, none of us do," said Jeff.

"That's too bad. You can't travel through eternity. We travel to 1839 to work during the day. A bunch of us do. We are all very particular about our food. You can't grow anything these days with the pollution and the spraying of the chemicals. We found the best time to grow is back in the eighteen hundreds. The animals look different too because the hand of man hasn't turned them," said Martha. "It's amazing how we have manipulated the look of animals and food over the last hundred years."

Tom nodded his head. "Makes sense."

"Why do you work?" asked Tom.

"It's what we were created to do. Believe me, you need some purpose in life. Every few years we change jobs, times, education levels. Five years ago, I was running a lab in the lower levels. I worked on a camera lens you will see on phones soon. Gus sold the rights through a shell company. After that, I needed a break, and nothing's better than manual labor to soothe the soul."

"So, why are you all here?" asked Jeff.

"What?" asked Bill.

"Not here, but here, at this time?"

"I'll answer your question." Gus sat beside the group. "I haven't invited anyone here in years. I guess I forgot to explain to you how this realm works."

"Okay, so why now?"

"Let me get some food." He returned with a plate of bacon and two waffles. "Pass the syrup."

Jeff slid it across the table. "Real maple syrup from your country, Simon. The trees this came from are likely cut down and the roots are covered with a subdivision or mall now."

"Dare I ask?" asked Simon.

"You can. But to save you, it's from trees in what you call Quebec. We harvested it back in the 1790s on a small farm."

"Of course."

"It's fantastic," said Jeff.

Gus smiled at Jeff. "Okay, so why now? I can't believe I forgot this. It's kind of important. The Earth, this realm, is the master realm, the Creator's realm. Everything feeds off here. This is the master clock that God started billions of years ago. This is, for lack of a better term, ground zero. Everything, dimensions, realms, and all our ports feed out from and back into this realm, even the portal itself. Here, this realm or dimension, time can't be changed, and nothing can stop it, yet. The Fallen are trying to end it and live in another realm. They know if they can gather all those with original blood and move them to a secondary realm, then this one will close in on itself. Closing our creator from us. Then they can rule the new realm, with no fear of God intervening. No one knows what would happen, or if it would even work. We must prevent that from becoming a reality."

Simon shook in his chair. He took a drink of water, then a mouthful of scrambled eggs. He shook his head. "This must be a dream, an amazing dream, nevertheless, a dream."

"No, it's no dream. You are right where you need to be. Cindy here, she works in the basement. She is one of the realm controllers keeping the ports stable," said Gus. "You might see her later, when you go through."

"Keep talking, enjoy the food and come see me when you're ready," said Gus to Simon, Tom and Jeff.

"When you live for as long as we have, you need to travel, educate yourself and work, or life becomes very boring without purpose. No one ever retired in the Bible. I think there's a reason the public die before one hundred. It's not that our bodies wear out, but our souls become bored. A little piece of us remembers where we came from. But when we are born with these meat suits on, it blocks those memories. As we age, we remember again, then realize the only way back is to leave the meat suit here. You will see what I mean. Or maybe you already do," said Bill. "Keep drinking your water."

Tom smirked and swallowed more water. "Are you saying we won't die drinking this water?"

"It's a little different for you with regular blood. But look at Gus and his age, you can last that long, too. Just don't become bored. Learn and challenge yourselves daily."

Simon poked the fork into his forearm.

"It's not a dream. Oh, and if you do poke hard enough to cut yourself, well, guess what happens?" asked Martha. "We all have tried. It's weird. You heal quickly, without scars." She looked at the clock. "We have to leave. It was nice meeting you three. Enjoy your day."

Bill followed Martha out the door.

"Get the water in you, Tom. I can't wait to see what we're in for," said Jeff.

CHAPTER FORTY-ONE

They stepped out of the elevator and followed Gus to a room full of doors. April met them there. She held three vials in her hand. Each one had a name on it.

"Okay, gents, a couple of things to review. First, did you drink all the water I told you to?"

They nodded.

"Second, I have to give you this small vial of golden blood. You won't feel it, but it works with the water. Without it, you'll suffer the opposite of the last couple of days. You'll age at a sped-up rate."

"Seems like an important detail to forget until now?" said Simon.

"Just like your lack of trust in us, some things we had to hold until you needed to know. But now here you are. We trust you."

"If you didn't, would April have sent us through the port without the blood to age and die?" asked Simon.

April glanced at Gus.

"Okay, I hate needles. Isn't there a pill?" Tom laughed at his comment.

"No, the good news is you only need this top up every six trips," said April.

They took a seat and extended their left arms. April took each needle and injected the blood into them.

"Good, good, now we wait. Fifteen minutes will do it," said Gus.

"Where are we going?" asked Tom.

"This is your first trip. We have sent three of our men over—Kenny, Noel and Peter. You have met them before. They usually travel together. We're sending you to a remote part of Canada. Sending you home, Simon. I know you wanted to see your kids, but Helen prevented you from doing that. But if she hadn't, we wouldn't have met."

"To Canada? To see my kids?" asked Simon.

"Yes, I thought it might help you. You're heading to Elliot Lake, Ontario. There's a fire watchtower overlooking the town. Your ex-wife is traveling back to Guelph. She is visiting her parents and then with the kids and her boyfriend, they are continuing down east."

"Elliot Lake, I know of it. I biked it a few years ago with a friend."

"Remember, you are in a different existence. Just a shift over, right? Beside them, just off center," said Gus. "Like you have seen us, and the parents see their kids. Only they won't see you."

"This is how you do it?" asked Jeff.

"Yes, through a port. We set the coordinates and you step through the door. It sounds simple but..."

"I'm sure it's not simple at all," said Tom. "Hopefully it will make sense when we pass through. Is there anything else we should know? In the movies there is dimensional illness or lightheadedness."

"What color are your eyes?" Gus looked at Jeff. "Jeff, you have blue eyes, you need to be careful. Usually blue-eyed people will..."

"Gus, stop. Travel humor, or a poor attempt at it," said April. "You might feel thirsty, even though you have drunk so much water. We have bottles waiting for you."

"And you will lose all your hair," said Gus, still laughing at his first comment. "I'm just trying to lighten the mood. It's tense in here."

"No, *no*." April looked at Gus. Her eyes said to stop with the humor.

"Ah, you will love this. You can stay the night if you want to explore, or go into town. It's a bit of a hike. Your kids will be at the fire tower. We estimate about an hour after you arrive. That will give you time to adjust and—give our guys the chance to put you back together if..."

"Gus, enough!" April laughed at his comment.

"When you return, we will need to have a talk about the future and your role in it. But, for now, enjoy the day. On down time, you can sit on beaches, ski, whatever you like. You will see people, but they won't see you. Unless they have a bit of clairvoyance. They might feel you. But don't worry about that."

"All right, that should be enough time. Who wants to go first?" asked April.

The excitement of the moment died, and no one stepped forward. Tom looked at his shoes, Jeff looked April in the eyes, pleading not to be picked first.

"Fine, right, let's go. I'm heading in. What do I do to see my kids?" asked Simon.

"Don't trip on the step, but just walk through. It will tickle a little. If you stumble, Kenny is there to grab you. There is a meter of darkness to reach through," said Gus.

"April stuck her hand through the door. Her arm disappeared. Then she pulled it back.

"What did you do there?" questioned Simon.

"Oh, I just waved at the guys, so they know we're sending one of you over."

Simon stepped to the door. He stopped and turned, looking at the others, and smiled. "Well, keep your stick on the ice." His leg was absorbed by the blackness, then his waist. He leaned forward and in a blink of an eye disappeared.

Jeff stood from his chair. His face was flipping between shock and confidence. "Cowabunga!" He stepped through the door without hesitating.

Tom stood. "My mind still can't sort this all out."

"Tom, I am hundreds of years old and can't figure it all out. There are still many secrets hidden from me. Go and enjoy yourself," said Gus.

"I have one question left for when I return. I would really like to know the answer. How did you figure all this out, the water, the blood, the ports and who has golden blood?"

"Simple. It was all those meetings through the portal. They told me everything. You need to go. They are waiting."

Tom moved to the door and stepped through it, into darkness. With his left leg, he took a second step. He passed through a green wall of light. Then in a flash, wind blew through his hair. The heat of the sun touched his skin. Noel took his arm and balanced him. He looked around. Jeff sat on a park bench, his legs crossed, and arms spread across the backrest. Simon stood with Peter and Kenny looking over the side of the outlook. The green trees and landscape went for miles, only broken by the gray buildings of Elliot Lake. Blue and green lakes, roads and trails cut through the woods.

"How was it, mate?" asked Noel.

"Are you okay, Tom?" asked Simon.

"I'm fine." Tom looked behind him. Nothing was there. He expected to see a wave or some form of deflection where he stepped through.

A car parked to his right, and a family exited the vehicle. The kids screamed as they ran from their parents.

"So, how do we get back?" asked Jeff.

"Not now, Jeff. Enjoy the moment," said Tom.

• • •

Simon wandered around the parking lot. He walked to the edge and looked out over the vast greenery of Northern Ontario. "Beautiful, isn't it? This is Canada when you leave southern Ontario," Simon said to Jeff.

Beside him, Jeff looked down at the sprawling landscape. He walked down a set of steps to a small gazebo. "How far do you think we can see?"

"I have no clue, but it's spectacular. I wasn't expecting to see so much green, I forgot how beautiful it was. We should come back mid-September when the colors change on the trees. I think the water on the horizon could be Lake Huron. As beautiful and green as England is well..." He waved his hand in front of him.

Simon looked back at the parking lot. Tom stood with Noel and Peter. "Hey, something's not right. We better go see what Tom's upset about."

Jeff stole another look before following Simon up the stairs. They approached the group and overheard an animated Tom. "No one said that before we crossed to here. How about we get all the rules and side effects before we travel? This need-to-know attitude isn't funny."

"Tom, what's the matter?"

"We can't go back," said Tom.

Simon turned to Noel. He raised his hand to stop Simon from reacting.

"We can go back, but there is always a one hour reset. Standard. Nothing to worry about. Really, it's now a fifty-one-minute reset. Or we can stay for three days. Why would you travel just to go right back? Gus told you about how time is different for us here, too?"

"Mate, no one told us we couldn't..." said Tom.

"Tom," Simon put his arm around his shoulder. "We can travel anywhere in the world for free. Come look at this view. Stop worrying about it and come over here. Plus, my kids will be here soon."

Tom stepped to the edge of the parking lot and froze. "I don't like heights or high places. This is close enough." He pushed back from Simon.

Simon turned and looked at him. "How about we sit there on the park bench? It's away from the edge."

Tom sat. He was shaking. Simon sat quietly beside him, enjoying the cool air and the view. Others passed by, not noticing the pair sitting on the bench. A couple walked to the bench, then decided not to sit.

Noel sat beside Tom. "Times up. If you're ready, we can leave."

"No, my family should arrive shortly," said Simon.

A vehicle crawled to a stop. Two kids stepped out of the back doors. Simon sucked in the air. "There they are." He smiled at them, forgetting they couldn't see him. Helen stepped out of the passenger door. Simon looked at her. She had lost some weight, and he saw something he hadn't seen in the last two years of his marriage.

She smiled.

The driver's door opened, and a man stepped out. He waited for Helen and grabbed her hand. "You two be careful at the edge," he said to the boys standing at the safety wall.

Simon watched as they gathered by his kids. They stood, looking over the landscape.

"All right, mate?" asked Jeff.

"Yeah, I think I am. She looks so happy. The kids look happy as well. Yeah, I'm okay."

With his arm around Helen, Tony leaned in and kissed the crown of her head. She turned to him and looked him in the eyes. They looked deep into each other's eyes and kissed.

"Mom, Tony, you can see the entire world from here," said Kyle, the youngest.

"I'm sure it's not easy. Go to your kids and see them," said Tom.

Simon stepped toward his children. "It's as beautiful as you said, Tony," Helen said.

"I told you, we came here every summer to visit my aunt and uncle. We had to stop on the way. What do you think, boys? That in the distance is Lake Huron."

"Kyle, this is so cool," said Richard.

Simon reached his hand towards them. He pulled his hand back when he touched them. Kyle turned and looked.

"What's wrong?" asked Helen.

"Not sure, Mom. It felt like someone touched my shoulder," said Kyle.

"I felt it too," said Richard.

"They say that feeling can be a loved one thinking of you," said Tony.

"Really, Tony? I wonder if it was Dad?" asked Kyle.

Simon stepped back. Tom approached him and put his arm on his shoulder. "Hey, no one said this would be easy."

"I know," said Simon, tears gathered in his eyes.

"Just think, you can do this when you want. I hate to say it, but they all look happy," said Tom.

"Yes, yes, they do. And I have seen them more now than in the last year."

Jeff stood beside Simon. "Nice kids. You doing okay?"

His friends surrounded him as tears dripped from Simon's chin. "Well, I've lost my family. I have no one to blame but myself for putting my job, and now this adventure, before them." He looked at Jeff and then Tom.

"Susan and Robin don't deserve this feeling. You can help or not, but they will get their kids back. None of this dimensional difference. They will see, hug, and hold their children. In the proper dimension."

Helen turned and looked towards him. Then back to Tony. His boys ran past him. He reached out to touch them.

Simon sat through watery eyes and watched Helen and Tony take selfies. They asked a couple to take a group photo.

Simon stepped behind his kids and hugged them. They didn't move as he squeezed.

"Stop it," said Kyle, swatting Richard's arm.

"What? Don't touch me," said Richard.

"Then don't touch me."

"I didn't."

"Boys, stop it. I want one good group photo, then you can go and check out the outlook station. Fifteen minutes, then we're leaving," said Helen.

"It's okay. Give them a break. They've been stuffed in the car for five days on our crazy cross-country trip."

"I guess." She pressed her head into Tony's shoulder.

Simon dropped his head and returned to the group.

"I know it's difficult, Simon. But we have all had to say goodbye to someone through this dimension," said Kenny.

"You did?" asked Simon.

"Yes. Back in 1890, I said bye to my dad as he passed. Then two years later, to my mom."

"Thank you for this. It might not seem like it, but seeing them happy puts my mind at ease," he said to the group. "Before we go back, I have one question. If I was to fall off the side here and died, what would happen?"

Noel looked at him quizzically. "You would die."

"And my body?"

"You would return to Guelph, likely found in a car or something. We don't control that."

"Quickly, so you can say bye to your family. When one of us dies here or in the first realm or any other one, Gus passes the body through a special door. No living person has been through it except Gus, that I'm aware of.

STEPHEN W. BRIGGS   349

Whoever is there accepts the body and returns it to the time and place they came from. Now go see your kids before they get in the SUV," said Noel.

Simon looked at him, then turned. His kids ran around the vehicle laughing. Helen and Tony walked to them, hands clasped together and arms swinging. Tony opened the door for her, then gathered the kids into the vehicle. Simon ran to the window and looked in. He watched his boys turn on their tablets and loaded a game. As Helen passed, he blew her a kiss.

She looked out the side window, stealing one last look at the scenery. He raised his hand and waved as they drove away. He stopped waving but didn't lower his arm.

Goodbye, boys. Daddy loves you.

Wiping his cheeks, he walked back to the group.

"I'll let you know. But yes, there was a vote," said Noel.

"What did I miss?" asked Simon. "Vote for what?"

"Do we invite you into the manor or bury you in the woods?" said Noel. "Especially after what happened to Nigel."

"Is the woods still on the table?" asked Jeff.

"No, well, no. I would say no." The doubt in Noel's voice made the trio nervous. "You two are in good standing, but Simon, please let it go. The twins and all other children need to stay with us. Please, Gus has asked those that have interacted with you about your commitment. We are all concerned about your desire to take the children. Please understand they are safe at the manor. He arranged this for you to show you how easy it is to see your family."

"I appreciate that, but I would rather hold my sons in the flesh, not like a ghost."

Noel shook his head and turned to look at the view.

"So, what do you do here? I can't imagine with all these battles going on that this is just a realm to come to for a vacation?"

"No, we usually have an assignment to work on. Like finding the Fallen's labs, or protecting young kids with golden blood. There is plenty to do daily. The worst days are when we interact with the hoodies. It means that we have been exposed or they have. Those days usually end in some form of a fight. But the good days, when we save a child from their grasps, make it all worthwhile. It takes a lot of work to find those hidden labs. A lot of research and tracking. Then we have to work in the Creator's realm to rescue them."

"Is that what we are being asked to do?"

"No, I don't think so. Maybe you Jeff, but not you two. Don't worry about that now," said Kenny. "There are some fun things we can do to manipulate the first realm. Watch this."

He stood behind a family standing along the railing looking out. The youngest daughter was standing on the safety rails' bottom bar. She was on her tippy toes, straining to see down the edge. Kenny stepped to her, and with a gentle pull, had her slip off the railing. She landed sure footed on the ground and looked around. He turned to the group, laughing.

Turning to the father, he whispered in his ear.

The man took one last look at the landscape and turned. He pulled out his camera and took a photo of the empty park bench.

"What are you doing, hon?"

He spun and looked at her. "I just thought it would be funny. I don't know why but..."

"Dad, you're so silly sometimes," said the boy.

"Yeah, we can be that little voice in your head. It helps sometimes. Bit of a carnie trick, but we use it a lot, especially when the others try to assassinate a person. We are behind a lot of the conspiracy theories. Not theories but truths that are hard to prove in the first realm, because of what we do in this realm."

"Do we want to hike down to the town or go back?" asked Kenny.

"If we go into town, do we have to come back up here to go back?" asked Tom.

"No," said Kenny.

"I'm up for a good hike," said Simon.

They descended the steep hill, controlling their speed, trying not to slip or fall on the freshly laid gravel. They stopped at a lake to take in the beauty of it. A large rock had a turtle sunbathing, and on the far side, a moose bent and drank from the lake.

"This really is beautiful here," said Jeff.

"It is," said Kenny. "There are many places around the world to see. Knowing what you now know about our world, tell me how any of you could say no to an offer from Gus."

"I agree. But what is his offer?" asked Tom.

"Here's something I just thought of," said Simon. "If we accept his offer, what happens to our houses, cars, clothes? Us?"

"Well, we have people that would sell or donate those items. Obviously, you can take keepsakes, but everything else would be gone. Simon for you, a trust would be created from the sale of your house and property. Gus would hold it for your kids' education or whatever."

"We don't get the money?" asked Simon.

"Why would you? You will never need a pound or dollar again if you stay with us. None of us need anything," said Noel.

They left the lake and continued down the road. Birds flew overhead and a cool breeze picked up.

"Okay, what about us?" asked Jeff.

"We told you, Gus has roles for you," said Kenny.

"No, our story. We have a large audience for the podcast. I have a job and Simon does, too. We all have friends. I don't think they will all just forget about us."

"Right, well, that gets complicated, as you can imagine. But we have a team that will deal with it. I'm just not sure how. I would assume for you three it's not as easy as a kidnapping of a child. Sorry to use that example," said Peter. He pointed ahead. "Almost down."

They turned onto a highway and walked on the shoulder towards town. Jeff and Simon dragged behind, thinking about what they were just told. Tom walked with Kenny, talking about having him as a guest on his podcast.

"Look." Peter pointed into the woods. A family of deer watched them pass.

"They can see us?" asked Tom.

"Yes, animals can see us," said Peter.

"Well, this is a lot longer hike than I thought," said Tom, sweat bubbling on his forehead.

"Another question. When I touched my kids, they felt something. How come they couldn't see me?"

"Simple. It's in the door's programming," said Kenny.

"Kenny, if they don't have golden blood, can they be seen?" asked Noel.

Kenny stopped and rubbed his chin. "Good question. I don't know the answer."

"I don't think they can. But that's a question for Gus," said Peter. "Plus, it would really mess with the story of you all missing, if you appeared in places."

"So will doing a podcast."

"Yeah, good point. I am sure Gus has figured it out. It's not my job to worry about those details, thankfully."

They turned into a parking lot beside a beach. "Can we take a break there?" asked Simon.

They walked to the beach and sat on the sand. Jeff looked around the area. Multiple families were enjoying the fall day. A toddler left his parents and stood in front of Jeff and stared.

"Hello," said Jeff.

"Hi, you look strange. What's…" The toddler's mother grabbed him by the arm and pulled him back to his blanket. She scolded him as he sat staring back at the group.

"Yeah, I forgot kids are born with the ability to see through the realms. But as they grow, they lose the skill, or have it taken away by being told we don't exist. Usually by five or six. We are everyone's imaginary friend."

They looked over the waveless water to the trees and hills in the distance.

"I think I'm ready to go back. Would you guys agree?" asked Jeff. "I don't have a jacket and I'm getting a chill."

"Fully," said Simon.

"Oh yeah, I'm more than ready," said Tom.

"Can we go back?" asked Simon.

Kenny took out a small blue ball. Placed it on the ground and stepped on it. He took three steps back and stopped. "This way, fellas, same as when you came over."

Tom stepped through, followed by Jeff. Simon turned around and stepped backwards. He watched as the world he was in turned to darkness, then he was back in the room, lying on his back. He had tripped, missing a step.

April and the rest watched as he appeared horizontal, then dropped to the floor. She stood at his head. "Lesson learned? There's always one that has to be a showboat going through."

Kenny appeared and stepped around Simon, as did Noel. Peter stepped on Simon's thigh.

Simon smiled at her. He rolled onto his belly and pushed himself up. "Is it me, or are you guys hungry?"

"Starved," said Jeff.

"The dining hall will have food for you, then Gus wants to see you," said April. "Here, take a bottle to drink. Always have a bottle of water with you, especially as soon as you get back. Finish this one and get another one drunk before dark."

"April, luv, we're still new. How do we get up to the main level?" asked Tom.

"Follow me," said Kenny. "You'll get your bearings the longer you are here."

She grinned. "You haven't even seen half the levels yet."

CHAPTER FORTY-TWO

Gus met them in the dining hall. It was full of kids and adults in blue tunics.

"How was your trip?" asked Gus.

"Trippy, for lack of a better word," said Tom.

"What do you think about all this? Intrigued? By midnight, you have decisions to make. I'm asking, would you three join me and the quest to keep this realm as we know it? Unfortunately, I can't offer you eternal life, but I can offer a long life full of adventure and mystery."

"Robin and Susan sent me here to find those twins. The ones sitting at that table. Can they be returned to their parents?" asked Simon.

"No." Gus said sternly. "The answer will always be no, Simon."

"I'm in Gus, sir. I'm all in. There's nothing to lose. No one waiting for me at home. Where do I sign?" said Jeff.

"Thank you, Jeff. There is nothing to sign. There is no pay, no pension, just service and worlds to see. Jeff, after you eat, go with Noel. He'll give you the rest of the tour and set you up."

"Gus, the kids, they need to see their parents. The parents need to see their kids, is probably more the truth. And not just see them, but touch them. I appreciated getting to see mine and, emotionally at least, saying goodbye."

"Let us travel to Guelph and talk to Doug and Don's parents. Explain what is happening. Then see what they do. Is there anything that could happen?"

"Plenty and again, the answer is *no*."

"Then we need to go to our room and think if we want in. What you have shown us is spectacular, despite that, there are kids who need their parents. You will have your answer by midnight, as requested. Come get us at half-past eleven," said Simon.

•   •   •

Simon and Tom sat in their room, discussing their options. By nine, Tom was struggling to stay awake. He lay on his bed, needing a minute to rest. Ten minutes later, he was snoring.

Simon left the room, wanting to tour the property for himself. Seeing his kids earlier only motivated him to get the others back to their parents. He walked through the third floor and then the second. Further down the eastern wing, he heard children laughing. He followed the sound to a door. With his ear pressed against it, he tried the handle. It turned with ease. He opened the door and peeked around it. There on the floor were the twins and seven other children playing a board game. He checked over his shoulder and along the hallway, then stepped into the room.

"Hello, Doug and Don. What are you guys doing up?"

"Simon," said Doug. "We don't have a bedtime. And some days when we travel, we all have a tough time getting to sleep, so we have sleepovers."

Simon looked at the other kids. Images of kidnappings, parents worried about their kids and siblings being killed, ran through his mind. He waved Don and Doug over to a window.

"Boys, I'm here to take you home. Get a coat and come with me."

"We don't want to leave, Simon," said Doug.

"We can't leave," said Don. "Gus warned us you might come to take us."

"Your parents want to see you, hold you, and be with you. That's why I'm here. Please quietly come with me. You can come back in a few days. Your parents just want to see you, and hug you again."

Don looked at Doug. "I want to go. I want to see Mommy again. She said today if you try to get us home to go with you." He tried to control his tears, but they flowed. He grabbed Simon's hand.

"I don't think this is good, but you can't leave me here alone," said Doug. "And you will bring us back to where we are safe?"

"Yes, of course. We'll only be gone a few days."

They ran to their room and gathered their coats and a teddy. Simon waited for them in the hallway. He stepped down the stairs towards the front door, with the twins trailing behind him. The grand entrance was empty and dark. He ran to the front door and swung it open with the kids on his heels.

Too easy.

He looked around as they entered the garden. In the distance, he could hear the dogs barking. At the main gate, he followed the brick wall holding the kids' hands. Where the wall ended and hedges took their place, he found a small opening to crawl through. The children asked to go back, but he encouraged them, dangling the gift of seeing their parents for their hard work escaping. On the main road, lights broke over the hill. He stepped onto the road and waved his arms frantically.

•   •   •

Gus sat in the security room with Kenny, Noel, and Jeff. They watched as Simon ran from the house.

"Just like we expected. My gut tells me to stop him," said Gus. "His selfish actions shouldn't bring harm to the children."

"I think this is the only way he will learn," said Jeff. "It's why he's here. I think a little scare will help him see what danger is out there."

"He is putting those kids, himself and the entire manor at risk," said Gus. "You three are sure you can handle this?"

"Yes," said Kenny. "I'll have teams on guard in all realms. The children should feel sick in twelve hours. He'll have to return with them then."

"Don't engage unless needed. He needs to see the consequences of his actions." He looked at Jeff in his new blue tunic. "Take care of Simon. You know him better than anyone else."

CHAPTER FORTY-THREE

Three days later, Simon waited in a hotel close to Heathrow Airport. Don and Doug sat on the queen-size bed, looking at the door. They repeatedly asked Simon, "How much longer?"

Finally, an hour later than expected, there was a knock on the door. Doug jumped off the bed and ran to the door.

"No Doug, stand back. Let me check first." Simon looked through the peephole and confirmed who was knocking. He opened the door and welcomed Susan and Robin.

"Mom, Dad," Doug yelled. He wrapped his arms around them, and they pulled him in tight.

Don ran into his brother, trying to get his arms around the three of them.

"Come in and close the door," Simon said, checking the hallway. They carried their children to the bed and tossed them on it.

Susan hugged Simon. "Thank you."

Robin shook his hand and thanked him.

"I'm going to leave. You guys get reacquainted," said Simon.

"No, we'll come too. We've been stuck on planes for the last twelve hours with delays and layovers. Some fresh air and exercise sounds wonderful. The three of you can tell of your adventures," said Susan.

"I asked you to think about the next steps. Did you?" asked Simon.

"Yes, we agree with you. We need to go to the authorities and, like you said, not the local police but someone bigger than that. I guess Scotland

Yard. Or even our embassy. They have no passports and neither do you," said Robin.

"We need to get our friends' children back, too. I couldn't live with myself if we didn't try."

"You didn't..."

"No, no one knows we are here. Not even Gary and Mark," said Robin.

The twins sat quietly on their parents knees cuddled tight to their chests.

"Okay, why don't we head to the embassy," said Simon.

"We saw a park beside the hotel. Could we take the boys there for a bit? Let us stretch our legs before we are stuck in a car and then, I assume, small offices being grilled with questions?" asked Susan. "I think once we leave here, we won't be able to enjoy a park or much privacy for a while."

"Sure, we haven't left the room since we arrived a few days ago. Fresh air sounds great," said Simon. "But we need to be careful and not spend too much time outside."

They left the hotel with five men in blue tunics watching them from a different dimension.

•   •   •

The children played on the swings. Simon filled in the gaps he didn't reveal during the multiple phone calls to the Easton's over the last few days. From the shadows of the trees, they were watched. The sun hid behind dark clouds, and rain fell from the sky. Susan called the twins to her and placed jackets on them.

"We should head back, I guess," said Simon.

"Who are those men?" Robin pointed into the trees. Susan and Simon strained to see any movement in the shadows.

In an instant, an arm slid around Simon's neck and squeezed. He shook his body to break free, but the arm tightened, cutting off his air. A man held a gun to Susan's head, as another man in a black hoodie assaulted Robin from behind.

Black dots filled Simon's vision. He stood and, using the bench, pushed forward, falling. It broke the grip of his attacker. Then, from above, a body landed on him, a man in a black hoodie. Simon struggled to get him off. He watched as the twins were picked up and taken.

What have I done?

He threw his fist up at the attacker's chin and connected. The man dropped to the side, unconscious. Simon scrambled up and ran towards the twins, but two men pointed guns at him.

"That's enough, Simon," said the one man in a hoodie. Over his shoulder, Simon noticed Jeff, Kenny, Noel, and four others appear from the parking lot. Three ran at the men holding the children. More men in black appeared from the tree line.

Jeff and two others sprinted across the field. Three more men in tunics appeared from behind parked cars. With the pop of a gun, one man in black fell. Simon dropped to the ground as more bullets pierced the air. He reached up and yanked Susan to the ground as well. Robin threw himself over Susan, shielding her body with his own.

The men who grabbed the twins lay on the ground motionless, with the twins trapped underneath them. Two men in blue tunics fell as bullets pierced through the air. A man in black dropped a glowing ball and stepped on it. He dove through the port. A bullet caught his leg as he disappeared. Others ran to his location and jumped at the opening. The remaining two men in black approached the twins. With their guns drawn, they pulled the children to their feet.

Jeff tackled the man holding Doug, and they rolled on the ground with Doug rolling away. Kenny slammed into the second man. He held onto Don as he stumbled backward. His gun fell. From his pocket, he revealed a blue ball. Kenny kicked at his hand, knocking the ball to the ground. Then, from behind, Noel snatched Don.

From the ground, a muffled shot was heard. Kenny looked at Jeff lying on the ground, the man he tackled lying tight to him. Blood seeped out between them.

"*Jeff,*" Kenny yelled.

Kenny's assailant grabbed his shoulder. Kenny kicked him in the stomach. He folded from the hit—Kenny grabbed his shoulders and drove his knee up into his foe's head. His opponent dropped to the ground.

Kenny pulled the man off Jeff. Seeing blood, he panicked. He dropped beside Jeff and searched for the source of the blood. Jeff looked at him and gave him a thumbs up. They stood and scanned the park. All men in hoodies had either disappeared or were lying on the ground.

Jeff, Kenny, and Noel circled the twins with guns drawn.

Simon crawled to Robin. A pool of blood grew beside him. Simon shook him and pulled his arm, then reached for Susan. Blood dripped from her mouth and nose. "Are my kid's, okay?" she asked.

Simon looked around, then back at Susan. He nodded. She expelled her last breath.

This is all my fault.

He dropped his head on her shoulder. "I'm sorry. I thought I was doing the right thing. I was only trying to help."

He stood and looked around. Jeff and Noel approached him, each carrying a child. He waved at them to stop. He pointed to Robin and waved them away. Noel looked at Susan and Robin, then back at Simon.

Simon could see the disgust on his face.

Two other men lay in the field, their blue tunics darkened over their chests.

Sirens approached as the group gathered away from the bodies of Robin, Susan, and three men in hoodies.

"Happy, Simon? *Are you happy about this?*" asked Jeff. "Look around you. You caused all this." Jeff raised his gun at Simon.

"Not now, Jeff," said Kenny. "We lost two good men. Both were over two hundred years old. And here they are dead on a field because of your selfish intentions, trying to be a hero. I feel like knocking you out and leaving a gun in your hand. Let you take the fall for all of this."

Simon stood staring at the twins, his eyes widened. "I just—I just thought I was doing what was best for them."

"We have to go. The police are seconds away," said Noel. He dropped a ball and stepped on it. "Help them. We don't leave anyone behind." Simon followed the two men to the bodies on the ground. He grabbed the wrists of one body and dragged it across the grass. He looked for the port.

Noel's head appeared. "Here Simon, here. It's going to be rough for you since you haven't had water in a few days. You will be unconscious when you arrive on the other side. If you're lucky, we'll revive you."

Simon dragged the body towards the port. Looking at Robin and Susan's motionless bodies, he stepped backwards into the darkness.

CHAPTER FORTY-FOUR

Gus paced behind his desk. Simon sat across from it. His head was down and aching. Traveling without water caused him a migraine and arthritic pain in all his joints. April had assured him once he got a few bottles of water through his system, he would feel better. She delayed giving him the water for a few hours, letting him suffer. He wanted Gus to speak. The silence was too much for him. He looked at Gus. His anger filled the room.

"Gus, I'm..." Simon said.

"No, not good enough, Simon. What did I tell you? I blame myself too. I let you leave. For some reason, I thought letting you go would help you understand the seriousness of our situation. As the children became sick after a day, I thought you would learn a lesson. Needing to bring them back here. But no, you medicated them, helping them through the pain. Why would you take them to a park? You were all safe in the room. I still don't know how *we* weren't prepared for the park. I'll deal with Kenny and Jeff later. Right now, I need to deal with you. Simon, you had to be the hero. Had to *finish the mission*." With his fist, he pounded the desk. Simon jumped from the noise.

"How can I make this right? Can we go back in time?"

"No, Simon, there's no going back in time to fix this. Because of your actions, two loving parents are dead and two of my longtime friends will be placed back in time. That's the consequences of your selfish actions, Simon. The twins are traumatized, and my staff are angry at me for letting this happen. They are upset at the team for allowing you back. I sent you away to see your kids, to make inner peace with your family situation and this, this is how I am thanked! Your colleagues have decided to stay and work with me."

"That option for me has been pulled from the table, I assume?" he asked.

"You would think, but no. I have been around too long to be that quick to judge. I know what you did and why. I should have stopped you, but sometimes the lesson we learn from letting things play out is remembered long after a chat or scolding. You now know why we keep them here. My words weren't good enough for you, but now seeing the threat up close and what they will sacrifice for the precious golden blood, do you believe me?"

"Gus, I promised—I promised to bring their children home to them."

Gus turned and looked out a window. "I am over you and your stories of keeping your promises. Funny, you didn't worry about the promises you made to your wife or children. But a family of strangers you will die for."

"That's not fair Gus. Not fair at all."

"*It's the truth*, Simon. I'm sorry, I'm the only one being honest with you. But it's the truth." He turned and looked at Simon. "Now, where does that leave us? I don't think you made too many friends with your antics over the last few days. So, you will need to address that. I need to keep you close until I feel I can trust you again. You have a lot to prove, Simon."

"Huh, I can still be part of this?"

"You tell me. Do you want to be part of this, or just return to Canada? Right now, Canada would be the simple choice."

Simon stood looking out a large window at the fields around the manor. "I want to stay. My ex has moved on without me, and my kids looked happy earlier. I need to watch those two orphans grow up. I owe that to Robin and Susan. I need to stay to help you Gus, and your work here. I am sorry."

"Seems the consequences of your actions over the last few years are settling into your heart and mind. This is good."

Simon dropped his head.

"It won't be easy gaining their trust."

"I need to deal with what I have done. I feel I owe it to you and the others. This is all I have to offer, Gus. I messed up. I want to be part of the team."

"Simon, I have lived a long time. All I can say is you thought you knew better, thought you could outsmart us. You didn't. Now you have people's blood on your hands. My suggestion—take the night, think about it. Then you go down to level three tomorrow and see Carol, talk to her, she'll help you. To live a long, happy life, you can't think of the past. The only thing you can control is now."

"Thank you, Gus. I'm so sorry about all this."

"Simon, show me, don't tell me."

Simon looked through the window. The rows of wheat moved and bent. "Gus, do you have patrols outside? Why are the dogs barking like that?"

"No, there is no need. We are invisible." He stood beside Simon.

"Look there and there." Simon pointed to the fields. "Is that normal?"

Gus hastily moved to his desk and pressed a red button on the phone. "April, lock us down. Peter, it looks like we have been discovered. Lock us down and defend the building. Get your teams ready for an assault on the manor." He looked at Simon. "I know you are suffering from dimensional illness, but to prove your loyalty to me and the others, we could use your help right now."

"Of course, thank you, Gus."

Simon stepped out of Gus's office to a flurry of people armed with rifles heading to the exits and roof. He watched Jeff shuffle out the back door. Simon pressed himself against the wall as a group of twelve people pushed past him, moving to the front door. He watched as children and staff moved to the elevators. He stepped into the dining hall, where weapons covered the tables. The kitchen staff loaded the rifles and distributed them. Simon overheard one man say to the man behind him, "I haven't been in a battle since the Boer War began in 1899."

Outside, they heard gunshots, and bullets bounced off the stone walls of the building.

Tom entered the dining hall. "Simon, I was told I would find you here."

"Do you know how to shoot one of these?" asked Simon.

"Yes, but I was told to grab you and head downstairs. It's safe there."

"No, I need to help outside. They're here because of me."

"I don't think so. I learned a lot the few days you were away. We have a lot to catch up on, a lot. But for now, I need to help you to the lower levels. You're not fit enough to be doing anything just yet."

"I agree there," said Simon. "I still have sea legs from the port."

"Shh—everything's gone quiet," said a staff member loading a magazine into a rifle.

Simon moved to the hallway. The back door swung open and three people in blue tunics marched in. They entered Gus' office and closed the door.

Jeff entered the hallway and walked to Simon. "Where were you? You missed all the fun."

"Are you all right?" Simon asked.

"Very well, mate," he patted Simon on the shoulder as he passed him. "Stand back, Simon. We're bringing in a couple of prisoners."

Noel approached Simon. "I wanted to leave you in London earlier, but without you looking out the window, we would have been caught with our pants down. Thank you."

Three men in black hoodies entered the hallway, with Peter and Kenny following.

"Hey, hold on," said Simon, placing his hands on the chest of the first man in a black hoodie.

"Simon, what's the matter? We need to get these guys downstair in case they have a tracker implant," said Kenny.

"I know, I know. There's just one thing I need to see."

Simon swung his arm, his fist smashing against the man's stomach. He bent over, reaching for Simon. Growing up in Canada playing hockey, Simon grabbed the hoodie and pulled it over the man's head. He stood him up straight. Under the thin white tank top, Simon pointed to a tattoo.

"That's what I wanted to see. Look Tom, the same tattoo we have seen since I arrived in England."

"Simon, they all have it somewhere on their body, the farmers, those within the church, and those in the ancient societies."

"I knew it," said Simon. He pulled the hoodie down around the man's body. "There we go Tom, one of the last questions we wanted answered."

He pressed himself against the wall to allow Kenny to push his prisoners forward.

"What happens to them?" asked Tom.

"We will search them, run some tests to see what's in their blood, then an interrogation, and..." he ran his thumb across his neck.

Simon and Tom nodded.

April appeared from the elevator. "Simon, Tom, Gus wants to talk to you two. Peter, can you find Jeff, please? He wants all three of them."

Peter nodded and walked into the dining hall.

•   •   •

"Simon, Tom, there are many advantages to living a long life. The one disadvantage is witnessing the deaths of family and friends. But we all must move on from the loss of those."

He lowered himself to Simon's eye level. "I knew this day was coming. The science has gotten ahead of my team. But what do you expect when they are all over the hill?"

"Gus, we have no background in any of that. I'm a washed up cop who hit the pinnacle of his career," said Simon.

"Yeah, and I'm a podcaster. Did your team release the one I did the other day?"

"Yes. With a growing list of listeners desperately waiting for your next show. You had over ten million downloads on your last show. We might have funded some advertising." Gus smiled at them. "I have hidden in the shadows for too long. It's time I reveal some of my secrets to the public. We can't go mainstream. They would never allow it. But you, you will have the best podcast equipment, talking points and guests. We need to prepare the people for 2020."

Jeff entered the room and sat beside Simon. "What have I missed?"

"Nothing son, you already know your role," said Gus. "I just want the three of you together, my new team."

"Huh? What about me?" asked Simon.

Gus looked at Jeff and winked. "Simon, I want you to head up a new department for me. I have always worked quietly, defensively, and secretively. But as we know with technology, the internet, and more people believing conspiracies to be real…"

"Umm, Gus, they are real. Just look around you," said Tom, laughing.

"What are you asking of me, Gus? You want me to be a spy?"

"One of many things, with your own team. We need to stop the others from ruining this realm, especially as we get closer to 2020. I fear what could happen in that decade. I need locations of labs, churches, and something I never was able to access, the other portal. Then there are those in Antarctica. I need your team to infiltrate them. The Mayans predicted the end of the world in 2012. They were right. But not the end, but the beginning of the end. We need to be aggressive as 2020 closes in on us. This blood needs to be protected. We need to aggressively work to find those with RHnull and protect them. Without it, the Fallen will win and there will be no way for us to protect this realm or the portal. We must save mankind and keep our souls connected to our Creator God."

"That's a lot to put on me."

"Simon, I chose the three of you long before you came together in a farmer's laneway. You all have common ancestors that meant the world to me."

"What?" asked Simon. "We're all related?"

"Yes, distant relatives, but yes," said Gus.

"Gus, are you our great, times ten or so, grandfather?" asked Tom.

Gus nodded, acknowledging Tom's question. "I have so many things to tell you, but we need to get through the important items first. Here's what I need from you. I need you to stop things that are to happen in this realm because of the Fallen's actions. Plus, when you can, Tom needs a co-host for his show."

• • •

Tom sat at a desk with Simon beside him. He opened his new laptop. "I assume we'll have a few hundred emails." He opened the email app and logged in. The number beside his inbox reached one hundred, then one thousand. It ended with nine-thousand eighteen new emails. "Well, that's a surprise." He opened a few emails. They were mostly the same.

"Where is the new show?" "They got you, didn't they?" and *"I am spending my vacation looking for you three."*

The last random email he chose had a video attached to it. He played the video. It showed Susan and Robin being killed and their children being taken. The camera panned to Noel, dropping the blue ball, and the group disappearing into it.

Tom slammed the laptop closed. He looked at Simon. "Now what?"

"We tell Gus, and get to work. We have a world to save."

END

ABOUT THE AUTHOR

Stephen W. Briggs is the author of *Family of Killers—Memoirs of an Assassin* and *Lies Lead to Death*, part of the *Family of Killers* series. For his third book, Stephen took a break from the *Family of Killers* series and wrote a supernatural mystery, *Beside Us*.

His only addiction is cycling, something he does regularly. He has been told that he owns too many bikes. That is a matter of opinion, mainly his family's. The longer the ride, the better for Stephen. He uses the time on his bike to create new story lines, develop characters or just let his mind wander as he challenges his best times on segments in the area.

STEPHEN W. BRIGGS

FAMILY
OF
KILLERS
Memoirs of an Assassin

NOTE FROM STEPHEN W. BRIGGS

Word-of-mouth is crucial for any author to succeed. If you enjoyed *Beside Us*, please leave a review online—anywhere you are able. Even if it's just a sentence or two. It would make all the difference and would be very much appreciated.

Thanks!
Stephen W. Briggs

We hope you enjoyed reading this title from:

www.blackrosewriting.com

Subscribe to our mailing list – *The Rosevine* – and receive **FREE** books, daily
deals, and stay current with news about upcoming
releases and our hottest authors.
Scan the QR code below to sign up.

Already a subscriber? Please accept a sincere thank you for being a fan of
Black Rose Writing authors.

View other Black Rose Writing titles at
www.blackrosewriting.com/books and use promo code
PRINT to receive a **20% discount** when purchasing.